Praise for Maeve Haran

Having It All

'Dazzlingly accomplished. It will make you laugh, cry and rethink your life' Jilly Cooper
'Warm hearted and fun' *Daily Mail*
'Realistic, compassionate, but still as pacey as they come' *Cosmopolitan*

Scenes From the Sex War

'Essential reading for every woman who has ever felt that she will turn into a serial killer if she has to pick up one more dirty sock' *Sunday Express*
'An entertaining writer, with a delicious lightness of touch' *Sunday Times*
'Witty, highly readable' *Woman's Journal*

It Takes Two

'Fast, furious and gripping' *Options*
'Uncomplicated and jaunty . . . funny and realistic' *Daily Mail*
'Plenty to laugh at and a strong, compelling plot' *Independent*

A Family Affair

'Maeve writes as she is: funny, warm and wry' *You* magazine
'Haran's mini-saga is so busy it hums' *Saturday Telegraph*
'Haran writes lightly, crisply and entertainingly' *The Times*

Maeve Haran shot to fame with her first, bestselling novel *Having It All.* Since then she has written a number of other successful novels, including *Scenes From the Sex War*, *It Takes Two* and *A Family Affair*. A former journalist and producer, she is now a full-time writer and lives in North London with her partner and their three children

All That She Wants

MAEVE HARAN

WARNER BOOKS

A *Warner* Book

First published in Great Britain in 1998
by Little, Brown and Company
This edition published by Warner Books in 1999

A CIP catalogue record for this book is
available from the British Library.

ISBN 0 7515 2259 7

Typeset in Adobe Garamond by M Rules
Printed and bound in Great Britain by
Clays Ltd, St Ives plc

Warner Books
A Division of
Little, Brown and Company (UK)
Brettenham House
Lancaster Place
London WC2E 7EN

For Stephanie Leigh, a warm and generous friend, who gave me the first splinter of inspiration for this story and also for her daughter Becky, the originator of the wonderfully apt pun, Oldtimers' Disease.

Chapter 1

'Blast it!' Francesca swore, staring at the huge photograph of her former fiancé and his simpering bride which took up half the front page of the *Woodbury Express*, the rival paper to her own. Underneath it was a nauseatingly detailed description of every item the bride wore, right down to the blue satin suspenders she flashed at the wedding guests after six glasses of Asti Spumante.

What infuriated the journalist in Fran was why the picture was on the front page at all. Weddings might be the staple fare of local papers but they usually made the front page only if one of the bridesmaids was a tiger or the couple had arrived by heli-ski. Francesca strongly suspected it to be a dig by Jack Allen, the *Express's* editor and the bane of Fran's life. Jack had trained on her father's paper and had never quite forgiven her for being the boss's daughter and inheriting his crown. Nepotism, in Jack's book, was a very dirty word indeed and he never gave her the chance to forget it.

Fran studied the photograph again, honest enough to recognize her emotion as rip-roaring jealousy. Even the fact that the bride, bedecked in ribbons, bows and ruched tulle, bore an uncanny resemblance to the wedding cake she stood beside, failed to cheer her up.

She tore out the offending page, screwed it into a ball and threw it with characteristic good aim into the bin. It wasn't that she'd wanted to marry him herself for, rising young businessman or not, he had also turned out to be a rising young shit. What upset her was that she didn't have the capacity to make her relationships *last*. Unlike the blushing bride, who actually seemed to believe that men were godlike superior creatures, Fran tended all too quickly to detect their feet – and not only their feet – of clay.

Consequently at thirty-four, although tall (too tall, Fran thought) and slender, with hair the colour of a new penny and startling green-grey eyes, Francesca had never got beyond the magic six-months mark and remained decidedly single. Her mother said it was because she was too lippy and that men didn't like clever women. At which point Fran would catch her father's eye as he quietly shook his head. And when, on his retirement, Fran had taken over her father's job editing the paper he'd founded, her mother said that was that. What man would want a woman who cared more about deadlines than Daz?

None of this fazed Fran too much. She adored her job editing the *Woodbury Citizen*, had her own flat and a cat, which she loved passionately since it hated pubs, didn't tell boring stories in which it had the starring role, and wasn't interested in football, golf or cricket.

But lately something scandalous had been creeping up on Fran. Where once her fantasies had been of scoops and takeover bids, the thoughts that disturbed her work-filled nights were of fragrant kitchens, homely hearths and even, she was deeply ashamed to admit, a frilly cot plus canopy with embroidered figures from Beatrix Potter on it.

This lethal information she had hidden from everyone, especially Stevie, her second in command. Stevie Grey, the paper's news editor, fifty and female, had about as much interest in babies as an alcoholic does in a glass of milk.

As if on cue, Stevie's head, with its uncompromising iron grey haircut, appeared round her door. 'Psssst!' Stevie hissed loud enough to attract attention three miles away. 'The enemy is here!'

Fran edged her way out of the splendid office that had once been her father's. At the far end of the newsroom, casually perched on the desk of their newest and prettiest trainee, was Jack Allen. No doubt he was offering avuncular advice on how to get on in journalism and the silly girl – far from recognizing it as one step from sexual harrassment – was lapping it all up.

At least he had the sense to get up when he saw Fran wrathfully approaching, but without the slightest hint of apology in his laughing blue eyes.

'What are *you* doing here?' Fran demanded ungraciously. 'Haven't you got an edition to get out or are you delegating everything to your minions these days?' Jack's fondness for delegation was notorious. It made young reporters flock to him, eager for their big chance, but Fran suspected it was, at least in part, laziness.

'Spoken like the true boss's daughter that you are. You, of course, had to *earn* your spurs by pure graft, didn't you?'

'Come on, now, boys and girls,' Stevie chided. 'A healthy rivalry's a good thing but don't let's get carried away.'

'Sorry, teacher.' Jack winked. Stevie was one of his favourite people and he would have doubled her salary to get her away from Fran. But Stevie, he knew, would never dream of leaving the *Citizen*.

'So, Mr Allen,' Fran drew herself up until she was almost the same height as Jack. 'What does bring you here apart from trying to take advantage of our trainees?'

'I haven't come to gloat over Woodbury's Wedding of the Year,' he challenged, knowing how it would annoy her. 'Though you would have made a far lovelier bride. Ivory, I think, rather than virginal white, and a few less flounces. You're too big-boned for the Scarlett O'Hara look.'

Behind them Stevie snorted into her coffee and had to go and look for a paper towel.

'I knew you made that wedding your lead story deliberately,' Fran accused, forgetting that she had meant to be calm and disdainful.

'Nonsense.' Jack's eyes widened in mock shock. 'Adrian Blake's wedding was of great local interest. His father employs a lot of people round here.' Fran had the infuriating impression that he was laughing at her. 'Actually I came to congratulate you.'

Jack's smile was so charming she was instantly suspicious. 'What for?' Even to herself Fran's tone was none too gracious, but then the *Express* was always trying to steal their hard-won scoops.

'Your coverage of that dodgy bus firm, of course. It was terrific reporting.'

'No thanks to you, then.' Fran pointed out. 'Your reporter was so damn eager to get the story first he very nearly screwed it up for both of us.'

Jack smiled. 'Hard to hold these young bloods back. They'll go to any lengths for a story. Rather like you used to yourself, if I recall correctly.' He raised one eyebrow raffishly. 'Remember that leather skirt you wore to go drinking with the cops? It got you some of your best leads, didn't it?'

Fran blushed. There had been a brief period at the beginning of her career when, eager to prove she wasn't just Daddy's girl, she had indeed used her allure and six inches of black leather to obtain tip-offs from the local police. It was thanks to these that she finally persuaded the other reporters on the *Citizen* that she was capable of even lower cunning than they were so she'd been accepted as one of them. Except by Jack, of course. All the same, she'd die of shame if she saw that skirt now. It had offered all the modesty of a couple of wide elastic bands. Trust Jack Allen to remember it.

'Are you carrying any more about it tomorrow?' He glanced over at the back bench where tomorrow's paper was being assembled.

'No,' Fran said cautiously. Jack was clearly up to something. He would sell not only his grandmother but his entire family for a scoop. 'All wrapped up for the moment. Why are you suddenly so interested?'

Before he could answer they were interrupted by a sharp mewly cry. Fran turned to see Eileen, one of their old switchboard operators, down the other end of the office holding out a small, noisy bundle in a red matinée jacket, its tiny head encased in a knitted hat hardly bigger than a doll's. Eileen handed it to Stevie, who stood looking as helpless as a reverend mother with a condom. 'Here, Fran, you have a go.' She plonked the baby, which on closer inspection turned out to have an unappealing red rash, into Fran's astonished arms.

Fran gently removed its hat and, ignoring the white scurfy cradle cap, tucked its small head under her chin. The sense of physical connection was so strong that she closed her eyes and rocked it gently.

The baby, however, seemed not to share Fran's serenity and oneness and continued to bellow louder than ever.

'Come on, let me have a go. I can see this isn't exactly your forte.'

Fran was too amazed to be angry when Jack took the baby from her and held it firmly against his shoulder, its face so deeply buried in the scratchy cloth of his jacket that Fran feared it would suffocate.

She could picture Jack Allen propping up a bar after a long night chasing an elusive story, winkling information out of unwilling public officials, or persuading aged ladies to tell their story to the *Express* instead of the *Citizen*, his celebrated charm polished and gleaming for the occasion. What she would never have imagined was Jack Allen offering his little finger to be clutched tighter than a vice, his tweedy shoulder to be puked onto, or murmuring lullabies in a newborn ear. But either the baby was addicted to after-shave or Jack had a genuine knack, because in thirty seconds flat it had stopped crying, attached itself to him with leech-like enthusiasm and even stared with its unfathomable dark blue gaze into his crinkled and cynical pale blue one. Fran suspected, with a sliver of ignoble irritation, that if it had known how to, it would probably have smiled.

Jack handed the baby back to Fran. 'You'd look good with one of those once you'd got the hang of it,' he threw in provocatively. Before Fran had time to snap back he waved his hand at the array of typewriters which ranged from relatively modern electric to one pre-war Remington with the 'e' missing. 'Still using old technology then?' Unlike Fran's paper, the *Express* was part of a profitable group and had gleaming new computer terminals on every desk in its office.

'We may not be hi-tech,' Fran pointed out loftily, not admitting how hard she'd lobbied recently to get the *Citizen* on-line, 'but at least we have our independence.'

'Nice of him to drop in.' Stevie watched Jack's departing back fondly. It had been such a pity when he'd left the *Citizen,* but Jack Allen wasn't the type to keep the seat warm for somebody else, especially the boss's daughter. 'I used to wonder whether one day you and he might . . .' Stevie let the outrageous suggestion hang in the air.

'You must be mad!' Fran protested, handing back the baby before it let her down and started crying again. 'I wouldn't go within ten yards of him. Jack Allen's testosterone levels are probably a health hazard.'

'I've always thought,' Stevie looked at her sneakily, 'what a good father he must be.'

Fran scanned the older woman's face. Did Stevie suspect the truth, that she was at an advanced stage of maternal longing, only one step from pram-snatching?

'If he's such a good father,' Fran demanded, 'why did his wife bugger off back to Australia and take their baby? He must have done something pretty terrible to merit that.'

Stevie's lined face softened marginally from its usual briskness. 'His son opted to stay with him, though, didn't he? And if you ask me there's more to that story than meets the eye. Carrie Allen never liked Woodbury. She was always pushing Jack to move to London, but he liked it here.'

'You sound as though you're half in love with him yourself, Stevie.'

Stevie shot Fran a conspiratorial look. They both knew the truth. Stevie had stayed single because she was in love with someone quite different – Francesca's father. And the fact irritated the hell out of Fran's mother and had done so for thirty years.

'He phoned, by the way,' Stevie's voice softened in the way it always did when talking about Ralph. 'He says there's a nice runner in the two-thirty at Chepstow he wants to tell you about. Oh, and could you bring him a bottle of malt whisky? The Macallan would do, and don't tell your mother about it.'

Fran laughed. The secret pact between her father and herself went back to childhood. Ever since she'd been six years old Ralph had taken her on outings either to the paper or to the races. Both places, it seemed to Fran looking back, had been wonderfully exciting, with the added bonus that they got her away from her mother and her stifling protectiveness. A protectiveness not borne, she suspected, of maternal love but of fear of further inconvenience. Having done Fran the immense honour of giving birth to her, her mother had expected her daughter never to trouble her again. It was her father who had supplied the magic and the fun and made her feel that she was bright and beautiful enough (a subjective view this, but he'd somehow made her believe it) to do whatever she wanted in life. The result was a bond stronger than that between any other father and daughter she knew. And this her mother mightily resented.

'Your trouble,' Stevie pointed out, 'is that you'll never find another man like your dad.'

'I know,' Fran agreed. 'But then neither will you.'

A brief smile sealed their complicity.

Stevie turned back towards the crowded office. 'Right then, you two,' she turned to the two nearest reporters who might just have been within earshot, 'haven't you got better things to do than eavesdrop on other people's conversations?'

'But, Stevie,' complained Mike Wooley, the younger, cockier of the two, 'I thought that was what journalists were supposed to do.'

'I'm worried about Franny,' announced Fran's oldest friend Henrietta to her teenage daughter Sophie. It was seven o'clock and outside the sky was a deep velvety blue, matched only by the deep velvety blue of the warmed bath towel Henrietta was holding out for her six-year-old daughter, Lottie, who was splashing happily away in the bathroom of their Georgian rectory. Lottie had been both an afterthought and also a welcome insurance that Henrietta could continue her pampered life, untroubled by thoughts of having to work for at least another ten years.

'What's she done now?' enquired Sophie.

'She puts men off.'

'You mean she puts off the kind of men you want her to like,' pointed out Sophie from the wisdom of her sixteen years. 'She's much less conventional than you, Mum. Not that that'd be difficult. Maybe she just likes being independent and doesn't believe in legalized prostitution like you do.'

Henrietta was about to protest at this description of the holy state of matrimony when the doorbell rang and Fran herself arrived, running up the stairs to join them in the bathroom.

'Auntie Fran!' squealed little Lottie, dangerously jumping to her feet and showering her mother with water. 'Will you take me to Old McDonald's?' At six, Lottie had not yet mastered the cultural convergence of hamburgers and nursery rhymes.

'Of course I will!' agreed Fran. 'But let's make it another day, shall we, when you've got some clothes on?'

'Time to get out, Lots,' insisted Henrietta, wrapping her in the huge bath-sheet.

'Can I dry her?' asked Fran, picking up the giggling, squirmy body and enveloping it in the warm cotton. Lottie's head fitted snugly and blissfully under her chin. 'Do you think I'll ever find anybody to make one of these with?'

'For heaven's sake, Fran,' scolded Henrietta, who considered men more important than children in the eternal scheme of things. Children were fine in their place but they couldn't pay the Harrods bill. At least not until they grew up and married well. 'Find a husband first. You're ridiculously romantic about children. Stay for hair drying, then you'll see the truth.' She advanced menacingly on Lottie who screeched at the sight of the hairbrush as if it were the Iron Maiden of Nuremberg.

Fran cuddled her tighter, suddenly struck by a revolutionary thought. 'Do you think I *have* to have a man? I mean these days –'

'Of course you have to have a man,' interrupted Henrietta, deliberately misunderstanding her. 'They have this *thing* you see, and they sort of stick it up you and . . .'

'She means sexing,' pointed out Lottie pityingly, delighted with the distraction and the chance to show off her superior knowledge. 'You have to sex with a man if you want to have a baby, Auntie Fran. Everybody knows that.'

Fran giggled. 'I mean a permanent man. A man-in-residence.'

Henrietta, rarely lost for words, was scandalized. 'You can't really mean . . . ?' She saw instantly that this was precisely what Fran meant. 'You couldn't. It wouldn't be fair on the baby. Babies need fathers.'

'Bollocks,' sixteen-year-old Sophie commented, with the perfect enunciation imparted by her private schooling. 'Loads of people have babies on their own nowadays.'

'Not in Woodbury they don't,' sniffed Henrietta. 'And

don't use that word to me. Here am I spending two thousand pounds a term on an expensive private school and you use language like that. Where did you learn it?'

'At my expensive private school, of course. Come on, Mum.' Sophie sometimes thought her parents, living as they did in a six-bedroom house in the posh part of Woodbury with a gardener and a cleaning lady, were on another planet. 'You're so out of touch.'

'No, your mum's right,' Fran conceded. 'Having a baby just because you want one would be incredibly irresponsible.'

Later on, when Fran had gone, Henrietta, who liked a challenge and was bored with fund raising for the usual pukka charities, lay in bed and thought about Fran's words. Matchmaking was one of her hobbies but she'd never had a mission like this. Finding the perfect father for Fran's baby might be quite an interesting challenge.

'But you've been trying to find her a man for years,' murmured her husband Simon, trying his best to interest Henrietta in sex. 'They all fall for her like flies, Fran tells them to get lost and they never talk to you again.'

Henrietta could feel her husband's prick starting to poke her in the thigh, his usual subtle prelude to seduction.

'This is different. That was husband material. This is father material.' She looked him in the eye. 'I don't suppose you want to volunteer?' That would put paid to his erection, she could bet on it. Unexpectedly Simon's organ became twice as insistent.

'Simon!' Henrietta gasped, shocked. 'You randy old bugger. I didn't know you fancied my best friend!'

*

Fran checked the car clock and decided that since she'd been too busy to call her father back that afternoon – a big burglary story had come up via the police radio – she'd slip in on her way home and see her parents. Her heart sank at the thought of the lecture her mother would deliver on the advantages she'd thrown away by not agreeing to be Mrs Adrian Blake but she had to get it over with.

The doorbell rang with a satisfying jangle through the rambling house. It was, she noticed, beginning to look run-down but then on her father's pension life these days must be much more of a struggle. To her delight it was her father who appeared at the door.

'Franny! What a treat.' The affection in his face warmed Fran like the sun on a winter's day. Seeing him always instantly cheered her. There was an energy and enthusiasm in her father she'd never found in anyone else. His hair might be white, but at sixty-five he still had a lean and boyish look, as though he might don shorts and sandals and depart at any moment on one of life's great adventures. Quiet by nature, but as steady and determined as a rock, Ralph had given her a strong sense of love and security so solid that it had made her ready to face anything in life. They both knew this but rarely acknowledged it in words. Between them what was left unsaid counted most.

'Where's Mum?' she asked.

The sitting room was untidy for once, with a comfortable male sprawl about it. A half-eaten pork pie – she recognized it as one of Singer the Butcher's famous home-made ones which her mother would instantly dismiss as high-cholesterol – sat on a plate with two tomatoes and a pickle. Ralph had managed to track down some racing on a far-flung cable channel. The *Sporting Life* was folded neatly by the side of his chair. 'Wednesday. Bridge night.'

Fran eyed his lonely supper and felt a twinge of annoyance at her mother. Phyllis had treated his retirement from the paper with a barely concealed air of martyrdom, as though the decision had been taken expressly to annoy her. It never seemed to cross her mind what it might be like for *him*. Fortunately Ralph, always a popular figure locally, was much in demand as an advisor and non-executive director for numerous good works. Fran knew, though, that he missed the paper like hell. Being Ralph, he would die rather than say so.

'You should have rung me.' She pointed to his supper. 'We could have gone out for an Indian.'

'My darling girl. Wednesdays are my favourite night.' He grinned his infectious grin, the one that must have won her mother's heart all those years ago. Phyllis had actually, according to the family photo album, been young and pretty once, with a country girl's bloom about her. Clotted cream instead of the sour old yogurt she now resembled. 'Racing on the telly and I had three pickled onions instead of the one the Commandant allows. Congratulations, by the way. Great story about those bastards at the bus company.'

The quick smile that passed between them acknowledged her debt to him. He had trained her well. Whenever she was working on a tricky story, and someone in officialdom was lying, she always asked herself what her father would have done. Even now the sticker on the back window of his ancient Volvo didn't bear the exhortation to join the Rotary club, find Jesus or vote Tory. His simply said, in catchy red capitals, QUESTION AUTHORITY. Her mother hated it and always parked as near as possible to the wall in Sainsbury's car park.

Sometimes the fact that her parents had stayed together for over thirty-five years impressed her. And sometimes, when she thought how much happier they both might have been with someone different, it appalled her. They must, she concluded, have done it because they loved each other once.

'Thanks, Dad. Actually, Jack Allen dropped in to congratulate me too.' She paused, remembering her suspicions over Jack Allen's motives.

'How is Jack? Best journalist I ever trained.' Her father's face clouded over for a moment. 'That reminds me. I wanted to talk to you about him.'

Oh no, thought Fran. Not you as well. 'You're not trying to pair me off with him too, I hope.'

'No, I wouldn't suggest you went after Jack. He's not your type. Too masculine. He acts before he thinks. You need someone more subtle. You should watch out for him all the same, though. Rumour has it the *Express* wants to launch a free paper and they've asked Jack to edit it.'

Fran felt a shockwave of anxiety. As she'd said so sarcastically to Jack, the *Citizen* had independence and a loyal readership, but in these tough times would their loyal readers be able to resist the lure of an entirely free paper? Especially one with an editor of Jack's quality.

'I can't see Jack agreeing.' Fran sounded more confident

than she felt. 'I've often heard him say freesheets are glorified adverts, not journalism at all.'

Ralph patted her hand reassuringly. 'You're probably right. Let's hope so.'

Fran was about to leave when she remembered the bottle of whisky hidden in her handbag. She'd have to give it to him before her mother got back. It was the Macallan, her father's favourite.

She handed it over with a conspiratorial wink. 'Only a drop now or Ma'll get the Alsatians out.'

Ralph fell on it with enthusiasm. 'Terrific. Your mother's hidden all the spirits. You'd think I was a damned alkie, the way's she's going on.'

'Come on now, Dad, you did have a heart attack. She's quite right to ration you.'

'Yes, but she doesn't have to enjoy it so much, does she?'

Neither of them needed to comment on the truth of this.

Ralph raised his glass. 'To the best paper in Woodbury. You know I'm really proud of you, the way you're running it.'

Fran clinked glasses, glowing in the warmth of praise from the one person she respected.

Wheels crunched on gravel outside and they both laughed and hid their glasses under the sofa.

Chapter 2

When Henrietta eventually found the perfect man for her friend Fran, she was at a distinct disadvantage. Anyone else but Henrietta, while lying flat on their back with their feet in the stirrups and their vagina facing due south with a posse of medical students staring up it, might have been discouraged and tried to think of other things. But Henrietta was made of sterner stuff. She focused her mind instead on the white-coated doctor she had just glimpsed in the foyer. He was, she reckoned, in his mid-thirties, a nice solid age, and while most hospital doctors shared a pallor like so many pork chops on the butcher's slab, this one had a post-skiing tan. His hair was corn-coloured. A pair of gold-rimmed half-glasses perched mid-way down his nose, giving him an engagingly serious air. And, Henrietta noticed, when he spoke even his older colleagues had listened in respect bordering on awe.

So excited was Henrietta with her discovery that she didn't notice the steely kiss of the speculum or the freezing sensation of gel on metal as it was removed. Afterwards the nurse handed her a strip of hospital paper towel and told her she could now get dressed.

No sooner had Henrietta whipped her silk knickers back on than she rounded on the astonished nurse.

'That doctor out in reception. Youngish. Blond hair. What's his name?'

'There were at least ten doctors in reception,' pointed out the nurse huffily.

'You know the one I mean.' Henrietta was sure every nurse in the hospital knew the one she meant. 'The one who looks like Robert Redford when *he* looked like Robert Redford.'

'Well . . .' The woman's voice took on a tone of saintly reverence as if she were discussing Mother Teresa or the Pope. 'You could be thinking of Dr Westcott. He runs the hospital's infertility unit.'

Henrietta sighed with content, luxuriating in the thought that this man's calling was to bring joy and fulfilment to childless women. Why not make one more childless woman joyous too? Fran's particular situation might require a little more intervention than was perhaps usual by a doctor, but in Henrietta's mind that was simply a minor detail.

The one drawback to this fantasy suddenly hit her in the face.

'This Dr Westcott. Is he married?'

The nurse sighed. 'Dr Westcott has given himself body and soul to the clinic.'

Henrietta smiled beatifically as she buttoned up her

cream linen suit. Everything, in that case, was possible. If he ran a clinic it was bound, in the nature of things, to be short of money. And raising money was one thing Henrietta was extraordinarily good at. The relationship, in Henrietta's mind at least, had practically been consummated. All she had to do now was get the pair together.

She made for the door, her shoes click-clacking on the new marble-effect NHS Trust floor. At the door she stopped, realizing there was one important detail she'd forgotten. 'What's his Christian name?' she enquired.

The nurse made a face as though this were classified information. 'Laurence,' she said finally.

'Laurence,' Henrietta whispered, savouring every syllable. 'Laurence.' Fran might be entertaining the idea of having a baby on her own but once she met someone suitable she'd soon see sense. It was the natural way of things. 'Laurence,' she repeated to herself. 'Dr Laurence Westcott, Dr and *Mrs* Laurence Westcott.'

The nurse watched Henrietta leave, repeating the mantra of Dr Westcott's name. Maybe the woman was a loony. Care in the Community had a lot to answer for. Just because she wore a cream linen suit it didn't mean she wasn't a dangerous schizophrenic who would tear off all her clothes and stalk Dr Westcott when he clocked off tonight. Maybe she should never have divulged his name.

Oblivious to the nurse's suspicions, Henrietta smiled as she walked towards the car park. She could feel romance in the air.

At the traffic lights at the edge of Woodbury, bang opposite the council estate, two small Squeegee bandits,

Henrietta's old enemies, lurked with their filthy sponges. Too late for her usual tactic of turning the wipers on as soon as she saw them, Henrietta was obliged to have her windscreen dirtied. With immense satisfaction she realized she had no small change and she was damned if she was going to give them a fiver. 'Here.' She picked up a paper bag on the seat next to her and handed it over graciously. She could afford to feel happy with the world and all who lived in it now that she'd spotted Dr Laurence Westcott. 'Take these. They're croissants.'

The boy peered into the bag, mystified as Henrietta roared off. ''Ere, Shane!' he yelled to the other urchin. 'What's a bleedin' cwassong?'

'Am I speaking to Miss Francesca Tyler? Or should I say *Ms* Francesca Tyler?'

The sarcasm in the voice made Fran sit up and stop typing her copy. It was probably an irate resident ringing up to complain about ramblers abusing his right of way or dog owners not using pooper scoopers. The paper got a lot of those, though most of them fortunately didn't find their way through to Fran. 'You are indeed.'

'The editor of the *Citizen*?'

'That's right.'

'Then I've got a cracking story for you. Family firm established eighty years ago is having to lay off thirty staff tomorrow. Maybe you'd like a photo opportunity.'

'Are you in Woodbury?' Fran's instincts made her reach for her pad.

'One of the staff has been with us fifty years.' There was

something unpleasant in the caller's tone that put her on her guard. 'He's not getting a gold watch though, not even one from Argos.'

'What's the name of the firm?'

'I can't afford to pay them a penny, you see.'

'You haven't told me your firm's name,' Fran pressed.

'We're down by the bypass. Wadey's Buses. Recognize the name now?'

Fran's breath speeded up. It was the boss of the dodgy bus firm.

'Thirty people thrown on the streets. Because of you. You're scum, you are.'

Fran wanted to put the phone down but it felt glued to her ear.

'Sanctimonious scum.' The man's voice was rising now, getting shrill with venom and hate. 'You think you're pretty clever but you're just a dumb tart. You should watch yourself, *Mizzz* Francesca Tyler, or you might have a nasty accident one of these days. Bump into a bus or something.'

The loathing in the man's voice seeped out of the phone and Fran wanted to drop it. She had to take hold of herself. What had her father always told her? Stand up to bullies and they'll back off. They're the real cowards.

'Are you threatening me, Mr Wadey?' Fran did her best to inject a steely toughness into her voice. 'Because I record all my calls as a matter of course.' It was a lie, it would be wildly uneconomic, but he wasn't to know.

'Sod off then, and I hope your fucking paper goes out of business and you'll know how it feels.' He slammed the phone down.

Fran closed her eyes. She knew they'd been right to print the story. It had been a good story and Wadey's Buses had been taking risks with the public. It still felt shitty being yelled at, though. Even worse putting people out of work. Tears pricked at the back of her eyes. Thank God none of the reporters were around

Fran felt a hand on her shoulder and jumped.

'You did brilliantly. It's why we're here, Fran. Don't forget that. Someone could have been killed.' Fran had been so wound up with her own emotions she hadn't heard her father arrive. 'Come on, you haven't got a deadline today. What about that Indian you promised me?'

Fran reached for her jacket. She needed to get out into the winter sunshine and feel Woodbury's clean cool air, the air that was even more refreshing since the *Citizen* had campaigned successfully for a bypass. That had been her achievement too and it had genuinely improved people's lives, though she supposed even then there'd been the odd business that had suffered and cursed her. Damn it, she'd end up under a bus like the unpleasant Mr Wadey had suggested if she didn't pull herself together.

Everyone shouted greetings to Ralph as they walked along the High Street, its half-timbering carefully disguising Boots and the Body Shop, but still beautiful and surprisingly unspoiled.

The waiter in Bengal Bertie's was Ralph's friend of old. He didn't bother to show them the menu. Fran always chose Chicken Dopiaza and Ralph the hottest curry they made. Once the Lamb Vindaloo had been so powerful that the chef and kitchen staff had come to cheer as Ralph polished it off without a word. The waiter insisted on buying him a pint of Kingfisher Indian beer afterwards.

'Your father,' stated the waiter in an orgy of political incorrectness, 'should have run Empire. Then we wouldn't have to throw British buggers out.'

'Dad,' Fran waited until the kolfi arrived before broaching another subject that was worrying her, 'if the *Express* does start a free paper, it's going to be rough on us. Our margins are tight already.'

'I know,' Ralph reassured, 'but we'll survive. You're a great editor with wonderful instincts for what people care about. Good journalism always counts.'

Fran laughed. He was so wonderful at making her feel good. If only there was a man out there like him. The trouble was she knew from bitter experience that there wasn't.

'Come on,' Ralph reminded. 'If I keep you out any longer Stevie will have me for breakfast.'

Stevie was indeed lying in wait for them on their return, leaning on her desk ignoring the yells for her attention all around her. To Stevie, noisy newsrooms were more relaxing than aromatherapy massages.

'How are you, Stevie?' Ralph kissed her on the cheek and held her hand just a fraction longer than normal. Stern Stevie, who favoured a selection of identical skirts and blouses in unappealing man-made materials, all of which looked as though they'd been put on in a darkened room, plus no-nonsense shoes with thick tights, blushed like a young girl at her first party.

'Fine. At least I was till I saw this.' She held out a copy of the *Express*.

To Fran's disbelieving rage, their rival paper had splashed with a story about Wadey's bus firm – *their* story! Fran had just been through insults and abuse for that story and the *Express* had stolen it.

'The cheeky sods.' Stevie, though as angry as Fran, could appreciate clever journalism when she saw it. 'They've only hired one of his death-trap buses and taken it to Trading Standards for a safety inspection. It failed on every single count. Wadey's are going to be prosecuted from here to Kingdom Come. Why didn't we think of doing that?'

'Because we're not as devious as Jack Allen,' snapped Francesca. 'How *dare* he steal our story? That must have been why he was in here yesterday. Come to congratulate me, my arse!'

'You must admit,' Stevie held up the paper with its headline THIS BUS COULD KILL, 'it's a pretty good wheeze, though, isn't it?'

'Stevie,' Fran removed the paper from Stevie's hold and tossed it in the bin, 'whose side are you on? You know perfectly well we couldn't blow hundreds of quid on hiring one of those damn buses.'

She was never going to forgive Jack Allen for this. In fact she was going to face him up now, while she was still blazing.

Stevie watched her go while Ralph retrieved the paper from the bin and spread it out. 'He's a clever lad, Jack, isn't he? I wish I were a fly on the wall in his office when Franny gets there. Anyone who managed to get those two to work together would have quite a paper.'

'Yup,' agreed Stevie, 'except that the sparks between them would probably burn the building down.'

The rival locations of the *Citizen* and the *Express*, it seemed to Fran as she drove across the bustling town from one to the other, summed up their differences. The *Citizen* was in the High Street, a prime location, but rents had soared and the space was cramped and parking was non-existent. You could, on the plus side, see the roof of the cathedral from its diamond-paned windows. Over the years Fran had become deeply familiar with its gargoyles and flying buttresses. Her favourite gargoyle had a long, lugubrious face and looked as if he had a permanent hangover. Rainwater spewed ceaselessly from his mouth, a telling comment on the folly of modern man hundreds of feet beneath, queuing to get into McDonald's or the multiplex. To Fran, though, the cramped conditions of the office were worth it because they were in the heart of things.

The *Express*, on the other hand, was in a flash purpose-built office on an industrial estate, between 21st Century Computers and an electronics superstore. Fran told herself it was faceless and dull, even if it did have its own fleet of pool cars with THE EXPRESS – THE PAPER THAT GETS THERE FIRST emblazoned, in her view highly inaccurately, on their sides, chilled water fountains on every floor, and off-street parking.

To Fran's intense irritation the off-street space earmarked by a large sign saying 'Editor' was noticeably empty. Unless Jack had jogged or biked to work, he must be out. Fran was taken aback by just how disappointed she felt, and told herself it was because she was geared up for a fight. She sublimated her sense of loss by adjusting her lipstick in the wing mirror. Behind her a peremptory hoot jogged her into adding a line reminiscent of Picasso's red period, the one after the blue, from ear to nose.

'You're blocking my space,' Jack Allen pointed out cheerfully, as she backed out. 'Nice face paint. Has it taken over from body piercing in terms of personal decoration?'

Fran swore. Jack Allen always seemed to find ways to put her at a disadvantage. It was quite a skill. If you happened to be a skunk. She reached for a tissue, then got out of the car in what she hoped was a graceful but assertive manner.

'You bastard,' Fran greeted him. 'That was our story and you knew it. No wonder you were looking sheepish the other day. Sneaking round to see if we'd got there before you. Well, as a matter of fact, I don't believe in the narrow scoop mentality.'

Jack opened the door of his ancient convertible Saab, a car he'd had for as long as Fran had known him. 'Oh, don't you? Then you must have gone soft. You used to kill for a story. Or at least expose three feet of thigh for one.'

Fran ignored him. 'I happen to believe we should all pull together to improve this town, not compete with each other to nail cheap villains.'

'Ah.' He grinned infuriatingly so that Fran wanted to hit him. 'In that case you won't object to this.' He handed her a letter. 'The *Express* and the *Citizen* have both been shortlisted for best regional weekly.'

'I just hope the better paper wins,' Fran said grandly as the offside door opened. She hadn't known he had passengers.

Or in this case passenger.

A pair of very long legs encased in a very short skirt, not too dissimilar from the one Fran had once worn herself, swung out of the car, followed by a body of waif-like proportions and a heartstoppingly pretty face. Slightly slanted dark eyes under a spiky gamine fringe surveyed Fran, making her uncomfortably aware of her smudged lipstick.

'I don't think you've met Miriam Wolsey.' Jack, ever the gentleman, had made no attempt to open the newcomer's door. Miriam, on the other hand, looked as though she might see door-opening as an insult tantamount to wolf-whistling or being told 'you could drive a bus through there, darlin'' so it was just possible that Jack was showing unusual sensitivity. 'Miriam has just joined us from journalism college.'

That made her, Fran decided, all of twenty. Twenty-one at the outside. Too young for Jack. She trusted Jack was mature enough to see that.

Miriam and Jack headed for the *Express* building. 'Surely there's no doubt the *Express* will win.' Miriam's voice floated to Fran across the tarmac. 'The *Citizen*'s one step up from a parish magazine, surely? I mean, for God's sake, people say they still use typewriters.'

'If you agree with her I'll kill you, Jack Allen,' Fran murmured under her breath.

'Miriam, let me tell you one thing,' Jack began, and for once Fran forgave the edge of patronage in his voice. 'Journalism isn't about technology; it's about instinct, a feeling for what readers care about. They do damn well on the *Citizen* considering they only have a man and a dog to run it.'

Fran slammed the door. How typical of Jack to turn a compliment into an insult.

If I'm a dog, Fran promised herself as she accelerated out of the car park, judging the distance between the two striped poles of the exit perfectly, then one day I might just up and savage you.

Jack, who had grabbed Miriam and hauled her onto the pavement as Fran revved up, let her go. The encounter with Fran had made him a few seconds late for his meeting with the group chairman, Murray Nelson, a man to whom punctuality was a religion. Damn! Sometimes he envied Francesca Tyler a lot more than she suspected. At least she had the freedom to make the mistakes she believed in.

Murray Nelson was already sitting in the bare and functional meeting room when Jack arrived, one minute and forty-three seconds late. He suspected Nelson had counted each one.

Jack sat down. He had adopted a policy of Never Apologize, Never Explain with Murray Nelson. It didn't make the man like him any more but at least Jack held onto his dignity. In fifteen years Nelson had risen from tele-ad salesman to chairman of the whole Express Group, embracing twenty regional papers and a dozen local radio stations, and he hadn't done it by being Mr Nice Guy. Jack was widely acknowledged as Nelson's only serious rival, but it wasn't this that made the senior man so tough on him. What Nelson most held against Jack was that everyone, from the motorbike messengers to the cleaning staff to the battleaxe on front reception, liked him. That Nelson found unforgivable.

'Right.' Nelson looked at his watch as if he were allocating precisely fifteen minutes at the outside to the business they were to discuss. 'The new paper. Can I assume you'll agree to edit it?'

Jack had been thinking about this for days. He knew as well as anyone that Woodbury would be too small to support three papers. One of them would end up going under, and because it was under-funded and had no group financing to support it, it would probably be the *Citizen*. On the other hand, in the cut and thrust of the competitive world it was up to newspaper editors to find a way of moving with the times and surviving. Part of the appeal of newspapers was their element of risk, otherwise you might as well go and work in a bank. If Francesca Tyler couldn't see that then she deserved to go out of business.

'Certainly.' Jack could be as brisk as him. 'On two conditions.'

'Yes? And what are those?'

'That I continue editing the *Express*.'

Nelson nodded. That would be a cost benefit. 'And?'

'That you give me a marketing budget to make a splash with this paper – organize some events that will grab attention for it. If I do it I'm not prepared to do it at half-cock.'

Nelson grinned at him sleazily. 'Doing things at half-cock isn't what you're famous for, Jack, or so I gather.'

Jack ignored the innuendo. 'I'd need five grand.'

'Poor old *Citizen*. It won't know what's hit it. You used

to work on it, didn't you, Jack? This wouldn't be settling an old score would it?'

'Of course it isn't. I simply want to give the new paper a decent chance of making an impact, that's all.'

'Don't get me wrong, Jack. I'm all for competition, the unfairer the better. I'm right behind you on this. It's nothing to me if the *Citizen* goes under. I might even acquire the title cheap. But what about Francesca Tyler? People say she's very attractive.'

'If Francesca can't stand the competition, she shouldn't be editing a paper.'

'Is she that rare animal, a woman who's turned you down, Jack?'

'This is purely professional. I happen to enjoy taking risks.' Jack looked at Nelson as if he were a particularly unpleasant form of bacillus.

'Just as well you're bloody good at your job, Allen.' Murray Nelson's voice was low and almost caressing. 'You like going near the edge, so people say, that's what they admire about you. Don't lean out too far, though – that's my advice.'

Jack was halfway to the door when Nelson spoke again. 'We all know the story, you know. How you were offered the big job in Fleet Street, then they heard the scandal about you and withdrew it. So don't get too uppity, will you, Jack? Or you could end up editing the Muckspreaders Bulletin.'

Jack decided it wasn't worth an answer. Nelson wouldn't understand the truth anyway. It had been far more complicated, and a lot messier. In fact he had been the one to turn down the job, not the other way round but he was damned if he was explaining himself to Murray Nelson.

His wife Carrie had walked out and taken their daughter Louise, but Ben, his beautiful son Ben, had opted to stay with his father. How could Jack have abandoned him for the big time in London and a job where he would never see his seven-year-old son? So he'd said no. And being with Ben, seeing him grow up, having the kind of relationship with him that few fathers ever had with their sons, had been more than worth it. Besides, he liked Woodbury and wanted to give it the best paper he could.

'Thanks,' Jack's tone and smile were deadly. 'I'll bear your advice in mind.'

Entering the newsroom after a meeting on the executive floor, Jack decided, was like shopping in a crowded street-market after the cold anonymity of an out-of-town superstore. Everyone shouted at you and wanted a view, a decision on a headline or an OK for a photo spread. There was noise and buzz and excitement, especially if the deadline approached. To Jack it was home.

It was well after six before people began to pack up their stuff. Jack was about to switch off his computer when he remembered to check his E-mail. There, surrounded by a jazzy graphic, was a message from his son. DON'T FORGET, read the electronic reminder, TONIGHT'S VIDEO NIGHT.

Every Tuesday for as long as he could remember, Jack and Ben had followed a time-honoured ritual of video and pizza together. When they'd started it had been *Postman Pat* and now it was more likely to be *The Postman Always Rings*

Twice, but the habit had remained. Jack was secretly rather flattered that his cool, almost-grown-up son wanted to stay in with him when the phone seemed to ring constantly for him. In fact, so constantly that Jack had considered getting him his own line.

The only problem, Jack mused as he rifled through the plastic boxes half an hour later in their local video shop, was finding films that both of them wanted to watch. Ben favoured the latest horror blockbuster while Jack's taste ran to black and white French films about love and loss. In the end he selected *Nosferatu* – the original vampire film in shaky black and white. To Jack the threatening atmosphere it achieved was everything a horror film should be.

Perhaps, since a black-and-white silent film with subtitles was a tad indulgent, he ought to choose something more modern as back-up.

'What are teenagers getting out at the moment?' he asked the fat girl with piggy eyes who sat, surrounded with piles of romance magazines, behind the counter. She had, he'd found in the past, excellent taste and a lively knowledge of movies.

'How old?'

'Fourteen.'

'The scarier the better.' She handed over a black cover with green neon goo dripping from a skull. 'Don't worry. It's all pretty fake. Just ask your son to come and tuck you in if you get a nightmare afterwards.'

Jack laughed. 'Thanks. Sounds perfect. But then you always get it right. You should be a critic.'

The girl glowed, her eyes brimming with pleasure in her

otherwise plain face. She really looked forward to Tuesdays when Jack came in.

By the time Jack arrived home the pizzas, with extra mushrooms (just how Ben liked them), were just beginning to cool. But he and Ben were maestros of the microwave and in no time at all were ensconced in front of the television as the titles to *Nosferatu* rolled.

To Jack's disappointment, Ben chomped his way through the chilling and sad tale of the first cinematic vampire with almost no reaction. The trouble with kids, Jack stopped himself nagging, was that they were interested only in flashy violence by Quentin Tarantino. They had no understanding of cinema's history. 'So, what do you think?' he finally ventured. 'Better than some manufactured pap from Hollywood?'

'Not bad,' conceded Ben, his pale blue eyes crinkling just like his father's, 'in fact a classic example of German expressionism. Now where's that other film I saw in your briefcase?'

Jack gave in, asking himself at what precise moment his son had learned to patronize him so effectively.

'Now,' Ben zapped the video into lurid action and settled back comfortably, 'tell me what you think of a *really* classic chiller thriller.'

After the last skull had been decimated by alien invaders dressed, for some reason Jack couldn't quite fathom, like medieval monks from the fourteenth century, Jack announced he was going to bed. Quite often these days he found himself going to sleep before Ben and wondered if this also happened in conventional two-parent families. Tonight, though, he couldn't sleep with his usual ease. The sight of a furious Francesca Tyler in the car park kept coming back to him. Had he been unfair to follow up a story the *Citizen* so clearly saw as its own? He did feel perhaps a whisper guilty, but surely all was fair in newspapers? He began to drift off, realizing that the problem was less to do with unfair rivalry between the two papers and far more to do with the *Express*'s editor finding himself increasingly attracted to the *Citizen*'s counterpart. A brief image of Francesca, her lustrous hair loosened from its usual restraints, filled his imagination. It was interrupted by a strange sound of scrabbling, followed by shushing noises. He sat up. What the hell was going on? He grabbed his bathrobe and crept downstairs, fear clutching at him for Ben's sake. Silently he snapped on the kitchen lights.

Ben knelt on the floor, his arms around a dog that seemed to be an unhappy marriage between a bearded collie and a lurcher. Around its scruffy neck was tied a red and white spotted bargee's bandanna. It was, by anyone's estimation, a disgraceful dog.

'Ben,' his father accused, seeing years of vet bills, chewed upholstery and doggy paternity suits flash in front of his eyes, 'where did that animal come from?'

'Please let me keep him,' pleaded Ben. 'One of those grungies left him tied to the market cross and he was going to be taken off and locked up.'

Instead of the grown-up teenager with his Discman and his rollerblades, Jack saw only a sad seven-year-old after his mother had left, begging ten times a day to be allowed a puppy. Jack, already finding it hard coping with job, child and a string of Finnish au pairs, had felt unable to face even a shred more responsibility and refused. He hadn't counted on the guilt that would lie in wait for him, fiercer than any Rottweiler.

'I suppose so,' Jack conceded and knelt down beside Ben. The creature immediately covered him in disgusting kisses. 'I don't suppose he has a name?'

'As a matter of fact he has. It's on the tag round his neck. He's called Wild Rover.'

'Wild Rover,' repeated Jack weakly, 'of course it is.' He pushed the dog away and into Ben's delighted arms. 'And with a name like that I'm glad it's you not me who's going to be calling him in the park.'

Francesca lay luxuriously back in the bath and thought about what she was going to wear tonight. She'd been surprised when Henrietta had invited her to a 'little fund-raising dinner for the local infertility unit'. Infertility, especially if it didn't involve infertile celebrities, wasn't on Henrietta's usual list of charitable concerns. Henrietta's benefits were usually in favour of Distressed Lloyd's Syndicates or the Gertrude Jekyll Society for Arthritic Lady Gardeners. When she'd hosted a strawberry tea for the Church Restoration Fund, Fran had to explain to her that it was nothing to do with restoring the Book of Common Prayer instead of the frightful modern liturgy, but simply replacing the slates on the roof.

And when Henrietta had casually mentioned that the star guest tonight was one Dr Laurence Westcott, Fran had been pleasantly surprised. She'd already heard of the man and that he was doing trail-blazing work at his clinic and had even wondered whether she might ask him for an interview. From his reputation, she imagined a man in his late fifties, charismatic and pioneering, who would hold the dinner party in the palm of his hand and have them waving their cheque books before you could say sperm sample. Maybe tonight she might even approach him for a story.

There was just time to wash her hair. Fran doused herself in Jojoba and began to sing 'Gonna Wash That Man Right Out Of My Hair'. The rather sweet memory of Jack Allen holding the baby imprinted itself briefly on her mind, chased instantly away by the reminder that he had stolen her story and was now barefacedly on the point of trying to put her out of business with his free newspaper. She rinsed her hair until it squeaked satisfactorily, then gave it a final masochistic soak in freezing water and wrapped it in a turban. Her bare unadorned face caught her eye in the bathroom mirror. Like this, without make-up, her resemblance to her father was striking. They shared oval faces with high, almost Slavic cheekbones – had some handsome Tartar once raped and pillaged her ancestors' womenfolk? Unlikely since as far as she knew they came from Surrey, the kind of county where even the Tartars drove Jags. Her nose was a shade too long and her eyes a mite narrow. It was a striking face, she knew. Not pretty but memorable. With the full mouth she'd inherited from her mother and hair the colour of a new penny, she could, on a good day, look fairly attractive. Except that she was always an inch or two taller than every man she met. If most men wanted to gaze admiringly into her eyes, they'd need a stepladder. You'll do, her father had told her when she was going to her first party, but with so much suppressed pride that, on a good day, she was occasionally able to believe him.

She wondered how dressy Henrietta was likely to be in the cause of infertility. Henrietta could range from Shirley Bassey glitter to nun-like understatement and it was sometimes hard to know where to pitch oneself. Short and black, Fran decided. That did for every occasion. This particular example looked best with a Wonderbra, but Fran decided too much décolletage might detract from the seriousness of the occasion. The man was coming to raise funds for childless couples, not gaze at her topography, or top-off-graphy if the Wonderbra did its stuff.

Fran zipped herself into the tightly fitting dress with the assistance of a coat hanger – a tip her mother had passed on to her from the *Jimmy Young Show* along with 1001 things to do with laddered tights. Fran blushed at how sniffy she'd been about it and now here she was using it. She hoped to God her mother never found out.

A blast of perfume and she was ready. Would Laurence Westcott live up to his impressive reputation, she wondered, giving herself a last check-up in the hall mirror or, like most men, turn out to be more interested in himself than anything else? In spite of years of experience which should have taught Fran that she ought to know better, she felt a small but decided sliver of anticipation.

Chapter 3

'Do we really have to go through all this just to get your friend fixed up with a test-tube father?' Simon complained to Henrietta. He hated having to wear a suit on a Saturday night when he could have worn his favourite Guernsey sweater and the ancient blue jeans he reckoned, erroneously as it happened, made him look young. Nothing he liked better than a cosy evening tucked up in front of the television.

'He wouldn't be a test-tube father,' Henrietta corrected, hesitating between decorous black and statement scarlet. 'You've got the wrong end of the stick as usual. He runs an infertility clinic, that's all.'

Simon brushed up against her, placing her hand on his ever-eager organ. 'Why don't you find the right end of the stick for me then?'

Henrietta grabbed her hand back irritably. 'Because our guests are arriving in twenty minutes and I don't want them standing on the doorstep listening to you coming like an oversexed whale.'

'Did you know,' Simon enquired, 'that sperm whales have orgasms that last twenty minutes?'

'My God,' Henrietta blenched, 'thank heavens I'm not a female sperm whale.'

Downstairs Henrietta surveyed the table. Just right, she decided. She'd spent hours wrapping all the napkins into water lilies just like she'd been shown on her Entertaining at Home course. In each one she'd hidden a tiny gold Biro as the smallest hint about what everyone was doing here tonight.

The table plan had been a nightmare. She had to give Fran the chance to shine without it looking as though she were being thrown at Laurence Westcott, and yet she had to separate the husband and wife GPs she'd also invited and put them at a safe distance so everyone wasn't treated to a riveting evening on the pros and cons of GP fund holding. Then there was the question of Simon and damage limitation. Where could she seat her husband so that he ended up offending only some of the guests rather than all of them? In the end she'd given up on that one as an impossibility.

The doorbell rang exactly on the dot of eight. Who would be so crass as to arrive on time? Luckily for them, her hostess course had told her always to be ready fifteen minutes early for just such an eventuality.

'We'll go,' chorused two voices. Damn. She'd forgotten to check what Sophie and Lottie were wearing. Knowing Lottie it could range from nothing at all to one of her mother's less suitable nightdresses.

When Lottie led Jim and Judy Williams, the two local doctors, into the sitting room, Henrietta heaved a sigh of relief. Six-year-old Lottie was looking fetching in a spangled net petticoat complete with wand and tiara. Then Sophie followed and Henrietta gasped. It wasn't her clothes, which were for once both smart and restrained, it was the diamond nose-stud that glittered in her left nostril. She must have had it done this afternoon and saved the unveiling for tonight, when Henrietta was powerless to protest, the little beast.

'I'll talk to you later,' hissed Henrietta just as Simon's business partner and his extremely rich wife appeared, followed by Fran herself who looked, in Henrietta's view, at her very best. Fran's russet hair fell across her face in the surprisingly shy gesture she adopted when meeting new people, then she flicked it back as her confidence built. She was an odd mixture, Henrietta reflected, of strength and vulnerability, like a pale, delicate rose that looks as if it would never see the autumn but outlasts all its robust-looking rivals.

It suddenly struck Henrietta that none of her guests had drinks. Where the hell was Simon? Just as she was about to bellow, he appeared at her elbow, genial and charming, with a tray of Kir Royales. She had to admit, he did have his uses. While all her girlfriends struggled to know their husbands' innermost thoughts and believed in working hard at their relationships, Henrietta had no such illusions. Her own marriage to Simon flourished because neither of them gave it a second thought.

'You look good enough to eat tonight,' Simon complimented Fran in a low voice so that his wife wouldn't overhear.

'Thank you, Simon.' Fran knew that, thankfully, although Simon often chatted her up, he actually loved his wife devotedly and had never, as far as she knew, strayed from the straight and narrow. 'What are we eating, as a matter of interest?' She steered him gently away from the subject of herself.

'Menu B. She only learned three on this course and she doesn't vary so much as a lettuce leaf. A is too posh, lobster and foie gras. Only visiting royalty get that. B is seafood salad and rack of lamb.'

'What about C?' Fran was intrigued.

'Shepherd's pie. For kitchen suppers. Made with only top-quality shepherds of course.'

Fran felt a tug on her frock and found Lottie, her tiara slipping, tongue poked out in concentration, offering her a canapé, closely followed by the nose-studded Sophie with the wine bottle.

'Auntie Fran,' Sophie whispered, 'could you nobble Mum later? She's livid because I had the tiniest little stud put in. The tamest thing imaginable. She should meet Rachel. Rach has had everything pierced. Ears, nose, lip and even her belly button.'

'My God,' Simon shook his head dejectedly, 'you beggar yourself saving up for their education and what do they end up with? Three grade As? No. More perforations than a bloody teabag!'

'Where's your guest of honour then?' Fran was surprised Laurence Westcott hadn't arrived yet.

Simon looked at his watch. It was quarter to nine, long after the acceptable band of lateness. 'Henrietta'll go ballistic if the man's forgotten. I must admit, I do think it's a bit rude when we're going to all this trouble.'

Ten minutes later the doorbell rang and Sophie and her mother headed as one for the door. 'Back to bottle duty,' commanded her mother, sending Sophie towards the drawing room again. 'The poor man spends his whole life creating children, he doesn't want to see what they grow up into or he might think again.'

Henrietta took her guest's coat and hustled him into the drawing room with great obsequiousness. 'Right, everyone, I'd like to introduce the man of the night, Dr Laurence Westcott.'

Fran shuddered for the poor man at the awfulness of the introduction, but he seemed remarkably unfazed. She studied him from behind the safety of Simon's reassuring bulk, fascinated at how different he was from her expectations. The most noticeable thing about Laurence Westcott was how extraordinarily good-looking he was. The second most noticeable thing was how he tried to play down that fact, as if beauty were somehow too frivolous for a man in his position. His corn-coloured hair was cut slightly long over the collar of his pale green linen suit, an unconventional choice of clothing for a doctor. He was lean and fit with pale gold skin of the kind that wasn't acquired sitting by swimming pools but by windsurfing or sailing or something gently athletic. He wore little gold glasses and Fran found herself wondering if they were real, or worn to give the gravitas the rest of his appearance lacked. Lastly, Fran noted with a little rush of pleasure, he was taller than she was.

'Mrs Norton,' he took the glass Henrietta was proffering, 'I can't apologize enough.' As if he'd guessed what Fran was thinking he took off his glasses and rubbed his eyes briefly. Fran saw then how tired they were and kicked herself for her stupid speculations. Whatever else he was. Laurence Westcott was genuine and, Fran had no choice but to acknowledge it, genuinely attractive. 'I would have been on time but we had an emergency egg collection.'

'Ooh,' Lottie dodged under his arm, clearly imagining the newcomer holding a basket, and perhaps a fireman's outfit for the emergency bit. 'Why was it a 'mergency? Would the eggs have hatched?'

Laurence laughed and ruffled her hair. 'They would one day, and turn into little girls like you.'

Lottie was clearly mystified.

'Dr Westcott is a special doctor,' announced her mother, 'who helps ladies who want babies but can't have them.'

'Like Auntie Fran, you mean? She's always saying she wants to take me home because she hasn't got one of her own.'

Simon muffled a laugh and Fran kicked him, wishing the ground would open up under her.

'I think it's time,' Henrietta announced, giving her husband a quelling look, 'that we all went into dinner.'

'Absolutely,' Simon took Laurence's glass out of his hand and put it on the tray. 'Dr Westcott,' he went on before Henrietta could stop him, 'why don't you go first?' He glanced back boldly at his wife. 'After all, we wouldn't want to give you the impression that you're on the menu, would we?'

Simon, knowing it was more than his life was worth to vary the seating plan, placed Laurence at one end of the table and himself at the other. Henrietta was to sit beside Laurence on one side, Fran on the other and the four other guests ranged down the table. Sophie, much to her annoyance, now that she'd glimpsed Laurence, was despatched to put Lottie to bed. 'Dishy, isn't he?' she murmured to Fran, who had slipped into the kitchen to help bring in the first course. 'I wouldn't mind his speculum up my –'

'Thank you, Sophie,' interrupted her mother firmly, gesticulating towards the other room, 'and don't go to bed with that stud in. It'll ruin the duvet cover.'

Finally they were all settled with their food in front of them. 'So, Laurence,' Henrietta invited briskly, 'perhaps you could tell us all a little about the work your unit does?'

Laurence put down his fork patiently with only a slight look of longing at the delicious seafood on his plate. Clearly he was used to singing for his supper. 'We treat the full range of infertility in women via hormone treatment and fallopian surgery but I suppose our significant achievements have been in test-tube fertilization – IVF and GIFT.'

'My God,' Simon poured himself a large glass of expensive wine, 'whatever happened to good old-fashioned bonking?'

Laurence smiled gently. 'It's rather an inefficient method of delivery as a matter of fact. And don't let's forget,' he glanced at Simon, 'there's a lot more male infertility than there used to be.'

Simon looked startled. 'Why?'

'Alcohol.' Judy, the GP on his left, eyed him beadily. 'And tight pants. I hope you wear boxers.'

Fran stifled a laugh and caught Laurence's eye. He was enjoying himself. He had none of the pompousness of the great man she'd expected. In spite of herself, Fran felt a jolt of attraction, like two wires sparking. She even sensed he was feeling it too. Then someone else was talking to him and he looked away from her.

'But isn't infertility really just a problem for all these wretched career women who want to have their cake and eat it?' It was the wife of Simon's rich partner who'd probably never worked and never wanted to. 'I mean why should all the rest of us sub it?'

Fran waited for his answer, knowing that somehow it would matter to her very much indeed.

'You're right that fertility problems do kick in the later you start trying, and wanting careers has slowed women down,' Fran's heart sank. He was going to agree with the horrible woman. 'But personally I believe every woman has the right to hold her own baby in her arms however late she starts to try to conceive. It's one of the most primal instincts we have.'

Fran could have kissed him

The lamb arrived, pink and delicious, and Henrietta headed the conversation off to calmer waters. She didn't want her minutely planned evening to turn nasty.

Fran went on watching Laurence discreetly. He took all the implied criticisms from these stupid rich people with calm and humour. There was a kind of tranquillity about him that bordered on the monkish. It intrigued Fran, used as she was to pushy journalists. Unconsciously she found herself comparing Laurence's considered calm with Jack Allen's charm and swagger. Jack was all on the surface. Laurence Westcott, she suspected, would take time to get to know, but it would be worth it.

She felt a tap on her shoulder. 'Would you mind helping me take out the dishes?' prodded Henrietta.

Once the kitchen door was firmly closed, Henrietta pounced. 'Well, what do you think? Fabulous, isn't he?'

'He seems very pleasant,' agreed Fran guardedly. 'Where did you bump into him?'

Henrietta grinned. 'In the stirrups actually.'

Fran looked confused. 'I didn't know you rode.'

'I don't mean that sort of stirrups.'

The full horror of her friend's implication dawned on Fran. 'You *didn't*, Henry!'

'Yes, I did. I glimpsed him across a crowded cervix. I was having a coil fitted and I saw him in the foyer. He was too good to pass up. Just think what a good father he'd make. He'd nurture your eggs like a mother hen and he'd be perfect if you had any fertility problems. All the babies you had would be bound to be good at science.'

An awful suspicion began to reveal itself to Francesca. 'Henry . . . tonight . . . this whole dinner, you didn't . . .' She couldn't bring herself to answer her own question.

Henrietta glowed with self-satisfaction. 'Of course I did. Why else would I ask him? I hardly know the man. Yet.'

Before Fran could comment, her friend propelled her through the door with a cafetiere and a jug of milk. Laurence Westcott looked up at her, as if he'd noticed the exact moment she'd left the room and the exact moment she'd re-entered it. His green eyes held hers for a fraction of a second and Fran felt her backbone melt dangerously. She hung on to the coffee as if it were a life belt and made for the opposite corner of the room.

Later that night, the washing-up done, the evening dissected, Henrietta leapt on her husband as he undressed, and wrestled him to the bed. He was so surprised, he could only capitulate.

'So,' Henrietta demanded, undoing his shirt buttons with ruthlessly efficient speed, 'what did you think of Laurence Westcott?'

'Seemed a bit of a wimp to me,' countered Simon, slipping his hand up her skirt.

'Good,' Henrietta said, easing herself onto her husband's ever-ready erection, 'that means Franny'll go for him. She doesn't fancy rugger buggers like you.'

'All that rot about tight pants and infertility,' scoffed Simon, increasing his stroke. 'I've always worn tight pants and it's never affected my fertility.'

'Yes, darling,' Henrietta arranged herself in her favourite position for a satisfactory climax. 'I'm sure your sperm could swim the Atlantic. But then neither Sophie nor Lottie look much like you, do they?'

His revenge for this unworthy jibe was to turn her over and start again.

Fran sat in her office with its view of the noisy chaos of the newsroom beyond and thought about Laurence

Westcott. It was their news conference in a moment and there were any number of things for her to be doing, but she couldn't settle to any of them. He hadn't asked for her phone number. Too obvious perhaps. He wasn't the kind of person, she guessed, who would like his actions witnessed. There was something private about him. Then she wondered for one ghastly moment if he'd any inkling of Henrietta's motives in asking him. A flush of embarrassment fired through her, stirring up one of her worst-ever memories. At seventeen she'd been to a May ball at Cambridge, invited by the boy she'd fancied for months and thought too deliciously wonderful. It had been the most glorious evening, the best of her life. She'd worn a brand new Laura Ashley ballgown in black velvet, and shoes with little rhinestones on the buckle which had reminded her of Cinderella. They had danced quite literally all night and then punted along the silvery Cam as the dawn came up. All the way home in the train to Woodbury she'd glowed with the excitement of it all. Then she'd discovered he'd only invited her because her mother was paying for the tickets. Forty pounds each. She'd wept for hours and thrown her rhinestone shoes in the dustbin.

'Dr Fertility was that attractive, eh?' Stevie's words cut into her daydream with the brutality of a surgeon's knife. 'I'd heard he looked like something from Young Interns In Love.'

'For heaven's sake, Stevie,' Fran snapped guiltily. 'I was simply wondering whether we might do a feature about his unit, that's all.'

'And the dazzling editor of the *Woodbury Citizen* might write it herself rather than sending some crass young reporter? Speaking of crass young reporters,' Stevie's voice sounded suddenly serious, 'I think it's time for a bit of troop-rallying. Give them your Boadicea-before-the-battle speech. They've all heard this rumour about Jack Allen and the freebie paper. On top of his wheeze with the bus story they're wondering if there's any point coming in to work.'

Fran was shocked at herself. Normally she'd have been the first to spot any anxiety among the reporters. The first thing Ralph had taught her was to have an open door and make sure she spent at least as much time out of her office with the paper's staff as locked away being Editorial.

'Thanks for telling me. I'll raise it at conference.' She strode out into the middle of the newsroom. 'Right, everyone. Time for conference.'

One weekly conference was held to decide on ideas for the week's paper, another to firm up on which page each story should appear and where the picture stories should be placed.

Mike Wooley, their newest and cockiest reporter, made a dumb show of being stuck in a crucial conversation. Keith Wilson, the sports reporter, picked up his thermos of tea to bring with him. He disapproved strongly of the real coffee Fran had introduced into the office and never failed to make his views felt. He followed Stevie, the features editor and the chief sub into the crowded meeting room where they perched on every surface. Keith Wilson got out his Garibaldi biscuits and handed one to Stevie. Mike Wooley, who had finally put down the phone tried to help himself. 'Uh-huh, sunshine,' Keith shook his head. 'You have to join the Garibaldi club, mate. 10p a week.'

Mike Wooley rolled his eyes in disbelief. At that moment Sean McGee, one of the trainees arrived, still wearing the anti-pollution mask he used to fend off the fumes as he bicycled around Woodbury, giving him the air of a slightly anxious alien. 'Right,' he demanded, 'who's nicked my bike space?'

Fran faltered for a moment. They were all hard-working and one or two of them highly talented, but she couldn't help feeling the news conference over at the rival *Express* might be a whisker more hard-nosed.

'OK, what have we got for this week?'

They ran through the mix of local scandal, council decisions, drunk driving cases, car crashes, weddings, funerals and productions of *Annie Get Your Gun* that made up the staple fare of a small weekly paper.

'I think I might be onto something with a coach company that's been cutting back on its drivers and making them drive dangerous stints,' threw in Mike Wooley. 'Now that the *Express* has taken over our bus scandal.'

Fran saw her cue. 'Look, everyone, I know you feel bitter about the bus story and so you bloody well should. It was piracy. We did all the foot-slogging and the *Express* capitalized on it, but remember this: the *Express* is a flash and trash paper. What they're about is ambulance-chasing, not real reporting. They like nothing better than a death knock to some poor mother to get the quote on how she feels about the only son she didn't even know was dead. If Jack Allen starts a new paper it'll be more of the same.'

'Some people like reading flash and trash,' Mike Wooley ventured.

'Then they should stick with the *Express*, or work for it.' Fran's eyes were blazing with sparks of anger now. 'When my father started the *Citizen* it was to cover genuine local issues properly. Issues that affected people, not just blood on the road and exposing villains. They have their place, of course they do, but the *Citizen*'s about making things better, empowering people. News you can use. My father always says we're the Bible locally. That's why it matters that we keep in touch with the people who live here, understand their agenda, not provide some scoop-led Fleet Street crap. That's why it matters so much that we spell people's names right. And where they live.' She picked up a copy of last week's *Express* with its misspelling of one of the best-known streets in Woodbury. 'Accuracy spells credibility on a paper like ours.'

Sean McGee looked up from the feverish notes he was taking of Fran's words. 'There's a nice story out on the Fielding Estate, you know, the one where the police want to make it a no-go area. A group of mums have got together and are patrolling it to stop the joyriding. It's even better because one of the mums' son is at a detention centre because of all the joyriding he's done himself.'

'Great. That's just the kind of story the *Citizen* should be doing. You're a terrific team and the *Citizen* is a great paper. We still sell more copies than the *Express*, remember.'

'But for how long once they start their freebie?'

She knew it'd be Mike again. She'd better have a chat with him, see what was bugging him.

'And a last bit of good news. We've been shortlisted for the regional press awards.'

A murmur of pleasure rippled through the room, which Fran didn't dampen by the information that the other candidate in the running was the *Woodbury Express*.

'OK, let's get out there. I need some good NIBs . . . that one about the man who lost his keys and broke into his own home and ended up being arrested was brilliant. Congratulations, Mike.'

Stevie followed her into her office. 'How was I?' Fran asked the older woman.

'Great. I thought you were a bit tough on Jack Allen though. The *Express* campaigns too, you know.'

'Whose side are you on?'

They were interrupted by a crack of laughter from the newsroom. Sean McGee had stuck a sign saying 'ACCURICY SPELLS CREDIBILITY' on his pinboard and Mike Wooley had pointed out that if he wanted to be teacher's pet he'd have to learn to spell first.

'You know,' Stevie smiled at the laughter, 'I do sometimes miss the old days before it all got so serious. Reporting in the morning, a long lunch and leisurely afternoon. We used to go to this little drinking club where they had strippers . . .'

'Stevie!' Fran was amazed.

'They were wonderful old stagers. More lip than Roseanne. They did a running commentary on everyone they could see in the audience as they whipped off their knickers. Naturally,' Stevie dragged herself back to the present, 'we caught up with work in the evenings.'

'Next you'll come out with that old cliché about the editor having whisky in the filing cabinet.'

'Your dad did.'

'And I have a bottle of mineral water.'

'Everyone's the same these days. They all want to go home instead of to the pub.'

'Poor Stevie. I'll come tonight and prove editors can still put them away just like the old days. By the way,' Fran slipped in, 'you know I mentioned a piece about the Woodbury Infertility Unit? What do you really think of the idea?'

'Good thought. Though you never know,' she winked outrageously at Fran, 'Dr Kildare might even ring without the power of the press.'

Fran was about to protest and shove her out when their receptionist came through on the buzzer. 'Phone for you, Fran. A Dr Laurence Westcott. He said it was personal.'

'See what I mean,' beamed Stevie and headed for the door.

Fran tried to calm herself down as she picked up the phone on her desk.

'Hello. I don't know if you remember me? Laurence Westcott from the other night.' She liked him for his diffidence. Jack Allen would have just assumed he was unforgettable. 'Actually . . .' he paused fractionally as Fran's pulse raced, 'I wondered if you'd be interested in seeing round the unit.'

'I'd be absolutely fascinated,' agreed Fran, struggling to keep the excitement from her voice.

'Oh well,' Stevie commented as she shut the door, 'I suppose it beats showing you his etchings.'

Fran was humming five minutes later when Keith Wilson came to her with a proposition. 'It's the Sunday Football League. They want us to sponsor them. It's a bit pricey but they promise to give us exclusive coverage if we sign up. Then they won't even talk to the *Express*.'

Fran thought about it. Her father would never have agreed to it. He would have said there was enough competition in TV sport without bringing it down to local amateur level and of course he would have been right, especially in view of what Fran had just told the troops. However, Fran wasn't perfect and Jack had stolen her bus story.

'Done,' she said. 'Do you think they'd call it the Citizen Sunday League?' That would really annoy Jack.

'I'll look into it,' grinned Keith, 'for another two hundred pounds they'd probably call themselves the Spiders from Mars.'

'All right, everyone, this is Fran's round so order a double,' Stevie shouted over the noise of the pub. The Cathedral Arms was just across the road from their office, tucked down a close at the side of the cathedral, and it sported every emblem the heritage industry could muster. Blackened beams, inglenook fireplace, horse brasses, oak settles and a wobbly stone floor. The only difference between the Cathedral Arms and most pubs was that this one was genuinely ancient and had refreshed stonemasons, carters and grain vendors since medieval times. Some people said the plumbing hadn't changed since then either. The only difference between customers then and now was that instead of reeling back to their carts and relying on their horses to know the way home, the modern clientele phoned their wives.

Fran memorized the round and fought her way to the bar. As usual the chauvinistic barman took great pleasure in making female customers, no matter how power-dressed, wait as long as was humanly possible. By now Fran had worked her way to the optimum position where to ignore her could only be a deliberate insult. He managed it all the same and asked someone at the end of the bar with his back to her for their order instead.

Fran prepared to bellow when a voice cut in before her. 'I think you'll find Ms Tyler was before me.' He turned and smiled. It was Jack Allen.

'Here, let me take that for you,' he insisted when the barman handed her a tray loaded with a dozen drinks. 'We wouldn't want you to throw it over Seamus, much as he deserves it, would we?' He nodded towards the barman.

Halfway across the crowded bar he stopped for a moment. 'By the way, I had an irate sports reporter in my office not five minutes ago. He seemed to think you'd done the dirty on us over the Sunday football league.' Jack's pale blue eyes flashed with humour. 'But I told him he had to be wrong, that you didn't believe in the narrow scoop mentality, that the *Citizen*'s vision was a positive and co-operative one.'

If she could have reached them, Fran would have gladly poured the drinks not over Seamus, who wasn't worth the price of good whisky, but over the self-satisfied features of Jack Allen.

'Your drinks, lads,' Jack said, as he laid them on the table. 'I'm afraid I'm not buying this time. I'll save it for the night of the award. May the best paper win.'

'Francesca,' Stevie's tone was heavy with irony, 'you didn't tell us who else was shortlisted.'

'Is that the time?' Fran jumped up. 'I'm having supper with my parents. I'll see you all tomorrow.'

From his position at the bar Jack Allen watched her go. Francesca Tyler was a bloody good journalist but if she had one sin it was to be holier-than-thou. He'd finally caught her out and it felt wonderful.

It was only half a mile from the pub to her parents' house and Fran seethed every inch of the way. Jack Allen had a nerve. How dare he imply that she was being hypocritical? He was lucky to have got away without her drenching him. The brief picture of Jack Allen with dark black stout dripping from his hair, soaking that ridiculous tweed jacket with the leather elbows he affected, when in this day and age he must have to get them sewn on specially, enlivened her journey so much that she suddenly found she'd missed her turning.

She doubled back, a pleasant tingle of anticipation propelling her down her parents' drive. Should she tell her father about meeting Laurence? She knew he felt vaguely responsible that she hadn't settled down and would be thrilled that she'd finally met someone she was interested in. She stopped for a moment, firmly reminding herself of how stupid she was being. Laurence Westcott had simply invited her to see round his unit. It was quite likely that his interest in her was purely professional. He simply needed publicity to raise cash. On the other hand, he had said his phone call was personal . . . She suddenly remembered the way he'd watched her coming back into the room at Henrietta's, and how aware he'd seemed of her absence. She ran the few final yards like a six year old on her birthday.

From the outside, Five Ashes looked a welcoming house. You could imagine it stuffed with children, a log fire crackling in the grate, baking smells drifting from the kitchen, but a certain telltale neatness gave some warning. All Fran's life, Phyllis had made neatness into a religion. Plates were whisked away the moment the last mouthful had been finished, beloved toys tidied relentlessly out of sight, coasters dotted the polished surfaces like chicken pox. Even in her adult life Fran still had the odd habit of never putting down a half-eaten biscuit or slice of cake in case she never saw it again. The one thing she could never forgive or forget was coming back from college one day to discover that her bedroom had been turned into a guest room and her possessions piled into a cardboard box. The message had been clear: her mother thought it was time she grew up. To Fran there was one supreme irony: they never had any guests to stay anyway. Visitors had more sense and headed for cosy B&Bs.

Fran rang the doorbell, the familiar feeling of being more guest than daughter creeping over her. Her mother appeared wearing a flowery apron over a wool dress, her hair a soft grey, the picture of warm and comfortable motherhood except, Fran thought, that it was all a sham. Her mother was as warm as a packet of frozen peas.

'Hello, Mum.' Fran kissed the proffered cheek. On a good day she felt sorry for her mother, realizing that Phyllis's narrowness had blighted her own life even more than other people's. Today was a good day so she reminded herself that her mother had had a childhood far more emotionally barren than Fran's own. She shivered slightly. It was March and still cold, but her mother didn't believe in wasting the central heating. Her father's retirement had added new zest to her economies.

'You look happy,' her mother offered unexpectedly. 'Like you used to on one of those trips with your dad.'

There was a wistfulness in her tone that reached out to Fran.

She hugged her mother briefly. Phyllis stiffened, reminding Fran of a punchbag in a flowery apron. 'Where's Dad?'

'In his study. Supper's in ten minutes.' Her mother went back to her spotless domain in the kitchen.

Entering her father's study was like stepping into another world. Lit with small table lamps, it was dark but the darkness was kind and welcoming. Her father abhorred overhead lighting. The deep green walls groaned with books, an ancient wing chair with the stuffing coming out sat next to an electric fire in the shape of an Adam staircase. There were newspapers everywhere, ancient and modern. Trophies and awards from a long career in journalism adorned the top of his roll-top desk. Even the motes of dust swirling in the dim light seemed comfortable and at home. How he managed to protect it from his wife's hostile Hoover Fran never knew.

'Franny, love,' Ralph jumped up, 'I didn't hear you come

in. What a pleasure to see you. How's life in the frenetic world of journalism?'

'Frenetic. You were right about Jack Allen. Stevie made me rally the troops today. They'd heard the rumour too. By the way,' she looked at him slyly, 'what's all this about afternoon drinking clubs and saucy strippers? This is not the image of my father the pioneering editor I have lifelong treasured.'

'Ah.' Her father beamed reminiscently. 'Stroppy Susan. What a woman. How many exotic dancers can remove their bras while withering every male in the audience at the same time?'

'Sounds disgusting.'

'Actually, I did think of giving her a column in the paper but Stevie wouldn't hear of it.' The affection in his voice wrung Fran's heart.

'Dad,' Fran wasn't sure she should ask this. 'Did you love Stevie?'

Ralph looked into the fire. 'We understood each other if that's what love is.'

'Why didn't you leave then? I mean you and Mum aren't exactly a match made in heaven.'

'There is such a thing as duty, Francesca. Your generation doesn't believe in it, I know. Individual happiness is your God. But Stevie and I decided it was for the best.'

'Haven't you ever regretted it? I mean, for all these years you and Stevie have been such wonderful friends, yet you could have been so much more.'

'Friendship's no mean thing, you know. Who knows, perhaps we would have fallen out of love and caused all that pain for nothing. Love based on other people's misery can be hard to sustain, you know.'

Fran felt tears welling behind her eyes. Her father had made a terrible sacrifice. He'd given up the chance of love and warmth and shared interests with Stevie for the sterility of a life with her mother. He'd probably done it for Fran's sake too, though he would never burden her with the guilt of telling her so. 'Thanks, Dad. For loving me so much.'

Ralph touched her face lightly. 'I'm no martyr, Fran. I've had a better life than many. The paper, the horses, my lovely daughter.' He seemed to read her mind. 'You were worth it, you know. Look how well you've turned out. If only you could find yourself a decent chap and settle down.' There was a pause. 'Now let's talk about something dull and boring like the chances of Spring Story for the Gold Cup. What do you reckon?'

Their passionate discussion about racing form – imbued in her since her earliest outings to race courses at eight years old – lasted until supper was on the table. Phyllis was a surprisingly good cook, given that cooking seemed an art requiring love and attention, but she compensated by giving unnecessarily small portions. No wonder Ralph was so taut and lean.

Afterwards, Fran helped her mother with the washing-up. In the corner, in pristine condition and sprayed daily with Dettox, stood a dishwasher, glowering like a steely god worshipped by adoring natives, never defiled by use. It's not worth it for two, was her mother's continual refrain. On the rare occasion when it was used Phyllis spent so long pre-rinsing the dishes before putting them in that it would have been quicker to do the job by hand.

'I'm worried about your father,' Phyllis announced, putting on her rubber gloves with all the delicacy of a surgeon about to operate. 'He hardly ever comes out of his study. Especially now he's got this wretched cable television.'

Fran could see his point. If she lived in this house she'd move her bed in there. 'It's a comfortable room,' she offered neutrally. 'It probably reminds him of going to work.'

'Why can't he take up gardening like most husbands? Heaven knows, we need someone to do the weeding.'

'Mum, you know he's as interested in flowers as a gorilla is in the works of Flaubert. He's like me. He can kill a plant at ten paces.'

'He could do a bit of DIY then.'

Fran laughed. How could her mother live with her father for thirty-six years and know him so little? 'He's hopeless at that sort of thing. Why should retiring suddenly make him good at putting up shelves?'

But her mother was in full flow. 'And then, the other day, do you know what he did?'

It amazed Fran that the only person in the world who seemed impervious to her father's warmth and charm was his own wife. 'No, but I'm sure you're going to tell me.'

'He offered to do the shopping.'

Phyllis's tone was so affronted that Fran burst out laughing. 'But I thought you wanted him to be more helpful.'

'How helpful is it to come back with all the wrong things?'

That's the male way of doing things so as not to be asked again, thought Fran.

'And then there was this business with the kidneys.'

'What business?' Fran asked wearily.

'He bought four pounds of them.'

'But he doesn't like kidneys.'

'Exactly!' Phyllis clearly felt she was scoring a point. 'And when I cooked them he said surely after all this time I knew kidneys were the one thing he loathed.'

Fran shared her mother's mystification. Unless her father had decided to act up as some subtle form of revenge, and for that Fran wouldn't blame him at all, then certainly it was odd. But then he was entitled to a little eccentric behaviour. Probably her mother was making too much of it. All the same a slight sense of apprehension crept over her.

Chapter 4

The Woodbury Infertility Unit was nothing like Fran had expected. Somehow she'd imagined a gloomy, desperate place with an institutional, faintly forbidding feel to it. Perhaps even with a dash of that furtive guilty air of a VD clinic, where no one quite wants to admit what they're doing there.

The pop music that greeted her in reception dispelled such thoughts instantly. The small wing of the hospital where the infertility unit was housed was warm and brightly painted. Everywhere the walls were papered with photos of babies. Newborn babies swaddled so tightly only a triangle of face was visible, babies having their first baths, babies on the breast, babies in their delighted mothers' arms. The sense of joy and relief and gratitude flowing from their parents was so powerful it lit up the whole place. To Fran, the most touching of all was a blown-up photograph of one of the ugliest couples she'd ever seen holding a staggeringly beautiful infant, their faces humble and almost holy in the joy of this unexpected miracle. To her eternal embarrassment tears filled up her eyes.

'Hello,' Laurence's voice greeted her and she whipped round feeling foolish, wiping her eye and hoping he hadn't noticed.

'Don't worry,' he consoled, putting his hand lightly on her arm, 'it gets people like that. I'd much rather you were moved than a hard-bitten hack who thinks the infertile are selfish obsessives who ought to pull themselves together and get on with their lives.'

'Do some people feel that?'

'You'd be surprised how many. Like that woman the other night. They've no idea how wanting a baby can take over a woman's life. You can't believe how passionately some women want children. It becomes a burning need, and to deny it causes incredible pain and misery. They feel utterly incomplete.' His own voice rang with the passion of his indignation. 'Being a single career woman you probably find that hard to understand.'

Fran longed to tell him how completely she understood it, but she hardly knew him and anyway she was here as a professional. The faintly priestly quality Laurence had about him probably opened him up to countless confessions as it was.

'Look, come and have a cup of coffee and meet Moira, the Sister. It's her who really runs things. I'm just the token male around here.'

Fran noticed a striking nurse with red hair smiling at them from the far end of the corridor. They made their way past the shy-looking man who was trying to decide which to pick up from a discreet selection of girlie magazines. In the end he disappeared into the cubicle marked sperm samples clutching *Football Weekly*.

'Just like my husband,' winked Moira, leading her into a small side room, 'only able to think of one thing at a time.'

Fran found herself confronting a bed with stirrups banked by an impressive display of screens. Moira picked up a fierce-looking needle and attached it to something that looked like a curling tong. 'That's the probe we insert for egg collection. We use a condom, of course. I'm telling you, we get through more condoms than Warren Beatty in this unit.'

Fran giggled, amazed again at the relaxed atmosphere.

'We get the partner to do it, unless they're shaking like a leaf. Actually, they often need more sedation than the woman. Why does that not surprise me?'

She opened a stable door to the embryology lab. 'Show us an embryo, lads. And make sure it's a good egg, will you?'

Fran was aware of Laurence at her elbow, pointing at the screen. A perfect flower-like shape appeared.

'That one looks like a goer. You see the two little eyes? That means it's been fertilized. Next, they're frozen, to be implanted when the ovary's ready.'

'Laurence,' Moira interrupted, 'Mrs Sampson's outside. She wants to say goodbye and thank you.'

Laurence slipped out. 'Such a sad story,' Moira confided. 'He worked so hard for her. Let her have four goes at

IVF instead of three because she was so desperate. We all liked her so much. It's terrible when you fail in this business.'

'He seems amazingly dedicated,' Fran couldn't help commenting.

She had clearly hit upon one of Moira's favourite subjects. 'He's a saint, I'm telling you. He works himself to the bone for these couples. Every failure is his failure, he always says. He's always pushing us all to get up our success rate but I sometimes wish he had more of a life. All these babies and none of them his. Do you know, when one of the mums asked if she could call her wee scrap Laurence, he actually cried.'

This picture was almost too much for Fran.

The door opened behind them before she had a chance to answer. 'I hope you haven't been filling Miss Tyler's head with nonsense about my goodness and altruism, Moira,' Laurence chided. 'Moira thinks I'd make a good candidate for Pope.'

'You'd do a damn sight better job than the other fella. He can't bring himself to approve of test-tube babies, that one. Interfering in the divine right of creation, or some such nonsense. No matter that creation manages to leave a few thousand wombs barren and their owners with their hearts breaking. Like all men – except Dr Westcott – he thinks women should stop making a fuss and accept the hand that's been dealt them. Silly auld sod. Pardon my sacrilege.' Moira crossed herself reverently.

'Moira, you're a good woman but a terrible Catholic,' Laurence teased.

'I'd rather that,' Moira replied tartly, 'than the other way around.'

'Come on, Francesca,' Laurence steered her out of the room, 'come and see the best bit of all.'

In a tiny converted broom cupboard a blue-overalled technician leaned over an apparatus attached to a large screen. He took a tube out of the incubator and placed some of the liquid onto a slide. On the screen in front of them a perfect egg appeared magnified thousands of times.

'Now for the sperm,' Laurence said softly.

The technician jogged his elbow on the apparatus. 'Whoops!' he breathed. 'Nearly the end of someone's family!'

Six or seven sperm appeared on the screen as the technician attempted to catch one in his hair-thin needle, their tails waggling as they swam hopelessly in all directions. Clearly their primordial urge to find the egg had become dented somewhere along the line. Finally he caught one and injected it slowly and carefully into the middle of the egg.

'There you are,' Laurence pointed to the screen, 'the moment of conception.'

Fran held her breath. It was quite simply the most extraordinary thing she had ever seen. All the dynasties and dramas, Henry VIII's six wives, the women blamed over the centuries for their barrenness by kings and peasants alike, the heartache and the desperation, all symbolized in that single miraculous act. And here it was taking place in a converted broom cupboard in Woodbury. No wonder the politicians and the bishops were so worried. Why did you need God when you could make life in a laboratory?

'Good luck, baby!' Fran whispered leaning on the back of the technician's chair and willing it on to life.

She felt Laurence's eyes on her and flushed.

'You really care, don't you?' he asked softly.

'Of course I care! I think your work's wonderful. It makes me feel as though what I do is off the scale of unworthiness.'

Laurence laughed. 'We need journalists too.'

He opened the door and led her out. 'Thank you for coming, and for believing in us. Sometimes I only remember the failures and forget the happy endings. You've revived my optimism.'

Fran glowed with pleasure. There was something soulfully sad about Laurence and she yearned to find out what it was. Perhaps he'd had a blighted love affair or an unhappy childhood. 'Laurence,' she faltered, 'there's something I wanted to ask you.'

'Go ahead.'

'Would you mind if I wrote about the unit in the paper? Perhaps we could organize some kind of appeal for money or donors.'

'I'd like that very much.' The pain had gone. His light green eyes held hers and she felt that jolt of electricity she remembered from the other night run through her body. 'Especially,' he added softly, still holding her hand, 'if it means I'll be seeing more of you.'

Fran couldn't bring herself to answer. Until now she'd dismissed men as being pretty second-rate creatures. After her father they seemed to have broken the mould. But Laurence Westcott wasn't just extraordinarily attractive. He was a caring and selfless person, and he'd trusted her with a glimpse of his hurt. Maybe her luck had finally changed.

'So how was the gorgeous gynaecologist?'

'He isn't a gynaecologist.' For once Stevie's caustic humour irritated Fran. She unpacked her notebook from her shoulder bag and banged it down on her desk. 'He's an infertility expert, and he was absolutely fine. Inspiring in fact.'

'Oh, dear. Sorry my tone was insufficiently reverent. I have this innate distrust of authority figures, you see. Especially if they're wearing a white coat and poking metal up my fanny. I'm sure you're right. Dr Laurence Westcott is the exception that proves the rule. So are you going to write this feature?'

'Yes, I am as a matter of fact. I saw it as a double-page spread, perhaps with an appeal. I'd need to talk to Laurence at greater length . . .' Stevie's eyebrow raised a millimetre or two at the sudden use of Christian names, '. . . about the exact nature of that. He's already given me the phone number for a couple of success stories and one woman who failed, so I'm pretty well ready to go.'

'I'll leave you to it then, and go and hassle the reporters. I expect you'll need some privacy.' She made to close the door. 'Fancy a Garibaldi? I raided Keith's store.' Fran caught the currant y biscuit and realized she was starving. The unit, and its director, had been so fascinating she'd missed lunch.

'Thanks, Stevie. Could you have a peek in the cuttings

and see if there's anything on the infertility unit? I might as well make a start.'

'Absolutely. Strike while the sperm are still wriggling, I always say.'

There was one more thing Fran had to do before settling down to write the piece and that was to call up the women whose names Laurence had given her for the case histories. Annoyingly, the first woman was out so Fran left a message, but the second was not only in but could clearly have gone on talking about the wonders of Laurence Westcott all night. 'I had three attempts at IVF and they all failed,' she rattled on enthusiastically. 'The rule is no more after that, but Dr Westcott persuaded them to let me have one more go. Then, when it was all set up, we couldn't get the funding and do you know what he did? He won't want me to tell you this but I think it's time he got the credit.' Fran listened, fascinated. 'He sorted out the finances for me from some charity.'

Fran was amazed and even slightly shocked. Goodness like that was so unusual.

'And that time it worked. I think he's the most wonderful man I've ever met in my life.'

In the background Fran could hear someone, her husband presumably, make some comment. The poor man had probably heard enough about the wonderful Dr Westcott.

The cuttings file, when it hit her desk, was surprisingly thick, mostly with news stories about the unit's fight for resources, or stories about miracle babies. Nibbling her biscuit she started to read about Laurence's fight with the hospital trust for some piece of expensive equipment.

She mustn't start seeing the man as a hero. Fran Tyler, she told herself firmly, stop this. You are not a ten year old dreaming about the lead singer of Boyzone, you are thirty-four years old, independent, free and your own woman. She made herself concentrate on the article, pushing out of her mind the shaming notion that independent and free she might be, but what she really longed for was to be bound, chained and utterly enmeshed with another human being. Preferably called Laurence.

It was almost eight when she'd finished preparing her notes and had got to the last cutting. To her annoyance it was a double-page spread, not unlike the one she was planning herself, and it was in the *Express* of all papers. She glanced at the top right corner. Thank heavens, the article was seven years old – quite long enough in the past to have been forgotten. The editorial led with a passionate defence of the unit's work. Even then it must have been under attack or begging for resources and there were three case histories of women who had conceived with its help.

Fran was enthralled. The stories were told with such incredible poignancy that you couldn't fail to be moved. It was a brilliant piece of writing; committed and deeply evocative. In fact, it was so powerful that she felt the writer must have been through infertility treatment herself. She raked the paper for the name of the journalist. In a feature of this size and quality you would expect the writer to want their name emblazoned all over it. Instead it was nowhere to be seen. How odd. She riffled through the rest of the paper until she found the index in the inside front page. She was so astonished that she had to read the by-line twice. 'A passionate appeal to save the Woodbury Infertility Unit', it read, 'by the *Express*'s Editor, Jack Allen.'

Fran stared at it. Had Jack and his wife undergone fertility treatment themselves or was he just exceptionally talented at understanding the emotions of those who had?

She was so bemused by this unexpected side of Jack that when the phone at her elbow rang, she jumped, almost expecting it to be him, telling her that she of all people ought to know that good writing meant getting so much inside people's skins that the reader simply *thought* they must have lived through the experience themselves.

'Hello.'

She recognized the voice instantly as Laurence's. 'You're working late.' His tone was surprisingly hesitant. 'I half expected a machine. I should have asked you this afternoon but I didn't have the nerve. You may think this is a bit inappropriate and please feel free to say no, it won't affect anything,' Fran's hopes soared, 'but I wondered if you might have dinner with me sometime?'

Fran dispensed with the customary period of hesitation. 'Yes. I'd like that very much.'

'Good. That's very good. Next week perhaps?'

When Fran came out of her office she assumed that everyone had gone home and there would be no witnesses to the private can-can she danced around the coffee machine.

'He rang then, did he?' Stevie emerged from the sports department carrying some copy. 'Are you still going to bother writing the story?'

'Of course I am. I've already found out almost everything I need to go ahead. This is entirely separate.'

'I see. By the way, your father rang earlier. I forgot to tell you. There's some horse running tomorrow you've got to back. I think he said it was called Twinkle Toes.'

'I promise. Goodnight, Stevie, don't stay too long.' Fran slung on her giant shoulder bag and almost skipped across the newsroom floor. Her father's tip-offs almost always romped home and even if she only put on a couple of quid it would pay for their next outing to the Indian restaurant.

She dashed into the betting shop the following lunchtime and placed her bet just in time. For some contrary reason, Fran loved betting shops. The atmosphere was fraught and dirty and smoky and most nice middle-class people would run themselves over with their own Range Rovers before crossing the threshold. But there was a kind of desperate excitement that made them unique. Partly it was the people – raffish types who'd poured out of the pub clutching their dog-eared copies of the *Racing Post* or *Greyhound News*, each a world expert on form; old ladies putting a pound each way on the outsiders; young men bunking off work to place the bet that would save them from ever having to go back. Mostly it reminded her of some of the most special times she'd spent with her father, just the two of them, watching the racing on the television, her sitting on a leather pouffe tucked between his knees, Ralph with his 20 Players' Medium Navy Cut at his side. Even now, the heady mix of strong tobacco, the smell of leather and the sound of the racing commentary rising to its fraught crescendo still meant bliss to Fran.

She sat down between two old dears glued to the satellite screen. Twinkle Toes seemed an unlikely winner but Fran knew better than to doubt her father where horses were concerned. This time Ralph must have got it wrong. Twinkle Toes made a bad start from which it failed to recover. There were five horses ahead of it. Then, with the winning post in sight, a rider fell and his horse ran in the path of the leaders. Twinkle Toes came calmly up from the outside and streaked home. She'd won! In Fran's moment of euphoria it seemed like a good omen for her and Laurence. She felt a flash of calm certainty that they were going to fall in love and that a pristine new page was opening in her life.

The sense of exhilaration was so strong that she just knew she had to tell her father about Laurence now. She'd just have time to dash round there and get back for her next meeting.

She found Ralph sitting on a bench in the garden, apparently lost in contemplation of her mother's herbaceous border. Since her father couldn't tell a peony from a petunia Fran assumed his mind was elsewhere. She was about to rush up and surprise him but something about his manner stopped her. There was none of the usual vigour and impish gaiety she so associated with him. He looked like a tired old man sitting on a park bench. The thought that he was getting old struck her like a sudden cold draught, and that he wouldn't always be part of her world. A world without him, on the other hand, seemed a complete impossibility, like the sun covered by a permanent eclipse. She ran up and put her arms round his neck.

'Franny!' The sun came out from behind its veil. 'How lovely to see you. What brings you here at this time of day?'

'Just a flying visit. Two things. One: I've met a man and although it's really early days I just had to tell you.'

Ralph grinned, some of his old charm returning. 'He's very lucky then. I sometimes worry I've made you unmarriageable. Given you all my faults: an obsession with newspapers, an addiction to racing, too much cynicism for your own good.'

'Nonsense!' Fran kissed the top of his head. 'My problem is I'm pathetically romantic. I've just never met anyone as nice as you before, and if there's one thing you've taught me it's not to compromise on things that really matter.'

'So, this chap of yours, will I like him?'

Fran thought about this. They were incredibly different. She caught herself wondering what kind of father Laurence would make. Would he be like her own, incredibly generous with his love and his time, dedicated to making his children feel good about themselves?

'Yes, I think you'll like him very much.'

'That's a relief. I couldn't bear to lose you to a man I didn't like.'

Fran laughed. 'Early days yet. He's only asked me out to dinner.'

'Things can move fast when you're grown up.'

I do hope so, Fran caught herself wishing, I really do hope so.

'And now, the other thing I've got to tell you. Why I really came.' Ralph watched her with a faint expectant smile. 'That horse you recommended, Twinkle Toes, it came in. I made thirty quid. What shall we do with it?'

Ralph turned away, the pleasure leaching away from his lean and still boyish face, a look of sudden fear and panic in his eyes. If it hadn't been completely impossible, Fran would have thought that he'd never heard of Twinkle Toes in his life.

Chapter 5

'Quiet sophistication, that's the image you want to achieve.' Henrietta raked through her bulging wardrobe on her friend's behalf. 'Something like this.' She held up a spangled black tube dress which wouldn't have shamed Diana Ross. Fran and Sophie exchanged meaningful glances. Henrietta had about as much grasp of the word 'quiet' as a heavy metal rock band.

Fran sat down weakly. 'I don't think Woodbury on a Wednesday night's quite ready for that. We're only going to the Old Bell and Crown.' She should never have even told Henrietta about the dinner invitation, let alone enlisted her help in deciding what to wear.

'A tight white T-shirt, plus black mini-skirt,' advised Sophie, the light glittering off her nose-stud, 'so short it shows your knickers when you bend down. The waitresses at that new wine bar have to wear it as a uniform and men queue up for miles.'

'I'm sure they do,' Fran shuddered, 'but you don't think that might be a tad obvious on the first date?'

'Absolutely not. The days when women had to be all coy and modest are dead and buried. You have to lay it on the line, Auntie Fran.'

'You can borrow my net petticoat if you like,' offered Lottie generously. Fran was incredibly touched. Her net petticoat was Lottie's prize possession. 'And even my tiara if you promise to look after it.'

'Thank you, Lots,' Fran picked up the little girl and put her on her knee. 'That's the kindest offer I've had all day but it looks too nice on you. I wouldn't want to spoil it.'

'Yes,' agreed Lottie, 'you'd have to be really careful, especially if you're going to sex with him.'

Fran tried not to laugh. 'I think I'll stick to chatting just this once. It might be an idea to get to know him first.'

'Sophie doesn't. She says sexing is more fun than talking and that most boys' brains are in their –'

'Thank you, Lottie. Sophie,' Henrietta puffed up like a cobra, 'I trust you're only trying to shock, as usual.'

Sophie's huge luminous eyes took on a defiant sixteen-year-old glint. 'How're you going to find out? Ask me questions on the Kama Sutra?'

Henrietta chose to ignore her. 'So what time's he picking you up tomorrow?'

'I'm meeting him there.'

'How very modern. Don't forget to take change for the phone and your taxi fare home, that's what my mother always used to tell me. "Stick a fiver down your boot, Henrietta, then you'll always be all right if the man gets fresh and you have to leave suddenly." I've done it ever since.'

'Even when you go out with Dad?' smirked Sophie. 'I can just see him getting fresh and you hopping on the number twenty-nine bus home.'

'Don't mock, young lady. The way you dress you may need a fiver down your boot any day now.'

'But why would I need a fiver? Dad's given me a mobile phone and an account with Readycabs.'

'Whatever you do,' Henrietta counselled her friend in despair, 'don't have children.'

'Correct me if I'm wrong, Ma,' Sophie said patiently, 'but wasn't that the whole point of this exercise?'

'Yes, well,' Fran was beginning to feel hideously embarrassed about all that.

'Sophie,' her mother hissed threateningly, 'go away. There must be something unsuitable you could be watching on television, surely?'

Sophie slunk off, pulling net-petticoated Lottie in her wake. 'Have a nice time, Auntie Fran.'

'Yes,' agreed Lottie, who was an even more determined individual than her older sister, 'and if you want advice on sexing, just ask Soph.'

Wednesday, as well as being the date of her dinner with Laurence, was also deadline day at the paper, and to Fran's great relief it passed in the usual comfortable chaos. Sometimes a big local story broke mid-morning and they had to change the front-page splash, which was hell but gave them the rare pleasure of getting to a story before the evenings and dailies did. Conversely, if a story broke *after* they'd gone to press they had to seethe powerlessly for a whole week watching their rivals chew up every detail until there was nothing left for them.

Today there were just the usual minor corrections, last-minute News-In-Briefs, and Keith Wilson running around like a headless chicken with the sports results. By lunchtime the paper had safely gone to bed.

'Why don't you go off home,' Stevie counselled at the end of the afternoon, 'and have a nice long soak before your Big Night Out?'

Fran decided there was no point fighting on. She felt as if everyone in Woodbury were coming on this date with her. She might as well give in gracefully and take Stevie's advice. Tomorrow would be soon enough to tackle next week's stories.

'Have a nice time,' Stevie called to her departing back, 'and don't ask for a sperm sample on the first date. He won't respect you for it.'

By the time she finally arrived at the Bell and Crown dressed in a plain black trouser suit without a single spangle or suggestion of knickers, she was so nervous she felt like turning straight round again. But the sight of Laurence, already sitting in a wing chair by the fireside in the lounge, glancing nervously at his watch, both touched and reassured her. She had somehow expected him to be more at home in places like this but perhaps the unit kept him too busy for dining out.

The firelight accentuated both the dull gold of his hair and also the deep lines in his cheeks which gave his classic features a touch of humanity and imperfection that Fran found infinitely endearing. She liked him for not flourishing his looks, for even seeming a little uneasy with them as if they were more an inconvenience than a blessing.

'Laurence, hello.'

He jumped up, almost spilling his drink.

'Fran. Nearly a dreadful waste of Macallan. What can I get you?'

She took in with quiet pleasure that he drank her father's favourite whisky. It was silly, she knew, to see it as significant. She might as well notice that he wore Church's shoes, like her father, or smoked the odd Romeo y Julieta, when he could afford them. But the whisky seemed personal. She hated to think what Stevie would make of such nonsense.

He brought her a glass of wine just as the waiter arrived with the menus. They were so huge that neither could see over the top.

'My father always says, "The bigger the menu, the worse the food."' Too late she realized she was insulting his choice of restaurant and tried to claw back her mistake.

But Laurence just laughed. 'Absolutely right. And the more adventurous the dishes, the greater the need to stick to something simple.'

'Did your father say that?' Fran teased, but Laurence's face closed up suddenly.

Fran was glad of the diversion as the waiter appeared at his elbow.

'Your table is ready now, sir,' the man practically scraped the ground in his practised humility. As she stood up Fran had to stop herself from swearing. At the other side of the lounge, just beyond the sweeping red-carpeted stairs that led up to the hotel, Jack Allen sat in heated conversation with his boss, Murray Nelson. The thought of her first dinner with Laurence being spoiled by Jack's larger-than-life presence appalled Fran. With his famous sensitivity, Jack might even take it into his head to join them for coffee or something equally gruesome. To Fran's eternal gratitude they had their backs to her.

'Actually,' she insisted to the waiter, who was holding his arm out with a quite unnecessary flourish to direct her to the dining room, 'I'd rather go round through the garden. The daffodils are lovely.'

The two men hesitated for a moment. It was March and freezing outside.

'Of course, madame,' his subtext shouting that only a complete fool would consider such a detour, 'as you like.'

'I do like.' Fran slipped quickly towards the side door, praying it would be open. It was.

'So, you enjoy wandering round freezing muddy gardens in black satin shoes, I take it?' Laurence laughed as they stepped out into the cold damp air.

Fran tried to stick to the gravel. She'd forgotten her damn shoes. 'Isn't it wonderfully fresh?'

'Actually, all I can smell is exhaust fumes from the car park, but I expect you love exhaust fumes.'

They were just turning the corner towards the restaurant when Jack and Murray came out, deep in argument, and walked to their cars. Thank God. Now she could relax finally.

'Absolutely.' She held his arm for a moment until the two men were safely out of sight. 'Exhaust fumes. Petrol. Pipe tobacco. I don't think I'm a very girlie girl.'

'I'll remember that if I ever need to get you a present. A nice pot of axle grease.'

All Fran's fears of going on a first date soon evaporated. That process of courtship whereby each offers only those aspects of themselves they deem attractive proved completely unnecessary with Laurence. Laurence laid out his strengths and weaknesses almost as if he were going for a job interview. 'The word everyone uses for me is dedicated,' he told her seriously, 'and it's true, I am. The unit is the centre of my life. I started it and it takes its whole direction from me. The down side of that is that I don't have much else.' He smiled his modest, likeable, cards-on-the-table smile. 'I'm really a pretty dull chap.'

But Fran didn't think he was dull at all. His dedication to what he believed in reminded her of one person: her father. He had the same passionate commitment to a worthy cause, the desire to change things, to make them better for people. She'd never really expected to find a man, in this cynical and materialistic time, who would possibly feel all that. And here he was sitting opposite her.

'I know this probably isn't the way things are done,' Fran felt a leap of excitement at his words, 'but I don't have a lot of time to waste on social life. I'm not asking for a firm commitment, I know that would be stupid, but could you . . .' he stumbled slightly and Fran's heart went out to him, 'that is if we do find we get on, potentially be interested in a serious relationship?'

They were words that could have been inept or even strange after so brief an acquaintance but Laurence's obvious sincerity transformed them into something infinitely touching.

The delicious Dover sole the waiter had brought cooled on her plate. It took a very special man to make Fran forget her food. 'Yes, Laurence,' Fran said softly, 'I think I could.'

'So he actually asked you your intentions? How wonderfully, divinely Victorian!' Henrietta was in paroxysms of joy that her scheme had gone so much better – and certainly faster – than she could have ever hoped possible. 'He actually wanted to be sure you were serious?'

'So naturally,' Sophie's sloe-eyes slanted with mischief, 'you said, "Well, Larry, a quick screw was what I really had in mind but I'm always prepared to compromise."'

'Sophie!' chorused Fran and Henrietta in the same breath.

'Well, I think he sounds weird. It's like trying to get an agreement out of someone before they've got a clue what's involved.'

'That's because you're sixteen,' Fran pointed out. 'At thirty-four you're enchanted to get a commitment, even without knowing what's in the small print.'

'I think it's very romantic,' added Henrietta.

'And he's already asked me out again. He got his diary out at the end of dinner.'

'God!' Sophie made a face. 'This guy sounds worse and worse. Now he's depriving you of the thrill of waiting in by the phone.'

'Sophie,' Fran insisted firmly, 'at my age you have no desire whatsoever to wait in by the phone for anyone: I have better things to do with my time. Like running a newspaper.'

Sophie shook her head. 'I hope I'm never thirty-four.'

'So,' Henrietta sank back into the deep chintz of the sofa, flicking her daughter's Caterpillar boot off the cushion. 'So, did you, er, you know . . . ?'

'No, we certainly didn't.'

'Well, don't leave it too long. I thought you couldn't wait to get your hands on his gene pool.'

'Ma,' Sophie pointed out, 'this was only the first date. By the sound of this guy he'll book it in two weeks in advance anyway.'

Fran giggled.

'Anyway,' Sophie demanded of her mother, 'I thought you were against sex outside marriage. You're always telling me that.'

'That's because you're sixteen. I won't when you're as old as Auntie Fran.' She turned to her friend. 'So when's the next date?'

'A week on Wednesday. He's away at a conference this weekend.'

'Gosh, Auntie Fran,' Sophie banged her galumphing boots onto the floor so that zig-zag patterns of mud fell on the cream carpet, 'if it were me I'd have wanted to be showered with flowers, sung to on balconies, rung up every hour to hear how much he loved me. You sound like you've booked in a relationship as if it were a dental appointment.'

'Yes,' agreed Fran gleefully, 'isn't it bliss? That's what's so absolutely wonderful about it.'

Ralph Tyler walked past the delft-blue sea of hyacinths in the small park at the edge of Woodbury and breathed in the strong, sweet smell. He was never sure about hyacinths. A bit like lilies, they had a slight scent of death about them, as if they were there to cover up the smell of something putrid underneath. He loved this small park and liked to wander here every day if he could.

He strolled towards the pond, and finally sat down on a bench that, at first glance, looked occupied. But on closer inspection Ralph found the figure of the old man engrossed in feeding the birds was made of bronze. Ralph smiled, remembering the row when the figure had been installed, the gift of a young sculptor who'd grown up in Woodbury and was already on the road to fame. They'd had reams of letters complaining about it, how it wasn't art, that the stylized chunky figure wasn't realistic, that it frightened the children. Ralph had thought it was wonderful and had said so on the front page of the *Citizen*.

'Diabolical, isn't it?' The green-uniformed park keeper was addressing Ralph. 'I used to hope it'd get vandalized then we could get rid of it, but the vandals just leave it alone. They go and write their four-letter words in the playground instead.'

Ralph looked at the man's closed and joyless face. Why did people like this always take petty jobs in authority? 'I campaigned to have it kept, as a matter of fact, I think it's rather wonderful.'

The man rolled his eyes to heaven and moved on, leaving Ralph with his own thoughts. And today there was a certain matter he wanted to address. Something frightening was happening to him. It had started with odd lapses of memory. Then he'd begun to get small things wrong. He'd go and get the milk and find he'd come back with the sugar, or he'd go to do a task and find he'd already done it yet he had absolutely no memory of doing so. It was as though the connections in his brain were misfiring. Then there was that business with Francesca and the horse. There she was with a bottle of whisky to celebrate her winnings and he couldn't remember ever giving her a tip.

Something was wrong, he knew it. If Phyllis had been a different kind of person he could have talked to her about it, enlisted her help, but she'd been so bad-tempered since he'd retired and would just think he was making a fuss over nothing. He should probably go and see a doctor, but all his life he'd hated visiting doctors. He hated their patronizing air, as if they knew everything and even asking a question about your own health was an impertinence and an intrusion. He had preferred to develop a cheerful stoicism which had got him through everything until now, but not this. The awful thought of what it might be drifted around the edge of his consciousness but he shooed it away. 'Blast it,' he vowed with as much of his old determination as he could find, 'whatever it is. I'm not giving in to it.'

'First sign of madness, you know,' said a voice a couple of feet away.

Ralph looked round. A long, gangly windmill of a boy

in a vast baggy sweatshirt, even baggier trousers, a baseball cap and narrow streamlined roller skates attached to a kind of knee-high boot thing, stood a few inches from his elbow holding a dog on a lead.

'Sorry?'

'You were talking to yourself. First sign of madness, so they say.'

'And the second must be wearing evil-looking roller skates and truanting from school.'

'Rollerblades,' corrected the youth. 'And I'm not bunking off. I'm revising. I repeat French verbs as I skate.'

'Perhaps you'll give me a demonstration. Tell me, why do all the other lads wear these,' he tapped the boy's cap, 'the other way round and you don't?'

'Only nerds do that.'

'I see.' He considered the boy for a moment. 'It's odd but you remind me very strongly of someone.'

The gangly youth's face split into a cheeky grin. 'My dad. He used to work for you once.'

'You can't be Ben, Jack Allen's boy?' Last time Ralph had seen Ben he'd been about ten. Now he had to be fourteen or fifteen. A pang of envy bit into him. If only he had a great big grandson like this.

'And who's this?' he shook the disgraceful dog's proffered paw.

'That's Wild Rover, but if you like,' he offered generously, 'you can call him Rover.'

'How about giving me a demo of this rollerblading. Keep an old man in touch.'

Ben was delighted. Most park regulars tended to see

rollerbladers as thugs on wheels and he was only too happy to show that rollerblading was an art. He raced off then jumped in the air, twirled round in a terrifying parabola and landed gracefully on one skate, almost like a ballet dancer.

The park keeper watched grouchily from his stance lurking behind the bowls club. Unfortunately rollerblading was permitted in this park, a grave error in the parkie's eyes, and likely to lead to a further decline in moral standards.

Wild Rover suddenly emerged from the bushes and dashed towards his new master with such speed and enthusiasm that Ben was forced to take avoiding action and ended up in a spectacular tangle of long limbs in the hyacinth bed.

The park keeper rubbed his hands. Rollerblades might be allowed in the park, but dogs were not.

'Excuse me, young man,' he wasted no time or sympathy in asking whether Ben was all right, 'is that dog yours? If so I've got a good mind to ban you from this park –'

'As a matter of fact,' Ralph grabbed the disreputable dog by its lead, ignoring its yelps of protest, 'it's mine. I apologize but I had no idea dogs weren't allowed. Another narrow-minded decision by our revered local council no doubt. Come on, Ben, time you and I went off and bought ourselves a Big Mac.'

The wonderfully liberating thing about her developing relationship with Laurence, Fran mused a few weeks later as she chopped vegetables for a curry in his kitchen, was how easy and natural it felt. They seemed to have a rhythm that fitted effortlessly together. They both put their work first and enjoyed the same things outside it. Every book she picked up from his shelves was one she was interested in. Their tastes in films and music were so alike that whatever one booked they knew the other would enjoy. She had found his flat something of a shock at first in its monastic emptiness, but she was adding things quietly to soften its edges.

After only a few weeks Fran felt as if she'd known him forever. Except in one regard. To her slight consternation, Laurence was showing no hurry in swooping her up into his bed. He had kissed her several times, once or twice with real passion, but then seemed to rein himself in. She had even, at times of vulnerability, tempered with longing, entertained the fact that he might be gay.

Laurence, noting her preoccupation, leaned over suddenly and took the knife from her hand. 'It looks so right seeing you there,' he said tenderly. She felt his arm slip round her waist and his head rest on her shoulder. A scent of spice, cumin, garam masala, exotic and sensual drifted through the air. He turned her round, looking intently into her eyes. 'You've filled a void in me, Francesca, that I didn't even know was there. I thought my work was enough, but since I met you I know it isn't.'

Fran closed her eyes and waited, hardly breathing. Was this going to be the moment she'd hoped for since she'd first seen him that first night? Very deliberately he switched the gas off on the hob. He took the palm of her hand and kissed it, licking the soft fleshy mound until

Fran shuddered in anticipation. He had kissed her before but never like this.

'I think I'm falling in love with you, Francesca Tyler.' Gently but firmly he removed her stripy butcher's apron and led her into his bedroom.

Chapter 6

Now that the moment had finally come Fran expected to feel shy or embarrassed, but with Laurence's hot breath on her neck and the hardness of his body she was conscious only of relief. He did want her after all.

With surprising skill he undid each button of her white linen dress and slipped down each bra strap, then turned her round to undo the clasp. She almost made some joke about bedside manners but stopped herself in time. A sense of occasion had never been her strong point.

'You're lovely, Francesca Tyler,' he said simply, stroking the swell of her left breast. He leaned down and kissed the hardening nipple.

'So are you,' Fran replied, her eyes looking directly into his. Tall though he was, they were almost of a height. She reached for the belt of his jeans and he let out a sigh, like a rush of a breeze on water, and pulled her almost viciously into his arms.

Moments later they were in bed and he was inside her,

working at her with an intensity she'd never seen in him before, eyes closed, an almost holy expression on his face. And then he came in a sudden explosive shudder of release, leaving Fran shocked at the total separateness of his experience. Surely Laurence, of all people, wouldn't turn out to be a selfish lover? Then, as if he remembered her and his obligations towards her, he looked into her eyes. 'Sorry. I just wanted you so much.' And then he held her from him and touched her breasts gently with an exploring finger like a child marvelling at some wonderful new toy. She shivered under his touch, involuntarily pushing her mound towards his other hand until he slipped a finger inside and felt for her clitoris. Moments later she too came to a shuddering climax.

Immediately Laurence pulled the duvet over them again. 'Hey,' protested Fran, laughing. 'I want to look at you. Don't think I'm going to bed with the best-looking man I've ever met and not even seeing him.'

She uncovered him and studied his body shamelessly. He was long, lean and perfectly proportioned, his skin a pale caramel that reminded her of Cream-Line toffees, always a favourite in the sweet shop.

She kissed his knees and prepared to work upwards. 'I bet you were a wow on the football pitch.'

'Actually I wasn't. Too short-sighted and much too scared. I got teased for looking like a choirboy or, failing that, a swot. I used to go and hide in the science labs.'

'And look where that got you, Dr Westcott.'

She noticed a long scar on one knee.

'I fell off my bike when I was ten.'

She dropped her lips onto the still puckered skin, loving him for this one minor flaw. 'Did your mother kiss it better for you?'

Laurence's face closed over and he tried to pull up the bedclothes.

'How can someone so good-looking and successful feel so shy?' Fran teased, tugging at the cotton coverlet and laughing.

'You have to feel loved to see yourself as either of those things,' he said quietly.

The bitterness of his tone shocked and puzzled her. The fierce maternal streak in Fran burned suddenly bright and she wanted to soothe away whatever pain it was that had blighted Laurence's life and happiness.

He gazed up at her and fixed her with the intent look that was so much a part of him. 'You're so vibrant, so bright and bold and colourful. Sometimes the only colour I feel is grey.'

That's because you work all the time, she wanted to say, and have nothing else to fill the empty corners of your life. What you need is bustle and activity, a family. But she didn't say it. It was too soon.

Instead they put on dressing gowns and, suddenly starving, devoured the meal Fran had cooked before they went upstairs.

As they sat at his kitchen table feeding each other Fran decided that her chicken curry had never tasted so spicy, her poppadoms had never been crunchier. It was food from heaven.

At eleven o'clock Laurence glanced at his watch. 'Time

for bed, I think. I have an early clinic tomorrow.' There was a second's pause before he added, 'Do you want to stay the night?'

Behind the pause Fran sensed a flicker of hesitation. Laurence was used to having his own space.

She went upstairs and picked her things up from the floor where they looked out of place in their spontaneous abandonment. Even Sally Bowles would fold her clothes in Laurence's bedroom.

A sense of wild panic set in. Was that it? A quick fling and home again? How curious that to make love seemed less intimate than to spend the night together.

Downstairs Laurence was smiling. He looked even more beautiful in his bathrobe than in his clothes. 'I wondered,' the shyness was back but now it seemed boyish, engaging, not as it had a moment ago, a means of keeping her at arm's length, 'if you might like to come and meet my mother.'

Fran felt a disgraceful rush of relief. This was an important step, she could feel instinctively.

That night her own bed, which normally felt warm and welcoming, felt wide and cold. She thought of Laurence and his unexpected vulnerability and she knew she wanted to fill whatever there was in him and make him feel loved. This time, she told herself firmly, nothing was going to make her screw it up.

Fran tried to find out as much as she could from Laurence about his mother over the coming weeks before they met, but he seemed oddly reluctant to talk in any depth about her. She was called Camilla, Fran discovered, and she had lived alone ever since her husband had died ten years ago.

The invitation, when it came, was to Sunday lunch. It turned out to be a glorious morning, one of those sudden gifts in mid-April when it feels almost like summer. The house was in a pretty grey and white timbered village five miles outside Woodbury. It was set back from the road, with a classic garden path in front cutting through two large flower beds. Camilla, Laurence pointed out, won first prize every year in the flowers and produce sections of the Woodbury Show. The house, though extremely pretty, was tiny.

'Don't say that to Ma,' Laurence advised. 'She makes Keeping Up Appearances into a religion. I'm afraid she's a frightful snob. She was teased at school for not being good enough and she's taken it out on life ever since. Actually the one person it hurts is herself because it makes her hard to get to know. So don't worry if she's a bit distant.'

Feeling anything but reassured, Fran followed him up the garden path. Camilla was waiting for them. Fran couldn't help thinking Laurence's mother would have looked more at home in Sloane Street than in a tiny village in the east of England. Her hair, though white, was perfectly cut to chin-length, and held in place by a dark blue velvet hairband, revealing large earrings which exactly matched her silk shirt and skirt, contrasting elegantly with a pale peach cashmere blazer. Fran wished she'd ignored Laurence's advice and worn something smarter than the sweater and jeans he'd told her looked fine.

Camilla stood in the doorway and offered an expensively powdered cheek to Fran. She seemed friendly enough but it was to Laurence that her whole being was directed. She was, Fran decided, like a lightbulb that was switched on only in his company. Laurence was clearly the centre of her neat universe.

And yet, oddly enough, Laurence didn't seem to reciprocate this river of love, but simply to let it flow round him like a rock in mid-stream. As she watched them Fran remembered his words of their first night together. How can you feel successful and good-looking if you don't feel loved? And yet Camilla seemed to love him, if anything, too much. She fussed and fidgeted over him, failing to notice that every caressing gesture, every word of flattery seemed only to make him uncomfortable. Fran wished he could pretend a little more to return her devotion, but Camilla didn't even seem to notice.

'Lunch is ready. Your favourite. Red roast beef, Yorkshires, roast potatoes and horseradish.' She sounded as though she were laying down gifts in front of a potentate. 'Have you brought your washing? I could put it on now and it would be ready by the time you go.'

'Ma,' Laurence reminded her patiently, 'I'm thirty-seven. I use a shirt service.'

The table in the dining room was immaculately laid out with cut glass and linen napkins, making Fran feel even more uncomfortable about her inappropriate clothes. She got the impression, though, that having something to disapprove of would suit Camilla.

Fran sat down at the polished table, marvelling how the women in Laurence's life all thought he was God's gift. She would have to be the one who didn't, who brought him down to earth a little. Or at least reminded him he was only a medium-ranking divinity.

'You work for the local paper, my dear.'

Fran sensed that to say actually she edited it wouldn't go down too well.

'Isn't it frightfully dull? All those weddings and giant marrows.'

'We do have other stories in the paper occasionally.'

Her irony was lost on Camilla. 'Anyway, I gather you're doing an article on Laurence.'

'Not on me, Mother,' Laurence cut in swiftly, 'on the unit.'

'He isn't appreciated nearly enough,' Camilla persisted. 'But it must be wonderful to feel that in a sense those babies are only there because of him.'

'I just wish he'd produce some by more conventional means.'

Fran flushed and looked away.

'I'm sorry,' Laurence said in a low voice as they cleared the lunch things. 'I don't often bring a girlfriend home, so she's on all stations go.'

'How often is not often?' teased Fran.

'Now that you mention it, I haven't brought anyone home for seven years.'

Fran was intrigued by how clearly he remembered. 'And what happened to her. How did she get away?'

Laurence turned away abruptly, accidentally knocking a cut glass decanter of sherry so that it shattered all over the stone floor of the kitchen.

'I'm sorry,' he bent down to pick it up, 'I'm very careless

sometimes. Look, Francesca, I've been meaning to ask you. Would you come away with me for a weekend? There's a very special place I know where we could get away from everything and really spend some time together. Will you come?'

Fran bent down and helped him pick up the pieces, their heads touching. 'Of course I will. I can't think of anything nicer than spending two whole days with you.' And nights, she thought, but didn't quite dare say it.

'Well, kiddo, if you weren't worried about Jack Allen's new venture, then it's about time you started. It's absolutely bloody brilliant!' Stevie slammed down a dummy of the new paper onto Fran's desk.

'Look at that,' Stevie pointed to the front page which, in vast type, heralded the paper's CLEAN UP OUR STREETS campaign. 'He's only telling the readers to collect any litter they find in the streets and dump it on the Director of Refuse's home doorstep.' Stevie chortled with glee at the chaos that would ensue. 'Bastards. Serve them right.'

'Stevie. Don't give me that All Councils are Evil stuff. Anyway,' she studied the paper, 'it's highly irresponsible.'

'Quite.'

'And probably illegal.'

'Bloody good wheeze, though.' Stevie sat on the edge of Fran's desk. 'I might even dump some myself.'

The awful thing was that Fran had to agree. It was even the logical, if rather extreme, extension of the ideas she'd been promoting herself. That local papers shouldn't just be in the business of finding villains, whether private or municipal, but should get the community involved directly in changing things for the better. She found herself smiling at the thought of the Director of Refuse, an unpleasant individual known to loathe journalists on sight, opening his front door to find it blocked by a pyramid of litter.

'He's only suggesting it because this paper's a dummy. He wouldn't if it were the real thing.'

'Want to bet?'

Whether Jack would actually dare incite people like this or not, Fran knew it was time she confronted the reality of the new paper and the impact it might have on the *Citizen*. The *Citizen* already struggled to keep ahead of the *Express*, on a fraction of its funds. Could it survive this new onslaught?

Bloody Jack Allen. How come his timing was so perfect that he'd lobbed her into a crisis just when she was planning a romantic weekend with Laurence? Anyone would think he knew.

In fact, across the other side of Woodbury, in the flash offices Fran so envied, bloody Jack Allen was fighting a battle of his own, not unconnected with Fran herself.

'What do you mean, you're not coming?' Murray Nelson raved at his editor, starting to turn the colour of a ripe damson. 'I've booked this lunch with Ronnie Newlands expressly for us to sweet-talk him. Newlands Estate Agency is the *Citizen*'s biggest client, he more or less keeps them afloat single-handed, and I've almost talked him into bringing his advertising to us. It's a coup. All he wanted to do first was meet you and talk over a few things. What's wrong with that?'

Jack stayed firmly put behind his chaotic, but surprisingly efficient desk. He wanted no part of this. Competing with the *Citizen* for stories was one thing. Even starting a rival paper seemed part of tough reality. If Fran couldn't stand the heat of journalism then she shouldn't be in the kitchen. But this was different. Deliberately enticing the *Citizen*'s biggest customer smacked to him of unfair practices, especially when, from what he'd heard, there would be little profit in it for the *Express*. It was simply sabotage.

Outside in the bustle of the newsroom, Miriam Wolsey put down her phone to listen through Jack's ever-open door. She could tell from his exaggerated calm that this was something he really cared about.

'Why should you be so concerned about the *Citizen*?' Murray scanned the dummy of the new paper. 'You work for us. And as you well know, the new paper will live or die by ads. You need Ronnie Newlands as much as they do.'

'No, I don't. Look, Murray, when we dreamed the newspaper up I told you I would find new markets, that we wouldn't need to bankrupt the *Citizen*.'

'You're such a romantic, aren't you, Allen?'

'No,' Jack loathed the idea that he was some sentimental fool. He'd worked long and hard on his business plan for the new paper. 'I'm not a romantic. I happen to think it's good for this town to have the *Citizen* and the *Express*. We keep each other on our toes. Without the *Citizen*, the *Express* could come out with – if you'll pardon the expression – any old crap.'

'I'm not cancelling this lunch, you know.'

Jack wondered for a split second if he ought to go, whether Nelson would do more damage without his editor's moderating influence, but he wanted no part of the deal.

'If this paper fails, Allen, you go with it. Have no illusion about that.'

'Thanks for that vote of confidence, Murray. I've always said you're an inspiring leader. It's the way you canvas people's opinions in order to shit on them I especially admire.'

'You'd better watch it, sunshine.' Jack thought the grog blossoms on Murray's purple nose might actually burst and he wondered what would emerge. Graham's Late Bottled Port? 'No one's irreplaceable, you know.'

'What, Murray,' Jack enquired innocently, 'not even you?'

A smothered giggle from the newsroom prompted Murray Nelson to pull himself up to his full five foot seven and do up the buttons on his double-breasted suit which, hand-made and expensive though it was, failed to conceal the origins he was so desperate to leave behind.

'You really should be more careful of him, you know.'

Jack looked up to find Miriam leaning on his door. 'Oh come on now, Miriam, the *Express* has already had two owners since I've been here. Nelson won't last. He'll find a better investment to move on to. He doesn't care whether he produces newspapers or toilet rolls. I just wish he'd choose the latter.'

Miriam laughed. The concern in her huge, dark eyes

warmed him. Trying to be a good father to Ben and a decent editor at the same time took up almost all his energy, but there were moments when loneliness chilled him as if someone were walking over his tomb, reminding him of how fast time was passing. He knew he had the reputation of being a womanizer, only interested in the quick fling, but that had been because of his son. He hadn't wanted to foist another mother on Ben before he'd even coped with losing his real one, so he had kept his relationships brief and friendly.

By some extraordinary stroke, Miriam reminded him of Carrie – the same elfin beauty and small, almost childish frame. He smiled back at her. 'Thanks for caring,' he said gently. And he wasn't sure what would have happened next if the news editor hadn't put his head round the door. 'Jack, bit of a crisis on the land infill story. Could you spare a mo'?'

'Isn't that piece on the infertility unit ready yet?' Stevie chided. 'I was hoping to get it subbed this afternoon.'

Fran, who had been in her office since seven trying to finish the article, sort out next week's paper, commission a supplement on Young Chef of the Year, and chivvy Keith Wilson to come up with at least one dynamic new thought about women's rugby that didn't refer to O Sir Jasper, was exhausted. Her throat was so sore that she'd worked her way through a whole pack of Fishermen's Friends, extra strength, which is more than most fishermen could do. Her joints ached all over, a clear indication that flu was on its way.

'Yup. Here it is.'

'So where's the good doctor taking you?'

'No idea, but he said it was his special place.' It was typical, Fran grumbled, that she should feel so terrible just when they were going off for a romantic weekend. Why did you always get flu, or a cold sore as big as the Ritz or, best of all, the curse at moments like this? God clearly had something against good food and good sex and enjoyed nothing more than putting his divine spanner in the works. Sex! On the whole she'd rather have a Lemsip.

'What time's he picking you up?'

Fran looked at her watch. 'In ten minutes,' she screeched.

'Then you'd better go and do your hair. You look like Morticia Addams on a bad day.'

Fran pulled a brush frantically through her hair and grabbed her coat.

'By the way,' Stevie's voice was at its most chocolatey, 'I saw Jack Allen the other day. He was with a small dark-haired girl, very pretty. Do you know her at all?'

'I have absolutely no idea who Jack Allen spends his time with, and no desire to know. He probably finds them in the Yellow Pages under A for Available.'

'Mia-oww!' chided Stevie. 'I suppose it's just as well you don't feel the same way about Jack as he feels about you.' Stevie pulled some of the balls off her ancient cardigan, a task like painting the Forth Bridge, since she always seemed to have just as many the next time. 'After all, you know the old adage, never marry a journalist.'

'*What* did you say about Jack Allen just then?'

'You heard me,' Stevie barked, picking up Fran's bag and shooing her towards the door. 'Now for God's sake get a move on or there'll be no point going. By the way,' she rooted in the depths of her pocket, 'here's some Oil of Olbas for you.'

Fran sniffed the pungent scent and reeled. 'What is it, some kind of aphrodisiac?'

'It's for catarrh actually, so you don't sneeze on him at the moment of ecstasy.'

'The only moment of ecstasy I've got in mind is an early night and a hot toddy.'

'Let's hope he's brought a good book then, or he could be in for a nasty shock, couldn't he?'

Laurence's special place turned out to be an ancient little oak-beamed hotel set in its own grounds complete with a small lake. Just as they arrived, a flock of Canada Geese swooped upwards and flew in perfect formation into the sunset, their wings burnished with red.

'It's glorious,' Fran breathed, trying to forget how ghastly she was feeling.

'Thanks. I laid the geese on just for you. We should just have time to dash up and change for dinner.'

The meal was delicious and afterwards Laurence suggested a brandy which he promised would do her the world of good. Instead it keyed a raging headache. She began to shiver violently and knew she had to get to bed.

'I'm so sorry to do this on your special weekend,' she apologized.

'Don't worry.' The amazing thing about Laurence was

that he really didn't seem to mind. Jack, who was so much less a gentleman, would have been furious.

Fran didn't notice the pretty chintz curtains on the four poster, or the fact that the duvet had been turned back and her nightdress arranged on her pillow in the shape of a flower. Instead she turned off all the lights and slipped into the seductive arms of sleep where she remained for nine solid hours.

When she finally woke next morning she could tell it was late. Laurence was already up. She sat up tentatively feeling her head. It was better. And her breathing had cleared. In fact she felt wonderful.

'Have we missed breakfast?'

'I went down earlier. I thought you needed your sleep. Do you want me to order you some?'

'There's something I'd rather have than food,' Fran said, surprised at her own daring.

Laurence put the 'Do Not Disturb' sign on the door and leaned on it watching her. The expression in his eyes made the straps of her nightie slip spontaneously from her shoulders.

By the time they left their room two hours later the sun was so warm they could take a drink out to sit by the lake.

'This is perfect,' Fran pronounced, watching a pair of swans gliding on the lake. 'Do you know that swans –'

'Mate for life?' Laurence completed her sentence, laughing.

Fran blushed at her predictability.

'They're also prepared to gangbang spare females until

they drown, so I'm not sure I'd hold them up as entirely model citizens.'

'Aaah,' Fran protested, 'you've shattered my romantic illusions.'

Behind them a young couple struggled to feed a toddler sitting in its buggy, complaining quietly at the absence of highchairs.

'Really,' Laurence remarked, 'you'd think they'd ban children from somewhere like this.'

'Laurence!' Fran was shocked. Another romantic illusion slipping. 'I thought you of all people would approve of children.'

'In their place. Which isn't a five-star hotel.'

Fran stared back at the swans, disappointment clouding the beauty of the day. She really didn't know Laurence at all. She'd simply assumed that, since he cared so passionately about fertility, he'd love children and be wonderful with them. Instead they seemed to make him grouchy and tense.

Later on they walked across the fields in the warmth of the afternoon sunshine and Fran told herself not to care about such a silly little incident. It was true that you came to places like this to relax and other people's children could intrude. Laurence was simply being protective about his hard-earned peace. All the same, she would so much have preferred it if he'd congratulated the family on their bravery.

At the end of the afternoon they went back to their room just as the sun was beginning to dip behind the line of trees. Fran stood looking out silently.

Laurence was suddenly behind her. 'I'm sorry for getting

annoyed with that child,' he apologized. 'It obviously upset you.'

Fran turned and studied his handsome face, glad that he'd brought it up. 'It's just that you're so brilliant with babies. Don't you want any of your own?'

He pulled back abruptly, as if she had held out a flame to his flesh. A long moment passed before he said a word.

'Look, Francesca,' the words cut into her, 'if it's children you want, perhaps I'm not the man for you.'

They drove back to Woodbury in silence the next day. Fran felt as if there were a screen between them. Had she raised the issue of children too soon in their relationship and scared him? Or was Laurence, despite his goodness and generosity to other people's, too damaged by whatever it was that was still hurting him to want any children of his own?

'Right,' Sean McGee, the gentle young reporter did his best to look aggressive, 'who's stolen my bicycle clips?'

'Gee, boss, you want me to cover the Saint Valentine's Day Massacre instead?' the cocky Mike Wooley demanded of Stevie in a mock-Chicago newspaperman drawl, the offending bicycle clips holding up his shirtsleeves. 'But that happened over a hundred years ago. The *Express* may have got the story first.'

Everyone in the office roared with laughter and Fran managed to sneak in unseen by everyone except Stevie. It would be conference in a moment and she devoutly hoped to avoid Stevie's beady gaze till then. No such luck. Stevie had ten-mile antennae for unhappiness. Especially where Fran was concerned.

'So, things didn't go swimmingly with Dr Kildare?'

'I wish you wouldn't call him that.'

'Maybe you should have rubbed the Oil of Olbas into his back after all. Was it the food? The conversation? The sex? Does he have disgusting habits his patients don't know about?'

'They were all fine.' Fran closed the door. 'My big mistake was asking if he wanted children.'

'Oh dear.' Stevie shook her head. 'And he took one look at the Pampers signs in your eyes and disappeared to an unknown destination?'

'But I don't have Pampers signs in my eyes,' Fran insisted, 'do I?'

Stevie ignored this one. 'Come on. It's time we went and ran a newspaper for a change.'

To her immense relief the demands of the paper swallowed her up and spat her out each night too exhausted to do anything. It was almost a week later when she decided that if Laurence was going to dump her he could at least do it civilly.

Her hand was on the telephone when Stevie knocked on the door puffing a Players and carrying a letter. 'This just came for you,' she handed it over. 'A Dear John if ever I saw one, the bastard.'

Chapter 7

Stevie was right. In one page of immaculate italic script Laurence informed her that things had moved a little too fast for him, that he thought she was a wonderful woman but he felt the need to cool things down a little, just for now.

Stevie picked up the letter. 'Why do they always do it in a letter? Anyway, look at his handwriting, he can't be a doctor, it's far too good. The man's clearly an impostor. Perhaps he's a plumber in a white coat. I think we should expose him.'

Fran crumpled the letter and threw it at the bin. For once it missed.

'Look,' Stevie insisted at the end of the afternoon, closing the door behind her, 'I really think you should go home.'

'No,' insisted Fran. 'I'm fine. I really am.'

'Then why is that copy of the paper all soggy? Sean's story of the tabby cat marooned up a tree is touching but not that touching.'

'Oh, Stevie . . .'

Stevie opened her arms and Fran buried herself in the bobbly softness of Stevie's ancient cardi. The familiar aroma of tobacco and fabric softener was infinitely comforting.

'Go on. Go home. We've got days till the edition and if we put out last week's paper again only half the readers would notice. One thing though: promise me you'll come to Sean's birthday drinks on Thursday at six. I don't want you moping. Men aren't worth it. Not even your father.'

'All right. It's a promise. Thursday at six.'

By the next day Fran had taken hold of life again. The paper was like a womb, pulsing with life. Just the noise of telephones ringing, questions bellowed across the room, reporters swearing at the coffee machine for boiling dry again when they were in fact too lazy to refill it, the constant demand for decisions left no room for misery. Decisiveness, her father had once told her, was the key to being an editor. Never say 'that's a tricky one'. It didn't even matter if you made the wrong decision, provided you made some decision. Fran found that if she simply concentrated on being decisive she could keep at bay the grey tide of unhappiness at seeing another relationship – and one she had been convinced was the right one – founder.

By Thursday that week's edition had safely appeared – and not a bad one at that – and the stories had been allocated for the following week, to be reviewed again on Monday morning. Fran felt an ominous tickling in the back of her throat. The damn flu was probably coming back. She'd probably have a lost weekend in bed, a thought that filled her equally with longing and panic. The last thing she wanted to do was go to the pub for Sean's birthday drinks. But Sean would be hurt if she didn't and she liked him a lot. There was something infinitely endearing about the way he ignored the macho joshing of the other reporters and stuck to his Green issues. She just hoped the others hadn't planned some horrible surprise for him like a Strippagram disguised as an Eco-Warrior who would undo his anorak and douse him in baby oil. They probably wouldn't dare with Stevie around. Stevie, though quite prepared to join in a laugh, had a nose for bullying and would sentence the perpetrators to three months of covering parish council meetings or reviewing amateur performances of *Calamity Jane*. The very thought of such purgatory kept them in line.

When she opened the door of the Cathedral Arms, she almost went straight home. The noise and hubbub hit her aching temples a hammer blow. It was one of the most popular after-work haunts in Woodbury. Whenever anyone uttered those dangerously deceptive words, 'Fancy a swift half before going home?', it was to the Cathy that they inevitably repaired. More marriages had probably been sabotaged in this hostelry than by all the mistresses in history.

Fran scanned the crowd for the *Citizen* contingent and eventually spotted them tucked away in the far corner. The two tables they crowded round were already crammed with empty glasses and Sean, clutching a jug of ominous-looking orange liquid, was topping them up. 'Fancy a sangria, Fran? They're on me.'

Fran shuddered at the thought of this disgusting con-
coction, which in her opinion should have stayed safely in
Spain, and longed for either a dry white wine or, better still,
a mineral water, but Sean was still holding the jug hopefully.

'All right,' unsuspectingly Fran uttered the words so well
known to the landlord of any similar establishment, 'just a
little one then.'

Actually, it didn't taste too bad. The sweetness and the
remote aroma of orange were surprisingly soothing to her
throat.

'Come and join us, Fran,' Stevie made room for her on
the banquette. 'These two dedicated reporters,' she indicated Mike Wooley and Keith Wilson with the fluffy
bumble-bee cocktail stirrer that had come with the sangria, 'are trying to decide which was their all-time worst
story. Reporting the Woodbury Dene Parish Council's decision to buy a new watering can after a mere two-hour
discussion or having to sit through two performances in the
same week of *The Sound of Music*?'

'And then instead of saying they're both a heap of crap
and that amateur dramatics ought to be outlawed along
with drunken driving and kerb crawling, you have to find
inoffensive words like "enthusiastic" to describe the
acting!' Keith Wilson, Fran noted, was pretty lively
already.

'And "spirited", don't forget "spirited",' cut in Mike, 'as
in "The Woodbury Dene Players gave a spirited performance of *Annie Get Your Sodding Gun*."'

Fran giggled. 'And do you remember the time when

someone called to say there'd been an accident on the bypass and Stevie asked, "How many dead?" And the guy said, "None, thank heavens," and Stevie said, "That's no good then"?'

Stevie blushed into her sangria. 'You know what I meant, I wasn't trying to be heartless.'

'I know,' Fran refilled her glass from the jug that, like the loaves and the fishes, seemed to be miraculously replenishing itself, 'that's what makes it so funny. We all know exactly what you meant!'

Fran, Stevie saw with relief, was finally relaxing. It was unusual for her to come for a drink with the troops, let alone to knock it back with such enthusiasm, but it was probably exactly what she needed. On the other hand, it might be a good idea if they all went and ate something soon to soak up the deceptive effects of this damn punch. She was just about to suggest it when another jug arrived out of the blue.

When she protested that they hadn't ordered it, the barman pointed into the noisy throng. 'From the gentleman over there!'

Stevie craned her neck and finally made out Jack Allen at a small table by the door. He was with Miriam Wolsey and Miriam was hanging on his every word.

'It's from Jack. Look he's over there with that girl again.'

Fran, beginning to feel both woozy and fluey in equal parts but determined not to let it show, squinted in the direction of Stevie's pointing finger.

'Really,' Fran's voice took on a tone of prim disapproval that made Stevie smile, 'Jack ought to be ashamed of himself.

She's only about twenty-one and she works for him. It's practically sexual harassment.'

'She doesn't look very harassed to me.'

Fran had to admit the truth of this. Miriam was wearing a neat reporter's suit with nipped-in waist and short skirt but instead of the usual opaque tights most women favoured, a flash of lacy stocking was showing at the top of her thigh. Fran, coming from a generation that felt wearing stockings spelt submission and discomfort, not to mention chapped thighs, was outraged. What had Emmeline Pankhurst and Gloria Steinem fought for? Probably, said a voice in her head, the right to choose lace-topped stockings or policewoman's tights at will, but after six glasses of sangria Fran decided to ignore it.

She leaned back suddenly against the wall which, being next to the coat rack, was cushioned by macs and overcoats, and almost went to sleep. She must pull herself together. It was flu, that was all.

'Oh, my God,' she hissed as Jack Allen extracted himself from the elfin clutches and walked towards them, 'he's coming over!'

Stevie patted her. 'Don't worry, he's not dangerous in public. You'll be all right.'

'Celebrating something?' Jack asked, looking down at Fran with amusement, 'or is this your normal Thursday evening consumption? I must admit I like a woman who can hold her own with the lads.' With all the resolve she could muster, Fran sat up.

'Actually,' Stevie answered for her, 'it's Sean here's birthday.' Sean flashed a fuzzy smile at him. 'In fact we're just off to Mamma Cucina to grab a bite. Why don't you join us?' Stevie raised an eyebrow. 'And your friend of course.'

'Sounds fun.' Across the room Miriam looked as though this were the last thing on earth she had in mind but she clearly wasn't releasing Jack into such risky company alone.

Fran stood up and concentrated all her energies on the challenging task of putting on her coat.

'Here, let me help you,' offered Jack, trying to maintain a serious expression.

'I'm perfectly all right, thank you. Just a touch of flu making me woozy.'

'I see. So, are we walking? Probably just as well in your . . .' He paused, catching Stevie's eye, 'flu-like condition.'

Fran was grateful for the sharp evening wind and was careful to keep her distance from Jack and his piercing gaze. It occurred to her that she hadn't had any lunch, not even a sandwich. No wonder she was feeling strange. They threaded their way through the narrow backstreets of Woodbury, past the cathedral and across the old wool market to the welcoming bright lights of the Italian restaurant.

The 'Mamma' of Mamma Cucina turned out to be a dour and thin woman in her fifties, and she looked anything but thrilled at the sight of a dozen noisy people weaving their way into her restaurant at almost eleven o'clock on a Thursday night.

'Sorry,' she began, 'too late. The chef has gone home already.'

Fran groaned. The only thing that could save her now, she'd decided, was a plate of pasta.

They started to file out dejectedly when Mamma C caught sight of Jack standing at the back of the crowd talking to Stevie.

'Mister Jack!' she shouted. 'Are these friends of yours? Come in! Come in!'

The party trooped back in while the proprietor, her thin features suddenly alight with pleasure, promised them she would cook them a pasta herself.

Looking back, Fran decided it was that final glass of wine that did it. She tried to turn it down but the woman looked so offended, insisting it was from the family's own vineyard, that she had to give in. The conversation buzzed around her as Keith and Mike traded tales of how low they'd had to sink to get a story. Long before the pasta arrived Fran's eyes began to close, her head slipped backwards onto the soft banquette and within a minute or two she was fast asleep.

Jack, who had been watching her with amusement, leaned across to Stevie. 'I think somebody had better take the editor home.'

Stevie sighed and reached for her coat. The most wonderful fragrant smells were drifting out of the kitchen. 'You're right. She's had this bug all week and it's weakened her defences, poor lamb.'

'That's the nicest description I've ever heard of passing out.' Jack took her coat away from her. 'Look, Stevie, you don't even have a car. Are you planning to carry her home? I'll take her.'

Miriam reached for her handbag instantly.

'Do you mind staying here? The fewer witnesses the

better when one's feeling like this. And Mamma Cucina will kill me if we all troupe out.

'This one's on me. Happy Birthday, Sean.' He slipped a large note into Stevie's hand. 'Don't let her tell you it's on the house. Tell her her son'll never get through college if she gives food away. I'll get back as soon as I can, but I doubt it'll be in time to catch you. And do me a favour and stop looking at me like that, will you, Stevie?'

Oblivious to all but the pleasant sensation of being half-walked, half-carried along, her cheek aware only of the rough kiss of a tweed shoulder, Fran would have been happy to get into anyone's car, no matter what their intentions. Not suspecting, because she'd never felt like this before, that this blithe sense of irresponsibility was what fuelled the sales of strong liquor and explained much of the male willingness to shell out for it, she simply nestled back in the comfort of Jack's velvety passenger seat.

'Where are we going?' she asked eventually, as if expecting the answer 'Paris' or 'Monte Carlo'.

'Home,' Jack said firmly, 'bed.'

'Oh good,' Fran reached out a hand, 'are you coming too?'

They pulled up outside Fran's flat and Jack leaned over to open her door. With great deliberation, like a walrus in stilettos, she stepped out. 'I'm fine now,' she announced, 'you can go back to the others.'

'I'd rather just see you in.'

He followed her at a discreet distance up the garden path whereupon Fran delved into her bag, eager to prove she was more on top of things that he thought. Even in her befogged condition she knew that the keys lived in a special pouch just under the zip. It was hideously empty. She rummaged again. Nothing. And then an image appeared, so clear it was almost encased in dazzling light like a vision, of her bunch of keys sitting on Stevie's desk after she'd locked up her office.

'I know,' she volunteered, 'why don't I climb in?' She put a hand out towards the virginia creeper that covered the front of the house.

'No!' barked Jack. 'At the moment you're just drunk. You don't want to be drunk with a broken leg.'

'Drunks are notorious for falling out of windows and not breaking anything. It's only a few feet.' She grabbed the creeper and started to pull herself up. 'Anyway,' she looked down at him from her foothold two feet from the ground, 'I am not drunk.' Deciding that some music would help her ascent Fran broke into a rousing verse of 'Onward Christian Soldiers' and was still singing it when the creeper parted company with the wall and she tumbled down six feet knocking Jack over in the process.

'You'd better come back with me before we're both killed,' he announced grimly, limping a little as he guided her back to the car.

Halfway to his house Fran's elation wore off and she began to feel very much the worse for wear. They were in the middle of overtaking something when she screamed, making him wobble dangerously and very nearly hit the other car.

'For God's sake! What is it?'

'I think I'm going to be sick.' There was no time to pull

in or open windows. Jack showed the presence of mind that had made him rise to the top at the *Express* group. He grabbed Fran's handbag, unceremoniously emptied the contents onto the floor and held it out for her.

Fran, too grateful to notice anything except that here was a way out of her problem, made good use of it and promptly passed out.

Jack pulled the car over to the kerb and shoved the bag into the back. He sat watching Fran with tenderness and exasperation.

'So, lovely Francesca, what the hell am I supposed to do with you now?'

Chapter 8

A small chink of light filtered its way mercilessly through heavy curtains and lit the wall behind Fran like some Egyptian guide using a mirror to reflect the sun down a dark passage. Except that the passage wasn't deep enough or dark enough for Fran. She opened one eye, but her head hurt so much she quickly closed it. She knew only that she was ragingly thirsty and that she wanted to die. Then the memories inched their way back into her consciousness like the developing plot of a horror film. She'd been drunk. So drunk that someone had had to take her home from that Italian restaurant. They'd all seen her. Stevie, Mike Wooley, Keith Wilson, Sean and everyone else on the paper. She would never be able to tell any of them what to do ever again. They'd just laugh. But that was only the first reel. There was worse to come – she had just remembered who had driven her home. Instinctively she clutched at her clothes. She was still wearing them. He had simply laid her on the bed and put a cover over her.

The door opened an inch and Jack Allen, looking ludicrously cheerful, appeared with a cup of tea. 'I thought you might need this.' He put it beside her with a couple of paracetamol. 'I thought of force feeding you with Alka Seltzer last night but you might have taken me to the Court of Human Rights for cruel and inhuman treatment. How are you?'

He sat on the end of the bed – his bed, she realized with a shock.

'I'm not sure. You seem very proficient at all this.'

'Years of training.' He was in such a good mood she wanted to kill him.

'Jack . . .' A truly terrible thought invaded her consciousness and she sat up, almost spilling her tea.

'Yes?'

'Last night, you and me, we didn't, er . . . ?' her voice trailed off in hideous embarrassment.

'Make mad passionate love? You don't remember the draining board then?'

Fran paled. 'What draining board?'

'That scene in *Fatal Attraction*. You said you wanted to re-enact it.'

'I didn't!'

'No,' he agreed, enjoying himself hugely, 'you didn't. And call me old-fashioned but I do prefer my partners to be conscious.'

'So we didn't do anything at all?'

Jack thought he could detect the tiniest tinge of regret in her voice. 'Not even a little bit. As a matter of fact, you seemed very unhappy to me. Want to tell me about it?'

The warmth of his sympathy washed over her in deep, seductive waves. All she could do was lie down in them and luxuriate.

'I was having a relationship. I thought it was going to be permanent . . .' She couldn't believe she was talking like this to Jack Allen, journalist, world expert in extracting sob stories from downtrodden mothers, hardened criminals, and stonewalling council officials. 'But it wasn't. He wrote and told me it was over.'

'Nice way to do it. He's clearly a man of principle.'

Tears began to slide down Fran's face and she wiped them away angrily. 'But he *is* principled. That was why I liked him.'

'His principles must have made him blind then.' He touched her face with one finger. 'If you were in love with me, I'd never let you go. I wouldn't let you out of my sight for an instant.'

Very gently he leaned forward and kissed her on the lips. Fran felt the freshness of his newly shaven skin, surprisingly soft against hers, and caught the heady aroma of subtle, spicy cologne mixed with freshly laundered shirt, and found herself responding, not sure if it was pure comfort or the urgency of her own body. Jack needed no more encouragement. He kissed her hard then, folding her body tightly against his, pushed her back into the pillows. 'Are you sure you're fully conscious this time?' he asked softly.

Fran pulled his head back to hers.

Neither stopped to think after that. Somehow they got out of their clothes and under the covers and she felt the warmth of Jack's body next to hers. He was kissing the soft base of her neck, stroking her, chasing away her pain with his strong desire. Already she could feel him, big and hard, but he held himself away from her, delaying the moment, his hand slipping downwards, thinking of her pleasure. Instead she took hold of him and guided him until he was inside her, filling her up, driving into her so that they forgot everything except here and now.

Afterwards they fell apart, but their eyes still held each other fast. 'Francesca Tyler,' Jack picked up her hand and held the palm against his face, 'you have no idea how long I have wanted to do that. My only excuse for the unseemly speed. It was unforgivable, if understandable.'

Fran gazed up at him brazenly. 'If that was bad,' she answered truthfully, 'I can't wait for good.'

He snorted. 'To think I had you down as an innocent.'

She traced the lines of his chest with her finger. He was heavier than Laurence but with a compact, masculine strength she found surprisingly attractive. 'You're a lot fitter than I expected. With all that phone-bashing and liquid lunching I'd expect a paunch at least.'

He leaned towards her. 'I work out at a gym. Don't tell Stevie or she'll never speak to me again. She thinks she and I are joint winners in the maximum unfitness stakes.'

'Don't worry. Your secret's safe with me.' Fran lay back, pinching herself at how comfortable she felt with Jack, of all people. She waited for the shame to land blackly on her shoulder and gnaw at her for her outrageous behaviour, but she felt only heady, disgraceful happiness.

And then his lips were on her breast, his tongue stiffening the pink centre of her nipple, and his finger gently probing the damp knot of her pubic hair. Fran felt as if an electric current had wired the one centre of pleasure to the other, doubling her delight until she was hardly able to bear it and begged him to come inside her.

This time their climax was different from any she'd felt before. Like a pebble thrown into a pond it rippled on and on. Worn out by its intensity, finally they collapsed into each other's arms.

'I think I may have been wrong about you, Jack Allen,' she admitted.

'You mean you always thought me handsome and witty and now you find me even handsomer and wittier? But I've always known what you really think of me.' His tone hardened for a moment. 'You think I'm an irresponsible womanizer who takes advantage of young reporters, and who lost his wife and child and probably deserved to.'

Fran flinched at the edge of bitterness in his voice. She wished she could argue, deny it all, but she couldn't. It was true. That was precisely what she had thought of him. Until this moment.

With an unerring sense of timing, Fran knew there was something to be dealt with of even greater importance than her misconception about Jack. She needed a pee. Desperately.

She slid from the bed, noticing for the first time what a characterful room it was. She wouldn't have associated Jack with red walls and rich oil paintings but Jack had surprised her in all sorts of ways.

'Where are you going?' His wary tone implied that with

Fran one never knew. She might be about to perform the dance of the seven veils or summon a minicab.

'To find the loo.'

'Second on the right,' he answered with relief. 'Watch out for the bikes and skateboard.'

So happy and confident was Fran of the tenderness in Jack's voice that for once she didn't think about covering up. Jack found her beautiful. 'Back soon.'

'Hurry up,' he patted the vacant bed, 'I miss you.'

Fran hummed as she strode across the carpeted floor and flung open the door.

Standing in front of the washbasin, wearing an Oasis T-shirt and baggy shorts, headphones plugged into a Discman, a tall young man stared in the bathroom mirror singing 'You're my Wonder Waa-alll!'

At Fran's entrance he whipped round, almost knocking over the wooden towel rail, blushing like a traffic light.

Conscious suddenly of her nakedness, Fran grabbed a towel and covered herself.

'Sorry,' Ben apologized, scrabbling for his things. He'd told his dad he'd be staying with his friend Mark but Mark's mum had thrown them all out for drinking cans of beer. He hadn't wanted to confess this to Jack so he'd thought it'd be OK to sneak in. Now there'd be hell to pay. He tried to make up for the ineptness he felt by affecting an exaggerated cool. 'Nice to meet you. I'm Ben.' And then, as if stumped for further conversation. 'Would you like a toothbrush? Dad keeps a supply in the cabinet. Oh and there's a wrap too on the back of the door.' He didn't think of adding that it belonged to Jack's sister who had been staying recently.

Conversational ploys exhausted, he grabbed his Discman and belted out of the room, at least as embarrassed as Fran. If he'd known Dad had a girlfriend here he would have talked Mark's mum, furious though she was, into letting him stay there. But how was he to know? In the last seven years Dad had never once brought a woman here for the night. It was for his sake, he knew, and he'd wanted to say, Don't worry, Dad, I can cope, but in fact he'd rather liked it, always knowing the house belonged to just the two of them. Now his father had broken his own rule. It must be serious. Ben flushed again at the thought of Fran's naked body. He'd never actually managed to see more than a small flash before, peering into the girls' changing room with another boy for a dare. He hoped to God he hadn't acted like a twit or said anything stupid. The shock of seeing Fran had been so great that he couldn't any longer remember what he *had* said.

Still stunned from her encounter, Fran opened the bathroom cabinet and saw a neat row of brand new toothbrushes. There was deodorant on the shelf too. White Musk. Not the kind an adolescent boy or his father would use. She sat down on the side of the bath, her joy ebbing away like the bathwater she could hear gurgling its way down the plughole. He must do this a lot. His son hadn't even blinked at the sight of a strange woman, stark naked, fresh from his father's bed. How old was he? Fourteen? Fifteen? The age when most boys would die of embarrassment at the word breast, let alone encounter the reality without flinching.

And how could Jack be so irresponsible? To bring women back and let them wander gaily around naked when he had a young son? Jack Allen had to be everything she'd ever imagined and worse. The tenderness had been all a con. Jack was just a particularly subtle operator who understood his prey. With that girl Miriam he probably had another line altogether. The father figure who could further her career not because she'd slept her way into a promotion but because of the wisdom he could impart to her young and fertile mind.

A sharp sense of shame at her own part in all this hit her like cold water in her face. Here she was blaming Jack but if she hadn't got so disgracefully wrecked he wouldn't have brought her here. And who, after all, had forced her to make love to him? She had been entirely free and willing.

Fran broke open one of the toothbrushes and brushed until there was no more aftertaste of the night, or what came after it, left in her mouth. Still wearing the towel, she had a sense of how Eve must have felt after she'd eaten the apple. Lost innocence and instant cellulite consciousness were a lot to cope with at once.

Jack lay in bed, still smiling, with no premonition of Ben's disastrous encounter, but one look at Fran's tight reined-in face told him something had gone wrong. She was like a prize bloom hit by sudden early frost.

She gathered her clothes and quickly put them on.

'Fran, what's the matter?' Jack demanded.

'I met your son in the bathroom. Remind me to wear some clothes next time.'

'Damn and blast him. He was supposed to be at his friend's house.'

'It is his home too, I assume. He was very polite.'

'Probably more shocked than you were.' Jack tried to hold her.

'As a matter of fact he took it very calmly.' She didn't elaborate about the wrap and toothbrushes.

Jack could feel her closing up against him and wanted to shake her. Instead he got dressed and together they went down to the kitchen. Ben was nowhere to be seen.

'Would you like breakfast? Since I wasn't expecting you I'm afraid it's not croissants and freshly squeezed juice. Unless you fancy sprout-and-turnip. We do a fine Rice Crispies though, I'm told.'

But Fran wasn't in the mood for laughter. She glanced round the warm homely room where books and news-papers and wellingtons vied for space with rollerblades and an alien bike wheel. On the capacious sofa a black and white dog with a dreamy expression and a ludicrous red scarf round its neck lounged as if in canine heaven. For a weak moment the thought of turnip juice and Rice Crispies held a brief temptation. 'No thanks, I've got a meeting.'

'And you wouldn't want to be late for it, would you?'

Fran ignored the angry edge to his voice and looked around for her handbag. This was a scene where she needed to make a quick exit and she cursed herself for losing it now of all times. It reminded her of the moment at seventeen when she'd very publicly given the boot to her boyfriend for snogging another girl then had to crawl humiliatingly round the party room on hands and knees in the pitch dark looking for her evening bag. 'Have you,' she refused to meet his eyes, nervous of what she might see there, 'happened to see my handbag?'

Disconcertingly Jack barked with laughter and disappeared for a moment. 'It was in the airing cupboard,' he handed it over.

'What on earth was it doing there?'

'You were sick in the car and that was all there was to hand. Don't worry, I washed it for you.'

This time Fran couldn't resist a small smile. 'How very resourceful of you.'

'Leonard Woolf did the same thing for Virginia, or so I read. Only in her case she needed a pee and it was a rolled-up newspaper. Apparently it sealed their relationship.'

'I imagine it might. Look, Jack . . . I . . .' and Fran might have apologized and all might have been well had not Ben, shy, big-hearted Ben, gone and scuppered things once more by choosing that moment to blunder into the room looking for the dog.

'Rover!' he yelled, clinking its lead temptingly. Rover dived under the sofa and tried to disguise himself as a stuffed toy. 'Obedience classes!' Wild Rover made a mad dash for the garden door and squeezed himself with great difficulty through the last owner's cat flap.

'Making progress, isn't he?' asked Jack.

Ben, with Wild Rover in his arms, finally struggled back into the kitchen. 'Oh, by the way, Dad, that girl Miriam rang from the paper. She said she needed some advice from you about an urgent interview and wondered if she could come round.'

'Bye, Jack,' Fran said wryly. 'I wouldn't want to come between you and an urgent interview.'

With one glance at the thunderous expression on his father's face, Ben and the dog made a beeline for the garden door. Sensing real trouble when he saw it, for once Rover did what he was told and the pair scuttled out leaving Jack to an empty fridge and the bitter taste of disappointment. Had Ben screwed up his chance with Fran deliberately?

Businesslike as ever, Fran wasn't going to let Jack get in the way of her meeting with Stevie, but halfway across Woodbury she realized her head ached and she had completely forgotten what the meeting was about. Ignoring all thoughts of Stevie's likely suppositions if she didn't show up, she headed safely back to bed. It wasn't till she was outside her front door that she remembered the reason she'd ended up at Jack's in the first place. She'd forgotten her keys. She leaned on the front door, hating herself. Couldn't she do anything right? The sudden thought that her neighbour had a key for safekeeping revived her spirits, but then she remembered he was never in at this time. However, the patron saint of hopeless cases was clearly on 24-hour standby because he was not only in but remembered that her spare key was in his cat-shaped teapot.

Once inside she made straight for the duvet and tried, in a masochistic sort of way, to recall the words Laurence had used in his Dear John letter. But nothing came. Instead all she could think of was Jack's face when he told her the story of Virginia Woolf peeing in the newspaper. And it struck her what an incredible force love was, that you could see someone at one of life's least advantageous moments and cherish them all the more.

As if in recognition of this fact, Fran's stomach, recalling its recent ordeal by sangria, began to heave unpleasantly and she was forced to dash for the bathroom. As she chucked up the rest of the wine and the orange juice and the cheap Spanish brandy into the toilet bowl, one thought drifted into her mind. She was alone again. There was no one here to hold out a handbag. This time she'd really excelled herself. To lose one lover might look like carelessness but to lose two took a really special talent.

Chapter 9

'I'm really sorry, Dad,' Ben crept back into the kitchen after he'd watched Fran depart, 'I get the impression I royally screwed that up for you.'

Jack Allen, staring out a bowl of porridge and losing, saw the look of almost parental concern in his son's eyes and couldn't feel angry with him. Ben leaned awkwardly on the door, standing on one foot, like a teenage crane, yearning to grow up yet terrified, especially at moments like these, of the painful pitfalls adulthood seemed to hold.

'Don't lose any sleep over it. I probably screwed it up for myself. I should have checked whether you were here. It's just that I had my mind on other things.' Jack, always sensitive to his son's feelings, tried to see the encounter from his point of view. 'It must have been a shock for you too, meeting Fran like that.'

Ben blushed furiously, remembering Fran's naked body, the first he'd ever seen except in dog-eared girlie magazines.

Overcome with shyness he sat down at the table and poured out half a packet of Bran Flakes. 'She's very pretty.'

'Yes,' agreed his father, 'she is. Very. By the way, far be it from me to discourage healthy eating, but you absolutely loathe Bran Flakes.'

'So I do,' agreed Ben, still munching. 'You don't suppose . . .' He paused for a moment. Jack held his breath wondering if the moment had finally come for Ben to ask him some hideous question about sexual technique or, worse still, what had really been behind his parents' divorce.

'You don't suppose,' Ben continued, 'she might give me a work placement on her paper? I've never asked you because it'd look like favouritism.'

Jack laughed out loud at the mercenary nature of youth. Here he was wondering whether Ben would be scarred for life by this Oedipal encounter and all his son was thinking about was career paths. 'Why don't you ask her?'

Ben merely shook his head. 'You know her far better.'

'Yes,' conceded Jack, 'but in my case that's a disadvantage. Francesca Tyler is convinced that I'm a shit, charming perhaps, but still a shit.'

'I thought women liked charming shits. All those women's magazine articles about why women love bastards. Treat 'em mean, keep 'em keen. All that stuff. Maybe you're not being shitty enough.'

'That's old hat now, Ben. Your generation is supposed to treat women as equals.'

'Why?' Ben helped himself to a second bowl. Food seemed to melt when he was in the house and Jack was continually having to replenish the cupboards the day after he'd filled them. 'The girls at school treat us like some-thing the cat's sicked up. They're cleverer than us, they pay more attention in class, get better A levels. Men won't be necessary soon, Jodie Smith says. They're just sperm banks with cheque books and soon women won't need them either.'

Jack retreated behind his copy of the *Woodbury Express*. Clearly the sex war had taken a nasty new turn. For once he was grateful for being middle-aged.

Maybe all this explained why Fran had such a very low opinion of him, but he had a feeling there was more to it than that. Perhaps he'd canvas Stevie on how to proceed next.

There was one thing he was completely sure of. After last night – and this morning – he wasn't going to just give up. Fran was the most delicious woman he'd ever made love to.

The other side of town, Laurence Westcott and his mother were having breakfast in her morning room, full of spring flowers, and reading the *Woodbury Citizen* which featured, in an impressive double-page spread, the article Fran had written about Laurence's unit.

'You know, darling,' Camilla enthused, 'she's really caught the essence of you in this article. Your selflessness. Your generosity. In fact I'd say you come out of it sounding really rather saintly.'

'What you really mean,' Laurence had the grace to look embarrassed, is that I sound like a heady combination of Albert Schweizer and Bob Geldof.'

'Well, you are, darling,' Camilla said proudly.

Laurence heard the love and pride in Camilla's voice and wished, as he always did, that he could return it. She wanted so little from him, but he couldn't give even that. He'd tried hard enough but no spontaneous feelings of affection ever came. Pretence would have to do. It was, after all, better than the truth. He reached over and squeezed her hand. 'I'm only what you made me.'

Camilla turned pink with pride. 'You never told me why you stopped seeing her.' Camilla knew she was on dangerous ground. 'It seemed such a pity. You really should settle down.'

Laurence resisted the temptation to say it was none of her business. The truth was he had been missing Francesca enormously. She was so lively and full of ideas. It was as though he had all his life been watching the world in grainy black and white and Fran had skipped in and with a flick of a switch she had adjusted his vision into glowing colour.

Laurence, when he was in an honest mood, knew that he was something of a dry well, but Fran seemed to be able to lower buckets and come up with things he didn't know were even in him. The truth was, her departure had left a hole in his life that he'd found very hard to fill.

'Why don't you give her a ring?' suggested Camilla. 'Tell her you liked the article?'

Laurence was not a man usually given to grand emotional gestures yet this morning, much to his surprise, the idea appealed to him. Perhaps he'd been too hasty. It had been that question of hers about children. It had panicked him. He ought to be fair and tell her that children were out of the question for him. They were simply not on his agenda. But if he told her that, he suspected, he might end up losing her altogether.

He spread his toast with Cooper's Oxford and cut it accurately in half. Would it really matter to her so much? She wasn't like the women he saw at the clinic, hung-up and desperate, unable to think of anything else but babies. She had her career as well as a full and busy life.

'That's not a bad idea, Mother,' he conceded. Camilla looked as thrilled as a budgie with a new bell. It wasn't often her impressive son ever took her advice, or even listened to her at all.

Stevie was reading the article about Laurence too by the time Fran finally made it to the paper, but decided he came over more sanctimonious than saintly. Saintly people, Stevie assumed (not having come across that many in her life as journalist in Woodbury), did good things without expecting acknowledgment. Laurence did good things and gave you the phone number of the people he'd done them to. It might be in the greater cause of his clinic, but it was self-serving all the same, in her view.

'Any phone calls following it up?' Fran asked

'Lots,' continued Stevie, ignoring the sounds of chaos from the newsroom outside caused by someone feeding Sean McGee's mineral water to the Yucca plant. 'This won't do us any harm in the Regional Press Awards. Any more news about that by the way?'

'We don't submit, they choose.'

'And every year the bloody *Express* beats us,' Stevie pointed out gloomily.

'Not this year though. They may have come up with a cheap wheeze but we were the ones who got that bus company bang to rights. Even the judges are bound to see that.' The memory of Jack's solidly masculine body filled her mind for a moment. Angrily she pushed it away. 'Bloody Jack Allen. That man had all the sensitivity of a surgical appliance.'

Stevie wondered what had gone wrong. It had all looked so promising.

'By the way,' Fran added casually, 'he hasn't rung, has he?'

'Aha,' Stevie tapped the side of her nose, 'I forgot to enquire. How was your lift home last night?'

Fran looked away, hoping desperately that Stevie had absolutely no idea what had happened and never would. 'Actually I threw up in his car.'

'Poor Jack. Not on his precious leather seats.'

'Don't worry about poor Jack's precious car. He emptied out my handbag and gave me that as a sick-bag.'

Stevie guffawed. 'I like it! That man's got style.' Stevie, knowing Fran very well and liking her even more, had a pretty shrewd idea that something had happened between her and Jack. She would make it her business – subtly in so far as she was capable of it – to find out what. Jack and Fran were two of her very favourite people and she was damned if she'd see either of them miss out on the chance of happiness that she and Fran's father, Ralph, had sacrificed.

Fran did a quick tour of the office, checking that everything was on course, but Stevie had done a good job.

Stories had been allocated, phones were buzzing, press releases checked through, the daily police briefing held. Some wag had attached a Post-It sticker to Sean McGee's ponytail saying 'Cut Me'. Sean, blissfully unaware, was deep in conversation about shortfalls in the community care budget. Life went on as usual.

Fran retreated to her office and closed the door. She was feeling a little better. Had she stayed a little longer at Jack's he would no doubt have come up with some cast-iron hangover cure. Jack was the type who would know about such things. Garlic up the nostrils or a whole coat of the dog or eight pints of water or maybe just a couple of Nurofen with hot, sweet tea. Instead she had found her bathroom cupboard bare and the only brandy in her house was ten-year-old Metaxas, which, unlike posher brands, did not age with grace. The best use for it, Fran decided when she'd gingerly undone the stopper, was cleaning drains.

Thinking about Jack, she began to smile in spite of herself. Stevie was right – faithless and unreliable he might be, but he did have style. The memory of his face, all tender concern as he brought her a cup of tea, would stay with her for a long time. When the phone interrupted her thoughts she even wondered if it might be him.

In fact it was Ronnie Newlands, senior partner of Newlands, Woodbury's biggest estate agency and the *Citizen*'s biggest advertising client.

'Ronnie,' Fran enthused, 'what a nice surprise!' Something in his voice – embarrassment? exaggerated formality? a careful choosing of words instead of the usual

Newlands I'm-a-plain-man friendliness – warned her that something unexpected was coming.

But even that didn't prepare her for the full extent of the blow when it fell.

Ronnie Newlands had rung to say that he was about to transfer the agency's entire business from the *Citizen* to the *Express*.

A wave of panic ran through Fran as she tried to mentally compute the loss this would mean to her paper.

'I'm sorry, Francesca, I'm fond of you, and Ralph and I go back a long way, but business is business. The Express Group offered me a deal I couldn't refuse.'

The full extent of the betrayal opened up before her like a black hole. Jack had to have known about this. In fact, while he'd been screwing her in bed he'd been screwing her professionally at the same time. Fran wondered briefly if he had taken pleasure in this knowledge. If it had seemed a particularly fine coup. God, she hated him. After the bus story she should have known he'd stoop to anything.

'Thanks for letting me know, Ronnie.' Fran was amazed that any words came out at all.

She picked up the nearest thing on her desk, a mug with YOU'RE NOT A CITIZEN WITHOUT THE CITIZEN, a somewhat clumsy line from an ad campaign in her father's day, and flung it against the wall, where it narrowly missed the glass of the door as Stevie opened it.

'What in the name of God's going on?' Stevie demanded.

'Bloody Jack Allen! You want to know what honourable

Jack who doesn't take advantage of unconscious women has done now?'

Stevie grinned at this confirmation of her suspicions and wondered what had happened when the woman in question had regained consciousness. 'No, but I have a premonition you're about to tell me.'

'He's only stolen our single best client! Ronnie Newlands has been made an offer he couldn't refuse and he's taking his business – every des res and studio flat not big enough to swing a cat in – over to the enemy.'

This Stevie had to concede was a crushing blow. She knew as well as Fran how close to the wind the *Citizen* sailed. A squall like this could sink them forever.

'And the new paper isn't even out yet. That won't help. We're going to have to start fighting back.'

'I know. And it needs to be radical, not a little re-jig nobody notices.'

Their gloomy deliberations were cut short by the arrival of Mike Wooley, informing Fran that there was someone to see her urgently downstairs.

For once Fran wished they could afford a secretary to put off unexpected callers like this, but the *Citizen* ran to no such luxuries and she could hardly take Mike off a story to find out what the caller wanted.

Reluctantly she traipsed down the two flights to the reception desk, pushing her way past leaning towers of newspapers, Sean McGee's bike and a double buggy which presumably belonged to someone placing an ad in the classified section.

'He's waiting outside,' whispered Elaine on reception dramatically.

From her reverent tone Fran assumed it had to be the mayor or at the very least some visiting pop star doing the rounds of the local radio station. For a brief and disgraceful second she wondered if it could be Jack, come to explain about Newlands.

The possibility that it might be Laurence didn't occur to her at all.

He leaned, hands in pockets, against an adjacent bus shelter outside the paper's front door, reading the *Lancet*. His smile, when he saw Fran appear on the doorstep, was sheepish and quite devastatingly attractive. She had, she realized with a jolt, forgotten how amazing his looks were. With his blond hair and his startling eyes it was another Laurence he suddenly reminded her of: Laurence of Arabia.

'Francesca . . .' Peter O'Toole couldn't have rolled more meaning and emotion into the word, even after nine pints of Guinness and a snog of the Blarney stone. 'Will you come for a walk?' He made it sound as if it were round the garden of Eden he was proposing instead of Woodbury on Friday lunchtime.

'I do have a paper to edit.' Fran's anger at the way he'd treated her flooded back into her memory, giving her strength and stature.

'And I, for the first time in my entire career, have left a clinic of patients in the lurch.'

Fran pictured all those hopes and dreams, sperm samples wasted, eggs remaining unfertilized, and all because . . . Here her imagination failed her. *And all because what?*

'I had to see you, Francesca. I had to tell you now, not

waiting even a minute longer, what a stupid mistake I'd made.'

Fran's heart lurched. He was going to tell her that he loved her after all.

'Let's go down to the river. Please.'

Fran agonized only briefly. The paper's troubles would still be there when she came back but Laurence might not. 'All right. Just for half an hour.'

They made their way silently through Woodbury's narrow back streets, grateful that they were so quiet that hardly any traffic disturbed them, down past the edge of the park and through the watermeadows to the river bank. It was extraordinarily peaceful with only the odd dog-walker to remind them they weren't alone in the world.

Laurence took her hand. 'I love you, Francesca. I suppose it's taken the stupidity of letting you go to show me that.'

Letting me go, Fran wanted to protest, cut the crap, you dumped me, let's speak plainly here. But Laurence was in full flow.

'You must think me a cold bastard to have run like that when you mentioned children,' to her astonishment his eyes shone with unshed tears, 'but there is a reason.'

He looked away as if what he had to say were so painful that he had to draw himself in and gather strength to say it. 'The thing is, Francesca, I'm adopted and I only found out when I was twenty-one. It came as a complete shock. I'd always been so close to my mother, and then,' his voice cracked under the weight of his pain, 'I found she wasn't my mother at all. My own mother had given me away. It felt like the ultimate betrayal.' He looked back at her, his eyes raking her face for understanding. 'It's why I chose the job I do. I suppose I thought I could make up for my own mother not wanting me by helping women who desperately want babies. I'm so sorry, Francesca, but it affects everything I do, it makes me test people, make them prove how much they love me. I suppose that was what I was up to with you. I'm so sorry. I should have tried to explain all this instead of leaving you to think it was all your fault when you're the most wonderful, vibrant woman I've ever met.'

He reached out and stroked her hair tenderly. 'Can you ever forgive me? Francesca, I want you to marry me. With you beside me everything will be different. My God, how I've missed you. Say yes, Francesca, please say yes.'

Fran allowed herself to be pulled into his arms, carried along by his certainty and her irresistible feeling for the underdog. He needed her and he had been badly hurt. He was a good man who was capable of helping so many other people, righting so much tragedy. He was also, she felt instinctively, a reliable man. He would not, as Jack had done, lose his wife and child. But there was one question she had to resolve before she could give her answer.

'When we were away last weekend you said that if I wanted children you weren't the man for me. What did you mean? That you don't want children of your own?'

Laurence saw the look of pained dismay in Fran's eyes. This was the moment of truth, the moment he'd dreaded so much. Yet if he were completely open with her she might go, leave him forever, she would be entitled to after all. And he couldn't risk that.

'I meant . . .' he faltered momentarily, 'I meant that I might not be a very good father.'

'Is that all?' Fran breathed. 'Everyone fears that. I might be a bloody awful mother, drop the baby on its head, not spot its meningitis, be bad tempered during quality time, but with a doctor around the place . . .' She took his hands, feeling that a huge weight had been taken from her. He was just frightened of being inadequate, but he'd probably make a much better father than he thought. A baby might be just what he needed to get in touch with all those emotions he'd battened down. It was in Fran's crusading nature to love a cause and Laurence, it struck her, was a very worthy one. She could save him for humanity.

'So,' he took her in his arms tenderly, 'now that we've got that sorted out. Francesca Tyler, will you marry me?'

Chapter 10

Fran looked into Laurence's eyes as he waited for her answer and saw hope struggling against fear in them. There was no shred of the easy confidence Jack Allen would have conveyed, the assumption that any woman would want him. But when Laurence loved, she felt instinctively, he loved forever.

'Yes,' she replied, more certainty flooding into her with every word. 'Yes, Laurence, I will marry you.'

'Lovely, lovely, Francesca.' And then for no reason he could rationally explain, he added, 'You'll never regret this, I promise you that.'

The first person Fran wanted to tell her wonderful news to was her father. For once the paper could wait, Stevie would manage brilliantly in her absence and enjoy every minute.

On the way back to get the car they stopped off at an old-fashioned baker's. Knowing her mother, the cupboard would be bare or stocked with only low-fat, low-cholesterol, low-taste biscuits. Instead Fran bought a home-made walnut cake, the kind with white frosted icing and chopped walnuts throughout, so sickly you could eat only one slice. They were her father's favourite. He used to sneak in and buy one for their most special outings together. Epsom Downs and the Derby would have been unthinkable without a frosted walnut.

All over Woodbury the schools were spilling out their laughing, chattering pupils, some uniformed, others having created their own uniforms of baggy trousers and bomber jackets over plaid shirts. Fran smiled at them. She also smiled at lollipop ladies, babies in buggies and even a traffic warden who was so disconcerted he wrote out his ticket wrongly and had to start again.

She couldn't remember feeling this ludicrously happy in years. It even lasted all the way up her parents' drive and survived the little lurch of apprehension at seeing what her father and Laurence would make of each other.

'Francesca, what a surprise!' Her mother took in Laurence's tall figure and softened somewhat. 'Come in, come in.'

'Mum, this is Laurence Westcott . . .' She trailed off, not quite sure what status to accord him. 'Where's Dad?'

Her mother's expression changed subtly. 'In his study. He spends most of his time in there. The past's more alluring to him than the present. Why don't you take your friend into the sitting room while I make some tea?'

The sitting room, as Fran expected, was cold and musty and damp. Only her mother could own a house with a gloriously sunny garden and never open the windows to let in the light and air, or pick a single flower to brighten her window ledges and little tables.

Fran flung open the French doors and the May sunshine instantly cheered the room. Her mother arrived with a tray of tea and biscuits. There was no sign of the cake. 'I'll get your father.'

When Ralph came into the room, Fran had to pinch herself with shock. It was only a few weeks since she'd seen him yet he had changed subtly. He seemed older and more aloof.

'Franny!' Her presence finally broke through his dreamy distance. 'How lovely! What brings you here? It isn't the weekend, is it?'

'We came for tea. This is Laurence, Dad. I think I mentioned him to you. He's in charge of the infertility unit at Woodbury Hospital.'

'Not an administrator, I hope? Can't stand administrators.'

Laurence laughed. 'Actually I'm a doctor.'

Obviously Ralph couldn't remember her talking about Laurence after all. 'Pa, we've brought you a little surprise.'

She slipped off to the kitchen and came back triumphantly holding the cake. 'It's a frosted walnut! Do you remember when we took one to the Derby and ended up sharing it with all those punters and they gave us a lift back in their open-topped charabanc? It was like the feeding of the five thousand.'

Ralph smiled non-committally, and Fran stifled a sharp sense of disappointment that her treasured memory meant nothing to him.

'Talking of surprises . . . Laurence and I have another one. We've just decided to get married!'

'How marvellous!' responded Ralph. 'I hope you'll be very happy.'

Francesca was stunned. The words were right but her beloved father had delivered them as if he were talking to a stranger. She had expected a strong reaction. Delight perhaps, mixed with a little apprehension that he didn't know Laurence better before this news was sprung on him. But this rather distant congratulation! It was almost as though he were talking to an employee, not his own daughter.

Laurence, however, didn't seem to have noticed anything amiss. Phyllis offered him tea and he sat down. Ralph, deciding something more was required of him as a host, jumped up and asked if he'd like milk or sugar. And when Laurence replied just milk, he proceeded to hand him the sugar and put down the milk.

'Milk, Ralph!' screeched Phyllis, making them all turn. 'Laurence said he wanted milk not sugar. Can't you get anything right at the moment?' She countered their surprised stares defiantly. 'Well, you try and live with him when he keeps putting his pyjamas back on in the morning and getting dressed in a suit to go to bed and see if you deal with it any better!'

Fran patted her father's hand. He was looking near to tears. This wasn't at all the happy, joyous family occasion she'd longed for.

Sensing her distress, Laurence engaged his father-in-law to be in quiet conversation while Fran followed her mother into the kitchen.

'Don't look at me like that, Francesca. He's driving me mad. He keeps wandering off to the park and not coming back for hours on end. You have to tell him everything ten times and he still forgets it. I don't know what the hell's the matter with him.'

And couldn't care less, thought Fran bitterly, except in that it inconveniences you and your bloody bridge.

'So when are you planning to actually get married?' her mother asked finally.

'We haven't really decided. It's all been a bit sudden. Anyway, I really ought to get back to the paper, I suppose.'

Phyllis laid a tentative hand on her daughter's arm. 'I'm sorry it wasn't more festive. He seems very nice.'

'Thanks, Mum. He is.'

Ralph followed them out and held her tight, just as he had when she was a child. His familiar scent, worn tweed, ancient aftershave and faint tobacco, transported her back for a blissful second to their happiest times together. 'Come again soon. And next time bring your young man. I'd very much like to meet him.'

Fran clung to him to hide her tears. Something terrible was happening to her beloved father. He was turning, almost as she watched, into a formal and distant stranger.

'Here,' said her mother quickly, handing over the white cardboard cake-box. 'Take it back to the office and have it there.'

It was her walnut cake and it was entirely untouched.

As she walked back to the car, she couldn't hide her tears any longer. 'I don't know what's the matter with him. He seemed like a different person.'

Laurence stilled her pace and held her for a moment. 'I'm no expert, but I'm afraid it looks to me like the beginning of Alzheimer's.'

The horrible, harsh word reverberated its tragic notes in her head.

'Fran, I'm so sorry. But if you want him at the wedding, I think it ought to be soon.'

Fran couldn't answer. She could only think of the terrible, nightmarish process that had started to destroy, if Laurence was right, the human being she loved most in the world.

Jack Allen stared at the glossy, full-colour ad for Newlands Estate Agency as it flashed onto the made-up page for tomorrow's paper and swore. He knew that one of the fundamental rules in newspapers was that advertising shouldn't be allowed to influence editorial content, and also that it constantly did. But this, to his mind, was different. He knew exactly what level of discount Murray Nelson had offered Newlands to get their business, and that the *Express* would be losing money on the deal, at least at first. Nelson had lured him away from the *Citizen*, threatening its future viability, for absolutely no profit, and very probably a loss.

'Murray,' he barked at his employer when he finally pinned him down on his mobile, 'this is madness. You're giving this space away.'

'Ah,' wheedled Nelson, 'maybe I am. But when other advertisers see that Newlands are coming over to us, they will too.'

'Look, Murray,' Jack threw a dart at a photograph above

the door featuring Murray Nelson showing round the Duchess of York at the opening of their offices, a fine pair. 'I don't need it. The new paper's picking up plenty of extra accounts.'

'Never say you've got enough in this business. You're going soft, Jack. Could it be that your judgement's been affected by the attractiveness of your rival editor? I hear you and she have been sharing more than your contacts book lately. Just keep your mind on the new paper, only two months to launch, remember. I'll remind you, shall I, that you said you had plenty of advertising when the margins don't deliver. Goodbye, Jack.'

Jack couldn't believe it. How could Nelson possibly know about him and Fran? Unless someone present the other night had told him. But there had been only one other person from the *Express* there. Miriam. Would she do that? He'd better be more careful of Miriam.

Especially if he intended, which he certainly did, to start pursuing Francesca in earnest. He remembered that he'd meant to get Stevie's advice. With luck he might catch her at the Cathedral Arms later this evening. First he had a pressing appointment. Ben had taken him aside and given him a lecture on father-and-son bonding, then promptly handed him a pair of second-hand rollerblades. Jack had felt like Cinderella sitting at the kitchen table with Ben slipping a delicate size eleven onto his foot. He'd secretly hoped it was his turn to be the Ugly Sister and that the slipper wouldn't fit. All those cool young dudes gliding around while he floundered about like a haddock. But the boot had slipped on. Perfectly.

Jack grabbed the rollerblades and shoved them into a macho-looking adidas bag. He sincerely hoped that none of the lads in the newsroom took a short cut past the rollerblading arena.

Two hours later, exhausted but surprisingly invigorated, not to mention mighty proud of the femur-threatening manoeuvre Ben had just taught him, he dragged Ben on a detour to the pub.

'Can I just go and get Rover from the car? He needs a run around. He and I can always sit outside if you want to talk shop.'

Jack noticed a large group of foreign students, mostly female, mostly teenage, and mostly microskirted at the next table. No wonder Ben was feeling so unusually thoughtful.

He glimpsed Stevie deep in conversation with the three young reporters from the *Citizen* and headed for their table. 'Anyone for a refill?'

Stevie and two of the reporters nodded enthusiastically. Sean McGee gestured to the bottle of mineral water strapped to his belt.

'The landlord must love you.'

'Actually I'm on a three-day purification programme.'

'Who needs water purifiers when you've got Sean?' demanded Mike Wooley. 'Seven times round our Sean and you could drink it straight from the tap.' He indicated Sean's skin-tight cycling shorts.

'Which is more than can be said for you,' Stevie reminded him. 'Mine's a whisky. Mike won't have one. He's still working on a story.'

Mike looked mutinous and raided her packet of Pork Scratchings.

On his way to the bar Jack's progress was impeded by continual pats on the backs and offers of drinks. Jack always did have the common touch, Stevie noted. It was what made him such a good editor. He came back through the crowded bar and put the drinks down without spilling a drop. Stevie liked that in a man. He also seemed to have a spring in his step she hadn't noticed before, like someone who had suddenly decided what it was he wanted from life and was about to pursue it singlemindedly. If so, Stevie concluded, his timing was pretty disastrous.

'So,' enquired Sean McGee innocently, raising his glass of mineral water. 'What's the toast. The editor's happiness?'

Stevie sent him a quelling look.

'Why on earth should we be drinking to that?'

'Haven't you heard?' Sean failed to notice the silence that had suddenly fallen at the table. 'Francesca's just announced she's getting married.'

'Married?' The colour drained from Jack's face until he matched the pickled eggs on the bar. 'She can't be. Who the hell to?'

'To the doctor who runs the infertility unit,' Stevie said quietly. 'His name's Laurence Westcott.'

Jack felt his chest tighten over and his breathing speed up almost as if he were having a heart attack. Francesca was getting married. And to Laurence Westcott of all people. Not only present but remembered pain seared up through him taunting him with the memories of the past and the thought that, once again, he hadn't acted soon enough.

He would lose the woman he loved. For the second time.

'Congratulations, Franny darling!' It was bath time on Saturday but the news was so good Henrietta went off to find a bottle of wine from her capacious fridge. Not, it had to be said that Henrietta ever needed much excuse. She came back with two vast goblets large enough to satisfy some medieval lord back from lobbing arrows at Crécy. 'When's the wedding? Can Soph and Lottie be bridesmaids?'

'Yes, please!' thrilled Lottie. 'Can I have a cream dress with pink bows on it and lace tights and pink satin ballet shoes and real flowers in my hair like Samantha did?'

Lottie was at the stage where the only thing that counted in life was keeping up with the Samanthas.

'Sam says it isn't a real wedding unless you have six bridesmaids and a karaoke at the reception.'

Fran giggled. She couldn't somehow picture Laurence singing along to 'Staying Alive'.

'Mu-uum, honestly!' Sixteen-year-old Sophie found her mother's brashness hideously embarrassing. 'Let Auntie Fran decide whether she wants us as bridesmaids. She might want to get married in a register office.'

'Of course she won't, darling. That's for next time round, isn't it, Fran? When you realize you made a God-awful mistake with number one and don't want to draw attention to your second in case that's a disaster too. Not that it will be, of course,' she added hastily, 'not with the divine Dr Westcott.'

'Of course I'd love you to be my bridesmaids. I thought

maybe I'd have a Flower Fairies theme. Lottie could be the Fuschia Fairy in pink and purple and, Soph, I thought perhaps the Nasturtium Fairy for you in orange and green, or would you prefer to be Pansy and Columbine?'

Sophie, Lottie and their mother all gaped at her aghast. 'Don't worry.' Fran was enjoying herself. 'To tell you the truth I haven't given it a second thought but my instincts would be to keep it simple and choose something you could wear again.'

'Oh, Fran,' wailed her friend, 'you're so hopelessly practical. I hope *you're* not going to choose something you can wear again. A nice jersey trouser suit that will do for work? Be frivolous for God's sake!'

'Have you decided on a date yet, Auntie Fran?'

'Fairly soon, we thought.' Fran's face lost its sparkle momentarily. 'It's my father, you see. He's really not well and Laurence thinks he may get worse.'

'Fran, how awful! Your father always seems like the fittest man in three counties. He's so full of energy whenever I see him he makes *me* feel old.'

'I know, but he's changing, Henry.' She paused, unsure how much detail of her father's condition she should reveal. He was so proud, he would hate people to pity him and yet she needed the comfort of telling someone herself. 'Laurence thinks it's the beginning of Alzheimer's.'

'But isn't that awfully gradual? I mean people don't go gaga overnight.' Henrietta flushed, realizing this might not be the most tactful of statements.

'He's been changing a lot over the last few months. He just didn't want us to tell everybody.'

'Oh, Fran,' Henrietta put her arms round her friend briefly. She knew how much Fran's father meant to her. 'How awful. He's such a wonderful man. Anyway, he must be thrilled that you're getting married at last.'

'I'm not *that* old, you know,' Fran replied. 'You make me sound as though I've been on the shelf for years.'

'Well, not years exactly, but you are getting a bit old-maidish. When did you last do something really spontaneous and wicked and exciting?'

A sudden vision of Jack Allen reeled through her mind, his mouth on her breast and his fingers sending a wildfire of excitement through her whole body. Stop that, she ordered herself and tried to insert some other more suitable image. None came.

'It's funny, isn't it?' Henrietta mused smugly. 'You wanted a baby and you found a husband. Perhaps Mother Nature knows what she's doing after all.'

Fran refrained from pointing out that if Nature knew what it was doing then it had a pretty strange plan, but Henrietta's thoughts on the Unseen Hand That Guides Us All were something she could do without at this moment.

Henrietta knelt on the edge of the huge Victorian bath and soaped Lottie's back. Early evening sunlight drew a pattern on the rich Burne-Jones wallpaper behind her. 'I suppose,' Henrietta blew a kiss of bathfoam in her friend's direction, 'the next invitation will be to the christening.'

Fran shook her head. That was one thing she had given some thought to and she had already come to a decision. It would be unfair to Laurence to get pregnant five minutes after the wedding, especially given his caution about children. She had to pave the way very delicately indeed.

'Actually I've decided to have a coil fitted.'

Henrietta looked stunned.

'What's a coil, Mum?' Lottie was fascinated.

Henrietta didn't even blink. She and Simon had a policy on enquiries like this: squirm-inducing honesty. 'It's a small device, usually made of copper, which the lady puts up her vagina and it stops the egg she produces every month embedding in the wall of the womb so the Daddy's sperm can't fertilize it.'

Lottie gave her an old-fashioned look.

'Really, Mum.' Sophie winked at her little sister. 'You don't have to make up things like that, and we don't believe a word of that fairy story about vaginas, do we? Me and Lottie know babies are brought by Mr Stork like in Dumbo, don't we, Lots?'

'So where's the wedding going to be if your dad's not well. I know,' Henrietta's eyes shone with Joan of Arc enthusiasm, 'why don't you have it here? We could easily seat two hundred in a tent. You could have a disco in the evening and breakfast at dawn.'

'Henry . . . it's really kind of you.' Fran could already envisage a marquee done up like a gilded birdcage, so many lilies you choked on arrival, hot and cold running staff and Henrietta queening it so disgracefully that Laurence's mother would never speak to Fran again. And then there'd be the twenty grand bill. 'But that's not really the kind of wedding we had in mind. Neither of us wants the full

Godfather number complete with Sicilian folk-band. We'd like something a bit quieter.'

'Ah,' corrected Henrietta pompously, 'but that's the first lesson you have to learn. Weddings aren't for the bride and groom anyway. By the way, what's his mother like?'

Fran attempted to describe her mother-in-law to be, leaving out the bit about Laurence being adopted. You might as well be done with it and take out an ad in the *Citizen* as tell Henrietta anything secret.

'Come on, Franny, shape up. You can't have ten people and a dog to celebrate the most important moment of your life.'

'Actually,' Fran was beginning to see why so many couples disappeared off to the Seychelles to get spliced in secret. 'I thought I might not invite the dog.'

To Fran's enormous relief, the next couple of weeks were so busy she had no time to even think about veils or venues. The Regional Press Committee was holding a press conference to officially announce its shortlist, and she also had to decide on the winner of the *Citizen*'s Beautiful Baby Contest, an event which made the Balkan Wars seem like a little local difficulty. When she eventually had five minutes to call the birth control clinic, she felt a perfect fool to be told, at the age of thirty-four, that it was advisable to have a coil inserted when you had a period. Damn, now she'd have to work out when her next one was due and make an appointment then.

The press conference announcing the shortlist was to be held at the 500-year-old Cathedral Court, Woodbury's one four-star establishment, recently taken over by Heritage Hotels, who specialized in giving history an en suite bathroom. This they did so effectively that one bemused businessman desperate for a G&T got locked in the priesthole and had to drink his way through the minibar before anyone realized he was missing.

Fran jostled her way through the crowd of familiar faces. Drinks and canapés were offered, which meant that every self-disrespecting journalist in the county had turned out. Fran found herself wedged in a corner with probably the dullest newspaperman for fifty miles and had to distract herself by admiring the wonderful stone fan-tailing of the ceiling. Even still she thought she might fall asleep over her Perrier when she felt a tap on her shoulder.

She turned round with relief, hoping it might be Stevie come to rescue her and found herself looking directly into the angry face of Jack Allen. 'I hear congratulations are in order.' The bitterness in his tone shocked her. 'Was I the hen-night stripper then? Warn me next time so at least I can charge.'

'Jack . . . I . . . look, all this has taken me by surprise as much as you.'

'So when's the happy event?'

'Soon, I think. It's my father. He's ill, Jack. They think it might be Alzheimer's. You won't believe how he's changed.'

The granite of Jack's features softened briefly. 'I heard from Ben that he wasn't well. They've become quite friendly at the park.'

Fran smiled at the thought of Jack's son and her father becoming close but there was no answering warmth from Jack. 'Offer my congratulations to your husband to be. I think you'll find he remembers me.' He turned abruptly and pushed his way through the crowd, not even staying for the announcement.

'Well,' Fran tried to calm herself after the savageness of the encounter and was grateful to find Stevie at her side. 'What on earth's the matter with him?'

'For Christ's sake, Francesca.' Stevie sounded almost as angry as Jack had. 'At least don't let's play games. If you weren't in love with Jack you shouldn't have bloody well gone to bed with him, should you?'

All around her, shoulders straightened and throats were cleared as her fellow journalists stared ahead and did a hopeless job of pretending not to have heard a word.

When the announcement was over Fran and Stevie drove silently back to the paper. Usually the hum of activity and the high-pressure buzz of the newsroom would have given Fran comfort, but she needed five minutes to herself. Suddenly it all seemed too much. Her sudden engagement, her father's illness, Jack's fury and now, the last straw, an attack from the one person who had been more like a mother to her than her own.

Do something small and routine, she told herself, as she usually did when fear or depression lurked, the kind of simple task that will give you a sense of achievement when you've done it. Like making her doctor's appointment.

Feeling much more like herself she opened her diary and tried to work out when her next period was due, wishing she'd been efficient enough to mark it down somewhere. She remembered it all now. The last one had come unexpectedly and she'd had to rush out of a court case they were covering to get some tampons. She leafed through her diary again.

A cold chill of panic swept over her. The court case in question had been over six weeks ago. It wasn't possible. She must have got it wrong. But the memory was too clear and vivid to be mistaken. She was over two weeks late.

Calm down, she told herself, there's some mistake. You're on the pill, it'll be all right. The pill suited Fran because she was reliable by nature, not the type to throw caution to the wind and jump into strange beds. At least not till now. And she never forgot to take her pills. This had to be a false alarm.

She had almost convinced herself of this by the time she got out her make-up bag and removed the packet of contraceptive pills. The foil of the packet neatly followed its daily pattern, each little arrow leading to the next. And there, unnoticed until now, two pills remained in their foil-covered igloos, the two days of her flu, when she and Laurence were away. The chill returned, redoubling into panic, three days later she'd had her encounter with Jack and spewed up everything in her stomach.

It was indeed possible that she'd been unprotected all that time.

Fran passed the rest of that afternoon as if someone else inhabited her body. She made decisions, selected the finalists for the baby contest, agreed to a special supplement on neighbourhood policing but it was as though some other, far more efficient person – the kind of person who didn't fail to take her pills in the middle of the month and sleep with two men – were running the paper for her.

For two and a half hours she had been desperate to get to the chemist and buy a pregnancy test, but each time she was about to go something urgent had come up. And this was one task she could hardly delegate. 'Stevie, sweet, you wouldn't mind popping out and picking up a Predictor so I can tell whether I'm in the shit up to my ankles or my elbows, would you?'

In the end she ignored all demands for her attention and just left. The chemist shop two doors down was just closing up but Fran couldn't have gone in there anyway since they all knew her. She ran instead to the much larger serve-yourself chemist near the market, which always seemed to be staffed by bored school leavers who would sell you a kilo of weedkiller and a chainsaw without blinking an eyelid. The girl didn't even look up as she waved the bar code through her till. Even so, Fran felt obliged to explain it. 'Just need it for research purposes. I'm a journalist, you see.'

She did look up then and honoured Fran with an expression in which disbelief fought with disinterest and disinterest won. Fran held the bag to her chest and headed back for her car. In ten minutes she'd be home and in fifteen would know the truth. When her mobile bleeped from the depths of her bag she gasped so loud that a passing pedestrian asked if she was all right. It felt like God was on the line telling her to save her money, he'd give her the answer direct. No, she considered telling the unfortunate youth who'd enquired, I'm not bloody all right. I'm two weeks overdue, I forgot to take my pills and in all probability I'm pregnant.

'Fine, thanks,' were the words that actually came out of her mouth. The youth looked relieved. Fran answered the phone.

'Hello, darling, Laurence here. You haven't forgotten, have you?'

Forgotten? she wanted to shout. Forgotten what? To take my pills when you're terrified of having children? Yes. Silly me.

'We're due at my mother's. She's cooking us a celebration meal, remember?'

Fran toyed with the idea of cancelling but what was the point? It wouldn't solve anything. 'Sorry. Busy day.' You could say that again. 'What time is she expecting us?'

'In half an hour.'

Fortunately what Fran was wearing was smart enough to pass muster, and quite frankly she wouldn't have given a damn if it had been rubber hot pants or a ballerina's tutu. It would have to do. She picked up a bottle of wine from the off-licence and headed for Camilla's house.

Camilla, predictably enough, had pulled out all the stops. Expensive china, linen napkins, candles. The table looked as if it came straight from Harrods' wedding list. Maybe she was offering Fran a few tips on good taste as mothers-in-law feel it their right to do. Poor Camilla. Just when she wanted to dispense wit and wisdom on the importance of table plans, the only thing Fran wanted to do was get upstairs into the privacy of the bathroom and find out whether her world was about to fall in or the whole thing was a gigantic false alarm.

While Camilla put the finishing touches to the beef Wellington, Fran tore upstairs repeating the mantra so familiar to the female sex ever since Eve missed mankind's first ever period. *Dear God, please don't let me be pregnant.*

Chapter 11

The bathroom Camilla had directed Fran to was straight out of *House Beautiful*. A masterpiece of blue and white, the shining enamel of the bath and the pristine paintwork gleamed against the bluebell hues of hundreds of china pots lining the shelves. Any moment a door would open and a little Dutch girl would trip in wearing clogs and cap. To complete the picture a huge bunch of delphiniums – God, what would they have cost at this time of year? – stood on the cistern in a glorious antique jug. If you were going to get bad news you couldn't choose a more fragrant setting.

Fran unpacked her testing kit and laid it out on the vanity unit. A hysterical laugh escaped her. It was blue and white too. She read the instructions with shaking hands. Not once since she was a teenager had Fran needed to do a pregnancy test. Henrietta had always been the one with monthly dramas. When they were eighteen, Henrietta only had to look at a man to find herself three days overdue. Then there were the tears, the lighting of candles to the Virgin Mary in church, the vows never to even be *alone* with a man under forty, no, make that sixty, ever again. Then the blood arrived, red and glorious and forgiving. Or, if not, more candles, and a trip to the chemist. But Fran had been the careful one, the one who always remembered to take her pill, who even remembered *when* to take it, the same time each day, who infuriated Henrietta with her sense of responsibility and her brownie behaviour. But it was Fran who was sitting here in this blue and white boudoir waiting to see if the dipstick she'd just held in her urine would change colour and complicate her life beyond measure or provide the only bit of yellow in the bathroom.

God, who had clearly been on a Colour Me Beautiful course, went for the matching option.

The dipstick turned blue. Blue as in positive.

A cruel, clammy hand grabbed Fran's heart and squeezed. Not only was she pregnant, but what was terrible, far, far more terrible, was that she had no idea who the father was: Laurence or Jack?

Fran sat on the loo and sobbed. How could she, practical, sensible Fran, have let this happen? Worse still, how could she marry Laurence, with all his concerns over his own parentage, if she might possibly be carrying Jack's baby?

Downstairs, when she finally dabbed her blotchy face and dared to emerge, Laurence and Camilla were nursing a glass of very dry sherry, the kind that was so far removed from trifle sherry that it could strip paint.

Laurence leapt up, his eyes fixed on hers. 'Francesca! What's the matter? You look as if you've seen a ghost.'

He took her arm and gently led her to the sofa. It was one of those sofas so deep you disappear into it and can't get up without assistance or a pulley. 'Let me get you a glass of water.'

Fran wanted to blub. That white-coated bedside manner of his, two parts sympathy mixed with one part you-can-tell-me-I'm-a-doctor, was almost irresistible. To make it worse, by some primeval instinct he'd added a new semi-tone: patriarchal concern. He was suddenly treating her like a piece of that bloody china upstairs, precious and fragile. He could be right. She certainly felt as though, if dropped, she'd shatter into a hundred pieces and that how-ever hard anyone tried they'd never go back together again.

Fran would concentrate on one goal: to get through the evening and get home. Thankfully her pale colour had shaken them and the only reaction she got when she announced directly after dinner that she needed to get some rest, that she might be sickening for something, was polite concern and the insistence from Laurence, rather irritating since it would mean she'd have to pick up her car tomorrow, that there was no way she should drive tonight.

'Now hang on a minute,' Henrietta's tones had the firm but reassuring timbre of someone talking to a wayward child, 'it's incredibly unlikely that Jack Allen could be the father. I mean you only slept with the man once.'

'Twice,' corrected Fran, whose journalistic instincts demanded accuracy.

'You didn't tell me that. Anyway,' Henrietta continued, undaunted, 'if it was on the same occasion that doesn't count. It's about a million to one against.'

'Except that it was exactly when I must have conceived.' Fran took a gloomy gulp of the calm-you-down cup of strong tea Henrietta had handed her. They were sitting in Henrietta's bleached oak kitchen, which beamed order and domesticity even though Henrietta herself rarely did more than open the occasional jar of sun-dried tomatoes and mix them into pasta sauce already prepared by the daily. 'Do you think I should tell Laurence?'

'And what would you say, precisely? "Darling, I've got a little indiscretion to confess. I just happened to screw someone else the day we got engaged." Of course you shouldn't bloody well tell Laurence!'

'But I can't marry him if it isn't his baby . . .'

'Loads of women have babies they aren't quite sure are their husband's. They just ignore the passing resemblance to the milkman and get on with life. Anyway, am I hearing you right? Only a few months ago you would have stopped a tramp in the street and had his baby. We're talking about the man you love here.'

'But that's *why* I can't do it to him. All that was before I knew Laurence. The thing is, Henry, he's adopted and Camilla didn't break the news till he was twenty-one. He told me it had affected everything he ever did, so what would it do to him, not being sure whether a child were his or someone else's? It would matter desperately.'

'Don't tell him then. He'll come round to having kids. He just needs to get used to the idea. Men always do. It's the killer combination of vanity and inevitability. You present them with a choice: would they like to see their genes handed on to generation after generation or slooshed onto the scrapheap of humanity? You should have seen Simon's face when I told him I was pregnant with Lottie. He was absolutely livid!'

'But Simon adores Lottie.'

'*Now* he does. But at the time he went banging on about how we wouldn't be able to ride across America on a Harley Davidson. He's a middle-aged solicitor from Woodbury, for God's sake. He wouldn't know a Harley Davidson from a cheese roll. But once Lottie was there she waggled her little finger at him and he was her slave. Laurence'll be the same, you wait and see. Look at it this way, Franny,' Henrietta came and put an arm round her friend, asphyxiating her with Opium, 'You're going to have a baby. It's what you've been longing for. Can't you just be grateful for that?'

Fran's hand crept down to the flat of her stomach. Henrietta was right in a way. She had got what she'd longed for so desperately. But how could she accept it and enjoy it when it had happened in such impossible circumstances?

'Come on,' Henrietta could see from the pain in her friend's eyes that she wasn't convinced, 'you're a journalist. In these days of rent-a-womb and cloning it must be possible to find out who a baby's father is. If you're so worried why don't you look into it?'

Fran clutched at this like a raft in a stormy ocean. Could there be some test she could take to make sure that Laurence really was the father? If she could just get over that hurdle she had a feeling Henrietta was right, he probably would come round in the end. The trouble was, the one person who would instantly know if such a test existed was the one person she couldn't ask.

Laurence.

Jack Allen loved editing a newspaper. He loved the constant stimulation, the demands for endless decisions, the buzz of people all around him. He was a good manager because he knew how to make up his mind fast and because he didn't find ambition threatening in other people. He was happy to give them their chance to shine. In fact there was only one thing he enjoyed more than editing a paper. And that was editing two.

The roughs for the new paper were spread out in front of him and they looked pretty good. What really made him proud, though, was that he had found entirely new advertisers. With the exception of Newlands Estate Agents, whom Murray had signed up, the paper would be funded, just as he'd said it would, without forcing the *Citizen* into bankruptcy. Out of nowhere, depression swooped down on Jack, buzzing him like an angry wasp. What was the point? Why the hell should he try and protect his rival? All right, he owed it a certain amount of loyalty because he'd trained on the *Citizen*. It was a decent paper, and Ralph had been his mentor, the best journalist he'd ever met.

Admit it, you stupid sod, he murmured to himself. It's nothing to do with any of that. It's because of her. And where has it got you? She's chosen Laurence Westcott.

Resilient Jack, charming Jack, ducking and diving Jack,

suddenly felt like Jack the wimp. Then a flash of incandescent anger saved him. He wanted to kill Laurence Westcott. He wanted to ruin Laurence's career and sabotage his relationship with Francesca.

The thought that he could do it, that he had the power and the information was like a shot of a pure drug, heady and dangerous. But *should* he do it? Jack felt a powerful wish, just as he had done so often as a young reporter, to ask the advice from the one man in journalism whose opinion he respected, Ralph Tyler. The memory cut through him of what Fran had said the other day. Ralph was ill. Ralph probably had Alzheimer's.

A bitter sense of sadness and waste, of dreams destroyed, haunted him. Why did life have to be so bloody sad?

Out in the newsroom everyone was packing up to leave. Notebooks were tucked into jacket pockets, tatty carrier bags filled with press releases to read at home, mineral-water bottles stuffed into briefcases, phone numbers of hapless victims jotted down to try them later at home. Miriam, whose eyes had been fixed on Jack's closed door for the last anxious half-hour, wound up her courage and knocked.

'We're the last here,' she announced. 'Fancy a quick one? Drink I mean,' she added flirtatiously.

Standing in the doorway, with her extraordinary heart-shaped face, her huge eyes and her hopeful, youthful beauty, Miriam suddenly reminded Jack again of his ex-wife, Carrie, when they'd first fallen in love. He knew Miriam was attracted to him, and that her feelings were probably due to the most clichéd power-axis of them all:

professor and student, boss and secretary, father–daughter. He almost added doctor–patient but amended it to doctor–nurse. It was hero-worship, pure and simple, and he ought to know better than to go along with it. On the other hand – he buckled the soft leather briefcase that the staff had bought him for his birthday, complaining that his old one had made him look like a music teacher – just at this moment when jealousy and rejection threatened to pull him under, being admired and worshipped didn't seem such a crazy idea after all.

There was one obvious solution to her problems, of course, Fran told herself as she banged away on her ancient typewriter. As Henrietta had pointed out, she could opt for a termination. But what might seem the only way out at seventeen, when having a baby really could wreck your life, seemed entirely wrong at thirty-four when you had no such excuse. Especially if a baby happened to be the one thing you'd longed for and fantasized about till it was one step short of an obsession.

'Francesca Tyler, what has that poor machine ever done to you to deserve such a going over?' Stevie demanded, summoned into Fran's office by the deafening pounding of the keys and Fran's frequent four-letter words as she thumped them so hard a clutch of them stuck together in a steely embrace.

The truth was Fran felt utterly indecisive. She had no idea what to do next and her only solution was to pretend to do something – like writing this editorial on the pros and cons of sleeping policemen being laid across the High

Street, something that was hardly likely to set her fragile emotions alight – and to do it extremely noisily. Even here she was wrong. She'd already managed, without realizing it, to add an unusual degree of drama into this normally dull debate.

'There!' she pounded to a thundering full stop. The office seemed as quiet as Woodbury on a wet Wednesday when she'd finished.

'Let's see,' demanded Stevie, pulling it out of her type-writer.

'My God, Fran, we can't use this. "Should we risk our children's lives to madmen in motorized weapons or give them the protection they deserve by allowing a few bumps in the road to slow the bastards down? The *Citizen* says Hooray for Humps . . ." Fran are you on speed or something? We never write editorials like that.'

Stevie was right of course. With a shock Fran realized what was happening. Her hormones were taking over! Not only taking over, but writing her copy for her. Suddenly saving children's lives had zipped to the top of her agenda. If she wasn't careful she'd be recommending the castration of drunk drivers and putting paedophiles into a giant mincer. The thought of killing her own baby, she realized, was absolutely impossible. But what *should* she do?

The idea of the paternity test came back to her. If anyone could find out if such a test were possible, surely she could. As a reporter she was licensed to ask nosy and imper-tinent questions.

Like all journalists probably from the apostles onwards, she started by calling for the cuttings file. She read through the articles in the folder, noting down several names in the world of embryology. One of them, Professor Stephen Fay, occurred in almost every one. He was clearly the top man in the field. Feeling only a little guilty about telling a barefaced lie, she faxed him a letter announcing that she was writing a feature on fertility and asking if she could come and see him. He was obviously a very busy man. It would probably be weeks before she got a reply.

His return fax arrived next morning, offering her an appointment three days later.

Stevie knew something was up, Fran was sure of it. The busy editor of a busy paper didn't just up and take off for London just like that. Fran decided the best policy was to say absolutely nothing to Stevie, just go. Anyway Stevie liked being in charge and after all her years on the paper she could have run it for a year, not a day.

'Have fun,' admonished Stevie when Fran's taxi arrived to take her to the station. 'I know I will.'

'Just don't get power-mad and change everything just for the sake of it.'

Stevie got out her blue pencil ominously. 'Wouldn't dream of it.'

The Royal Hospital was in a tarted-up area of East London once populated by prostitutes and footpads and now by merchant bankers and stockbrokers. Some people thought the previous inhabitants preferable. Professor Fay turned out to have a thatch of unruly dark hair, a twinkle in his eye and the kind of accepting world-weary face that invited instant confidence. He also struck Fran as having an air of genuine goodness you encountered only very rarely in life. She would trust her womb to him any time.

It also occurred to her as she followed his reassuring white coat through his fiefdom – and it was precisely that with everyone bowing and scraping to him – that this man must know Laurence.

Professor Fay's office was tiny and very modern. There was a Formica shelf that served as a desk running along the far wall, two straight chairs and a priapic African god on whose erect anatomy Professor Fay hung his key ring.

'Were you expecting leather-bound tomes and chester-fields?' he asked, following her gaze. 'No need for that stuff now. It's all in the trusty laptop and you can't get leather-bound CD-ROMs thank God. Now what can I do for you?'

For a moment she yearned to tell him the truth. That she'd just got engaged to the man she loved and had found herself pregnant, possibly by someone she didn't. She was reasonably sure nothing would raise an eyebrow in that kind and lived-in face. Then the awful thought that one day she might meet him again, with Laurence, at some fertility dinner-dance jumped into her mind. She clamped down her confessional urges and got out her notebook.

At first she asked him the kind of journalistic questions he must have been expecting. How did he decide who should get fertility treatment? What if they were manifestly unsuitable? Did he ever feel that couples were trying too hard or had gone on too long? Or that the woman was too old? Had he ever told anyone to forget about children and get on with life without them? Were children a right that everyone was entitled to?

Fran could have listened to him for hours. His answers were so interesting that for a while she forgot why she'd come. It was only when he glanced at his watch and gently reminded her that he only had another ten minutes that her mind was wrenched back to its real purpose.

'Just one more thing . . .' She paused and caught his gaze, warm, dark eyes under his luxuriant thatch of hair, unshockable. All the same she almost lost her nerve and felt the temptation to run from the room with the question unasked.

'Fire away.'

Fran took her courage in her hands. 'In these days where everything seems to be testable, is it possible to tell the identity of a baby's father?'

Professor Fay seemed unfazed. 'Couldn't be simpler. As soon as the baby's born you just compare their DNA.'

'Actually,' Fran added softly, 'I actually meant *before* the baby's born.'

'Aha.' She felt his gaze on her again. 'Again dead simple. Via amniocentesis or chorionic villus biopsy. You'd measure the baby's cells against those of the prospective father. There is one problem though.'

Fran had somehow known there would be.

'You'd be hard pressed to find a lab to do it before the baby was born. They'd be nervous that the woman would have an abortion if she got the wrong answer.'

'I see.'

'You'd have to try the private sector. Plenty of labs in the

Yellow Pages, or *Pharmacy Today*. Now,' Professor Fay was on his feet, 'sad though it is, I have to go forth and inseminate, I'm afraid.'

'Thank you so much for your time. It's been riveting.'

'Send me a copy of the article. I'm very fond of Woodbury. Loveliest part of Britain. The light's unique.'

'Thank you.'

He held the door for her, his brown eyes smiling, almost as dark as a monkey's. 'Just as well they didn't have a test like that during the war or half the fathers at the front would have been in for a nasty shock. Oh, and by the way . . .'

'Yes?'

'Good luck with the dilemma. If I were you I'd go for a CVB. They do that between eleven to fourteen weeks so you don't have to wait so long before your mind's at rest.'

Fran was already outside the room before she realized he'd used the word 'you' and she flushed redder than the revolting hospital curtains.

At least Professor Stephen Fay was a man who seemed as though he could keep a secret.

There was a post office round the corner in the Mile End Road where Fran copied the list of lab numbers from the Yellow Pages. At least if they advertised there they had to be pretty commercial. The lab ads were an eye opener. 'Why worry and wait when you could come to us for an anonymous Aids test?' offered one. Fran suddenly felt her own dilemma wasn't so terrible in the great scheme of things. You'd need real courage to take an Aids test.

Afterwards she found a small park, got out her mobile

and worked her way through the list. Professor Fay was right. All the labs could do the test, but none was prepared to do it before the birth. Discouraged, Fran gazed out over the scrubby derelict spaces that surrounded the dazzling, spanking new office blocks. She only had two more to try. The news was bad again, but at least they gave her another number, a new clinic, the man said, with a reputation for innovation.

Fran closed her eyes as she dialled.

The technician she was put through to listened calmly to her request and told her that he couldn't see any problems.

If she'd been there in person, Fran would have kissed him.

'You would need to have an amnio or CVB privately then bring it to us.'

'Of course,' Fran agreed hastily, trying to contain her excitement in case she aroused his suspicion.

'Certainly. Then as soon as we get the putative father's blood sample we could go right ahead.'

Fran almost dropped the phone in her horror. A blood sample! That was one small point the professor had forgotten to mention.

She might as well give up the whole thing now.

Chapter 12

Fran had half an hour to kill before her train home. She watched the roller-bladers at Broadgate for a while, her gaze homing in on a mother and small child laughing and struggling to stand up, clinging on to each other, both as hopeless as each other. The extraordinary thought struck Fran that in three years' time that could be her. She was going to have a child of her own. No matter what the complexities and the mess, that one, wonderful, glorious truth shone through. She was going to be a mother.

She made her way back towards Liverpool Street Station, leaving herself enough time to buy some papers. Compared with Woodbury, the news stand in the station forecourt was like an exotic deli. The *International Herald Tribune* rubbed shoulders with *L'Express*, *Corriere della Sera* with *El Pais*, *Paris Match* with *Hello*. In London, even the local papers were almost as fat as the *New York Times*, bulging with free supplements. She gathered an armful and picked up the free-ads paper *Loot* as an afterthought.

Ensconced in the train she started to nod off, her thoughts drawn back to what the lab had just told her. The whole thing was mad. How could she possibly get a blood sample from Laurence or Jack? Invest in a syringe and murmur, 'Excuse me, darling, but I need to ask you a teeny favour.'

Perhaps she could tell Laurence it was for an Aids test? She'd read in America that couples checked each other out before marrying, and why not here? But somehow she couldn't see Laurence agreeing. He'd just tell her he wasn't in the habit of being promiscuous, so unless she was, they had nothing to fear.

It was hopeless. Unless . . . a thought occurred to her so simple that she couldn't believe it hadn't struck her before. She could just come straight out and ask Jack face to face. That way Laurence didn't have to know anything about it. Feeling comforted by this thought and lulled by the gentle rhythm of the rails, she fell asleep. She woke up just as they were just coming into Woodbury to find that she was sitting with her skirt riled right up with a mile or two of thigh showing and that the youth opposite was watching her while doing something unmentionable under the used-car supplement from one of her papers. Do you mind, she wanted to shout, have you no respect for a pregnant woman? Instead she gathered up the papers with great dignity.

'I wouldn't put your fish and chips in there if I were you,' she advised the youth frostily and stalked out of the train.

It was still only four o'clock and Fran decided to head

for the paper rather than home. She needed something to take her mind off the hideous mess she'd got herself into.

Stevie was hard at it, her sleeves rolled up and hair tied back with what appeared to be a pair of old tights, subbing a news piece on Woodbury's latest traffic crackdown. 'How was the mysterious away-day?' And then through some instinct borne of knowing Fran since she was a baby and caring for her deeply, she added, 'It was something serious, wasn't it?'

'You could say that.' She pulled Stevie into her office and shut the door. 'The thing is, I'm pregnant.'

'Oh, Franny, that's terrific! I suppose the timing could be better but you adore babies. Is Laurence pleased? I mean, he knows you're not the type to force him into a shotgun wedding.'

'Actually, I haven't told Laurence yet.'

'Why ever not? He's hardly going to warn you never to darken his door again, is he?'

The concern in Stevie's voice was too much for Fran. She had to confide in someone and there was the faintest hope that Stevie might understand. 'Because I don't know whether it's his or Jack's.'

Stevie's reaction was the last one Fran was expecting. She didn't look shocked or horrified or disapproving. She simply smiled. 'You poor girl. You have got yourself into a pickle, haven't you?'

'You could say that.'

'And now you don't know whether to go ahead with the wedding?'

'I can't if it's Jack's, can I? The thing is, there's a test I can have but I'd need a blood sample from Jack. It struck me that maybe I could ask him for one. What do you think?'

Stevie eyed her incredulously. 'I think your hormones, at least I *hope* it's only your hormones, have temporarily deranged you. How do you propose to ask him exactly? "Hello, Jack, I wondered if you could possibly help me out here and hand over a blood sample so I can see whether you're the father of my baby. If you are I'll have it aborted so I can live happily ever after with someone else." For heaven's sake, Fran, Jack Allen's in love with you. You owe him a damn sight more consideration than you're giving him.'

Fran collapsed miserably into her seat. 'I know. You're absolutely right. I can't possibly ask him.'

'You'll just have to ask your precious Laurence. And doesn't it tell you something about them that you can consider asking Jack but not the saintly Dr Westcott? I'd think about that if I were you.' Fran had rarely seen Stevie so angry, but then she'd always been soft on Jack. 'And if you want something else to worry about, try this for size. The *Express* is slashing its cover price as from next week. What have you got in mind to do about it?'

As soon as Stevie left, banging the door behind her so that every head in the newsroom shot up, Fran buried her head in her arms. Maybe she should just forget this business about Jack and accept that it was almost certainly Laurence's baby and simply tell him. He loved her, after all. Henrietta was probably right. He'd be shocked but he'd come round. Then she could start to enjoy the joy and pleasure of finally having the child she'd wanted for so long.

And if the *Express* slashed its price and gave them real problems she could always contemplate giving up journalism and helping Laurence with PR at the clinic after she was married.

Her words even shocked herself. Was this her father's daughter talking? The one who'd stood up to the bus firm boss who'd called her scum? Pregnant or not, she had to fight back.

But how? With their already narrow margins on the *Citizen* they couldn't afford to cut the cover price and soon they'd have the added competition of the free paper. There was a stark truth behind all this that scared her so much she hadn't really faced up to it. In the face of all this competition it was possible, likely even, that the *Citizen* might not survive, and it would be under her editorship. How could she face her father if she were responsible for killing off his precious creation?

Outside her office there was an empty silence. Everyone, even Stevie, had gone home. Listlessly, Fran picked up her bag and followed them. There was something symbolic about the quiet, shut-down feeling of the place. A picture ran through her mind of it even emptier, the paper dead and the staff redundant.

'Gosh,' a voice behind her made her jump, 'I didn't know anyone was still here.' It was Sean McGee, stripped down to lycra cycle shorts and work-out top, adjusting his helmet so that it sat comfortably between pony tail and his line of silver earrings. Next to him was a large backpack which he fastened onto his mountain bike.

'You look loaded,' Fran remarked. 'Off for the weekend?'

'Actually, I'm cycling to Cambridge.'

'But that's seventy miles!'

'Worth it though. The bike of my dreams is in *Exchange & Mart* this week. A guy in Cambridge wants to get rid of it. Fifty quid cheaper than I'd get it anywhere else.'

Fran was stunned. 'And you'd go all that way. Aren't there any bikes nearer Woodbury?'

'I did think of putting an ad in the paper, as a matter of fact, but I never got round to it. It'd be hell of a lot easier than schlepping off to Cambridge. Never mind. Time I was off. I won't be there till midnight. See you on Monday.'

Fran held the door open for him and was about to follow him when a thought occurred to her that froze her to the spot. Maybe there were more people like Sean in Woodbury who wanted to find something but wished it were nearer. In London, *Loot* offered pages and pages of no-longer-wanted goods and it had been a huge success. What about doing exactly the same thing on a small scale here? After all, it would be the localness that would be the attraction. No one apart from a bicycle nut like Sean would travel miles for a mountain bike, but they'd probably bother to cross town for it. Just like Londoners, people in Woodbury had baby clothes they no longer needed, computer games their kids had got bored with, cars they didn't want to sell through dealers. Why not?

Fran felt the small hairs on the back of her neck tickle in the way they did when she was onto a really good idea. All journalists knew that surge of heady excitement when the pieces of a story finally began to fall into place. It was what kept them at their desks slogging away, making just one more phone call, when anyone with a smidgen of sense would have given up and gone home hours ago.

The *Express* probably thought they'd already won the battle, but she'd give them a run for their money. Her mind buzzed with all the practicalities. They had spare capacity on their presses here. They had vans that could deliver the copies. But how much investment would it take to set up? They would need phone lines and telesales staff to take the ads. Her excitement plummeted suddenly, like a bird shot down in mid-flight. She would have to talk the family trust into borrowing money. It was a risk. And maybe not one the trust might want to take. Her father might go for it but her mother and the family lawyer were more cautious.

She had to go and see her parents now this minute while the thought was still white-hot. Her father would understand that the *Citizen* needed a new idea – that is if he was still capable of it.

Fran was so eager to get to her parents' house that the journey across town in the evening traffic seemed unbearably long. She must organize another campaign about the traffic. Woodbury's rush hour was getting as bad as London's.

She zoomed up the drive, scattering gravel in a wonderfully antisocial way that would have curtains twitching all the way down the road. The front door was open, amazingly, given that her mother was more security-conscious than a Saudi sheik. There was no sign of her parents. A slight chill of fear breathed on her as she went into the house.

The sitting room and her father's study were both

empty. She steeled herself to go into the kitchen. Her mother sat at the immaculate work-top, phone in hand.

'Francesca, thank God you're here. I've just been trying to get you at the paper.'

'Why?' Fran felt her palms suddenly sweat like cheese wrapped in plastic. 'What's happened?'

'It's your father,' thankfully her tone was irritated rather than scared to death, 'he's behaving even more peculiar lately. Getting dressed when he's just gone to bed, forgetting what he's just said. And wandering off. He keeps doing it. It's the second time this week. And on my bridge night too. It's too much!'

Fran ignored her mother's querulous, nagging tone and addressed the situation squarely. 'How long's he been gone?'

'It must be a couple of hours now.'

'Does he usually go anywhere in particular?'

'The park. He feeds the birds there. I have to make sure the bread's damp and save bacon rinds.' She made it sound as if this were a completely outrageous demand, like bringing ten extra people home for supper.

'OK, I'll go and look for him.'

The park was only a ten-minute walk away, tucked into the side of the watermeadows behind the cathedral. Walking through the gates was like finding yourself in a timewarp, as if you'd somehow travelled back to the nineteen fifties, when all was ordered and safe and children were seen and not heard and everyone knew their place. The whole park was green, neat and litter-free. The flower beds, in garish colours that would have appalled Vita Sackville-West, were weeded and cheerful. Next to the paddling pool little girls rushed around in their knickers, screaming with joy, trying to get in a last splash before the sun went down. Mums sat nearby on rugs, chatting. It was a picture of suburban peace and order.

But there was no sign of her father.

She asked the park-keeper who grouchily recognized the description and thought he'd seen him earlier talking to a loutish boy with a disgraceful mangy dog. He remembered because the dog was wearing a red bandanna of all things and he'd wondered who would dress their dog up so ridiculously.

Fran allowed herself a beat of fear. Could her father have been talking to one of the grungies who, even here in Woodbury, begged and hassled and sometimes threatened you into giving them money? Her father, it had to be said, would befriend Bluebeard if the man was down on his luck. But they'd hardly take him along with them to join their squat or their double decker travelling round the country.

She ran back via a different route but there was no sign of him. Maybe by now he'd got home under his own steam and the panic would be for nothing. A few doors down from her parents' house she spotted the dog in question. He was tripping along behind a youth on rollerblades and beside them was her father.

'Hey!' she shouted, worried that her father might be disorientated or scared.

They turned round and she saw that the boy was holding her father by the arm, leading him tenderly like a small child. And then, when she saw exactly who the youth was, she wanted to run for it herself. It wasn't a grungie. It was a lanky young man in a baggy T-shirt and clown-like tracksuit pants. And the last time they'd met she'd been stark naked, fresh from his father's bed. Jesus.

'I knew he lived in this road but I didn't know which number,' Ben explained, flushing and not meeting her eyes. 'He had a funny turn in the park and couldn't remember where he lived.'

'Francesca!' The confused look in her father's face cleared at seeing her. 'How nice to see you. Are you staying long?'

'I'll take him,' she informed Ben, her tone sounding brusquer than she'd intended in her eagerness to get away. 'He'll be fine now.'

Ben, clearly as enthusiastic to disappear as she was, grabbed the disreputable dog's lead and rollerbladed off. It was only when he was halfway down the street that she realized she hadn't thanked him.

'Where's Ben gone?' Ralph asked, suddenly distraught, 'Where's my friend Ben?'

'He'll be round again soon. Let's go in, shall we?'

'He's Jack's son, you know.'

This was one fact Fran didn't need to be reminded of.

'He's done a good job on Ben, has Jack. He's got manners.'

Fran had to admit that, given his father's propensity for bringing back strange women every five minutes, Ben did seem to have survived. Probably just good luck.

'Ralph!' her mother shrilled from the driveway. 'Where in heaven's name have you been? You know it's my bridge night. It's really too bad of you! Anyway,' she tore out of the house clutching coat and bag, 'I'm off now. There's plenty of food in the fridge.'

Fran couldn't believe her mother's attitude. 'For God's sake, Mum, he can't help it. There has to be something very wrong. He's obviously ill. He hasn't done it to inconvenience you, you know.' Fran felt a powerful wave of anger towards her mother. Phyllis always treated Ralph as though he'd subtly cheated her, now she seemed to feel she finally had the evidence.

'Well it *is* inconveniencing me. I'll be back at ten.'

Fran watched her mother's departing back with fury. 'Come on,' she led her father inside, 'let's have a fry-up.'

She took him into his study and put on a video of the ten best Cheltenham Gold Cups. Then she knelt down beside him and put her arms round him. 'I love you, Dad.' She didn't usually say things as direct as that. Their love expressed itself more in actions than in words, as if the words weren't really necessary in the face of everyday proof. But today it seemed called for.

He held onto her tightly in return, the bewildered look coming into his face again. 'You know, Francesca, I hate to say this, but I think there might be something going wrong with my brain.'

Fran buried her head in his shoulder for a moment, so that he wouldn't see her tears.

After they'd eaten he fell asleep in his chair leaving Fran watching his face anxiously. That subtle transformation of roles had taken place when the child becomes the parent and instead of looking for protection, must offer it instead, frightening though that can be. She longed to talk to someone who would understand how terrible her loss felt. And she knew the person she longed to talk to. Laurence. She tried his number but there was just a machine on so she left a message. He would have left the hospital by now. She'd just have to sit this out alone, but she had to admit the thing that scared her most: the future.

Half an hour later Ralph woke up. 'Franny,' his still-alert eyes lit up with pleasure as if he hadn't seen her only half an hour before, 'how lovely to see you. What brings you here?'

This time Fran just smiled and took his hand. She was getting used to the pattern. The sound of gravel outside made her glance at her watch. Too early for her mother, unless she'd quarrelled with her bridge partner, a fairly regular occurrence. The only way either of them stuck it out together was because no one else wanted to partner them. Rather like a lot of marriages.

The doorbell rang and she jumped up to answer it. Laurence stood, handsome and concerned, on the front step.

'Laurence, thank God!'

He held out his arms to her and this time she did cry and made no attempt to hide it. 'It's Dad. He's got worse again. It's as if each time he sees me, he's forgotten the last time completely.'

He put his arms round her and held her to him. 'I know. It's very distressing. More so for the relatives often, although I'm sure that's no consolation.'

'But he knows! He just told me he thought he had something wrong with his brain.'

'That's encouraging then. He can't be too bad.'

'I can't bear it, Laurence. He still looks so young and his mind's always been as sharp as a razor. Will he get worse?'

'It's hard to know how rapid the decline will be. I'll talk to my friend who specializes in geriatrics. I really think you should take your father to see him soon.'

Fran closed her eyes. It was childish, she knew, but having his arms round her and his cool and comforting mind to reassure her, she felt infinitely better. He really did love her. Why on earth did she feel the need to keep the baby a secret from him?

'Laurence, there's something I think I should tell you.'

'Is there?' He smiled at her seriousness.

She looked into his steady, affectionate gaze, full of concern and love for her. 'Yes. You see I've just discovered I'm –'

Behind them a terrific crash from the area of the kitchen made them jump apart and run to see what had happened.

Ralph stood in the middle of the room, the bewildered look back in his eyes, the toaster in pieces at his feet. He looked up from the mess to his daughter. 'I'm sorry, Franny darling, I was just trying to find Radio Four on it.'

'As soon as possible,' Laurence whispered softly. 'I think you should try and see my friend as soon as possible.'

Ben rollerbladed the mile and a half that separated his house from the Tylers at breakneck speed. Ralph and he had got to know each other well over the past weeks and the old man had filled a gap in Ben's life that hardly knowing his own grandparents had left. He'd assumed, until meeting Ralph, that old people were disapproving of the young, whom they saw as rude and aggressive potential vandals. Ralph had been quite different. Fun and quick, and interested in Ben's thoughts and views as if five minutes, rather than fifty years, divided them. And rather than upholding petty authority in the form of the park keeper, he had constantly challenged it in ways Ben recognized as quite subversive.

'Great, Rover, look!' He indicated the light on in an upstairs room. 'Dad's home!'

Boy and dog dashed in the front door, pausing only for Ben to discard his blades. A welcoming smell of Bolognese sauce and garlic bread, his favourite, greeted them. Keith Jarrett's jazz piano filled the room, the volume louder than Ben was allowed it, he noted wryly.

They took the stairs at a speed that wouldn't have shamed the Grand National. In his study, Jack was hunched over his computer looking at designs for the new paper. Ben grabbed the dog back, biting back his disappointment. His dad had brought work home.

Some teenage guardian angel tapped Jack on the shoulder and made him turn swiftly round. The look on his son's face, sad and resigned at the same moment, had him up from his screen in no time. Jack was only too aware that it could be tough having a single dad.

'Hi,' he grinned, 'rough day at school?'

'Fine. Then I bumped into Ralph in the park.'

'You and he are getting to be old buddies. That's great.' He saw the sparkle of tears in the corner of Ben's eye, quickly wiped away on his Umbro sweatshirt. 'What's the matter?'

'It was awful. He didn't know where he was. He was wandering about with no idea how to get home.'

'Thank God he found you. Did you take him?'

'His daughter arrived. The one who you –'

'Yes,' interrupted Jack. 'Francesca.'

'She took him back. Dad . . . ?'

'Yes.'

'It's so bloody sad . . .'

'And unfair. He's a wonderful man. When I was training on the *Citizen* he seemed like a hero. He always stood up for what he believed in. And he really believed in local papers. He never wanted to run off to Fleet Street.'

'Dad?' Jack knew from Ben's voice the next question mattered. 'Did *you* ever want to run off to Fleet Street?'

Jack wrestled with the truth. He didn't want Ben to think he was some kind of martyr. Besides, he wasn't. He'd had a damn good career here. 'No, Ben. There was too much I wanted here.'

He could see that Ben was reassured. His usual cocky smile was coming back. 'I'd like to be like Ralph. Make a difference.'

'You never say that about me,' Jack fished outrageously.

'Oh you, you're just a boring old hack. Why would I want to be like you?'

'Come on,' he ruffled his son's hair affectionately, 'let's have tea before the dog gets it.'

An ominous sound of doggy lips being licked in the kitchen made them tear downstairs, yelling.

Wild Rover barked gratefully.

'Bloody dog. He's eaten the garlic bread.'

'At least he's left the spag bol.'

'Only,' Jack glowered threateningly, 'because there wasn't any Parmesan to go with it.'

Although she felt a little guilty at the speed with which they seemed to be jumping the queue, Fran was also deeply grateful to Laurence for getting her father checked out at once. He was as good as his word and an appointment at Woodbury Hospital was offered to them for the following week.

'What the hell's the point,' Laurence had reassured her, smiling, 'of me working fifteen-hour days for a pittance if I can't pull the odd string for the people I love?'

In the midst of the bustling hospital corridor, with her parents sitting behind, Fran had felt unbearably touched.

He kissed her on the cheek. 'I'll call you later to hear what happened. And would you mind if I had a chat with the consultant myself? He might be more upfront with me.'

She glanced over at her father, but Ralph was determinedly reading the paper. Last night he'd tried to protest that they were just making a fuss.

'But, Pa,' she'd reasoned softly, 'you know there's a problem too. It would be silly to avoid it or you'll never get better.'

'But that's the point, Franny,' and she'd seen the fear in his eyes then. 'What if I'm not going to get better, only worse? This could be a life sentence and in some ways I'd rather not know.'

'Come on, Pa,' she'd taken his hand then, feeling a

breath of his own fear, 'this isn't like you. You always believe in facing things head on.'

'Yes, Franny. But that's always been things I can do something about.'

There hadn't been anything more she could say then, only hope they'd all got it wrong and the doctor would confirm it.

'Mr and Mrs Tyler?' a surprisingly young doctor came out to collect them. Perhaps he was the registrar or perhaps it was just that consultants, like policemen, were starting to look young to Fran. He led them into a small room, crowded with equipment and charts. It was a warm day anyway, but the room was stifling.

'Now, Mr Tyler,' the consultant said gently, 'I'd like you to tell me the problem as you see it.'

'The problem,' cut in Phyllis, 'is that half the time he can't remember what happened five minutes ago and he keeps getting dressed to go out in the middle of the night. Then there's the wandering off.'

'Thank you, Mrs Tyler,' the man's tone took on an unexpected sternness towards her mother which Fran instantly warmed to, 'but I did ask your husband.'

Phyllis fell into grudging silence.

'I don't seem to be able to make the connections,' Ralph began, hesitant for once. 'I go to the fridge for the milk and come back with yogurt. I say something and then, I suspect from the expression on people's faces, I say it again. I get disorientated . . .' His voice broke slightly and Fran longed to put her arms around him and take his pain and fear away. 'Sometimes I can't even remember where I live. I'm frightened, doctor, that I'm losing touch with the person I am.'

'And how long has this process been going on?'

'That's the extraordinary thing. Only a matter of months.'

The doctor stopped writing notes on the form in front of him and looked at Ralph. 'I'd like you to go up with the nurse and have a brain scan, if you would, Mr Tyler. Then we can see if there's any visible deterioration of the tissue. After that we can talk about possible causes.'

Fran caught her father's eye as he stood up. It was obvious the doctor wanted to talk to her and her mother alone and Ralph had guessed that. 'See you soon,' Ralph made a weak attempt at humour, 'and don't tell him about the gin and the girlie magazines.'

Fran did her best to laugh, but it stuck in her throat. She knew he was trying to be brave, to joke it off, and she saw how utterly terrifying all this must be for him, he who had always been so sharp and incisive and who had lived by the acute perceptions only he had been able to make.

'All right, doctor,' Phyllis began almost before her husband was out of the room. 'You can tell us the truth now.'

The consultant shrugged, not warming to her. 'I wish I could, Mrs Tyler. I wish it were as easy as that. First there are a number of tests we can run to eliminate physical causes. A minor stroke, depression even, can have similar manifestations. As can alcohol abuse, but I assume that isn't relevant here.'

Chance would be a fine thing with her around, thought

Fran bitterly. In some ways it was her mother who would be more prone to secret sherry drinking.

'And if none of those things are the cause?' Fran asked quietly.

'Then it could be Alzheimer's. But that isn't an easy diagnosis to make. One can only really be sure after a post mortem biopsy.'

'And is there any treatment?'

'If that's what it is, then I'm afraid not.'

'What's the prognosis?' Fran asked, dreading what his words would be.

'Hard to tell. He is young for the disease and his decline, over a matter of months from what you say, is unusually quick. Change tends to be cyclical. He'll improve and then decline.'

'He knows it's happening, that's the worst thing.' Fran had to hold onto herself. It was so bloody unfair. Her sharp, funny father. Why couldn't this have happened to someone else?

'Yes. Well if it is Alzheimer's he will gradually become less aware. In that sense it will be easier. For him at least.'

But not for them was the implication.

'Of course, if that is the eventual diagnosis, you may have to brace yourselves for odd and even antisocial behaviour. Anyway, let's not assume the worst yet.' The consultant's voice lost its warm, sympathetic note and took on the brisk impersonal edge which presumably came in part from self-preservation. He couldn't afford to carry the burden of other people's tragedies.

As they came back out into the waiting area Fran tried to

put her arms round her mother. It was she, after all, who would be most affected by all this.

For once, Phyllis allowed it. 'Oh, Fran, he doesn't deserve this.' For a brief moment mother and daughter were able to give each other what each most wanted – comfort. Then the old Phyllis reasserted herself. 'I'm not looking after him, you know. I couldn't stand the strain. I've seen people with it before. They don't even know who you are. You give them your whole life and you could be anyone. They don't know you from Adam.'

A shockwave hit Fran at her mother's words. 'What do you mean?'

'I mean if that's what it is, I'm going to look for a place for him. Somewhere where they know how to deal with these things.'

'For God's sake, Mum,' people around them stared as Fran grabbed her mother's arm, 'you can't put him in a home. He's fine most of the time. You owe him more than that.'

'And what about you?' demanded her mother. 'Don't you owe him something too as his only child? Why don't you give up your brilliant career and look after him if you're so conscious of duty?'

Fran was silent. It was fair comment.

'Anyway,' Phyllis's voice took on a tone that was part crowing, part shameful, 'you might find you have time on your hands. We've had an offer for the paper. From the Express Group. They want to amalgamate the *Express* and the *Citizen*.'

'Ma!' She gripped her mother's arm so tight it would

probably bruise. 'You can't be serious. They'd just close us down after five minutes. In a year our name would have gone from the masthead. Dad can't possibly be considering it.'

'Maybe not. But he's ill, Francesca, and I've got to pay for his care somehow. If not now, then in a few years' time. How do you propose I do that?'

Fran had no answer. Except the certainty that the paper had been her father's life's work and she couldn't let it go under, now of all times. She'd just have to think of ways of making it more profitable.

'Ma, I need to talk to you and Dad about the paper anyway. I've had an idea that might be able to rescue it. I've already discussed it with Stevie and she's right behind it.'

Her mother flinched slightly at the mention of Stevie. 'Then you'd better call a trust meeting.'

Fran could see her father, being led back towards them by a cheerful nurse. He didn't look too awful. 'By the way, how much are they offering?' She was shocked at the answer. 'But that's an insult!'

'Maybe. But it would cover residential care with enough over for a bungalow.'

Fran found she was shaking. She knew that tone. Her mother had made her mind up already.

Chapter 13

'How is he?' Stevie jumped on Fran the moment she arrived back at the paper.

'You know Dad,' Fran was so frightened of breaking down that she couldn't quite look the older woman in the eye. 'Trying to get on with life. Pretending to be more interested in the racing results than his diagnosis.'

'And what was the diagnosis?'

Fran turned away to gather her courage. 'Alzheimer's. At least probably Alzheimer's.'

'Alzheimer's?' Stevie's voice was almost a whisper. 'Oh my poor Ralph!'

For a moment they clung to each other for support, both drawing balm from the other's neediness.

'They're doing other tests too, but it looks bad. I must find some help for Ma. She's finding all this very difficult to cope with.'

'There's a surprise.' The depth of bitterness in Stevie's voice appalled Fran. 'Phyllis found chicken pox hard to cope with. Except when she had it herself. Then the world had to stop on its axis. She's a neurotic, Fran.'

'Yes, but a neurotic with a genuine worry this time.'

'I'm sorry, perhaps I sound like a heartless bitch, but my sympathies are a little more with Ralph. He's the one whose brain's deteriorating.'

The brutality of the words hung in the air.

'Stevie, she wants to put him a home.'

Tough, unsentimental Stevie, whose ancient cardigan had soaked up countless tears wept by other people but never her own, sat down roughly and began to sob.

The sight was shocking.

'She's never appreciated him, let alone loved him. His brilliant journalism, his campaigns for this town. She just thought his job was a minor inconvenience that might annoy the admissions secretary at the Golf Club.' Stevie's spare, lined face looked up at Fran in anguish. 'Oh God, I'm sorry, Fran. I know she's your mother. I shouldn't be saying this.'

For answer, Fran put her hand lightly on Stevie's, feeling the raised veins under the warm dryness of her skin. The disloyalty didn't have to be put into words. 'In her defence, I don't think she's been happy either. Her narrowness has imprisoned her as much as anyone. And she had a very unhappy childhood.'

'So did Hitler.'

'Their tragedy is that they were so *wrong* for each other. I hope to God they didn't stick it out for my sake.'

'And my little tragedy is that I went along with it. I should have fought for him. Fran, whatever the risk. We loved each other. All those years have been wasted. And now this . . . She can't put him in a home! You can't let her, Fran. Surely he needs to be somewhere he knows, with all the things that mean something to him around him.'

'I won't let her, no. Not if I can find a way to stop her. Maybe she's not serious. Oh, God, Stevie, I forgot. Another bombshell just when we need it. The *Express* is trying to buy us up.'

Stevie snapped out of her self-pity at the first whiff of danger. 'How can they? Jack's never even hinted about it.'

'Maybe he doesn't know. Murray Nelson's quite devious enough to do it behind his back.'

'He'd have warned us if he'd known. I know Jack.'

'Yes,' Fran had to concede, 'I think he probably would. Anyway she's agreed to a meeting of the trust so I'd better get working on the facts and figures for this new venture. What do you think we should call it? I thought about *Fair Exchange*.'

Stevie slammed her emotion away like the closing of an untidy drawer. Fran waited for her verdict. Stevie's instincts about titles were worth more than hundreds of pounds of market research.

'Not bad. It makes it clear what the product is. People like that.'

'*Fair Exchange* it is then. One good thing,' Francesca added.

'Fire away. We need all the good things we can muster.'

'Laurence was brilliant. Got us in to see the specialist in three days and he's ringing the consultant to find out what he really thinks.'

'I should think so.' Stevie wasn't about to hand any praise out without a fight. 'What's the point of having a fiancé in a white coat if he isn't prepared to elbow a few geriatrics out of the queue?'

'Stevie!' But she couldn't help the ghost of a smile at the image. The old acidic Stevie was coming back to life.

'Have you told him yet? Dr Kildare? That you're going to be a ravishing but pregnant bride?'

'I have had a few things on my mind.'

'Of course you have. Like the fact the baby may have brown hair, crinkly blue eyes and wear leather elbows on his jacket like Jack Allen instead of being an Aryan god with no sense of humour and a science degree.'

'Stevie!' Fran couldn't help giggling. 'Laurence has a perfectly good sense of humour. It just isn't yours.'

'Or anyone else's.' Stevie escaped into the hubbub of the newsroom before Fran had a chance to retaliate.

Fran took out the file she'd started on costs and practicalities for *Fair Exchange* and looked for her calculator. But other, more urgent questions buzzed into her head. Should she try and postpone the wedding? But if she did, her father might be too ill and she couldn't contemplate doing it without him there.

Suddenly she felt utterly, totally ravenous. And it was the kind of hunger that needed a bar of chocolate or a buttered scone to assuage. This, she realized with a shock, must be how it felt to be pregnant.

'Have you thought about a date for the wedding?' Camilla wrapped her long elegant legs underneath her on the chintzy sofa and, from somewhere in its capacious depths, produced a diary. 'I mean it's June already and I assume you don't want to go for a winter wedding? So gloomy somehow.'

Fran was shocked to realize that she'd never thought about the actual process of getting married. She tended to be the kind of guest at other people's weddings who, instead of sniffling at the back, wondered how long it would be before the happy couple got fed up with each other. Camilla was still rattling on. 'We'll need three months at the bare minimum to organize it, and of course August's out, so really September would be ideal. We might get one of those wonderful Indian summers. What do you think, Laurence?'

Hearing his name, Laurence looked up from the article on Gamete Intra-Fallopian Transfer. 'September sounds fine to me. What do you think. Francesca?'

Fran could feel Camilla's proprietorial instincts moving in on her wedding and resisted. 'I haven't really thought about it actually.' She knew that would annoy them both but said it anyway.

'Mother's right that we ought to, you know.'

'It all takes time, you know, Francesca,' endorsed Camilla. 'Wedding lists, bridesmaid dresses, sorting out the catering. What sort of invitation did you have in mind? Might I see it too?'

She's the type who checks her invitations to make sure the print's embossed! thought Fran with irritation. And she thinks I'm the type who might choose silver with little wedding bells in the corner.

Maybe she *should* let Henrietta have the wedding at her house after all. That would really infuriate her snobbish mother-in-law to be. It was almost worth it.

'By the way,' there was no stopping Camilla once she got her teeth in, 'Laurence says your poor father's rather ill. Do you think he's going to be well enough to give you away?'

Fran was so furiously, steamingly angry at Camilla's insensitivity that she jumped out of her chair. The blood rushed to her head at the sudden movement and without a second's warning she crashed to the floor in a faint.

The blackness was terrifying and total, as if she'd been given a general anaesthetic and had counted to three, then an abyss. She began to rise slowly to the surface, taking in the figures leaning over her, feeling her legs being propped up on cushions to get the blood flowing.

'Laurence, darling,' she heard Camilla whisper. 'That was very dramatic. There's not something you're not telling me?'

'That she's an epileptic or something? Of course not.'

'I meant that she was pregnant.'

'Mother,' the annoyance in Laurence's voice grated through into Fran's consciousness. 'I can categorically assure you that Francesca is not pregnant.'

Laurence brushed Fran's hair back from her face guiltily. He'd been sharp with his mother because he knew this was something he and Francesca should have discussed. She had started conversations plenty of times but Laurence had always managed to give evasive answers. Perhaps he ought to tell her the truth now, before they went any further, about him and babies. But if he did, he might lose her.

He would tell her, of course. After the wedding.

Even though she was busy at work and worried about her father, Fran soon learned that when weddings are on offer, everyone wants to get in on the act. Resistance, it seemed, was useless.

'Don't you think you'd look lovely in that one?' Henrietta had dragged her the following week to a wedding dress boutique near the market where they kitted out the 'bride with a mind of her own' from tiara to toe. Henrietta was pointing to a hoop-skirted, white silk number, ruched like Odeon curtains with an off-the-shoulder neckline that even Scarlett O'Hara would have declared indecent.

Fran shook her head.

'OK then, how about that one? Perhaps that's more your style.' She pointed to a slender and stylish Catherine Walker with not a single frill or furbelow. 'Cool and unattainable in ivory satin. Perfect.'

Fran giggled, though she had to admit she loved the dress. 'It's hard to be cool and unattainable when you're up the spout.'

Henrietta's voice sank to a whisper. As with certain upper-class voices, this made it twice as audible. 'Look, Fran, you're not really going ahead with this test thing to find out who the father is, are you?'

'Probably not. It's too complicated.'

'Thank God. It's best to leave some things to fate and not go round tinkering with nature.'

The trouble with me, thought Fran, is that I'm leaving everything to fate and fate is notoriously unreliable. I really should take control of my life and come to some decision.

To the horror of the sales assistant, Lottie skipped up clutching a vast chocolate doughnut. 'Can we go and look at bridesmaid's dresses now, Auntie Fran? Pleeeeze!'

'This should be a treat,' promised Henrietta. 'Sophie's hoping for a crop top in white suede and Lottie's more into Fragonard meets Pocahontas. Why don't you just have the wedding at Eurodisney? You could probably hire Mickey to carry you over the threshold.'

'Oh, yes, go on, Auntie Fran, do!' squealed Lottie.

Fran shuddered, her mind filled with an image of a giant plastic mouse carrying her into her bedroom, looking passionately into her eyes and saying, 'And now, little Minnie, the moment I have waited for for so long . . .'

'I think you're making a big mistake, Murray, in slashing the price.' Jack held up a copy of tomorrow's paper with the price cut splashed across the banner. 'Look what happened when the other papers did it. They ended up cutting their own throats. Circulation rose for a while, but it damaged the industry in the long term.'

'Jack, Jack,' the odious Nelson tutted, 'you amaze me. You still think competition's a good thing, don't you?'

'Of course I do. Without it you start getting complacent and complacency is death to good journalism. You have to want to get the story, to get it right, and to get it first. If there's only one paper around, why should you bother?'

Murray stood up, his expensive suit not quite hiding his

paunch, but still showed no sign of going. Why the hell not? Jack wished someone from the newsroom would come in for a decision or a question but they all knew who was in his office and gave it a wide berth.

'Well, Jack.' He obviously had something up his sleeve, Jack knew it. 'You'd better get used to keeping your standards up without competition.'

'Why is that, Murray?' Jack knew he was being pulled into some game but presumably sooner or later Murray would get bored and enlighten him as to what it was.

'Because before long it'll be the *Express & Citizen*. We've made an offer for the *Citizen*. Ralph Tyler's out of it, hadn't you heard? Lost his marbles, poor old boy, and his wife's really quite interested in selling.'

Jack was furious. 'You really are a shit, aren't you? Did you wait for the diagnosis or just slap in the offer anyway?'

Murray sighed. 'I'm just realistic. The daughter won't survive the price cut and our new paper. We're offering the family a reasonable way out. Quite altruistic really.'

'You wouldn't even be able to spell the word. And I wouldn't write the *Citizen* off just yet. Francesca Tyler has a lot of her father's flair and talent.'

'Then she'd better hurry up and show it.' Nelson had had his say. 'Especially to her mother. I gather she's the one who's keenest to get out.'

Jack hurled the price-slashed paper at the closing door. Did Fran know, he wondered, that it was her own mother she'd have to convince?

He thought of Ralph, the closest thing he'd ever had to a mentor, the father figure who had been generous and wise when his own father had been cold and absent, and he wanted to rage at the unfairness of it. It was worse than the simple dying of the light. In some ways a short sharp death would be better than the long and semi-conscious voyage into disintegration he knew Alzheimer's to be. It would be a double tragedy to someone of Ralph's intellect. He pictured Ralph's still youthful, animated features, the capacity he had retained for making new friends even at his age as he'd done with Ben, the clear-eyed enthusiasm that had been such a part of the man. For a moment Jack lost his own taste for the thing they had both loved best: the thrill of creating a newspaper.

He switched on his computer and tried to lose himself in re-jigging the splash headline, but it was no good. Outside in the newsroom it was unusually quiet. Most people were out on stories or had gone for a bite to eat in the canteen or the pub next door. Jack paced around for a while then gave in. It was obvious he wasn't going to get any work done.

His beloved blue Saab gleamed at him from its Editor space. Usually it was loved more than polished, but Ben, who was saving up for some Nike Air trainers, had taken to giving it a weekly shine with dazzling effects.

It was crazy, he knew. She might be in conference, she might be out, she certainly wouldn't be expecting him and probably wouldn't welcome him. She might well distrust his motives or at the very least think he was interfering. Which he was. He went anyway.

Fran was deep into her lists of costs and figures when reception told her who was downstairs. She shuffled them into a file and then into a drawer. Had Jack Allen heard about *Fair Exchange* already and come to snoop? That would be typical of him. He had antennae that stretched right across town.

'Jack, hello.' She always forgot what a solid presence he was after Laurence's tall slenderness. It was like putting a rugby player next to a marathon runner, not that she thought of them in the same way. Laurence was the man she was going to marry and Jack had been a passing mistake. She flushed suddenly at the memory of quite how much of a mistake.

'Are you all right? You don't look that well.' He realized how tactless that must sound. She'd hardly be tap-dancing. She'd just heard that her father was seriously ill. 'Look, Fran, I came to say how incredibly sorry I am to hear about Ralph. You must be feeling bloody angry with life for doing this to him.'

'Yes,' Fran agreed, realizing that what he said was true. She *was* bloody angry but somehow she had too many responsibilities to admit it. 'It's the unfairness of it. Him of all people. I suppose that sounds stupid. I mean it's just as much a tragedy whoever it happens to.'

'Of course it is. But it's even more of a tragedy when it happens to someone like Ralph because there aren't many people like him around.'

Fran smiled gratefully, feeling a little less despondent. Jack understood. It didn't change anything about her father's situation but acknowledging her right to be absolutely goddam furious about it somehow made it easier to face.

'Look, Francesca,' the use of her full name, as Laurence always used it, jarred, reminding her of who she was talking to. 'This offer the *Express* is putting in for the *Citizen* . . .'

'Is it serious?'

'I think so. But look, I gather it's your mother who's pretty keen to accept.'

Fran could see exactly why. She panicked, wondering if her mother had already talked the family lawyer round to her point of view.

'Yes, I'm sure she is. Thanks for warning me, though.'

Jack looked at his watch. He was already late for a meeting. 'I must go.'

'Of course.' Once again she was conscious of his physical presence, the way it dominated a room. She imagined he always got what he wanted from his reporters. He had the knack, she'd heard, of getting them to sit through parish council meeting after parish council meeting believing that, like Clark Kent, their moment would come.

After he'd left she wondered for the briefest of moments what a child of his would be like. And then she picked up the phone and made a call.

Norman Jones, the Tyler family lawyer, was not someone who shared the usual adulation for the founder of the *Woodbury Citizen*. Although he would never have breathed a word to anyone except his wife, he had always found Ralph Tyler a troublemaker. Ralph had, early in his career, led a crusade against the high cost of conveyancing and even encouraged the citizens of the town to do their own, thereby threatening local solicitors' most dependable source of income. This had been almost twenty years ago, but lawyers had a long memory. Norman Jones didn't exactly think that getting Alzheimer's was a just punishment for this, but it did occur to him that there were many aged and retired lawyers in the town, often to be seen on the golf course breathing in the good fresh air, and that none of them was similarly afflicted. He felt the slightest twinge of satisfaction at holier-than-thou Ralph Tyler, Archbishop Ralph, as Jones had secretly called him, becoming so terribly ill.

'Is everything ready for the Tyler meeting?' he asked his secretary the following week.

'Coffee and biscuits all laid out in the meeting room. I've given you an hour and a half. Will that be long enough?'

'Certainly should be.' Norman Jones consulted the silver watch on its chain, a fitting adornment, he always thought, for the chalk stripe suit he inevitably wore to the office and which he was convinced looked hand-sewn, even though it was off the peg from Hector Powe. 'Anyone here yet?'

'Just Mrs Tyler.'

'We'll go through and have coffee then.'

'How many more expected?' Janice had opened a whole packet of Marks & Spencer's chocolate assortment and it sounded as though there might be a few over to liven up her low-cal lunch. Janice weighed in at fourteen stone but to the mystery of all was rarely seen eating anything fattening. It was just a thyroid condition. And a serious chocolate dependency.

By the time Fran arrived, absolutely on time, her mother and the lawyer were already deep in low-voiced discussion. They jumped apart like guilty lovers when she came into the room.

'Right.' Mr Jones was all brisk efficiency. 'As you know, the Express Newspaper Group has made the trust an offer, quite a tempting offer as a matter of fact, given that the *Citizen* isn't exactly the *Daily Mail*.' He laughed a snide coughing laugh which Fran thought for one blissful moment might lead him to turn bright red and lose his puffed-up dignity. Unfortunately he recovered himself. 'Your mother is, as is perfectly understandable, very worried about your father's future. She would like the security of some funds to care for him, should he need it.'

'Yes. In a residential home. But I passionately disagree with that option. And I know the last thing my father would want would be to sell the paper he founded to do so.' She fixed her gaze on her mother. 'Where is he, by the way? Did you forget to tell him about the meeting? He has a vote too.'

'Really, Francesca,' her mother fussed with the buttons on her suit rather than meet her daughter's eye. 'He's far too ill to make decisions like this. How do you expect someone who can't tell a wireless from a toaster to come to a meeting?'

'He's perfectly rational most of the time. The *Citizen* is his creation.' Fran was going to say the love of his life, but that would only incense her mother further. 'You have to consult him.'

'I think on an important issue like this, that's for me to decide.'

The door opened behind them. 'What's for you to decide, Phyllis? What's so important that you didn't feel the need to tell me about it?'

Phyllis gasped. Her husband, wearing a smart grey suit with a neat, perfectly knotted navy tie, followed Janice into the room.

'I'm sorry, Mr Jones, but he insisted. When I said he couldn't, he demanded to see the senior partner. Well, that's you, so I couldn't really stop him.' Janice smirked with just a hint of disrespect.

Ralph sat down at the head of the table, in the chair Norman Jones had temporarily left vacant. Fran's smiling eyes met her father's keen blue ones and her heart turned over. Today there was no sign of decline and disintegration. The father she loved was back as if he had never glimpsed into the abyss.

Ralph crossed his legs, revealing the only sign of disarray. One sock was a conventional muted wool; the other a raucous turquoise with the words Happy Birthday emblazoned on it. Fran's last gift to him only six months ago. She raised her eyebrow in its direction and Ralph, re-crossed his legs, masking the one with the other.

'Now, Franny, what's this I hear about a new venture of yours that might mean we can fight the *Express* instead of selling out to it?'

Fran reached for her briefcase and spread out the figures and graphs for *Fair Exchange* that had taken her every spare moment to prepare. Then she poured all her skill and enthusiasm into talking the group round.

'You see, Ma, it's not just a lost leader. The key to *Fair*

Exchange is being really local, but it doesn't have to be just Woodbury. We could open another in Westwold or Sawbridge. Once we have the system running, there are five or six towns big enough to support their own versions. In a year or two's time *Fair Exchange* could be worth far more than the *Express* are offering us. Just trust me. Give me a year. You will, won't you, Dad?'

Phyllis watched the easy affection pass between father and daughter as she had so many times before and felt the vicious mosquito bite of jealousy.

'What do you think, Mr Jones?'

Norman Jones saw the quicksands ahead. He had been deceived. He had assumed Ralph Tyler to be already a nodding, doddering wreck like those poor souls he saw when he visited his own mother.

'Phyllis, my dear.' Her father was sitting with his back ramrod straight now. Everyone knew what he was about to say mattered. He reminded Fran faintly of one of those statues of Rameses II about to issue a proclamation, but had any Pharaohs smiled? 'I know what's in store for me. I know I will get worse. Much worse, probably. But I don't want to sell the paper. If you must have me locked away, do it cheaply. Fran may have children of her own to pass it on to.'

Fran jumped. Had he guessed about her pregnancy? Was there something different about her skin, her appearance, did their deep affection mean he could sense the change in her? 'Please, Phyllis, I haven't asked much of you. Let Franny try her idea. If that fails, by which time I will be in the land of gaga, then sell by all means. That's your right.'

Phyllis glanced at Norman Jones but he was deliberately looking away. She was isolated.

'All right, then. A year to show the idea can work.'

'Done,' said Francesca. If she couldn't show some profits by then she'd have to question the whole venture anyway.

It struck Fran, gathering up her stuff, that her mother seemed reduced now that her brief taste of power was over. If only she'd had some achievements of her own, perhaps she wouldn't be so grudging about other people's. She was like a squirrel in brushed red wool, hoarding away other people's triumphs like acorns, refusing to let any go.

'Can I give you both a lift back?' Fran offered.

'I'd like to walk in the park for a while. Ben has invited me to tea at the Pavilion. Would you like to come, Phyllis?'

It was a great relief to Ralph when she said no.

Stevie was lurking in reception when Fran got back to the office, waiting to hear the outcome. 'So, how did it go?'

'We're not selling.'

'Grand news. But I thought your mother was set on it.'

'She was. So set that she forgot to tell Dad about the meeting. Absent-minded of her. So I had to remind him myself. He was brilliant, Stevie, just as wonderful as ever.'

Stevie's eyes leapt with sudden pleasure. 'Maybe the diagnosis was wrong. Maybe he just had a minor stroke. All this Alzheimer's stuff could be a ghastly mistake.'

Fran, hoping to God that Stevie was right, followed her up to the paper. It did feel wonderful and miraculous and for the first time in weeks she felt hope reach out a tentative finger towards her. There was one thing she owed her parents and that was to make a roaring success of *Fair Exchange*. Then there would never be any question of having to sell off the paper that had been her father's pride and passion.

During the frenetic weeks that followed, Fran had never been more grateful for Stevie's presence. Not only was Stevie able to take over the day to day running of the *Citizen*, but during the long nights when Fran had to work Stevie would plonk her reassuring bulk onto Fran's desk, admire the beginning of a ladder in her thick tights, offer coffee and wisdom and prove, as she always did, the perfect sounding board for new ideas.

'There are two options for a venture like *Fair Exchange*,' Fran mused, by now too exhausted to make up her mind unaided. 'One: the readers can pay for the paper and the ads are free. Or Two: the paper's free but people have to pay for the ads.'

'Easy,' Stevie stood up for a moment, shook out her skirt where it was particularly baggy over her generous rear, 'make the paper free. Everyone loves a bargain round here. Once enough people see their friends reading it, they won't mind paying for the ads.'

'But if it's free, how will we get newsagents to stock it? There'll be no margin in it for them.'

'Then you have to persuade them that *Fair Exchange* will be such a hot ticket that people will flock into their tatty old newsagent shop for their free copy and leave loaded with fags, *Fiesta*s and Cadbury's Flakes which they wouldn't otherwise have had the opportunity to purchase.'

'Stevie, you're a marvel!' Fran grinned. The argument actually sounded quite convincing. She took another swig of Stevie's almost undrinkable strong black coffee and moved on to address the question of where and how people could place their ads. The one advantage of their expensive and overcrowded offices sandwiched between Boots the Chemist and the cathedral was that it would be convenient for people to drop in with their orders. Even so, in this day of technology they would need a telesales department. And where the hell were they going to put it?

'Why not in here? Plenty of room,' Stevie suggested wickedly, gesturing with her mug at Ralph's specially designed editor's office. It had been Ralph's one act of bravado. Painted dark green and lined with bookshelves and awards, it was big enough to house a whole department. In an age of open plan and little boxes, Fran had often been faintly embarrassed to claim such a huge space for herself.

'Stevie! That's it! We could fit six phones along that wall and put a counter here for people to come in and work out what they wanted to say. You're wonderful!'

She hugged a startled Stevie, whose chin was wobbling in amazement like a turkey who's just heard of Christmas. 'You mean you'd really give up this fabulous office. Where would you sit?'

'Out with the troops. It's trendy management practice anyway. Some tycoons don't even allow themselves a desk, let alone an office. Fluid structures are all the thing. It keeps you in touch with what's going on on the ground.'

Stevie, who secretly aspired to the editor's chair herself, and would make sure it was vast, leather-bound and barricaded behind closed doors, suspected she might be becoming a bit of a dinosaur. In a more technological office than the *Citizen*'s she would be way out of her depth. Perhaps retirement and gardening beckoned after all. The trouble was she loathed gardening and the thought of a quiet life gave her the willies.

Fran's head was buzzing with possibilities but it was already long after midnight and her body was beginning to protest. 'Come on, I'll give you a lift home.'

She picked up her huge bag, stuffed with costings, print runs and staffing estimates, and switched off the light. The emptiness of the place was disconcerting. Papers are places that should be bursting with life, and the empty newspaper office was even quieter than a home full of sleeping children. The contrast made the silence seem deeper.

'One thing. Do you think you could find out the actual launch date for the *Express*'s freebie?'

'Certainly could.' Stevie looked round the office lovingly. It was more home to her than home. 'I already know. August the fifteenth.'

God it was soon. Could Fran get *Fair Exchange* together in that time and steal their thunder? She'd damn well try.

'Right. Then we'll aim for August the seventh.'

'Is that long enough?'

Fran grinned. 'It had bloody better be or we'll all be out of a job. Unless, that is,' she opened the car door for Stevie to climb in, 'you fancy being Cookery Editor on the *Express & Citizen*.'

'Now that you mention it, I do make a mean Victoria Sandwich. People cross three counties to avoid it.'

When she finally settled down in her pretty pine bed that night Fran tried to empty her mind and relax. August 7. It was a pretty significant date. Not only would she be launching a new paper. She would be about fourteen weeks' pregnant. The optimum time, according to Professor Fay, to have the test that would tell her whether Laurence or Jack was the father of her baby. If only she could find a way to do it.

'So, your new paper would be rather like a giant car boot sale?' Henrietta was struggling to understand the concept between sips of white wine – her second this evening, which was naughty. Her first had been while Lottie was in the bath, but she did so love bath time. 'So you could advertise all your own rubbish and swap it for someone else's?'

'Cool,' endorsed Sophie, immediately grasping the principle and approving of it. She adored thrift shops, jumble sales, and anything second-hand, and drove her mother mad by ignoring all the smart new dresses Henrietta bought her in favour of enormous tweed overcoats, miniskirts in horrible man-made fibre, and cheap and nasty blouses which came from cheap and nasty shops. To Sophie the name Laura Ashley was profane.

'Anyway,' Henrietta leaned forward conspiratorially, changing the subject. Anything to do with work, Simon's or anyone else's bored her rigid. 'How's the divine doctor?'

Fran leaned back in her wooden steamer chair and closed her eyes. It was early evening and they were sitting in Henrietta's garden, which looked as if it had been ordered as a job lot from the Chelsea Flower Show. 'He's fine. Except that I've been so busy I haven't actually seen him for a couple of days.'

'I must say.' She looked round to make sure Sophie wasn't in earshot, but she had agreed to play fairies with Lottie at the bottom of the garden. Lottie had, as usual, stripped off her pyjamas and put on her net Tinkerbell costume. 'Pregnancy suits you. I was sick as a dog and looked like shit from day one.'

'That's probably because I keep forgetting all about it. I've got so much on my mind at the moment.'

'Forgetting all about it?' Henrietta echoed scandalized. She had treated pregnancy rather as if she had just been told she had only nine months to live. She cosseted herself, went to bed at every possible opportunity, and worked her way through the entire Marks & Spencer's pudding range from Luxury Bread and Butter to Milk Chocolate Profiteroles. It had been bliss. Apart from the bolshy old practice nurse who had told her she had to get out of bed or she'd get a thrombosis in her legs. Whatever happened to a good, old-fashioned *accouchement*? Henrietta had wanted to know. But the bad-tempered old bat had said even *accouchements* only lasted two weeks and took place *after* the birth.

'And how're the wedding plans coming along? Do you still naively believe weddings are for the bride and groom?'

Fran laughed, shocked that she really hadn't thought

about it at all. 'I'm just leaving it to the mothers. Cut out the middle men, so to speak.'

'Francesca Tyler, you are the strangest girl –'

'And the most beautiful,' cut in Simon, who had just arrived home from work. 'You really do look absolutely gorgeous.' His voice leered so much that Henrietta gave him a quelling look. 'If this is what working does for a girl than you ought to try it sometime, Henrietta. Anyone for a top-up?'

Henrietta rose above this and held out her glass.

Simon, who had a good idea about how much she'd already had, pursed his lips and ignored it.

'What's for supper?' He pulled up a steamer chair, a little too close to Fran's.

'Cold poached salmon with mayonnaise.'

'As in cold poached salmon bought whole and ready dressed by the deli at vast expense, involving no culinary effort from you?' Simon asked scathingly. He sometimes wondered what his wife did all day.

'Will you stay for supper?' Henrietta asked, ignoring him. 'There's masses of cold poached salmon paid for by Simon.'

Fran wished she could. She'd hardly eaten all day and was starving. 'I can't. I said I'd drop in at Ma and Pa's.'

'How is your father?' Henrietta looked right through her husband, who was already beginning to repent, and would do so until he cravenly apologized.

'Actually,' Fran brightened, 'he seems amazingly much better. Stevie and I were wondering whether he might have been mis-diagnosed.'

'Oh, Franny, how wonderful.' Henrietta beamed. 'You mean it might just have been a false alarm?'

'That's what we're hoping. There are other things, minor strokes, that can have similar effects. I'll need to find Ma someone to help out anyway, though. I don't suppose you know of anyone?'

'As a matter of fact, I might. One of our neighbours has just popped her clogs and she had the most brilliant house-keeper. I'll get you her number.'

Henrietta went into the house, still ignoring Simon, who was beginning to melt a bit and remind himself of the very comfortable life his wife created around him. He had to admit he quite liked being the breadwinner and the centre of this female universe. Now and then, when he was working too hard or things were stressful, he tended to feel simply like a redundant drone. What was it someone had said? Men are simply sperm banks with a cheque book. That was him all right.

Henrietta, who could gauge her husband's moods to the millisecond, reckoned he was due to come out of this one and raised an interrogatory eyebrow at him as she showed Fran out.

'Bye, Fran darling,' she cooed, looking over her shoulder at her sheepish husband.

'Sorry, love,' Fran heard him say, very softly, as she got in the car.

'Right.' Henrietta's upper-class tones rang through the evening air. 'Say it properly. Down on one knee.'

Simon winced. 'Do I have to?'

'Yup,' commanded Henrietta mercilessly. 'Or no din-dins for you tonight.'

As Fran drove off it was to the incongruous sight of

Simon kneeling down on one knee as Sophie and Lottie whooped with delight, shouting, 'Who's a naughty boy then?'

After this ritual, she suspected, they'd go upstairs and have some excellent sex. Marriage, after all, did have its good points.

Her mother was in the garden deadheading roses, wearing a flowery apron and bright yellow rubber gloves. No doubt she would have bought flowery gloves if they made them. The sight of yellow rubber against the fragrant, delicate blooms was disconcerting.

'Where's Pa? In his study?' Fran asked.

Phyllis carried on snipping. 'He went for a walk hours ago. You know him, always wandering off.'

'You don't think he's got lost again?'

'I doubt it. He's seemed so much better anyway. He's probably with that boy he's so pally with, the one with the dog.'

'Jack's son, you mean?' The panic that had threatened to jump out at her subsided. Fran remembered how fond he was of Ben. They'd probably gone off somewhere together.

When Ralph wasn't back in another half-hour, even Phyllis was getting fidgety. Fran decided to check whether Ben was back.

There was an answering machine on and she was about to replace the receiver when Ben's voice cut in apologizing for the machine being on by accident.

'Ben, it's Francesca Tyler here, Ralph Tyler's daughter.' She tried not to let any of the embarrassment she was feeling seep into her voice at the memory of how they'd first met. 'Listen, have you seen my father today?'

Ben had wanted to talk about something entirely different, how much his own father liked her and what a mistake she was making in marrying someone else, but he hadn't got the nerve. 'I saw him earlier. After school. He was at the park. We were teaching Rover to get sticks out of the pond.'

Fran thought for a second. She didn't want to embarrass her father or make Ben think he was odd. 'Ben, I know this is a funny question, but did he seem OK to you? Not confused or anything?'

'He seemed absolutely fine. I told him I wanted to be a reporter and he was telling me all these funny stories about what it was like when he started. Isn't he home yet? Do you want me and Rover to come and help look for him? We know the park really well, where he likes to sit and that.'

'Would you?' Ben was being brilliant – sympathetic and genuinely concerned. How could Fran have ever thought he'd make crass remarks or tell his friends about his father's one-night stand? 'I'd be ever so grateful. See you there.'

In the end Phyllis insisted on coming too, still wearing her flowery apron.

Ben was nowhere to be seen, but Fran could make out a gaggle of people over by the duck pond and, oh my God, a police car was parked just inside the entrance. A sick and shaky feeling churned her up at the thought of what might have happened.

She half ran across the playground area and along the path by the water, her mother puffing to keep up with her a few yards behind.

The scene close up bore out her very worst suspicions. A young-ish and pretty-ish woman was talking to a police officer, her voice shrill and her finger pointing towards the panda car. In which, facing straight ahead, as if in some dream or nightmare, sat her father.

Chapter 14

Fran covered the remaining distance in seconds. 'What's the matter?' she demanded. 'What's happened? Why is my father in that police car?'

The young woman stopped her complaint and turned in Fran's direction. She wore a blue denim jacket over a tight bustier top and pink frilly ra-ra skirt revealing chunky thighs that brought to Fran's mind the three little pigs. Where her body suggested generosity her face was pinched and mean.

'Because he's a dirty old man, that's why.'

Fran disliked her on sight. 'Officer, what exactly has been going on?'

The policeman, young and raw and hideously embarrassed, hummed and hawed. Behind Fran, Phyllis puffed up.

'This young lady says that the old gentleman indecently exposed himself to her.'

'He was in the bushes over there,' insisted the busty girl.

She pointed at a clump of trees going down to the duck pond.

'Oh my God, Ralph,' squeaked Phyllis. 'How *could* he? He's been ill you know –'

'Look, Ma,' cut in Fran, 'we don't yet know what actually happened. Could I speak to him, please, officer? Just for a moment.'

Fran climbed into the back of the car. Her father's face was confused and very, very frightened. 'What's going on, Franny? Why is there all this fuss? I was caught short, you see, so I went into those bushes.'

Fran held his hand, her heart breaking. 'Why didn't you go to the gents, Dad? There's one just over there. You must have been there loads of times.'

The confusion settled on his face again. It was like talking to a frightened child who knows he's done something of which the adult world disapproves, but has no idea what. 'Is there? I just didn't remember. I'm sorry, Franny, really I am.'

A chill invaded the warm car as she remembered the doctor's words. *You may have to brace yourselves for odd and even antisocial behaviour.* But was this antisocial behaviour or a simple misunderstanding? Whatever the explanation Fran knew it would change everything. They could no longer fool themselves that a minor stroke would have so radically affected her father. The original diagnosis must have been correct.

Outside the car she saw Ben arrive. Jack was with him and he seemed to take in the situation instantly. Through the open car door she could hear the friendly but firm and

no-nonsense tone Jack always used with troublesome officials. Next he was talking intensely to the piggy girl in a low
but serious voice. The girl was nodding and Fran kicked
herself that they were just too far away for her to hear.

The blushing officer approached the car. 'The young
lady has decided not to press charges,' he told them with
obvious relief. His recent graduation from police college
clearly hadn't prepared him for dealing with well-known
Woodbury citizens accused of flashing at under-dressed
young women.

Fran's pulse, which had been shooting through the ceiling, levelled a little. 'Thank God. Can I take him home?
I'm sure this was all a silly misunderstanding.'

Her mother stood outside the police car, looking white
and stiff. She seemed too upset even to speak.

'Come on, Mum,' Fran had no time for histrionics now,
'help me take him home.'

They half lifted Ralph out of the police car and together
they walked as fast as they could to the exit where their own
car was parked. 'Thanks, for your help, officer,' Fran said
gratefully as the young bobby opened the gates for them.

'Don't thank me,' he said cheerfully. 'I couldn't calm her
down at all. It was the other gentleman, the one with the son,
who did it. He was terrific with her. You should thank him.'

Fran looked behind her but there was no sign of either
Jack or the dreadful girl. She'd have to thank him later.

Fran drove them home quickly, with her father strapped
in the front, looking straight ahead, and her mother point-
edly holding onto the arm rest looking like the heroine of
a Greek tragedy.

'I think I'd like to go to bed,' Ralph announced as soon as they got there.

Phyllis said nothing.

'Good idea, Dad,' Fran agreed. 'It's been a horrible shock. I'll bring you a cup of tea in a moment.'

Her mother, she sensed, was waiting for his departure.

'Look, Mum, Henrietta knows this wonderful woman who's been looking after an old lady, and thinks she might be free. I'll ring her tomorrow, shall I, and perhaps she could come and help you out.'

Phyllis brushed away an imaginary mote of dust. 'Call her if you want to, it won't make any difference. There's nothing you can say or do, Francesca. I just can't stand this. The worry. Risking our standing in the town.' Fran wondered which weighed more heavily and suspected the latter. 'I simply can't cope. He's going to have to go into a home. Somewhere they know how to deal with it.'

Guilt and pity threatened to smother her. Not her beloved father! There *had* to be an alternative. She thought of Laurence. He would understand. He would back up her plans for some other kind of care.

She caught him just as he was leaving the hospital and he promised to come straight round. As soon as she heard the doorbell she flung herself into his arms, and the tears, held back by sheer power of necessity, poured down her face.

Laurence stroked her hair and told her that everything would be all right, they would find the best solution. He listened quietly as first Fran and then her mother gave their versions of what had happened in the park. Fran was still convinced the girl had simply misunderstood a confused action, but she could see that her mother didn't care whether her husband's behaviour had been deliberate or not.

When she'd finished speaking, Laurence took Francesca's hand. His handsome face was caring and serious. She thought again of what a good man he was, how much of his life he'd devoted to helping people. 'Look, Francesca darling,' the 'darling' tacked onto the already formal Francesca made her spirits droop, 'this is serious. People with Alzheimer's do all sorts of things like this. They get dressed in the middle of the night. They disappear. They take their clothes off inappropriately. This could just be the beginning. I know you love your father, but I think he needs professional care. Anything else would be unfair to him.'

'But what about his home, the things that matter to him that he's collected over a lifetime? His family? Surely he needs to have those around him?'

'Francesca, listen to me. Your father is deteriorating fast. I know this is hard to face, but soon he won't recognize his surroundings, maybe not even you. That's the tragedy of his condition. I'm afraid I agree with your mother on this.'

Fran felt herself tumbled in the waves of Laurence's goodness and sincerity. If he really believed that, how could she disagree?

'Look, why don't I get some brochures of the very best residential places? Then you and I – and your mother of course – could go and look round them together.'

'What about Dad? Won't he get a say in his own future?'

Laurence's face softened into a smile of absolute concern.

'I'm not sure that would be a good thing. You're the parent now. That's the way you have to look at it. He'll know you've chosen the best for him.'

'Oh, Laurence . . .'

Laurence held her against his long, lean body. He was, she noticed for the first time, still wearing his hospital coat. He must have rushed straight here.

'I know how hard this is for you, but you have to see it from his point of view. People with Alzheimer's find structure and routine comforting. He may actually prefer it.'

It was such an alien thought that Fran couldn't find grounds to argue. Was she the one who was being selfish when she thought she was being the opposite?

'Excuse me,' she saw Laurence and her mother exchange a glance that could have been exasperation, 'but I promised Dad a cup of tea.' She walked slowly and sadly to the kitchen. Before long her father, to whom choice and individualism had been the guiding principles of his life, would be allowed such luxuries only when other people decided to allow them to him.

She hoped he couldn't taste the salt of her tears in his cup of Darjeeling.

Back in the sitting room, Laurence was waiting to say goodbye, his face creased with concern.

'Francesca darling, I think there's something else you may have to face. If you want your father to give you away I'm not sure we should wait until September. I think we should consider getting married as soon as possible.'

No one had ever seen anything like the whirl of activity at

the *Citizen*'s offices in the weeks that followed. Carpenters banged away to transform Fran's office into the Telesales department for *Fair Exchange*, their ghetto blasters blaring, ignoring all the poor reporters struggling to type their copy.

'I can't even hear myself bloody well think!' Sean McGee protested to a pony-tailed, earringed chippie, who reminded everyone of Sean himself, only with pecs.

'Sorry, mate.' The builder leaned down, exposing two inches of buttock in what the office girls referred to as bottom cleavage. 'But then you're a journalist, aintcha, so you don't need to think. You all just make it up anyway.'

The desk downstairs in reception was also being extended the length of the room so that the readers could come in and place their ads here too, which had put Elaine the receptionist's nose out of joint. From now on painting her fingernails and blow-job by blow-job analysis of her boyfriend's sexual prowess would be rendered off-limits by the presence of streams of Woodbury citizens asking her how many words they got for their tenner.

Fran had hired a dozen new staff, had flyers announcing the arrival of the paper delivered to every house in the town, and ordered newsprint for forty thousand copies. The number terrified her, but she knew that without it they had no chance of making an impact. Somehow they had to shift every copy so that the people who hadn't managed to get one felt they'd missed out. Then they would rush into the newsagent to demand the next issue. *Fair Exchange* had to become the hub of communication in the town, the modern parish pump, announcing every jumble sale, PTA meeting, car boot sale and carol concert, as well as providing Happy Birthday announcements, flogging second-hand saddles and Barbie-and-Ken collections abandoned in favour of Spice Girls sticker books.

'You don't think,' said Mike Wooley, jealous of all the attention suddenly going to this irritating new arrival, 'that this freebie of yours is cutting our own throats?'

'Aha!' Fran tapped her nose. 'What I'm trying to do is create a whole new market. Provide people with something they didn't know they wanted till I gave it to them. So they should still want both.'

'Good luck to you,' Mike muttered sceptically and went back to his exposé of council overspending. 'By the way,' he tossed over a copy of the *Express*, 'did you see this? Quite a good idea, I thought.'

Still grinning to herself, Fran picked up the rival paper. She almost gasped out loud. Her breath speeded up and her palms felt cold and clammy. How could he? How could Jack have betrayed her like this?

Across the whole of the front page was a photograph of the piggy girl from the park, her mountainous boobs and tree-like thighs discreetly hidden under a flowery dress, demanding that our parks were made safer places for lone women and mums from the risk of marauding males bent on one thing.

Fran scrabbled through it, heart racing, waiting for the mention of her father, but thank God there was nothing specific, only a passing reference to 'alcoholics and other unsavoury types who might be lurking in the bushes'.

All the time, when she'd thought Jack Allen had come to their rescue, he'd been talking that tarty girl into writing for his paper. How could he live with himself? To Jack Allen, getting the story really was all that counted. No wonder his wife had flown four thousand miles to get away from him.

She flung the paper back at the unfortunate Mike Wooley, her green eyes flashing. 'Cheap journalism,' she snapped. 'The *Citizen* would never stoop to anything so tacky.'

Mike watched her in frank amazement. Getting an ordinary young woman to suggest how she'd improve the amenities of Woodbury was exactly the kind of story Fran usually wanted. Women editors. Changing their bloody minds every five minutes. He thought enviously of his colleagues the other side of town and wondered what Jack Allen was like to work for. He'd heard good things on the grapevine. Next month there would be the announcement of the Regional Press Awards and the story Mike had worked so hard on, exposing the bus firm, was up to win. If it did he was going to find out if the rival paper had any jobs going.

The brochures for the residential homes, when they arrived, depressed Fran beyond belief. They were so glossy and posed, just like an ad for some weekend-break hotel promising smorgasbord and a swimming pool when you knew the reality was cheese sandwiches and a grimy bathtub. Both Laurence and her mother, though, were insistent that she visited them.

In the end they narrowed it down to two. 'Tawny Beeches', which offered the last word in geriatric luxury, and a more modest establishment called 'The Willows'.

Why, Fran wondered, did old people's homes have such gruesomely rural names?

Tawny Beeches wasn't far from the centre of town, not, she supposed, that the residents would ever be allowed out to go to the library or Boots. She and Laurence decided to walk there.

Not far down the High Street, she saw to her horror that Jack Allen was just coming out of the sandwich shop. He noticed her at the same time, took in who was with her, and started to walk determinedly towards them. Short of turning and running there was absolutely damn-all she could do but steel herself to meet him.

Laurence, holding her arm and still extolling the advantages of geriatric care, was too engrossed to notice her agitation.

'Hello, Fran.'

Laurence's head whipped round with a suddenness that startled her. Jack ignored him.

'Look, Jack, after that article you printed I don't think there's anything I've got to say to you.' She had to struggle with herself not to go for his face with her fingernails. 'It was the lowest of the low.'

'As a matter of fact,' Jack's face hardened, 'it was the only way I could talk her out of not pressing charges. It stuck in my throat to hand over half a page of my precious paper, but it seemed to me the alternative was worse. I apologize for my appalling journalistic standards. In a way you're right – it was the lowest of the low. But not in the way you think.'

Fran was feeling the smallest tinge of guilt. Beside her, Laurence appeared to have been struck dumb.

'Anyway,' Jack continued, 'I'm sorry. I thought I had your best interests at heart. By the way,' he indicated Laurence, 'aren't you going to introduce me to your, er . . .'

'Of course,' Fran relented a little. 'Jack Allen, editor of the *Woodbury Express*, this is Dr Laurence Westcott.'

To Fran's astonishment, Jack made no attempt to speak or to take Laurence's hand. She looked from one to the other, conscious of an almost physical tension between the two men, as if, under different circumstances, they might have hit each other instead of offering a greeting.

In the end it was Laurence who cracked first. 'I know Mr Allen, Francesca. Although I haven't seen him for a number of years.'

'Of course,' Fran remembered, 'you did that terrific piece on Laurence's unit, I'd forgotten.'

'Look, Francesca,' Laurence insisted, his tone suddenly urgent, 'we really are going to be late for our appointment at Tawny Beeches.'

'Tawny Beeches?' Jack cut in. 'That posh Colditz up on the hill? Why are you looking round there?' And then the truth dawned. 'Fran, not Ralph? You wouldn't do that to him?'

Before she could answer Laurence hustled her off down the street with Jack's accusing eyes boring into her back.

It wasn't until they were outside the pretentiously porti-coed front door of Tawny Beeches that Fran realized their appointment wasn't for another half-hour. Why on earth had Laurence been so keen to get away from Jack?

Tawny Beeches, so the brochure claimed, liked to see itself as the five-star end of the nursing home market. The entrance had swagged curtains over each long window and an enormous flower arrangement, which must have cost the families of the residents a fortune. Unfortunately the major flowers in it were lilies with their sickly-sweet association of death and decay.

'Miss Tyler!' An auburn-haired woman with a lot of gold jewellery descended on Fran with as much warmth and enthusiasm as if Fran were a health and safety inspector. 'And Dr Westcott. How nice of you to come. You're a little early but it doesn't matter at all. Out to catch us out in our natural state, eh? You'd be surprised how many people try that one. But we have no secrets here.' She laughed a tinkling little laugh that must have been attractive when she was thirty years younger. 'Would you like to see round our lovely establishment now?'

Once they were out of the reception area Fran couldn't help sniffing the air. Lilies might have been bad enough but through here there was a disgusting pot pourri of disinfectant, urine and air freshener.

'Now,' the auburn woman said briskly, 'Dr Westcott tells me your father is dementing. We have lots of others here, so he'll be in good company.'

At that moment a pair of old men shuffled in holding hands like overgrown schoolboys.

'Not through here now,' corrected the warden. 'Back into the lounge please.' The front one stopped and stared at her, rocking backwards and forwards on his feet. Standing next to the swagged curtains and the richly upholstered chairs he looked like an ancient alien who had suddenly found himself transported to the Ritz.

Fran knew for certain that her father would hate it here among all this hideous pretension. Even if he did stop noticing where he was, it still mattered that he was at least placed somewhere Fran could be sure they'd treat him with respect.

'Thank you very much for your time,' she gabbled at the warden, and grabbed Laurence's arm.

'But don't you want to see the croquet pitch and the swimming pool complex?'

'No thank you. I'm afraid I've got a very important meeting.'

'Right,' she said to Laurence as soon as they were outside. 'Where's the next one?'

'And what was the matter with that place? It has a terrific reputation. The trouble is, darling,' she knew he was trying to be patient and it suddenly annoyed the hell out of her, 'not everywhere, especially of that calibre, takes people with dementia.'

'There's nothing wrong with the place – except that it probably makes all the poor old incumbents wear black tie for their Bengers Food – it's just that I know my father and he'd hate it.'

'Francesca,' he stopped her and touched her face gently, 'you must stop seeing your father in one of these places as he is now. He'll change. I'm sorry, but there's no point avoiding the truth.'

Fran rushed on down the leafy drive, not wanting to listen. Surely if they simply accepted a prognosis like that, it was doubly bound to happen.

The next place, The Willows, wasn't so bad. It was

smaller with far fewer pretensions to grandeur. The public rooms were more cheerful and every resident had their own bed-sitting room. These, she was glad to see, weren't box-like conversions but higgledy-piggledy shapes that followed the design of the Victorian house. At least here the personalities of the occupants seemed as distinct and individual as their bedrooms.

She was just beginning to be able to picture her father as one of these engagingly dotty residents when the matron took them into the lounge. In the middle of one wall a large television was fixed with the volume on maximum. About twenty old people sat in rows, their heads lolling, their mouths agape, either fast asleep or watching *Home and Away*.

'It's not the best time to see round just after lunch,' the matron pointed out defensively, sensing Fran's horror, 'but they do like a bit of telly.'

Fran felt her throat close over at the thought of her beloved father as another lolling figure in that row of discarded old people.

'Are they allowed a TV in their rooms?' Racing on television might be the one thing that kept Ralph sane. *Home and Away* certainly wouldn't.

The matron shook her head. 'We discourage them from going to their rooms too much in the day. A bit of social life is what we believe in.'

Fran looked at the parody of social life in front of her and wanted to weep.

'So what do you think?' Laurence asked her as they drove back.

'Better than the other place. But still bloody awful. No matter what you say about not knowing where he is, he needs some sense of place, of his own history, or he certainly will go into terminal decline like all those other sad blobs.'

Laurence sighed. 'Right. In that case we'd better try and talk your mother into keeping him at home.'

Even though they were back in the middle of Woodbury High Street, Fran leaned over and kissed him, causing a young woman shopper, hopefully not one of his patients, to smile indulgently at them.

She knew Laurence was acting for the best and had taken valuable time off work to help her, even pulling strings to find Ralph a place, and all she seemed was ungrateful. A sudden wave of tenderness washed through her and she longed to simply tell him about the baby. It might not be the ideal moment, but perhaps there wasn't one.

'Laurence,' she began hesitantly, 'there's something I've been wanting to raise.'

But Laurence, who was unusually silent and unresponsive, even to her kiss, now that she thought of it, turned to her abruptly.

'Look, Francesca, how well do you know Jack Allen?'

'Why do you want to know that?' She hoped her tone didn't sound too guilty.

'I just don't like him, that's all.'

Fran had never heard that tone from Laurence before. It chilled her. What was it between Laurence and Jack that made them behave like this?

Whatever it was, her pregnancy could only make it worse.

God, what a mess she'd got them all into.

The next few weeks were just how Fran liked them best: so busy she didn't have a minute even to sit down and drink a cup of coffee, let alone ask herself why she was so happy to leave the plans for her own wedding to other people. She rationalized that if she allowed Camilla and Phyllis to make the decisions then they would at least be happy, and there would be the added bonus that they couldn't say they'd been left out. Fran simply had to order her dress and those of the bridesmaids.

The demands of setting up *Fair Exchange* with the added burden of at least overseeing the *Citizen* left her giddy and exhausted. Her pregnancy she didn't let herself even think about. It was, she kept reminding herself, a natural condition and not one that meant you had to take to your bed. Henrietta thought she was completely, utterly, barking mad.

'You're going to have to tell him.' Henrietta kept nagging her at every opportunity, with the slight variant of, 'Fran, *when* are you going to tell him?'

Fran didn't let herself wonder if all this frenetic activity was something she embraced so readily because it took her mind off that tricky question.

And then, out of the blue, she woke up one morning and knew Henrietta was right. What was it that was stopping her? She had hesitated long enough. She must tell him. She would do it tonight.

She hummed as she lay in the bath, stroking the slight mound that was just beginning to be noticeable. Now that she had decided to tell him, she felt the moral glow that confirmed she'd made the right decision, just like the feeling of self-satisfaction when you finally decided to go on a diet. What Fran forgot was that often that moral glow made you feel so much better about yourself that actually following it through no longer seemed necessary.

The weather was so glorious that she walked to work, savouring the friendly greetings from local shopkeepers and the lollipop lady outside the primary school. It was wonderful to live in a place where people knew you, not in some vast anonymous city.

The cathedral spire shone golden and tall against a bright blue sky. Already at nine in the morning it was being photographed by hordes of tourists. Later on, when it got really hot, they would crowd into it, drawn not by God but by the desire to get out of the sun. Fran ducked in too, something she hadn't done for years, and knelt for a moment in its dark spaces. She loved the atmosphere in here. Not so much because of the religion but because of the sense of continuity. People in this town had worshipped in these pews and aisles for seven hundred years, bringing their hopes and fears here and laying them down at this altar.

Fran realized she was no different. Let my father be all right, or at least let us do the best thing for him, she whispered into the warm darkness. And let me do the best thing for this baby. She just wished she could be absolutely sure what that was.

Almost to her relief, a party of noisy tourists invaded the place, breaking off her conversation with – who? God? The spirits of the people who'd worshipped here? Herself?

She felt almost furtive coming out. As if someone might come up and challenge her, the unbeliever – what were *you* doing in there? You haven't paid your dues.

Before anyone she knew could see her, Fran scurried over the road to the paper, eager to deal with the far easier questions of print runs and advertising rates. But her peace didn't last long.

'*There* you are,' Stevie accused. 'Working a half-day, are we? Before you get stuck in maybe you'd better look at this. The *Woodbury Free News*. If this hasn't got Jack Allen stamped all over it, I don't know what has.' She waved the paper tantalizingly at Fran.

'But it isn't due out for another two weeks!' squawked Fran, grabbing it.

'Maybe they heard about our little venture and decided to steal a march.'

Fran spread the paper out carefully on her desk, eager to take in every detail. It was an impressive job. Colour photographs on the front page, a bold readable typeface. It trod the tricky line of being cheerful without looking cheap. *Fair Exchange* would measure up beside it, because it too was new and bold, but put the *Citizen* alongside and her own paper would look like a rather maidenly aunt.

Fran read the index and saw that Jack had missed few tricks. There was a pull-out TV guide which could rival that of the nationals and yet he had played the local card brilliantly too. Panicking, she wondered if he might have wildly expanded the small ads section, thereby scooping the whole idea of *Fair Exchange*, but thank God he hadn't.

But the best idea of all was on the front page. The *Free News* fought off all charges of being cheap and nasty by launching its very own crusade. The stocks of blood at Woodbury Hospital, the paper revealed, were running dangerously low and across the whole of the front page, in an enormous splash headline, the paper exhorted its citizens to GIVE BLOOD!!

Special stations, the paper informed its readers, had been set up all over town where there would be tea, biscuits, balloons and a band playing. The whole thing was to be kicked off at midday by Nico Morgan, the area's one famous pop star, now a middle-aged sixties' rocker, who had recently remarried his first wife, had another baby even though his oldest son was thirty, and come back home to settle in Woodbury to lead a clean and blameless life, or so he claimed.

'You've got to hand it to him, Fran, Stevie conceded. Who'd have thought of asking Nico Morgan to start a blood donor campaign. This'll be all over the tabloids, you wait and see. Come on, girl, we can't miss this. It's the most exciting thing to happen in Woodbury since the Viking raids.'

The rest of the office had already deserted their posts, apart from Sean McGee, who was virtuously making the most of the rare silence to type his copy, and Elaine on reception who was sulkily looking out of the window, like the one child who has to miss the party.

There was a marquee all round the Market Cross in the

cathedral square, which Fran hadn't seen since she'd used the side entrance. On a platform at the far end was an unlikely figure wearing a country tweed jacket with blue jeans and cowboy boots, his hair tied back with a red elastic band. Stevie and Fran squeezed to the front. Nico Morgan was in the middle of extolling the virtues of Woodbury, its citizens, its wonderful fresh air and glorious countryside, and announced that he couldn't understand why when he was growing up here he'd thought it was a dull, hick dump with fuck all to do in the evenings.

The citizens laughed nervously, especially when a nurse arrived with an enormous needle and led him, mock scared, to a tent with a red cross on it. Orderly queues formed all round the square to follow suit. Jack saw them at once and came over.

'Here to spy on the opposition, eh? What do you think of the paper? Would your father have approved?' He saw her eyes cloud with unhappiness and wished he hadn't been so tactless. 'How is he?'

'Not too well. But the answer's yes. Not quite his style but I think he would have approved.'

Then she remembered how Jack had given space to that awful girl, and the smile froze on her face. Jack's charm and concern were only skin-deep.

'So,' he went on, noticing the chilly change in her manner but deciding to ignore it, 'what do you think of our rock star? Actually I wouldn't touch his blood if it were the last haemoglobin on the planet. God knows what it's got in it. In fact, it'd be a public service if I nicked it before it goes anywhere near the hospital. Oh, and I suppose I'd better offer up a few drops myself.' He waved them goodbye and disappeared into the tent with the red cross.

'Have we got any chance against all this?' Stevie murmured. For once she'd lost her bounce and looked her fifty-eight years.

'Stevie!' Fran needed her support too much to let her collapse now. 'Of course we do. Our idea's different. Come on, let's go and do something public-spirited. I'm always meaning to give blood. And we get free tea and biscuits afterwards.'

'You must be joking. I'm far too squeamish. Besides they don't want old soaks like me. There's too much blood in my alcohol stream. You go ahead.'

The queues had shortened by now, people were drifting off to shop and to work. She spied Mike Wooley, always first with nerve and front, cheekily interviewing the aged rock star right in front of Jack. Now it was her turn for the tent.

Giving blood was something Fran always enjoyed. If only helping the community was always so effortless. As long as you kept your eyes firmly away from the blood collecting in its neat sterile pack, then things were fine.

But Fran had more in common with Lot's wife than she thought, and despite all the promptings of good sense she couldn't help stealing a glance at her jewel-like offering.

The combination of the sight of her own blood and the fact that she hadn't had breakfast that morning were suddenly too much for her and the world span suddenly out of control.

When she came round the nurse was standing over her. 'Are you all right?'

'I think so. I know this sounds ludicrous but I'd forgotten I was pregnant.'

The nurse looked at her as though she were mad. 'But you should have filled in a form when you came in. How many months?'

'About eleven weeks.'

The nurse rolled her eyes. 'I'd better get the doctor to look at you. You shouldn't even be giving blood in your condition.'

'Sorry.' Fran felt like a toddler scolded for knocking over the bricks. While she was waiting she took one tentative step on the floor, but she was still shaky and had to squat down on her knees to keep her balance.

Staring her in the face, almost exactly at eye-level, was a row of the blood donations collected that morning. She was about to take a deep breath and stand up when one of them, labelled Allen, J., scorched itself onto her hazy consciousness like a brand on her skin.

She remembered Jack's joking words about stealing the pop star's blood and looked again.

God didn't give you many chances, and Fran had asked Him to help only this morning. To pass up an opportunity like this would look like ingratitude.

Chapter 15

Fran hesitated only for a moment. Then, looking guiltily over her shoulder, she slipped the blood into her vast shoulder bag and buckled it up just as the nurse came back into the room with doctor in tow.

'All right?' asked the doctor anxiously.

'Fine,' Fran replied cheerily, clutching her bag to her chest. 'In fact, never better.' She consulted her watch and remembered that today of all days she had an arrangement with Henrietta and her bridesmaids at the bridal shop in Market Street. 'Must dash,' she apologized to the startled doctor and nurse. 'I've got an appointment to try on wedding dresses.'

Henrietta, with Sophie and Lottie in tow, had clearly been in the bridal shop for some time. It was one of those tiny upmarket ones where everything was in tasteful cream and they gave you coffee in tiny china cups, probably deliberately tiny, Fran decided, watching Lottie rampage through the shop, to stop small children spilling bigger ones on the vastly expensive wedding dresses.

Fran tried on the newly altered Catherine Walker dress she'd chosen last time. Despite her tummy, she'd actually lost weight in the last few weeks.

The assistant fussed around her, straightening its simple satin folds, and fastening a veil with a single silk flower in Fran's red-gold hair.

'Will you be wearing it up or down on the day?'

'Up,' said Fran.

'Down,' said Henrietta. 'You already look like a Carmelite nun. Can't you at least have your hair loose for a bit of glamour?'

Fran decided to ignore this. Henrietta's idea of what to wear for a little light shopping in Woodbury was a shocking pink Jasper Conran suit with gold buttons, tights that looked like five denier max and gold slingbacks. 'Better to look like a Carmelite nun than Ivana Trump,' she insisted.

'That's a matter of opinion. Anyway,' Henrietta leaned forward confidentially so that neither Sophie nor Lottie could hear, 'I'm so relieved you've given up that silly idea of finding out who's the father of the baby.'

'Oww!' said Fran, as the assistant, apparently engrossed in adjusting the dress at the back, accidentally stuck a pin in her.

Back in the office Fran discovered a disconsolate knot of people with their feet on their desks, looking as if they'd just been handed redundancy notices.

'Come on, come on,' Fran pushed their feet off and sat there herself, 'what's all this?'

'We're depressed,' Keith explained. 'First the cover price, now this new paper and all we're coming back at them with is some rag where you can swap your marbles for someone else's old *Beano*s. Sorry, Fran, but it makes you wonder if it's worth going on.'

Fran recognized the need for a Boadicea speech when it bit her on the ankle. She should have seen this coming instead of swanning off buying wedding dresses.

'Of course it's worth going on! One: the *Citizen* is still the best paper in this town and for your information' – she pulled the circulation figures she'd specially requested that morning out of her bag, realizing with horror that the blood was still in there – 'our sales have *not* fallen since the *Express*'s price slash.' The assembled group looked a little more cheerful but not enough to send them back to their desks itching to nail another Woodbury wrongdoer.

'Look, chaps, *Fair Exchange* isn't just about marbles and *Beano*s. It's my belief that within a year or two it will be a serious moneymaker.'

'Yes, but it's not journalism, is it?' Keith Wilson insisted. 'You don't get Pulitzer prizes for advertising jumble sales and helping some masochist find a nice cruel sadist via the personal ads, do you?'

Fran battled on. 'Maybe not. But if *Fair Exchange* really does make some money the *Citizen* could be properly funded at last. We could go high tech. Computers for all. You could change your village cricketing results right up to the last minute!'

She saw Keith Wilson's eyes finally light up with a spark of something resembling enthusiasm.

'And don't forget. The week after next it's the Regional Press Awards and we're right up there with a chance.'

She was about to retreat to the peace of her office when she realized she didn't have one any more. She had to take her mobile into the loo and flush the cistern so that no one could hear. She nervously dialled the number of the Harley Street gynaecologist to make an appointment to have the simple test known as a chorionic villus biopsy which would enable her, with the help of Jack's stolen blood, to finally discover which of them was the father of her baby.

As soon as it was decently possible, Fran went to the office fridge and tucked Jack's blood, now discreetly hidden in a jiffy bag, at the very back on the bottom shelf. As she did, she sincerely hoped that his blood group was not a desperately rare one, and that there were no pile-ups on the by-pass tonight when lives could have been saved had it not been hidden in here behind the cans of Diet Coke and piccalilli, brought in to spice up people's shop-bought cheese sandwiches.

It was Ben and Jack's night in with a video and a pizza. On this occasion Jack had left the selection of both the film and the pizza toppings to his son. They were now halfway through *Pulp Fiction* and Jack hadn't laughed once, not even when the man in the back got shot, or during the discussion over what quarter pounders were in French. Ben felt cheated because this was the bit they always mouthed along to, falling about laughing each time they did, yet tonight his father didn't even seem to be watching.

The empty pizza carton sat greasily eyeing them from the coffee table in front of the TV. Absently, Jack got up to tidy it away, breaking another of their unwritten rules. On Boys' Night In no one was supposed to tidy up till the film showing was over.

'Dad,' Ben demanded, his concern so deep that he even put the video on Pause. 'Dad, are you all right?'

Jack just went on tidying.

'Planet Earth to Dad!' insisted Ben, pretending the remote control was the microphone on a powerful space craft coasting through the galaxy. In the end he had to fling one of the big soggy cushions with Marilyn Monroe on the front at him, the ones his mum had hated because she said they were tasteless, thereby condemning his father's choice. 'What's the matter? Did the new paper flop or something?'

Jack threw the carton at him, so that Ben had to duck, neatly catching it in one hand and frisbeeing it back.

'No, it did not flop. It's been a big success. Even the revolting Murray Nelson temporarily approves of me.'

'Cool. So what's the matter then? Is it Ralph being ill? I know how much you like him.'

Jack sat down next to him, conscious that it should be him who was trying to find out Ben's teenage problems, not the other way round. 'No, it isn't that particular Tyler who's getting to me as a matter of fact.'

'Francesca then. You really like her, don't you?' Painfully, he wished again that he hadn't been around that morning and intruded on them.

Jack was silent.

'If you really do like her,' Ben was choosing his words carefully, especially as his experience of women was limited to copies of *Penthouse* and the girl back in his primary school days who would flash her fanny for 50p, 'don't you think you're being a bit of a wimp, sitting back and just letting her marry someone else?'

Jack was touched at this fatherly advice. 'I don't think Francesca thinks I'm a very good bet. Stevie says she wants someone reliable. Not the kind of bloke who's in the habit of losing a wife and child.'

'But he's not reliable, is he, this doctor?'

Jack looked up sharply. 'What do you know about Laurence Westcott?'

Ben shrugged. 'Kids always notice more than adults give them credit for.'

Jack turned away, the memory of it all flooding back into his mind like filthy water. That was a sluice gate he'd kept closed for a long time now. It had been the only way to survive. 'I suppose they do, especially you. Nosy little bugger. Ben?'

'Yup?'

'Thanks for staying with me.'

Ben grinned. 'Pure self-interest. I knew you'd spoil me rotten because you were so guilty and Mum would be doubly strict because I didn't have a dad. No contest really.'

'Get out of here, you horror. And take *Pulp Fiction* back.'

'Don't need to. The man in the video shop gave it to us.'

'Why?' This didn't sound convincing to Jack, yet Ben

was normally so honest it made him hard to live with at times.

'Because no one else but me has had it out fifty times. He reckons we've paid for it several times over. *And* he wants me to come on their movie quiz team.'

'Sign of a mis-spent youth, knowing films as well as you do. I blame the parents.'

While Ben was taking *Pulp Fiction* up to his bedroom, Wild Rover came and laid his head on Jack's knee. 'So,' Jack leaned down to look in the dog's soulful brown eyes, 'is Ben right? Am I the last of the no-hopers? Should I be fighting harder to win the hand of the fair Francesca?'

For answer Wild Rover gave him a slobbery kiss so redolent of pongy dogfood that Jack expired quietly and lay on the floor with a cushion over his face until Ben came and prodded him. 'So, wimp-features, whaddya gonna do about it?'

Underneath his Marilyn Monroe cushion, Jack pondered. The trouble was, he hadn't got the slightest idea.

'What do you think of this layout, Stevie?' Fran was feeling quite proud of the bright front page she'd just assembled for *Fair Exchange*. 'Would you pick that up and stick it in your shopping bag?'

'I'd pocket a railway table for Aberdeen providing it was free.' Stevie gave the page her full and focused attention.

'Well! what do you think?'

'It's great. With real ads instead of these made-up ones we'll be laughing. How's the telesales office coming along?'

'Fine. Though naturally the phone lines haven't come through yet.'

'Bloody typical.' Stevie liked nothing better than a crisis. Only three weeks to go. Do you want me to ring them up and threaten them with exposure in the *Citizen* for rank inefficiency?'

'That would be wonderful. Or you could even try being nice.'

'*Nice?*' Stevie was clearly shocked at this extraordinary concept. 'Anyway, how's that other great event coming along, the Wedding of the Year? I thought we might make quite a splash of it in the paper. Editor Finds Love On Prescription . . .'

'You dare . . .' Fran threatened. For a brief moment she thought of confiding in Stevie that this afternoon at four pm she was booked into a London clinic for the test she hoped would resolve all her doubts about the wisdom of getting married at all. But maybe the less said the better.

'Look, Stevie, could you hold the fort this afternoon? I've got to nip up to town.'

'Lucky you. What a glamorous life you lead, unlike us poor drones. What is it this time? Wedding dress fitting? Colour counselling for your going-away dress?'

The truth might have shocked even Stevie. *Actually, I'm going to find out which of them is the father.*

The Windover Clinic had one of those grand rococo fronts, all balustrades and curlicues, that was supposed to fill you with proper respect for the medical profession and conclude that however much your visit was costing you, it had to be worth it.

Fran stepped into the reception area, ankle deep in Axminster, and thought about bolting back to Woodbury on the next train. Why didn't she simply let sleeping foetuses lie? Was this desperation she felt really for the best?

As if she detected the prospect of a fee changing its mind and legging it back to the provinces, the receptionist informed her in honeyed Harley Street tones that they were ready for her now.

Five minutes later Fran found herself, minus her clothes, wearing a blue hospital robe, lying on a bed with a friendly young woman next to her explaining that to ensure maximum safety they first needed to do a scan to find out where the baby was lying. On her left side was what seemed to be a TV screen. The young woman rubbed gel over Fran's tummy, apologizing for having cold hands.

'Sorry,' she smiled, 'that was the worst bit. Have you ever had a scan before?'

Fran shook her head.

A blurry grey picture appeared on the screen above them, which seemed to Fran a jumble of dots, as hard to make sense of as a weather map of the Eastern Hemisphere.

The young woman pointed to a vague shadowy line. 'That's baby's back.' The squiggle moved. 'Baby's lively today.' Fran followed the direction of the wand the young woman was pointing.

And then she saw it. The miraculous, shifting, but just discernible form of a tiny infant. Her breath stopped and she craned up to see better. It was almost inconceivable that those shapes were a baby and that the baby was living and growing inside her.

'That's baby's heartbeat.' The girl pointed to a regular pulsing beat. 'It's much faster in the womb.'

To her hideous embarrassment Fran's eyes welled up. How easy it was to create another human being, a simple act of carelessness, a pill forgotten, a condom not used, and in that casual unvalued moment another person's whole life began.

I'll love you, baby, she found herself promising. I'll make it up to you, I really will. You'll be wanted and cherished.

'Would you like a photo?' the young woman asked.

She handed Fran a blurry, ghostlike snap. But there, just as it had been on the screen, were the distinct lines of a small human being. Fran held it against her heart.

'Right.' The kind voice next to her penetrated her quiet happiness. 'The doctor will do the test now.'

Fran felt panic rising. What had seemed so sensible now seemed fraught with danger. What if something happened to the baby? What the hell did she think she was doing? And yet surely a baby also deserved to know who its father was?

The doctor sensed her anxiety and tried to calm her. 'Miss Tyler, I can see you're concerned but this is a very safe test. With effective scanning the risk of miscarriage is very slight and at your age the advantages of screening are significant. Just relax.'

And then, just as quickly, it was over.

'Take life carefully in the next day or so. No heavy lifting, just stay calm.'

'When will I get the results?'

'Slightly longer than usual since you're sending this off to a different lab.' He made this sound like a serious offence. 'Two weeks' time, maybe three just to be on the safe side. The nurse will see you out.'

In the train back to Woodbury all Fran could do was clutch her photograph and stare at its miraculous grey secrets. Whose genes had joined with hers to make it the person it was already programmed to be, Jack's or Laurence's?

'You're being very mysterious,' Stevie pointed out the next day as Fran attempted to slip in without being seen. She'd been up since first light, wandering down by the river, still wondering if she was justified in what she was doing. The last thing she felt like was close questioning from Stevie on her activities in London. 'Your mother's been after you. She's rung three times already. Naturally she wouldn't deign to tell *me* what it's about.'

Fran fought her way through the chaos of builders banging, typewriters clanking, Mike Wooley throwing paper darts made out of council press releases at Sean McGee, until she finally found a phone in a distant corner of the sports department. It meant staring at a full-frontal of a woman with boobs so large she must have been taking Growmore, but at least it was quiet.

What could her mother be in such a state about? She dialled their number, reining in her imagination about what could have happened to Ralph.

'Thank God I've found you.' Her mother sounded

unusually agitated. 'I've been trying to get hold of you since yesterday.'

'Is it Dad? What's happened?'

'Francesca, it was so awful. At the Rotarians' Cricket Match of all places!'

'What did he do?' From her mother's tone Fran pictured her father streaking across the pitch or mooning at the players' wives while they cut the cucumber sandwiches.

'He turned up in his silk dressing gown and panama hat!'

Fran fought the desire to giggle. 'Sounds quite sensible in this weather. Did anyone object?'

'Francesca that's not the point! They did their best to ignore him. The thing is, his behaviour has been getting odder and odder. It's all right for you with your precious paper to go to but frankly it was just too much. So I rang Laurence and he helped me get your father into Tawny Beeches.'

'How could you, Ma?' Francesca's knuckles whitened as she clutched the phone furiously. 'How could you put him in that ghastly place without even asking me? He'll hate it there. I could have got someone to look after him myself.'

'But you weren't here, were you?' Her mother turned the knife. 'It was the only alternative and we were very lucky to get it. It was only thanks to Laurence that we did.'

'How did Dad take it?' Fran could imagine her father's powerlessness and confusion.

'He'll settle in time.' The defensiveness in her mother's tone told her all she needed to know.

'He hated it, didn't he? Oh God, poor Dad, I can't bear it.'

'What about Poor Me? I'm the one who has to look after him. Why don't you spare a thought for poor me?'

Fran couldn't explain that if her mother had been less grudging and joyless before tragedy struck, she would have got more sympathy now.

After she'd said a painful goodbye to her mother Fran knew she had no alternative. She had to go and see him now.

When she arrived she was horrified to find that, although it was only eleven forty-five, it was lunchtime at Tawny Beeches and the lounge was deserted. 'But it's so ridiculously early. Whatever time do you have supper?' she asked the irritated warden.

'High tea is at four-thirty, biscuits and cocoa at seven.'

'But my father hates eating early. He's used to supper at nine.'

'Extremely bad for the digestion. No one should eat after six from a health point of view.'

Fran glanced through the open door of the refectory where the residents ate silently in rows, each with a glass of water beside them. Ralph had always loved a good wine. She caught sight of him sitting at the far table slightly apart from the others, marked out not only by his physical separation but by the youth of his features. She knew it was partly a trick of the years that Ralph had kept a kind of boyish eagerness about him, even into old age, but here it made him look as if he came from a completely different generation. How long would he keep that alertness in this place?

'Can I go in?'

'Not during meals I'm afraid. You can wait in his bedroom if you like. I'll make an exception just this once. Normally we encourage socializing after lunch. A whist drive or bingo or they all nod off.' Fran wanted to shake the woman and tell her that her father would hate enforced bingo, that he had all his life hated false jollity and enjoyed his own company, but she knew the warden would listen tightlipped and disapproving and ignore her.

Ralph's room was a white box, identical to a dozen others, as the result of 'clever' conversion. There was everything in it, closet, loo, shower compartment all fitting together in the minimum space. She thought of his cosy study at home which had, despite his retirement, kept something of the atmosphere of a newspaper office about it. Where were all his special things? The possessions that had marked important moments in his life.

'Why don't you bring some things in tomorrow?' The warden could see that Fran was one of those difficult relatives, the ones who wouldn't sacrifice their own life but criticized the way other people picked up the pieces. 'Not too many, of course. We find six is about right given the limited space.'

Fran half expected her to say it saved on dusting, but the woman wisely remained silent.

'I'll go and fetch your father now,' she announced finally.

Fran waited, struggling to remain in control. Her father needed her to think, not weep.

'Now, Mr Tyler,' she could hear the warden from

halfway down the landing, 'I've got a nice surprise for you in your room. Here now.' She flung the door open.

Ralph Tyler looked round the room, a confused but happy smile lighting up the features Fran so loved.

'Hello,' he shook her hand with a warm but quaint formality, and looked at Fran as if she were the honoured guest at a prize-giving. 'I know your face. We go back a long way, don't we?'

Fran thought her heart would break.

'Sorry, my dear.' For once the warden's voice held genuine sympathy, 'I'm afraid this happens all the time. It's hard to believe, but he still knows you're important to him.'

Stevie was waiting for her as soon as she got back to the paper. 'How was he?'

Finally, knowing she was with someone who cared for her father as deeply as she did, Fran let her guard down. 'Oh, Stevie, it was dreadful! He was there in the middle of all these automatons and it was as though he were the only one of them who was still alive. His whole life is organized for him, there's nothing to tell you who he is or how he's more than just a doddery old fool. And the worst thing of all,' Fran's throat closed over agonizingly as she remembered her father's unrecognizing face, 'he didn't know who I was!'

She buried her face in Stevie's woolly shoulder.

'He'd never have been in that place if I'd been married to him!' Stevie's bitterness hung in the air, almost frightening in its intensity. Abruptly she extricated herself and patted Fran's shoulder. 'Come on, Fran love. This isn't doing any good to Ralph. We should be using our energies to think of some way of getting him out of there. He wouldn't want us to be snivelling in a corner like a couple of old biddies. Can't you almost hear him? "Come on, troops, we've got a paper to get out!"'

In a way Fran was grateful that she didn't have a second to think about anything except the fact that *Fair Exchange* was due to appear in every newsagent in under a month. She didn't allow herself to think about what would happen if it was a flop and the loan she'd negotiated from the bank couldn't be repaid. The thought was too awful to contemplate.

'What amazes me,' Stevie remarked, as they worked their way through yet another set of costings, 'is how cool you're being about this wedding of yours. You're the only bride I've ever come across who's more interested in deadlines than duvet covers.'

Fran laughed. 'Don't worry. Laurence's mother is treating it as her lifetime calling. I know I'm the daughter-in-law from hell and I do try. I just can't help finding *Fair Exchange* more riveting than matching towels and toasters.'

'Poor Camilla.' Stevie fixed Fran with one of her fierce and unwavering stares, the kind that sent reporters running for the loo. Fran was like the daughter she never had, and there was something about her manner that made the older woman uneasy. 'All the same, don't you think you should be worried that you're not worried?'

'I'll start panicking nearer the time, when I'm less busy. At the moment just the thought of having Laurence permanently on tap is enough to get me through it. It'll be bliss.'

'Mmmm . . .' Stevie agreed, pouring them both a cup of glutinous black coffee from the inch or two that remained in the jug. As usual no one in the newsroom had bothered to empty it and refill it. 'Think, you'll never have to be insulted by your GP's receptionist trying to get an appointment ever again. You'll have your own free, on-the-spot treatment centre.'

'Except that I'm not sure fertility experts know any more than you or me about chicken pox and glandular fever, but if we're talking cervixes, I'm well in.'

'Fran . . .' Stevie paused and looked round her. It was so late there was no one left in the room but them. 'You do love Laurence, don't you?'

'Stevie! What a question! Of course I do. I'm just too busy to be all hearts and flowers about it, and to tell you the truth I think that quite suits both of us. We like the fact that the other's committed to their work.'

Stevie contemplated the implications of this depressing fact. It meant, as far as she could see, that this gave them a licence to see each other as little as possible. But then would she and Ralph have been any different? They certainly had a commitment to their work, but as they worked together that had given them a glorious sense of shared goals and passion. That, it struck her, was what was missing. She didn't sense any passion when Fran talked about Laurence. But then, she thought sadly, looking back on the desert of her own life, where had passion got her? It had probably spoiled any chance of ordinary happiness she'd ever had. Once she'd met Ralph it was him or no one. Perhaps passion was something best avoided. Stevie, she told herself, though she said nothing to Fran, you dishonest old rogue. You may be a down-to-earth old bag who calls a spade a shovel, and you may spend most of your time using it to shovel shit with, but you know passion's the only thing that counts.

Fran saw the doubt in Stevie's eyes and came over to her. 'Look, I adore Laurence. Stevie. Of course I do. He's the most wonderful man I've ever met. Handsome, caring, spending his whole life helping people. You're the one who's always telling me I should find someone like my father. For the first time in my life I have.'

'Good.' Stevie went back to the job Fran had delegated to her, if she said anything more she'd end up putting her size seven right in it.

But the mention of Laurence had jogged Fran's memory.

'Oh my God! Laurence! I'm supposed to be going to his mother's for supper tonight! Do I look OK like this?'

Stevie considered Fran's slightly unusual outfit of purple sleeveless tunic over dark green leggings. 'You look fine to me, but then,' Stevie indicated the tweed skirt and cardigan she wore 364 days of the year, 'the concept of day-through-evening wear has somehow eluded me. I suppose you could always say you've come as Robin Hood.'

'Thanks a bunch. I'll just have to plead understatement and overwork. Now I must dash. Could you be a love and bung those figures in the file when you've finished?'

If Stevie considered Fran to be a trifle underwhelmed by the wedding arrangements, then Camilla, her prospective mother-in-law, found Fran's behaviour totally infuriating.

The last thing she wanted, if truth were known, was to be told, 'Fine whatever you think. That sounds wonderful,' by a daughter-in-law to be who was more interested in her precious paper than in the most important day of her life.

What Camilla longed for was deep and intensive analysis, preferably over long giggly lunches, of every single tiny detail of the arrangements from the exact components of the bridesmaids' posies to whether 'Jesu Joy of Man's Desiring' was absolutely essential as wedding music or a tad overused these days. Instead of which, with only a month to go, Fran seemed to be calm and disinterested and totally happy to let her mother-in-law decide everything without even understanding that the discussion was a vital part of the process, just as the wedding didn't exist until it was duly captured in a leather-bound, perspex-lined photograph album.

And now, just to add to all the complications, there was this business about the girl's father. It was too much. Why couldn't Laurence have found some nice easy-going nurse who hero-worshipped him and who Camilla could have quietly dominated?

But Camilla said none of this when Fran arrived, breathless, in a strange principal-boy ensemble, and, instead of launching into wedding chat, immediately broached the subject of her father and the home he'd been admitted to. Really.

Fran, for her part, felt a warm glow of pleasure at the sight of Laurence, handsome and calm in a pale wool sweater and cotton slacks, sitting at one end of his mother's pretty chintzy sofa in his mother's pretty chintzy sitting room. It had rather surprised Fran, when she first saw this room, that so many different flower patterns existed. Along with the bunches of roses, peonies, and delphiniums in vases on every surface, you could almost think you'd taken a wrong turn and wandered into an edition of *The Secret Garden*.

Rather to Laurence's surprise, Fran flung herself into his arms, relishing his cashmere caress, realizing how much she'd missed him in the last few days.

'Darling Laurence, it's so lovely to see you. But there's something I really need to talk about.' Laurence too had hoped it was about the wedding. His mother kept asking him things he had no idea of the answers to and he felt with a flash of annoyance that surely all this was women's stuff. 'That awful place Dad's in. I went round there yesterday and I just couldn't bear it. I know he's confused and ill, but he'll just become a vegetable in a place like that. We *have* to find a better solution.'

A look of exasperation clouded Laurence's handsome features. 'Francesca, my love, these places are very hard to get into in your father's condition. Plenty of homes just won't take them, and your mother's adamant that she can't cope. What exactly have you got in mind?'

Fran didn't know. That was the problem. 'I could try and talk her into having him at home with a carer.'

'I thought you'd already tried that and she wouldn't consider it.'

'I did.'

'Well, then.'

'I thought . . .' Fran faltered for a moment at the

knowledge of what she was suggesting and decided this wasn't the moment for it. She'd wait until after the wedding when everything had calmed down. It was only a few weeks, after all, now that they'd brought it forward because of Ralph's health. 'Don't worry. Perhaps he'll settle.'

'I'm sure he will,' Laurence said with easy certainty. 'Now look, darling, there's a number of things we need to get sorted out.'

'Yes. Yes of course. Where shall we start?'

She sat up straight and with an almost imperceptible sigh – but not so imperceptible it missed Camilla – she gave him her fullest attention.

After two solid hours, Fran was totally exhausted. Why on earth did people put themselves through this agony instead of nipping down to the register office in their lunch hour? Weddings, she'd once read weren't simply private events but occasions that affected the whole community, and frankly it felt as if the whole community was being consulted. It was ten o'clock, they'd had coffee and she could see Camilla getting her second wind.

'Now, how about the ushers and the bridesmaids? What did you have in mind to give them as presentation gifts?'

'Well actually, Camilla,' Fran said cravenly, 'I'm afraid I've got to get back to the paper now.'

'But it's ten o'clock.'

'Is it really?' Fran asked innocently. 'That's newspapers for you. Not long now till the launch.'

And even less until the wedding and I can see which has

your priority, Camilla longed to add. Instead, she saw Fran out ungraciously. If you asked her this was quite unnecessary.

Back in the sitting room, Laurence was lounging elegantly on the sofa again. There was no point trying to get any decisions out of him. From nowhere an image of Francesca's father, Ralph Tyler, fluttered into Camilla's mind. Sad that he'd become so ill so quickly. He'd always been a very attractive, if difficult man, but then she rather liked those committed types whose life had a purpose. Unlike poor Harry, the husband she'd loved but had totally dominated. A chill thought struck her. If it had been she who was ill, would Laurence have packed *her* off to a home with such indecent speed at the first sign of failing?

'Laurence,' she sat down next to him, 'this business about Francesca's father is making me think. I would like to put away part of my money towards sheltered housing. Will you promise me one thing?' Camilla's pretty, exquisitely made-up face lost its air of being an upper-class doll and showed real fear. 'That you won't pack me off to Tawny Beeches. I really don't think I could bear it.'

'Honestly, Mother,' Laurence's tone hardened. 'You mustn't listen to Francesca. You'd think Tawny Beeches was the gulag. It's five-star luxury all the way.'

'Or five-star imprisonment. You've never forgiven me, have you, Laurence?'

'For heaven's sake, Mother, don't start that. I've had a long day.'

'You think I betrayed you. You think I should have told

you the truth.' Anguish shredded her voice. 'But people didn't believe it was right then. All this honesty and tracing your birth mother, it's new. We all thought it was better not to know. To make a fresh start.'

'Yes.' Laurence's back was ramrod stiff and the age lines in his face, usually only lightly etched, suddenly looked like deep runnels.

Pain gives his face character, Camilla thought irrelevantly. Makes him look like his father when he was young. Poor handsome Harry. He would probably have been happier with a different kind of woman too. Life was pretty damn sad all round.

'Laurence, there's something I've always wondered. Why did you choose to work in infertility? Was it because of being adopted? You seemed so utterly sure that's what you wanted to do.'

There was something she couldn't read in his expression when he looked back at her, then quickly away again. 'I suppose so. I just knew I wanted to help women who really wanted babies. Maybe to redress the balance of all those who got pregnant without thinking and aborted them or threw them away.'

'Laurence . . .' Camilla's voice almost broke up at the intensity of the memory. 'I wanted you desperately, even if I'm not your birth mother.'

Laurence's hand briefly touched her shoulder. 'I know, Ma. I know.' He didn't say what both of them were thinking, that their tragedy was that this fact still mattered so much and could never, no matter what either did, be forgotten.

*

Fran loved the *Citizen* offices when they were empty almost as much as when they hummed with frantic noise. She always found peace here. Even at two in the morning when it seemed as if she were the only person for miles, she never felt lonely or frightened. Partly it was because the spirit of her father was still so strong here. What, she wondered leaning on the door, would he have thought of his office, that had become her office, being turned into a room for six telephonists? The mementoes he'd handed down stripped from the walls and boxed up to be rearranged when Fran finally got an office back. She had a feeling he wouldn't have minded. The soul of a paper, he always said, was in its reporters; in things that moved them and made them angry, in the changes for the better they wanted to make in the world around them. And now it was her responsibility to keep that going. Now perhaps more than ever, as the light was fading in Ralph himself.

She brushed a tear from her eye and sat down. This was no good. This didn't help anyone. On a sudden whim, she opened her wallet and took out the grey and blurry photograph of the scan and propped it up on the desk in front of her. She needed something joyous and life-enhancing. Inspired by a rush of new-found energy, she got down to work. She had to get *Fair Exchange* ready and on the streets in less than three weeks. Then she could finally relax and enjoy her wedding.

The other side of Woodbury, Jack Allen was working late too, but he wasn't the only person left in his building. Miriam Wolsey was there too. All evening Jack had been aware of her presence. He kept expecting her to wave good-bye and leave, but she didn't. There were two conclusions he could draw from this. First, that she had a sad and lonely life and that the paper was the only thing in it, but picturing that perfect heart-shaped face and those huge dark eyes he didn't think so. There was also the small matter of the clamour an hour ago when a gaggle of young male reporters, some of whom he suspected of hanging on not so much because of their crippling workload, but because of the presence of Miriam herself, tried to talk her into coming to the pub. Miriam had refused. She could of course be working on a story that required her to burn the midnight electricity. Or it could equally be that she was waiting for him.

He packed his briefcase and turned off the light. 'Goodnight, Miriam. Your dedication is impressive, but don't work too late.'

For answer Miriam jumped up. 'Actually, I was about to stop. I'll end up with RSI if I go on any longer.' She loaded up her bag in record time and fell into step with him. In the car park he remembered that his car was in the garage and, with a big story breaking earlier, he'd forgotten to pick it up. Damn. It would be locked in by now.

'I'll give you a lift,' Miriam offered quickly. 'Woodbury's not that big after all. Where do you live?'

To refuse would have been ridiculous. The car was newer than he'd expected, a zippy red Peugeot convertible. Miriam must have private money. 'Nice car,' he commented, 'although I doubt you got it on what I pay you. How easy is it to put the roof down?'

'Dead easy.' She demonstrated.

Jack, thirty-eight and occasionally feeling his age, was instantly twenty-one again. He'd been too broke at the right age for a car like this and now he could afford it he found it unseemly. Old men in young men's cars were pathetic. Seducing women with the size of their sports car. He preferred his comfortable old Saab but this, he had to admit, was fun.

'Why don't we go for a drive?' Miriam turned up the music on the stereo and Jack laughed. Somewhere there was a faint misgiving, but the music and the sense of spontaneity drowned it out.

It was bad luck for Miriam that on her way towards the ring road and the route to Woodedge Hill, which boasted one of the most romantic views in the county, she happened to go via the High Street and passed the *Citizen*'s offices. It was also too bad that Fran happened to be standing at the window with the light behind her staring out.

'Sorry, Miriam,' Jack put out a hand to the wheel as they stopped at the next red light. 'It would have been fun but there's something I've remembered I've got to do.'

'At this time of night?' Miriam's eyes followed Jack's.

''Fraid so.' He climbed quickly out of the car before the lights could change. 'See you tomorrow. Thanks for the lift.'

Miriam roared off round the block and screamed to a halt. She tore off her earrings and the high heels she'd worn because they made her legs look thin and flung them in the back. Damn Jack Allen! Why couldn't he deign to take what most men would get down on their knees and beg for? The shocking truth of it all was that, sensible and sane girl though she usually was, his indifference only made her want him more.

When Fran heard someone opening the door she looked at her watch in surprise. It was a bit early for Flo, the cleaner, but Flo had a sick husband and they left it to her to choose her hours to fit in. Sometimes they were pretty erratic.

'Flo?' she called.

But it wasn't Flo who replied.

'I saw you burning the midnight oil and wondered if you might like to come for a drink.'

'At this hour?'

Jack grinned. 'There's places.'

'And I'm sure you know them all.' In fact, having just finished the task she'd been putting off for weeks, Fran was on a high. She would never sleep. And after all the worries over her father and launching the paper, she felt like doing something irresponsible. 'All right then, you're on.' She gathered her things together. Their eyes locked on the photograph of the scan at precisely the same moment.

Fran grabbed it before – please God let it be before – Jack had a chance to see the name typed in white letters along the bottom. 'Did I tell you,' Fran fluttered nervously, 'my friend Henrietta is pregnant again. The only thing is her husband's dead against it so she's having a terrible time deciding what to do.'

Stupid. She should remember what her father advised her. Never lie. And if you do, keep it simple. It's the embroidery that catches you out.

'Ah,' said Jack, suppressing the smallest of grins. 'Congratulate her for me. Though perhaps I'll get a chance myself. I often see her round town.'

'Oh no,' Fran panicked, 'don't do that. She's not sure she's going ahead with it, you see.'

'Ah,' repeated Jack infuriatingly.

The after-hours drinking establishment he took her to was hardly the den of iniquity she'd been expecting. No roulette and whisky and wicked women. The Feathers was a tiny pub in the back streets of Woodbury boasting only two small bars, each the size of a front room and decorated in suitably cosy style. Closing time, Fran noted, seemed to be a concept that had escaped it.

'The cops have an informal arrangement round here. They let one pub in the area stay open as long as it likes. They call it drinking-up time, though even Ena Sharples couldn't take three hours to finish up a milk stout. It's a quaint local tradition.'

The publican, a grandmotherly lady, came and took their order. 'Two pints of Guinness please, Dorothy.'

Fran was outraged. 'I loathe Guinness.'

'You can't order a fancy spritzer here. They probably opened the bottle in nineteen thirty-four. That is, if they have one. Besides, Guinness is good for you.' She thought for a fraction of a second he was going to add, 'in your condition,' but he didn't. 'So, what's all this I hear about your new venture?'

'Is that why you've brought me here? To find out what I'm up to in case it threatens the mighty *Express*?'

'Look, Francesca,' Jack's voice was suddenly serious,

'forget the paper for a moment. There's something I need to know.' He put down his drink and held her gaze steadily. 'Are you in love with Laurence Westcott?'

If he hadn't looked so deadly earnest, Fran would have laughed. He reminded her of the father of a virgin asking her young man his intentions. 'Of course I am. Why else would I be going to marry him?'

Jack's eye strayed downwards to her stomach.

What the hell was he doing? he asked himself. If Francesca really loved Laurence Westcott, then he had no right to interfere and try to change her mind. At the sight of her wide green eyes fixed candidly on his, Jack wrestled with his conscience. Finally he came to a decision.

'The thing is, Francesca, I knew Laurence Westcott quite well seven years ago. Carrie and I spent two years having fertility treatment with him.'

'But you already had Ben.'

'I know. It happens, or so we were told. A third of their patients already have one child and find they can't have another. Who knows why. Stress? Hormones? Anyway it was Laurence who –'

Jack stopped, mid-sentence.

Miriam Wolsey had just appeared by the bar, red lips flashing, earrings and high heels firmly back on. 'Hello, Jack, not as tired as you thought then. Can I get you both a drink?'

Her entrance seemed to wake Fran up. She had a feeling Jack had been about to unburden himself and she wasn't at all sure she wanted to hear what he had to say. 'I must go . . .'

'Fran, don't . . .' There was a note of unexpected pain in

Jack's voice that halted her for a second. But Miriam was looking at her expectantly.

'No really. I have to go. Have fun. And thanks for the Guinness, Jack. I'm sure it was good for me.'

Miriam sat down. 'I do hope I wasn't breaking anything up.'

Jack stared into his drink. 'It's all right. I think whatever it was broke up some time ago.'

Chapter 16

What was Ben's light doing on? Jack wondered anxiously, when he finally got back at close on midnight.

Ben appeared at his window, looking out and waving. He had obviously been waiting up. The usual emotions warred in Jack: pleasure at seeing his son, guilt that he should have been spending more time with him. It was the summer holidays, after all, which ought to be a special time, and a slight sprinkling of panic in case Ben might be wanting a heart-to-heart about some problem of earth-shattering importance like what could be done about the ozone layer.

Jack just hoped, whatever it was, he'd be able to scrabble together some answer that Ben, with his demanding teenage standards, found adequate. There was nothing quite like the lip-curling sneer that accompanied the words 'You're just saying that because you want to go to bed / go to work / read the paper'. Single mothers found it hard work and he had every sympathy for them. But they should try being single fathers.

'Hi, Dad.' Ben skipped downstairs to join him in the untidy sitting room. With a sinking heart, Jack guessed this wasn't to be the usual twenty questions, but something altogether more challenging.

'Wotcher, cock.' Jack patted the squashy sofa next to him. 'How's life?'

Ben's luminous dark eyes, so like his mother's it used to turn Jack's heart over, fixed themselves on his, then looked away. 'Fine.'

'Something you wanted to talk about?' Mistake. Too direct. When would he learn that there was a protocol to these things. It was just that he was so bloody tired. This was clearly going to be a diplomatic venture of Kissinger-like proportions. He hoped he had the strength.

'You'll go bald wearing that thing night and day.' He swiped Ben's baseball cap and ruffled his son's hair.

'Like you, you mean?' Ben indicated the very beginning of his father's receding hairline.

'Nonsense. My great grandfather had hair like Strewwelpeter right into his eighties. It's a family characteristic, along with enormous intelligence and Picasso-like charisma.'

'What about Mum's side of the family?'

So that was it. Ben rarely talked about his mother. He wondered what had brought this on.

The guilt that lay waiting for Jack whenever anything went wrong in his son's life jumped out from behind its tree. Should he have tried harder to patch up the marriage all those years ago? The thought of little Louise, the daughter he hardly knew, growing up the other side of the world, was a source of such unbearable loss that he tried not to think of her. She would hate him, or perhaps, for better or worse, he would simply be no part of her emotional landscape.

The cruellest blow of all had been that, when the marriage had folded, Carrie's parents had taken her side and had cut him from their lives. When Ben had opted to stay with his father they had simply refused to see their own grandson. For which Jack would never, ever forgive them.

'Come on, lovely, tell yer old dad what's worrying you. Are you missing your mum? She loves you, you know.'

Ben shook his head. 'Actually it's about Ralph. Mrs Tyler told us he was in Tawny Beeches so Rover and I tried to go and see him today.'

It took Jack a moment to realize Ben was talking about Fran's father.

'That was a nice thought. He's not very well, is he?' Jack suddenly saw how disturbing Ralph's decline must have been for Ben. He hadn't worked it out before, but Ralph had probably in some way become the grandfather that Ben had so cruelly lost. Now he was losing him too.

'Hey. Come here and have a cuddle. You've still got me and always will have, you know.' He made a promise to himself to spend more time with his son, paper or no paper. Murray Nelson could get stuffed. Preferably with old copies of the *Express*.

But Ben sniffed loudly and turned away. Jack could have

sworn he was crying. 'It was awful, Dad. Ralph is my friend and they wouldn't even let me and Rover in to see him.'

Jack considered the disreputable dog, made more raffish by the bargee's scarf Ben had insisted on keeping round his neck, and saw their point. They probably thought he'd lift his leg on a resident. But Ben at least should have been made welcome.

'The worst part was I looked through the window and saw him and he saw me too. He looked so pleased. Then they wouldn't let me go in. They said it wasn't visiting time.'

Jack cursed Tawny Beeches and its pretentious ways. Didn't they see it would do a sick old man more good to see Ben than a year of TV watching? These places were a scandal, many of them. Old people had to sell the homes they'd spent a lifetime buying just to get some boxroom in one of them and be charged an arm and a leg. Jack didn't have much sympathy for people who harked on about 'the good old days'. Mostly they weren't good at all, but the way old people were shuffled off by their families maddened him. The fact that Fran could have agreed to it frankly amazed him.

'Look, would it help if I went to see him myself tomorrow and fixed a time for you to visit him? You can leave Wild Rover with me.'

'Oh, Dad, would you? Soon?'

'Absolutely. Now, up to bed. I don't know about you, but I'm knackered.'

As he fell asleep, wondering when on earth he could make time tomorrow, one of his busiest days, to get to

Tawny Beeches, it struck Jack that Ben's own grandfather was a sad man. All that affection and love, which Ben was lavishing on Ralph, could have been his too.

'Can you promise me, one hundred per cent, no, two hundred per cent, that those phones will be operational by tomorrow?' Fran had to shout at the man from UK Telecom above the almost actionable noise-levels in the newsroom. Reporters shouted to make themselves heard over the sound of builders banging, which seemed to spur the builders on to bang even louder. It reminded Fran of one of those Italian paintings of hell. Thank God, unlike hell, it should be over in the next two weeks, or so they said.

'Fran,' Stevie bellowed in her loudest sergeant-major voice, 'that newsprint you ordered. It's stuck in Sweden. They can't deliver for a month.'

Fran took a deep breath and tried not to panic. Then she took another one because the first hadn't worked. Without the newsprint she would have no *Fair Exchange*. A month was too late. They needed it now. 'Let me talk to them.'

After a morning of frantic phoning she tracked down enough newsprint for the first four weeks of production. Now she felt like a large very jammy doughnut as reward.

But it wasn't to be. Jim Curry, the *Citizen*'s chief sales rep, who had been charged with the job of talking newsagents into carrying *Fair Exchange* plonked his portly behind, the product of too many fish-and-chip lunches grabbed on the hoof, on Fran's desk and announced with something approaching glee that the biggest chain in the area had refused point blank to carry it.

'What!' screamed Fran. 'How can they? We have hoardings all over this town promoting the thing, ads designed to tease and intrigue everyone, the punters are starting to talk about it, I've heard them.'

'I told you we should deliver it through people's doors like the *Express* are doing with their freebie. Or at least fold it inside the *Citizen*,' Jim informed her with satisfaction.

'No.' Fran was adamant. '*Fair Exchange* is a different market, potentially a bigger market. It has to be something people actively *want* because all their friends have it. I'll go and see the newsagent myself.' As a matter of fact, she'd just had an idea. She glanced round the room, looking for the right person. Her gaze halted on Sean McGee. He would be perfect. 'Sean, I need you for an hour, Stevie will release you from whatever scoop you're working on.'

Sean looked thrilled. He had been allocated to Woodbury Dene Parish Council that week and their riveting deliberations on whether or not to mow the graveyard. Woodward and Bernstein would not have been impressed.

The biggest branch of Morton's Newsagents was just a few doors from the *Citizen*'s offices, overlooking the cathedral square. Fran and Sean fought their way through the tourists, who were knee-deep on the pavement.

'We should be printing guide books for foreigners,' mumbled Sean, still mystified as to where Fran was taking him.

'Except that they come here for only six weeks a year. Now, Sean, have you any acting experience?'

'I used to go to drama club at school,' Sean replied, even more bemused. 'And I've watched enough Am Dram by the

Woodbury Dene Players since I've been here to last me a lifetime.'

'Right. This is what I want you to do.' She pulled him round the corner into the cathedral close.

'Ah, Mr Morton,' Fran beamed five minutes later as she swept into the large newsagent's shop, grateful that the proprietor was at least present. 'What's this I hear about you not carrying our wonderful new publication.'

'Hello, Miss Tyler.' Terry Morton watched Fran bearing down on him with a certain amount of misgiving. Her father had always managed to make him feel as if carrying the *Citizen* were less a choice than a duty, and it looked like his daughter was just as bad. 'The answer's very simple. Your new paper's free, so there's no margin for me. Why should I have it clogging up my precious shelf space when I don't make anything out of it, tell me that?'

In front of a fascinated audience of old ladies and mums with buggies, Fran held forth on why *Fair Exchange* was going to be something people bought not because they had a car to sell but because they'd find out exactly what was going on in Woodbury. 'You see, Mr Morton, people aren't interested in flower shows and village cricket any more. They want to know about jumble sales and PTA meetings and when the next car boot sale is. Everyone will want *Fair Exchange* and if you don't have it in your shop you'll be missing a wonderful opportunity to get people in to buy other things.'

Miraculously a ponytailed young man with bicycle clips that matched his earring appeared from behind the birthday cards stand. 'Excuse me? Can you tell me when you'll have that new paper they're advertising? The one that's about swapping things?'

Mr Morton looked on in awe as Sean proceeded to buy forty Silk Cut, an expensive computer magazine and one of those huge tasteless birthday cards in padded silk for his mother. It came to almost twelve quid.

Mr Morton watched him thoughtfully as he loaded up his booty.

'Look,' Fran moved in for the kill. 'Just take it for the first month. If you have any left over we'll come and remove them personally the next day. That's how confident we are. So they won't be clogging up your precious shelf space, will they?'

Grudgingly, like a customer who's just bought a knock-down dinner service from a market trader and suspects some of the plates are missing, Mr Morton agreed.

'Here, take this lot,' Sean McGee stuffed the goodies into Fran's hands as soon as they were round the corner. 'My heart was in my mouth in there. I was sure he'd remember me interviewing him at the chamber of commerce lunch, or guess how much I hate smoking or that my sainted mother's been dead for ten years now.'

'You did a grand job, Sean. Well done.'

They hurried back to the paper as Fran tried to push from her mind the image of having no paper to print the thing on, or of vast piles of unpicked-up copies falling on top of Terry Morton and suffocating him.

'How did you get on?' demanded Stevie as soon as they got back to the office.

Fran grinned. 'He agreed! For a month anyway, providing we pick up any copies that are still there next day.'

'Next day?'

'There won't be any, Stevie. Believe me.' She wished she felt quite as bullish as she sounded. 'And by the way, Sean and I are thinking of doing *Romeo and Juliet* next.'

'I can't wait.' Stevie handed her a piece of paper. 'Your mother-in-law to be rang. Can you call her back?'

Fran attempted the impossible task of finding a quiet corner to make the call.

'Hello, Camilla, you were trying to get me.'

'Yes. I thought you might like to hear the exciting news. The first wedding present arrived today. We thought it better to have them sent here, seeing as your father's unwell. Anyway,' she gushed on, 'isn't it wonderful! How are things going at your end?'

If truth were known the arrival of the first present had sent Fran into a mild state of shock. 'Oh, fine. Very good actually, we had a problem with our newsprint, I thought we'd lost it for one awful moment, and a little local difficulty with a wholesaler, but everything's fine now.'

'Actually,' Camilla's voice could have sheared through a steel bar, 'I was talking about the wedding.'

'Whoops!' Fran murmured under her breath when Camilla put the phone down, remembering that she was due at Camilla's with Laurence tonight. She'd just have to gush about all things weddingy then.

It was, of all days, Jack's deadline day today and there wasn't a spare second to sneak off and see Ralph until late afternoon when the paper had safely gone to bed. It was almost five by the time he parked the Saab on the well-levelled gravel outside Tawny Beeches. God, he hated places like this. Pretending to care for old people when it was really a money-spinning industry, a classic Thatcher spin-off, privatized geriatric care.

As he strode angrily towards the imposing front door, Jack made himself examine why he felt this strongly. Was it his crusading hackles rising because this was the kind of scandal he relished exposing, or something altogether more personal? His own mother had died from a straightforward stroke, the way she had always said she wanted to. His father had died when he was a child. And his wife Carrie's parents had simply cut them off. Consequently he had no difficult dilemmas to face himself and perhaps that coloured his views.

Even still, he told himself as he asked to see Ralph, I wouldn't have done this with them. The place was like an expensive hotel peopled by ancient aliens. They didn't need five-star luxury, Lucozade served in crystal glasses, they needed to be *part* of something. People here had no choices to make, everything was done for them, and it seemed to Jack that choice was what made people human. He thought for a moment about his own old age and saw himself by a fireside, reading a paper, creating little rituals for himself to structure the day: doing the crossword, gardening, pottering in the kitchen, drinking a good whisky, answering to no one. Yet none of that was possible for the inmates here; luxurious though the lifestyle might be, the one thing they didn't have was a freedom to decide anything.

'Mr Allen? Would you like to come with me now?'

The warden, chatting brightly, led him down the plush corridors to the lounge. 'Mr Tyler's in the chair at the end.'

Jack walked down the long row towards the big picture window. All the chairs faced the big TV screen except one. Ralph's. As if in the only small gesture of defiance permitted to him, he had turned his chair towards the outside world. To Jack it seemed unbearably symbolic.

'Hello, Ralph, old boy,' Jack took his hand and shook it warmly, looking into the bright, observant eyes of his mentor. 'Ben sends you his love. He's coming to see you tomorrow.'

A small glint of recognition, like mother-of-pearl thrown up on a muddy beach, flickered momentarily in Ralph's eyes. 'Will he bring his dog?'

'They won't let Rover in, I'm afraid. They don't allow riff-raff like him in here.'

Ralph smiled and made a move as if to get up. Maybe he wanted to go for a walk. Jack jumped up to help him, catching as he did so the strong, acrid smell of stale urine. 'Sorry, Jack,' Ralph looked at him fearfully, as if Jack might lose his temper.

It was too much for Jack. Ralph was the one person he'd genuinely looked up to in his life and he couldn't bear the hurt and apology he now saw on the old man's face. Fury burned through him like a lit fuse. 'Nurse!' he shouted, not caring whether this was the appropriate term. The warden reappeared, her mouth a cat's bum of disapproval.

'Mr Tyler's had an accident and been left here to sit in it.'

'Naughty boy!' wheedled the warden as if Ralph were a particularly headstrong budgie. It made Jack want to throttle her and he was sure the other residents would assist him by running her over with their wheelchairs. 'He won't sit on a pad, that's the trouble.'

'Then surely it isn't beyond the wit of your staff to take him to the lavatory occasionally? I'm sure the fees should cover it.'

'It isn't always possible. Residents have to fit in. Do their bit. Don't they, Mr Tyler?'

For answer, another little trickle appeared on the floor at Ralph's feet.

Jack suppressed a smile. Ralph had never liked fitting in, his career had been founded on rebelling against stifling small-town attitudes. Jack remembered the sticker he'd had on his car. Question Authority. It broke Jack's heart to think this was the only way he could do so now.

Jack had to fight the impulse to bundle Ralph into his car and take him away from here this very second. Instead he told him that Ben would be coming tomorrow. He waited until Ralph had been taken to his room to change then headed straight for the *Citizen*'s offices. He wanted to know from Fran's own mouth what she thought she was doing putting Ralph here in the first place.

It was after six and the newsroom was finally quietening down by the time Jack got there. For the first time all day it was possible to hear what someone else was saying to you. Which was why, now that Fran no longer had an office of her own, Sean McGee and Stevie both heard every word of what Jack would have preferred to be a private conversation.

The only warning Fran had was that Elaine on reception had buzzed her to say, 'Someone's coming up to see you,' in such a meaningful way that it sounded like trouble.

'Jack, hello.'

But Jack was too angry to waste time on small talk. 'How could you do it to him?' he demanded furiously. It took Fran a moment to realize he was talking about her father. 'I've just come from the retirement home from hell. Ralph was sitting there while the rest of the zombies watched *Blue Peter*, and, Fran,' Jack's voice cracked with emotion, 'his trousers were soaking and no one in that poncy prison had even bloody well noticed! Whose idea was it to put him there in the first place?' There was no stopping Jack now. 'The good doctor's I suppose? He wouldn't want the bride's father being an embarrassment at the wedding now would he?'

'Jack, that's not fair. Laurence has been incredibly helpful.'

'Helpful to whom? My God, Fran, there has to be a better way of coping with Ralph. If he were my father I'd find a way of keeping him in the family or, God help us, what are families *for*?'

The hurt in Fran's eyes made him want to take it back. But he couldn't. The memory of Ralph's humiliation was too raw. He left as abruptly as he'd arrived. Fran watched him silently, eaten up by guilt. The picture he'd drawn was brutal and yet in her deepest conscience Fran knew that it rang true.

She sensed Stevie standing behind her. 'Jack's a hothead. Never capable of seeing a problem from more than one side.'

'He's got a point though, hasn't he? And do you know, Stevie, I actually believe him. He wouldn't let it happen to his own father.'

Sitting in the car, Jack's anger subsided into depression. It was easy for him to say. He didn't have a father with Alzheimer's who was wonderful but incontinent. Maybe he'd been romanticizing.

Fran sat staring at her typewriter, thinking about Jack's words. The only alternative to Tawny Beeches she could see was that Ralph came and lived in her flat with a carer until she and Laurence were married. Then he would have to move in with them for a while.

'I thought we might lay the presents out here on this oak table in the hall.' The evening sun shone through the open front door, illuminating the little sign Camilla had made saying 'Wedding Presents'. A huge bunch of lilies dominated the empty space, apart from the lone gift strategically placed at one end.

Fran wondered for a moment if her own mother minded how Camilla was subtly taking over the arrangements. She hadn't said anything but perhaps Phyllis was simply daunted by Camilla's grande dame manner, or maybe the business with her father had hit her harder than she liked to admit, so she was happy to leave it all to someone else.

'Yes,' Fran tried her best to play the good daughter-in-law. 'That looks terrific, Camilla.'

It was actually happening! In three weeks she'd be married. The reality hit her with a sudden shocking force. Even trying on her wedding dress had seemed like a game or a film playing in her head. This – saucepans wrapped in gold paper with a matching label – was real.

'Feeling excited yet?' Laurence squeezed her hand. 'I know I am. Only three weeks to go now and you'll be Mrs Westcott.'

Fran couldn't fail to be touched by the pride in Laurence's voice. Being engaged suited him. He had softened somehow, and some of the fine stress lines had disappeared from his handsome face, leaving him looking younger, more optimistic. She imagined this was how he must have looked when he was just starting out in medicine, before the burden of so many people's sadness had been laid on his shoulders, and the inevitable sense of failure set in that he couldn't give a baby to each and every one of them.

'Of course I'm excited.' She avoided Camilla's eye, hoping she hadn't recounted their conversation on the telephone. 'I just wish I wasn't quite so busy.'

'Nonsense,' Laurence teased, looking ludicrously boyish and attractive. 'You love it! You'd be bored to tears if all you had to think of was wedding lists and reception lines. Leave that to the experts who really enjoy it, eh, Ma?'

'Camilla, I don't want to be tactless but do you think you could make a point of including my mother? She may be finding my father's illness harder than she lets on.'

'Of course, dear.' Camilla flicked her neat white hair, so beautifully cut it put Fran's own to shame, 'though every time I try she seems to be out at bridge. How *is* your poor father, by the way?' Her tone of slight distaste made it sound as if her father had a mild case of leprosy.

'Well, actually, I need to talk to Laurence about that. Tawny Beeches isn't working out. I'm going to have to move him.'

Laurence was listening intently. 'Francesca, darling, I think that would be a serious mistake.' He took her hand and pulled her into the sofa's chintzy depths. 'I know how much you love your father, so I've never dwelt on what may happen to him, but you need to understand how serious it is.' His tone rang with sympathy, almost like a vicar's talking lovingly about the perils of sin. She could see why his patients did whatever he said. 'He's not too bad now. He knows you sometimes. He may behave oddly but it's just about acceptable. But I'm afraid it'll get worse. His personality will change. And when that happens he won't recognize you any more. You'll lose him completely. Yet he'll be totally demanding. He'll take over your life, Francesca, and though it won't be his fault, he'll give you nothing in return.'

'Laurence, I know you're trying to help, but Jack Allen visited him today and he was sitting in the lounge with urine running down his legs. No one had even noticed. Laurence, he hates it there! Of course it's going to be hard, I understand what you're telling me, but I know a wonderful woman who will look after him.' Her eyes latched onto his, knowing how difficult her request would be for him. 'Laurence, I want him to come and live with us when we're married. Just for a while, at least.'

'Francesca,' Laurence's eyes had narrowed at the mention of Jack, 'you know that's a ludicrous idea. It wouldn't even be best for him. Believe me, he's better off with the experts.'

'The experts who leave him watching children's television in the trousers he's wet himself in!' Fran blazed, realizing the words she was using were Jack's own.

'Francesca, it isn't as simple as you think. We can't simply take your father in just like that. I respect that you love Ralph, but we can't cope with him living with us. And anyway,' the sudden coldness in Laurence's voice chilled her, 'what is Jack Allen doing getting involved in all this?'

'He was just being kind. He cares about Dad.'

'And I don't?'

Was that what she really meant? She'd thought Laurence would make such a good father because he devoted his life to trying to help people, but was it possible Laurence only cared about humanity on a grand scale at the expense of being able to put up with real messy individual weakness?

She remembered the other thing Jack had said, that looking after each other was what families were for. But then had Jack really looked after his own family? Having an affair and losing your child wasn't exactly a caring pattern of behaviour.

'I'm sorry, Laurence, whatever you think, I'm not leaving him in Tawny Beeches. As soon as the paper's launched I'm going to find an alternative.' Fran picked up her bag. 'I'm going now. I'm sorry, Camilla, but I'm not really hungry.'

'Well,' Camilla commented as she watched her daughter-in-law to be leave, 'she certainly likes getting her own way.'

Laurence wasn't listening. He was wondering instead how it was that Jack Allen had suddenly embroiled himself in Francesca's life and what he should be trying to do to get him out of it.

Next day, cocooned in the noise and bustle of the newsroom, in one of the rare moments when no one was shouting at her for a decision, Fran couldn't stop thinking about the DNA test and what it would reveal. If Jack turned out to be the father of the baby, then Laurence would back out immediately, she had no doubts about that. He was too sensitive about his own paternity to take on another man's child. But if Jack found she were carrying Laurence's baby, she had a feeling he might not stick a damaged goods label on her, but actually still go on loving her.

She couldn't stand the tension any longer; although they had said it might be three weeks, she was going to have to see if the results were ready yet. Sneaking off with her mobile, she dialled the number of the lab, conscious as she did so of an unsettling sensation. A few weeks ago she had been a hundred per cent sure she wanted the baby to be Laurence's. Now there was the tiniest element of doubt.

The result wasn't on the computer yet but, hearing the anxiety in her voice, the technician promised to go and look in today's arrivals. It was just possible it was in there.

Fran held on for five agonizing minutes until finally the technician came back to the phone.

'Miss Tyler? Your results are back.' Fran held her breath. This was the moment of truth. 'But I'm sorry to tell you the culture didn't take. I'm afraid we'll have to start again.'

'How long will that take?'

'About ten days, maybe two weeks. I'm really very sorry. This happens occasionally.'

Fran snapped her mobile off, her head racing. Maybe she should call the wedding off until she was sure of what was happening. She pictured Laurence's confused and angry face when he found she had betrayed him. She would lose him forever, a prospect she just couldn't risk facing.

Now, damn and blast it, she wouldn't get an answer until just before the wedding. She tried not to think about the strangeness of her reaction to this new development. Instead of the bitter disappointment she'd expected at being cheated of her answer, she felt a kind of relief.

Chapter 17

YOUR OLD TAT, proclaimed the giant poster plastered across the biggest hoarding in Woodbury, MAY BE SOMEONE ELSE'S TREASURE. SHIFT IT **FREE** IN THE FIRST ISSUE OF **FAIR EXCHANGE** THE LOCAL PAPER THAT COULD MAKE YOU MONEY.

Fran sat at the traffic lights, excited and exhausted, desperately hoping the risk she'd taken in buying that site and, even more, in going against everyone's advice and offering free ads in the first issue would pay off. The money men had said it was madness, but Fran's instincts, honed by years at the betting shop with her father, told her it was a risk worth taking. *Fair Exchange* had to disappear from the shelves from the very first issue so that the newsagents went on stocking it. If it didn't she'd have to spend her Sunday mornings picking up unwanted copies and the whole venture would fold, perhaps taking the *Citizen* with it.

There was no point worrying, she kept telling herself fruitlessly, because in two days the paper would launch and she'd know. And later this morning she had her other big gamble to reckon with: the publicity stunt she'd set up in the cathedral square at midday.

Three women who wanted to sell their wedding dresses would be walking down a mock aisle to the tune of the wedding march, each with a vast price tag on their frocks, to publicize the launch. Local and national press had been alerted and Eastwards Television had promised to send a crew.

But first she had to pay a lightning visit to her father to tell him that as soon as *Fair Exchange* was launched she was going to move him out of that awful place. He would just have to come to her flat for now and she would get the woman Henrietta knew to come in during the day. She didn't let herself think about the strain it would be running the papers, then going home to her father. It would just be temporary, until she found a better solution. Though what that would be, she hadn't the faintest idea.

It was too early for visitors and Tawny Beeches hadn't put on its glossy make-up yet. Breakfast time was clearly a war zone. The residents hadn't yet been drugged by sauna-like central heating and lethal injections of daytime television. They even seemed to retain some elements of their original personalities. An old lady in her dressing gown was steadfastly refusing porridge. 'Take away this muck,' she kept demanding imperiously. 'I want a crois-sant. With almond filling, dusted with sugar and nuts on the top. Now.'

Fran was staggered when she recognized this feisty ter-magent as the near-catatonic old dear who usually sat in her wheelchair only two inches from the TV set. Maybe she hated it and some particularly sadistic helper positioned her there deliberately.

Fran made a mental note to bring a bag of almond croissants on her next visit, even though the old lady would probably look at them in blank amazement and say, 'What's this muck? I want porridge.'

She searched around for her father and finally spotted him in the far corner, looking mutinous, his breakfast untouched. 'I'll eat it when my wife comes,' he was insisting with firm and stubborn dignity to a male care assistant.

'Well, that'll be a long wait because she hasn't been in this week, has she?' the man sneered.

Ralph's face collapsed into pain and panic. 'Hasn't she?' he asked. 'I can't remember.'

It was the gratuitous nastiness that did it. The impatience with a sad old man who was too confused to defend himself. Fran knew she couldn't leave him here for another moment, press conference or no press conference.

'Right, Dad,' she announced, briskly marching forwards, 'we're off on a little trip. You go out to the car while I do the packing.' She led him outside. 'I'll only be a moment. You get in and wait for me.'

It broke her heart that he had so little to pack. In two minutes the room was cleared of all his possessions and Fran ran down the stairs, dying to get away from Tawny Beeches and its veneer of gentility.

'His room will be snapped up, you know,' shouted the warden as Fran ran out of the front door. 'We have a waiting list as long as your arm. And you still have to pay a month's fees. I hope you know what you're doing, Miss Tyler.'

So did Fran.

Her father was already in the car, waiting patiently. Fran tried not to be thrown by the fact that he was facing backwards, straddling the front seat as if on horseback. 'Where are we going? Can we go to the races? We could take a picnic.'

For a moment panic set in. What the hell was she going to do now? Her brides would already be starting to arrive in the cathedral square.

Her father watched her, smiling and happy, totally trusting in her capacities. You're the parent now, she told herself and took three deep breaths.

What about Henrietta's? She tried to imagine Henrietta taking her father into her immaculate rectory, where the upholstery was winter-white silk, despite the presence of two children. Henrietta even had coasters for her coasters. No. Stevie would be a possibility except that she lived in a one-bedroomed flat. Then it came to her – Jack. Jack would know what to do. He felt just as she did about Ralph. Feverishly she dialled the *Express*. Jack, she was told firmly, was in conference. 'Then could you interrupt him, please? It's an emergency. Say it's Francesca Tyler and it's about my father. Thank you.'

Jack came on the line in a matter of seconds. 'Fran? What's the matter?' She could have hugged him for the urgency and concern in his voice.

'I've just sprung Dad from Tawny Beeches.'

'Good for you. That place stank. Literally and metaphorically.'

The next bit was harder. 'The trouble is I don't know where to take him now. I've got a press conference to launch the new paper in an hour.'

'I see.' As she waited for his reply, the enormity of what she was asking of him hit her. Jack had a paper to run too.

But Jack seemed entirely undaunted by the prospect of having Ralph thrust upon him. 'Right. This is what we'll do. I'll meet you at our house. Ben's in. He and Ralph are old friends. He'll look after Ralph until we sort this out. Thank God it's the holidays.' A brief pause. 'You did the right thing, Fran. It was a hellhole with plush upholstery. See you at the house.'

Fran relaxed for what seemed the first time in days. Ralph would love being with Ben.

Half an hour later they were settling Ralph into Jack's comfortable sitting room. 'What about the sofa?' Fran asked in a low voice. 'He has the occasional accident.'

Jack laughed. 'So does Wild Rover.' He clicked at the dog and it jumped up, nestling cosily next to Ralph. 'Now, let's see if we can find some racing on the telly.'

It turned out to be too early for racing. Ralph asked for the remote control and flicked through the channels until he hit upon an ancient repeat of The Wombles. 'There you are, Ben,' Ralph offered generously as if Ben were five not fifteen, 'you'll enjoy that.'

Ben winked and they both settled down happily, each with the excuse that they were putting up with Orinoco and Uncle Bulgaria for the other's sake.

Fran felt as if a vast rock had been lifted from her chest. The confused look had cleared from her father's face and he seemed totally at home. 'Thank you, Jack. You don't know what this means to me.'

'Yes, I do.' Jack opened the door of the sitting room for her. 'Ralph matters to me too. Now you'd better get to your press conference and I'd better get back to running the *Express*.' Murray Nelson had noted his departure with beady interest. 'Will you be all right, Ben?'

'We'll be fine. Maybe I'll teach Ralph to rollerblade later. Only a joke,' he reassured, catching sight of their faces.

'As a matter of fact,' Jack said as they were about to go out of the front door, 'there's someone I've got in mind who might be the perfect person to look after him. But it might take a little delicate negotiation.'

'Thanks for doing all this.' Without thinking, she put her hand on his arm. For the briefest of moments his eyes held hers and she thought he was going to say something.

Behind them the door opened. They sprang apart.

It was Ben. 'Thought you might like to know that Ralph just asked for a cup of tea and a copy of the *Racing Post*,' he informed them, 'so I think he must be recovering.' And then he disappeared, feeling, not for the first time, that where his father was concerned, his sense of timing left something to be desired.

The cathedral square was in complete chaos when Fran arrived. Two of the brides had turned up their noses at getting changed in the cathedral conveniences even though they were as clean as an operating theatre, and they were still looking distinctly unbridal in shorts and T-shirts. Stevie was trying to calm down a cathedral official who wanted to know who was responsible for this disgraceful performance on God's soil, and a posse of market traders who normally sold tasteful little snowstorm paperweights of the cathedral were whingeing noisily about disruption to their business. This happy scene was being witnessed by far more journalists than Fran could have dreamed possible. Most of them were gathered round the youngest and prettiest bride who was deep in negotiation with a tabloid photographer who had almost persuaded her to pose in a garter he'd produced from his pocket, showing more boob than Pamela Anderson.

Fran, trying to keep her temper, cut a swathe through the crowd and almost dragged the two recalcitrant brides into the Cathedral Arms to change. Five minutes later all was roughly as it should have been and the photographers happily snapped the bridal trio with their outsize price tags.

'Why are you selling the frock, darlin'?' demanded the cheekiest snapper of one of the brides. 'Didn't he live up to your expectations?'

'No,' she snapped back, 'but he did a better job than you would.'

The crowd of hacks hooted with laughter and snapped away for twenty minutes until one held out his watch. 'Gentlemen,' he announced, 'they have been open for one minute and twenty seconds.'

To Fran's intense relief they headed off in the direction of the Cathedral Arms, the youngest bride trailing along with them, still in her wedding dress. She looked as if she were having a better time than when she'd last worn it.

Through the crowds in the opposite direction, Fran caught sight of Laurence striding angrily towards her. 'Francesca, can I have a word?'

While Stevie organized the rolling up of the red carpet that had served as their aisle and arranged for the two remaining brides and their dresses to be ferried home, Fran led Laurence through the hot sun to the shady little bench in the middle of the small graveyard behind the cathedral. If she was to have a scene she'd rather it were witnessed by the peaceful dead than twenty nosy hacks.

'I've just had a call from the warden at Tawny Beeches. She was absolutely furious. I thought we'd settled this the other night. Your father needs proper care.'

'He also needs love. Something he most certainly wasn't getting there.'

Laurence's anger subsided. He touched her face, almost as if she were a member of a rare and soon-to-be-extinct species. 'It must be wonderful to love someone as much as you love your father.'

It was such an odd thing to say that it touched her deeply. Poor Camilla. It was clear that he didn't feel any such thing for her. Finding she wasn't his real mother seemed to have killed his trust and, along with it, his love. 'Could you ever love me like that? With that passionate, fighting force?'

It was a question she found almost painful to answer. Instead she held his hand to her cheek.

'I suppose you think I'm a self-centred bastard, not wanting your father to live with us.'

She knew this was an apology and smiled sadly in

recognition. 'And maybe I'm mad to think it's possible. Not to mention irresponsible.'

During the moment of silence that followed Fran felt the warm wind lifting her hair, exposing her still pale neck. Laurence leaned down and kissed it, as if he could somehow draw out of her the capacity to love so fiercely.

She hadn't seen it before, that despite all Laurence's achievements she was the strong one in this relationship. He seemed so godlike and sure of himself when he was at the hospital that it came as a shock finding the real man sometimes felt himself to be insubstantial. Curiously, the recognition of this made her feel closer to him than she had for weeks.

'So, what have you done with him? Plonked him back on your mother's doorstep?'

'Actually,' Fran hesitated, not sure how he would take this, 'he's at Jack Allen's.'

Laurence's head shot up as if someone had put a firecracker in his pocket. 'What the hell is he doing there?' The warmth and tenderness in his voice were frozen to ice.

'He and Ben, Jack's son, are good friends.' She looked at him curiously. 'Why do you mind so much?'

'Because he's got nothing to do with your father. Besides,' he avoided Fran's searching gaze, 'I don't like the man.'

'I'm sorry, Laurence, but my father's happy there, and that's where he's staying until I find a permanent solution.'

'Suit yourself.' It was as if something had closed up in Laurence. 'Now I must get back to the clinic. I'll send the warden at Tawny Beeches a bunch of flowers. She did me a favour getting him in at such short notice.'

'Fine,' Fran agreed, adding under her breath, 'just make them dead ones.'

Fran woke on the day of *Fair Exchange*'s launch, her senses reeling with excitement, spiced liberally with fear. What if she'd been wrong and no one was interested? She thought of all the work and investment and buried her face in the pillow. Then she remembered how her father had launched the *Citizen* almost singlehanded on the tiniest of budgets. Everything worth doing carried a risk.

She dragged a red suit from her wardrobe to make her look braver than she felt and ran down to the newsagent on the corner. Surveying the shelves with reined-in breath, disappointment bit into her. There wasn't a single copy on the bottom shelf next to the local papers where she'd expected to see it. Maybe they hadn't stocked it after all. She drew on all her courage and asked if they had a copy of *Fair Exchange*.

The man shook his head and Fran's heart plummeted.

'Too late, love.' He went back to stocking his shelves with Silk Cut. 'They walked out in the first fifteen minutes. Someone's on to a good thing.'

Fran bit her lip and restrained herself from kissing him.

'Jack, a moment of your precious time, please.' Murray Nelson pounced on Jack as he arrived at work, and pulled him into his office. The older man, in his shiny brown suit, made Jack think of a squirrel with its eye on a particularly glossy nut. Him.

'This new venture of Francesca Tyler's. I just sent my secretary out to get hold of a copy.'

'Good idea. And what's it like?' The truth was Jack had purloined one of the earliest copies and thought it a clever idea, though in his view it was too early to be sure of its viability. The ads in it had been free after all and she must have spent a lot of money on the first issue. The next few weeks would be make or break. Still, it was an incredible coup to get the newsagents to stock it without even giving them a cut.

'The point is, my secretary couldn't find one. Not in the whole of Woodbury. And do you know what the print run was? Forty thousand copies! *Forty thousand*, Jack. And how many have we been shifting of our very own free paper, the one we go to the bother of delivering through people's own front doors at enormous expense?'

'Thirty thousand.'

'So why didn't we think of the idea she had instead of employing all these expensive journalists?'

'Because we're a newspaper, Murray. And frankly if I'd tried to flog you the idea of a venture designed to swap three-piece suites for superannuated Action Man collections you'd have laughed me out of court. So that shows how wrong we can both be. Have you ever noticed how everyone says something's a good idea when someone else has taken the risk?'

'Well, you'd better pull your bloody socks up. And now I suppose all our small ads will disappear overnight, thanks to Miss Tyler.'

'You'd be surprised. What Francesca's done is create an entirely new market. It's the old adage: give people what they didn't know they wanted. We may keep even our level of ads.'

'I bloody well hope so, for your sake, Jack. The share-holders will be asking a few questions otherwise. Let's just hope we hold our heads up at the Regional Press Awards tomorrow. If we haven't got sales, by God we need kudos.'

For the first time in his working life, Jack had forgotten all about the awards. Murray Nelson, he knew, considered the award to be the property of the *Woodbury Express*. He drew no comfort at all in the knowledge that their closest rival this time round would be the *Woodbury Citizen.*

As soon as the brides had been matched and dispatched, Fran had to get started on the next issue. This time the ads would have to be paid for. She had a vision of walking into the *Citizen* building and finding the telesales office like the *Marie Celeste*, its phones as silent as an old maid's. She could hardly believe it when what actually greeted her were noise, confusion and chaos as the public queued up to part with their money for issue no. 2. The only people who had any complaints was Sean McGee, who couldn't get his bike past all the pushchairs on the stairs and Keith, the sports editor, who complained that the old biddies in the queue kept on saying, 'Hello, darlin', got any hot tips for us?'

It was after six before Fran called round to Jack's house to see that Ralph was all right.

'He's in the kitchen,' Ben announced, 'making us both tea.'

'For God's sake be careful,' Fran panicked, grateful that Ralph was being allowed so much independence but terri-fied he'd burn the house down.

'You don't think I should have let him start a chip pan, then?' Ben enquired.

'Oh my God, Ben!'

'Only joking. He's making cheese and pickle sandwiches.'

Fran laughed. It was so wonderful to feel Ralph was part of a family again, even if it was only for the short term. 'Ben?'

'Yup?'

'You'd better check they're not washing-up liquid and pickle sandwiches. Dad gets a bit confused.'

'No probs,' Ben assured her. 'As long as it's Fairy Liquid and not one of those cheaper brands.'

'Will he be all right for tonight? I've got someone ringing me tomorrow who can probably look after him at my flat.'

'Fine. Dad's made him up a bed in the study. He seems to like it there.'

She hesitated a moment. 'Is Jack here? I'd like to thank him myself.'

Her face had gone red, Ben noted with satisfaction, just like his own did when he asked a girl to dance. He must remember to tell his dad. 'I'm afraid he's not back. Some business dinner. He rang to check on Ralph ten minutes ago.'

'Are you sure you can cope? He can behave unpredictably sometimes. Wander off.'

'Dad said to lock the doors.'

'Francesca, darling, how lovely to see you.'

Fran turned in disbelief. Her father stood smiling by

the door of the kitchen wearing a blue and white striped butcher's apron. But it wasn't the father of recent months. Confused. Frightened. Looking as if he'd bought a ticket for Victoria and ended up on Mars. This was her real father, the one who'd made her childhood so special. She knew enough about his illness to understand that this was probably an illusion, a small step in the right direction, which could be chased in moments by rapid decline, but she wouldn't think of that now.

Instead she hugged him. 'Sorry I'm late. Working on the second edition of *Fair Exchange*.'

'Of course. How could I forget?' He sounded so normal it was uncanny, just as he had at the trust meeting. 'How is it going?'

'Wonderful. Copies were walking out on their own. I don't want to tempt fate but I think it could be a real success.'

'Congratulations. You deserve it.' He glinted at her mischievously. 'Your mother will be very disappointed.'

'Thanks, Dad.'

She remembered something that would take him back to his own days of glory. 'Regional Press Awards tomorrow. Keep your fingers crossed for me.'

And once again her real father answered. 'I will. You deserve to win this time. You really do. Are you staying for dinner? We're having a lovely casserole.'

Ben and Fran exchanged stunned glances and moved as one towards the kitchen.

On the worktop, assembled neatly enough to impress any television cook, was a row of carrots, onions, two potatoes, garlic, pepper and salt and two freshly opened tins of Wild Rover's rabbit supper.

'Thanks, Ralph,' Ben said, politely pointing him at the fridge, 'but what I really would prefer is a cheese and pickle sandwich.'

The medieval carvings of the Cathedral Court hotel were hidden under a vast banner announcing the Regional Press Awards and all the great and the good of the county plus a large slice of civic freeloaders had squashed themselves into the too-small room for the event. The organisers were obviously of the school that says a really good party is one where it takes you half an hour to push your way to the bar. Across about two hundred heads, Fran spotted Jack Allen and waved just as she took in the gorgeous and gamine Miriam hanging on his arm. Why was it that women who had giant eyes and tiny bones always had a haircut that made them look like a cross between Demi Moore in *Ghost* and Jean Seberg as Joan of Arc. Attractively victimish, until they suspected someone of being after their man, then complete tigresses.

Fran felt a disgraceful flush of pleasure when Jack detached himself and pushed his way towards her. 'How's Dad?' she asked when he finally made it to her side.

'Great fun. I think I might give his cooking a miss though. He put coleslaw in my tea this morning.'

Fran wanted to say how moved she'd been to see Ralph back in a family, and thank Jack again for his generosity. She might have added how wrong she'd been about Jack himself – the assumption she'd jumped to that he must be a bad father when the truth seemed to be the reverse. Over the last few days she'd had the chance to see him and Ben together, and their closeness was entirely genuine. She'd even come to suspect that the rumours of Jack's womanizing might be spread by women he'd rejected, not taken advantage of. In fact she'd been wrong about Jack Allen in a whole variety of ways.

'Have you heard any hints about today?' she asked, suddenly embarrassed at her own volte-face about his character flaws.

Jack, however, seemed faintly uneasy, but perhaps she was imagining it.

The major domo from the town hall, a man who looked far grander and more impressive than the mayor himself, began to get their attention for the award ceremony.

She sipped her glass of orange juice, knowing it would be the last she got in this squeeze until the awards had been announced. According to the programme, theirs was fifth on the list.

After the first couple of announcements everyone was wishing that the major domo *was* the mayor, and by the time he'd got through four sets of nominations, each spiced with its own bad joke, Fran's palms were damp and sweaty with tension. She let herself imagine the moment when she handed it over to her father, and pictured the pride shining through his eyes.

Finally it was their turn. 'And now, for outstanding regional reporting, we have two contenders, both as it happens from Woodbury. The *Woodbury Express* . . .' A loud cheer from Murray Nelson and the *Express* contingent.

'. . . and the *Woodbury Citizen*. This, I'm instructed to say was the hardest category of all.'

Come on, Fran willed him, spit it out!

'One of the papers came up with perhaps the year's most outstanding and sustained investigation . . . and that was . . .' he paused dramatically. Fran could almost see him put his hand to his ear as if he expected the audience to shout contributions. '. . . The *Woodbury Citizen* for its exposé of Wadey's Buses.' The applause drowned him out and Fran almost laughed out loud with relief. This was just what they needed. It would make her father happy in perhaps the last year he would be able to appreciate such things, and surely it would convince her mother that it was too good a paper to sell.

But the awful man was still droning on, looking more subdued now as if aware of an unexpected faux pas. 'However, the judges felt that the final *coup de grâce* in the investigation was provided by its rival, the *Woodbury Express*, and it is to that paper that they have finally given the award.'

Fran had to hang onto herself. She felt suddenly faint and sick and the room began to swirl about. Someone behind her caught her just in time. She edged her way through the throng towards the door, not caring what anyone thought. Surely Jack wouldn't calmly walk up there and accept the award. Not when he knew how many painstaking months they'd spent on that story, providing the dull digging for his fizzle of fireworks.

But calm was an understatement. Jack looked as if he were positively enjoying himself, like a schoolboy hugging a secret treat.

She had reached the exit by now. Jack was on the stage, his hand being wrung by the mayor. Fran gave him one more chance.

'First of all,' Jack didn't look shamefaced or apologetic. In fact he positively twinkled, the rat, especially as he caught the eye of the adoring Miriam who was practically spraining her delicate little wrists clapping, 'I'd like to thank the judges for what must have been a very tough choice indeed.'

Surely he was going to at least say that the *Citizen* had laid the groundwork? But if he did wouldn't she find that hideously patronizing? Like a congratulation for coming second when everyone knew coming second didn't count. In the event, she needn't have worried because Jack didn't mention the *Citizen*. He simply accepted the award and congratulated the reporter who'd come up with the wheeze.

Fran couldn't believe it. She seemed to have an endless capacity to be wrong about Jack Allen. She stumbled out, not caring how her sudden departure would seem. Too bad if they all thought it poor form. She had to get out before she really did faint.

So she wasn't in the room when Jack Allen unexpectedly stayed put on the platform and added that there was one more thing he wanted to say before he gave up the microphone.

'I don't know how many of you in this room have been lucky enough to have a mentor, someone older than yourself, someone who resisted the opportunity to make you look small because you were new and young and you thought you knew everything when the truth was you

316

knew damn all. A man or woman you could respect because they were principled, inspiring, wise, and most of all because they believed in a vision of journalism that was going to change the world – even if it was only in small ways. Ladies and gentlemen, I have been lucky enough to work for such a talent . . .' His eyes raked the room as if looking for one face.

Standing at the back, a Remy Martin in his hand, Murray Nelson stood tall on his size-seven feet and decided Jack Allen wasn't as bad as he'd branded him.

'For me Ralph Tyler, the founder of the *Woodbury Citizen*, was that man. The *Citizen* set standards of journalism in this town and the *Express* could only race to keep up with them. Ralph can't be with us today because he is suffering from the early stages of Alzheimer's disease.' There was a gasp from those in the audience who hadn't known. Jack's voice tightened as if he were struggling with strong emotion. 'But he would have enjoyed it immensely if he had been. Ralph loved awards.' Jack paused for a moment. 'That is, unless he lost them and then he declared that they weren't worth the certificate they were written on.' A laugh of recognition rippled through the hall from everyone who knew him. 'Ralph Tyler is a man of honour and inspiration and I suspect we won't see his like again, so it's to him that I dedicate this Eastern Counties Regional Press Award. Thank you, ladies and gentlemen.'

The applause went on for five minutes as people remembered the newspaperman they'd known and loved. Even a hardbitten hack or two had to pretend to sip their drinks in case they gave themselves away by an embarrassing sniff or tear.

Stevie, crushed up against the far corner, handily close to the bar, rubbed her nose on the sleeve of her cardigan and wished to hell that Francesca had been there to hear it.

But Fran was speeding recklessly out of the car park, convinced that her original opinion of Jack Allen as an ambitious, self-serving womanizer had been the right one.

Still in the hall, Stevie told herself firmly that she was a sentimental old turkey, gobbling up every little bit of recognition on behalf of her beloved Ralph. The irony was that even if the old Ralph, her Ralph, had been there, he would have hated listening. He always said that any achievement worth marking showed in the paper. But he would have understood Jack's need and desire to say it, and would have, in the end, accepted it with a modest twist of the lips.

She was making her way through the crowd to tell Jack this, and thank him anyway on her own behalf for describing Ralph's personality so vividly, when Murray Nelson got to him first.

The generosity – not to mention foolhardiness – of Jack's gesture suddenly came home to Stevie. She hadn't considered how his employers at The Express Group might take this spontaneous accolade for their greatest rival.

But Murray Nelson was smiling, reminding Stevie of a poisoned dwarf pretending to be genial. 'Congratulations, Jack, on a heap of crap. Listening to you up there I realized one thing. That kind of journalism's finished. It's Ralph Tyler's daughter who's got the right idea, not the old man. No one's interested in newspapers that carp on about how wicked the council is – or even the bus firm. You may have got the award today but that's because it's handed out by other dinosaurs like you, all in the sacred name of journalism. It took Francecsa Tyler to show me that the public doesn't give a stuff about reporting. They want to shop and spend. Francesca Tyler's new magazine is the future, not papers like the *Express*. I've decided to withdraw our offer for the *Citizen* and try to buy her freebie magazine instead.'

'For God's sake, Murray.' Jack was tired and irritated and he loathed his boss's capriciousness. 'You're making too much of this. *Fair Exchange* has only been on the streets five minutes. It may only last ten.'

'You can't cope with it, can you, Jack? The idea that something like that might outsell your precious paper, with its campaigns and its news values?'

Jack had had enough. He refused Murray's offer of a lift and walked back to the paper to give himself time to think. Opposite the hotel, the afternoon sun illuminated the intricate carving of the cathedral, its gargoyles standing like cutouts against the deep blue of the sky. The news vendor outside shouted a greeting but none of these things gave Jack his usual pleasure. For every delight he'd taken in working on a paper in this town – the extraordinary beauty of the place, the fact that he knew almost everyone on the streets and thought he understood what they cared about, that he ran a paper that gave them a voice – none of this blanked out Murray's words. *Was* he jealous of Fran's vision, her capacity to come up with an idea that might well outsell local papers and even replace them?'

Outside the cathedral primary school the lollipop lady smiled and called out a greeting. Jack pulled himself together. The lollipop lady herself was there because the *Express* had campaigned for her presence after the death of a child on his way home from school. Fran's magazine might have met a new need but there would always be a role for that kind of campaigning in a town like this. And he had a feeling that Fran knew that herself even if Murray Nelson didn't.

In spite of the heat of the afternoon, Jack walked briskly back, feeling like an alcoholic waiting for opening time. He needed a shot of the newspaper atmosphere he loved so much to put him back on course: two parts chaos to one part panic, spiced with a dash of intense excitement, stirred up with adrenaline, and flavoured with satisfaction.

He held the award high as he walked through the wall of sound that was the newsroom. 'Congratulations, everybody. We won!'

Still mid-telephone calls, the reporters in the sports department marked their pleasure by starting a Mexican wave which rippled joyously through the features desk, via the news reporters right up to the subs at the far end. Jack laughed, almost restored to his old optimism. Whatever Murray Nelson might think, there was nothing quite like the atmosphere of a newsroom.

'Congratulations, everyone. Come six o'clock, drinks are on me.'

'I think you might have to make that tomorrow.' Jack looked round in surprise to find Miriam leaning on his door. 'Your son rang in a bit of a state. He wants you to get home as soon as you can.'

'Did he give you any reason why?' Jack's thoughts went immediately to Ralph. He'd probably been damn stupid leaving him in Ben's care. Unfair to Ben as well. Ralph might be fine for ninety-five per cent of the time, but what if his confusion had turned into something harder to deal with?

'No. Just that someone unexpected had arrived and he thought you really ought to see them.'

'Right. I'd better get over there.'

Jack tried to think who such a visitor might be. Fran's mother, perhaps, finally deciding that she ought to play a more wifely role and look after Ralph? Fran herself? It was useless to speculate since he'd be there in ten minutes.

Ben was standing outside the house waiting for him, wearing a tracksuit with bare feet and an anxious expression. Instead of a mature fifteen, he suddenly struck Jack as looking like a small boy in adult's clothes and Jack's heart turned over. He should never have forced so much responsibility on the boy. What if something serious had gone wrong?

'Dad. Thank God you're here.'

'Ben, you look terrible. Whatever's happened? It's Ralph, isn't it? If it was, it wasn't your fault. I shouldn't have left you alone. I must be mad.'

'It isn't Ralph, Dad. Come inside.'

Jack pushed open the front door to find it jammed with suitcases. There were five, all expensive looking in dark green with tan leather trim, from a vast trunk-like case down to a small vanity bag. They reminded Jack briefly of one of those conveyor belts of gifts on gameshows, except that those were cheap and these would have cost an arm and several legs. Who the hell did they belong to?

'Whose are all these bags in the hall?' he shouted to Ben.

But before Ben had a chance to answer, a voice behind him made Jack swing round in shock. It was one he hadn't heard for seven years, and even now it felt like a knife turning in a raw, fresh wound.

Chapter 18

'Hello, Jack.'

Carrie leaned on the door of the sitting room, her dark eyes fixed on Jack's. 'How lovely to see you. You haven't changed a bit.'

It was she, of course, who hadn't changed. She was as exotically beautiful as ever, her eyes soulful and vast in her small face, which the faintly boyish haircut she favoured deliberately accentuated. She had always had the look of an Italian madonna, pale olive skin, dark brown eyes, a deceptive air of serenity. But it was the hint of something deeply unmadonna-like beneath, a hidden fire, that had driven men mad, him included.

'You don't look very brown.'

God knows why he'd said something so ludicrously trivial.

Carrie smiled a small smile, enjoying his discomfiture. 'It's winter there now. That's why I had to get away.'

He let it pass that there had been seven winters since

she'd left that day. Even now he could hardly bear thinking about it. Carrie would be here because she had a reason and being Carrie she would tell him what it was only when she wanted to.

'How are you, Jack?' The almost treacly concern in her voice infuriated him. What did she expect him to say? I suffered deeply but time heals in the end? Carrie had always had the capacity to overlook anything unpleasant, even – or perhaps especially – when it concerned herself. At first it had made her an enchanting companion. Always happy, always positive. Until he'd realized it was only her own happiness that she believed in pursuing.

'I'm fine,' Jack replied briskly, avoiding her eyes. Carrie's extraordinary brand of beauty and the vulnerability she could switch on and off were powerful weapons even after all this time. With Carrie it was too easy to forget the acid that bubbled under the marble, even when it had burned you once.

He tried to summon up the anger that had sustained him, kept him sane, but it was beyond his reach.

'I've got a surprise for you. In here,' Carrie nodded towards the sitting room, as if instinctively knowing which card to play. She stepped back, revealing a beautiful child, cast almost identically in the image of her mother, even down to the dark green velvet shirt that so flattered Carrie's colouring.

Jack's pulse raced. 'Louise?'

He wondered painfully if his daughter would ignore him or nod politely as if at some passing stranger. Instead she hurtled across the room. 'Dad?' There was a sadness in her young eyes that made Jack want to throttle Carrie. What story of cruelty and abandonment had Carrie spoon fed Louise during the years she had denied him access to his own daughter? Louise had every right to hate him. Instead, miraculously she seemed to forgive him.

Jack picked up her small body and held it so tight that neither of them could breathe. It was all he could do to fight back the tears. That and the sight of Ben's face.

Ben stood hunched on the periphery of the scene. This was his mother, for God's sake, and yet she seemed hardly to have acknowledged his existence. It was as if Ben stood outside the family circle, knowing that this event would change their cosy world forever, and not at all sure it would be for the better. Where Louise seemed able to forgive, Ben, in years so much closer to adulthood and maturity, was not.

Jack held out a hand to him. 'Here's your big brother. Have you two introduced yourselves?'

'Just a minute ago.' He held out his hand in forlorn formality. 'How was the flight?'

'I'm Louise, only please don't call me that. I hate it. Everyone I like calls me Lou. And the flight was crap. They kept treating me as if I was a baby and I'm seven.'

Ben laughed, his shoulders relaxing and losing some of their hostility. 'I can see that would be tough.'

'By the way,' Carrie arranged herself on the sofa, totally at home, tucking her legs underneath her in the childlike way Jack remembered so well, 'who's that strange old man in his dressing gown typing away in your study? Don't tell me you've opened a home for distressed newspaperfolk?

That would be so like you.' There was a caress in her voice Jack found both alluring and alarming.

'Don't laugh at him, Mum,' Louise chided seriously. 'Ben already told us. He's called Ralph and he's got Oldtimers' Disease.'

Jack smiled at his daughter, love mixed with relief. Being brought up by Carrie obviously hadn't blighted her. She seemed to have a natural tact, far outweighing her mother in sensitivity. Perhaps, Jack thought, the pain hitting him again, given Carrie's capacity for immaturity, she'd been forced to be the parent, not the child.

'Want to come and see the house?' Ben invited. 'I expect the adults have plenty to talk about.'

He didn't, Jack noticed, say Mum and Dad.

'So,' Jack carefully avoided the sofa and sat opposite Carrie, in the armchair, 'how long are you staying in England?'

'As long as I like. To be frank I've had it with Australia. As a matter of fact,' Carrie flooded him with her lagoon-blue gaze, 'I wondered if perhaps we could stay here.' She saw the slight flinch in Jack's reaction and rushed onwards. 'Only for a few days of course, until we find something permanent.'

For a moment Jack was paralysed by a storm of conflicting emotions. Furious anger, corrosive and dangerous, washed through him at the way Carrie had disappeared and stolen his daughter, not even telling him where she was, always promising to let him see Louise, then disappearing again before he could. And then there was Ben. How could any mother cut herself off from her child with such apparent ease? It was as if she were punishing him for choosing Jack by denying his whole existence.

Carrie, not usually attuned to other people's emotions, sensed some of this. 'I'm sorry, Jack. I think maybe I went mad for a while. I couldn't cope with my own hurt, let alone theirs. I was a bad mother. I had to get away for my own sanity.'

'It's Ben you should be apologizing to.'

Carrie played her trump card. 'That's why I wanted to stay here. So I could get to know him, try and make it up somehow.'

Jack knew he was beaten. How could he refuse Ben the chance to spend time with his mother? But he was damned if he was going to let Carrie think she could slip back into his life so easily.

'All right,' he conceded finally, 'I'll book a room for myself at the Cathedral Arms.'

He ignored the flash of disappointment in her eyes. 'You don't need to do that, Jack.'

Jack stared ahead. He knew exactly what a picture of soft seduction Carrie could be when she wanted something badly enough and didn't quite trust himself.

Then he remembered Ralph. She would just have to put up with him. That would be an interesting test of her commitment. Carrie wasn't in the habit of putting herself out for anyone. 'I'm afraid Ralph will have to stay. I can't chuck him out at such short notice. He's confused enough already and he likes it here.'

'You mean you're leaving me with that mad old man?'

'Ben will look after him. It's only temporary anyway.

He's perfectly harmless. The worst he'll do is make you a cup of tea with coleslaw instead of milk. You do have to stop him wandering off in the middle of the night, though.'

Carrie's face was a picture.

As soon as she got back from the awards, Fran got on the phone. She'd come to a decision. She was too furious with Jack for walking off with her prize to leave her precious father with him. She had to find someone proper to look after him and move him into her own flat. After the wedding, if Laurence still didn't see sense, she'd confront the future then.

Thank God the woman Henrietta had suggested was indeed available and Fran could go ahead with her plan to move him to her own place tomorrow. It was a pity because he'd liked it at Jack's but the solution had only been a temporary one anyway. Ben had his own life to lead and couldn't devote himself to Ralph for ever.

She was busy making a shopping list and working out what her father would need when Stevie came back.

'You were a long time,' Fran accused. 'I thought you would have followed me out when Jack Allen had the bloody nerve to pick up *our* award. Or have you been bad-mouthing him in the bar? If so I hope your insults were fittingly disgusting.'

'I could hardly rubbish the hero of the hour, could I, not after the tribute he'd just made to your dad, now could I?'

'What tribute?'

'Oh, Francesca, I wish you'd been there. He dedicated the award to Ralph for founding real journalism in this town and said how sorry he was that Ralph couldn't be there because of his illness. Honestly, Fran, there were hacks there so hardbitten they'd get their grannies to pose topless, and Jack had them brushing the tears from their eyes. Everyone in the bar had their own Ralph Tyler story. It was amazing.' Stevie sniffed into her hankie, her nose redder than Rudolf's. 'Murray Nelson was absolutely livid.'

Fran was trying to come to terms with this new turn of events when Elaine put her head round the door. 'We've just had your friend Henrietta on the phone, hopping up and down she's so cross. Apparently you're supposed to be with her trying on the bridesmaids' dresses and she says if you don't come soon she'll buy the white leather ones with a feather trim and matching thigh boots.'

'My God! I was supposed to meet Sophie and Lottie half an hour ago! Could you supervise these ads for the Personal Section? Some of them are so outrageous I think we'd better find out if they're legal. "Partner wanted for mutual piercing and fun" . . . in Woodbury?!!'

She grabbed her satchel bag and tore through the newsroom, colliding with Sean McGee who was carrying his bike up the stairs. 'I don't suppose I could borrow that?' she asked. 'I've got to be somewhere half an hour ago and I'll never find anywhere to park.'

'Fine. But it isn't the Tardis. And don't forget to take the front wheel off when you park it. It's been nicked twice already.'

Riding a bike might be a skill you kept forever, but Fran turned out to be the exception that proved the rule. It was another fifteen minutes before she arrived at the exclusive wedding dress shop, shaken, stirred and clutching the filthy front wheel of Sean's precious mountain bike.

'Fran! What do you look like?' screeched Henrietta. 'Your beautiful dress is ready and you arrive looking as if you've been under a juggernaut. Look, isn't it fabulous?' She pointed to a sophisticated ivory satin frock hanging on a scented silk hanger next to the floor-length mirror. An assistant had thoughtfully added a simple tiara to complete the arrangement.

All it needs now, Fran thought, panic taking over her chest as if a mad shiatsu teacher were jumping up and down on it, is a bride. Me.

Henrietta took the wheel away and gave it to a perfectly groomed assistant who couldn't have been more shocked if she'd been handed the Aids virus. Then she led Fran to the tiny ladies' loo to wash her filthy hands. Finally the dress was held up in front of her.

'I take it all back,' breathed Henrietta. 'You don't look a bit like a Carmelite nun. Not even Maria in *The Sound of Music*. You look wonderful. Laurence is a lucky man.'

For answer Fran let out a distinct sob.

'Francesca, for God's sake.' Down-to-earth Fran didn't behave like this. She left the histrionics to Henrietta. It had been Henrietta who'd gone into terminal decline every time a boyfriend had ditched her, and Henrietta who swore she'd never fall in love again, until five minutes later. Fran was the one who always baled her out with tea and sympathy or wielded the medicinal corkscrew. Henrietta had never, ever seen her friend burst into tears before. Especially over a man. 'What on earth's the matter?'

'Nothing much. It's just that I stole some of Jack's blood and went ahead and had that test.'

The two shop assistants stood stock still. They saw it all here. Panicky brides who thought they were making a mistake, grateful brides who knew they were lucky to be going down the aisle at all, practical brides who would rather be saving for a suite and grudged every non-returnable penny. But they'd never had a bride covered in oil who went round stealing blood.

'My God, Fran.' Henrietta clutched her friend. 'So you know which one's the father!'

'That's the whole problem. The culture didn't take and I'm still not going to know for another week.'

'But you're getting married then.'

'I know. And suddenly I'm not sure if I should be going through with it. What if Laurence isn't the baby's father? I could be walking down the aisle with the wrong man!' In her distress, Fran wiped her cheek, leaving a slash of oil all down one side of her face. The assistant shivered with panic in case it touched the dress. It sounded as if this perfect confection by Catherine Walker, representing hours of brilliant design and painstaking handstitching, might not find its way down the aisle after all. At least not on this mad woman. She discreetly removed it from Fran's hands and hung it back up.

'I mean,' Fran continued, the full awfulness of her situation hitting her, 'what if Jack's the father after all?'

'Look, Franny, it's really quite simple.' Henrietta was beginning to lose patience with her friend. 'Which one do you *want* to be the father?'

This was the question she hadn't ever allowed herself to really face. She closed her eyes and visualized the church, all decked out in Camilla's flowers, she heard the music, and forced herself to picture who she wanted to be waiting for her by the altar. It struck her that when you'd got as far as this, you had only one option left: to be scrupulously honest with yourself. So, which one was it?

Chapter 19

'I think, if I'm absolutely truthful . . .' Fran could hardly bring herself to make the admission even though this was Make Your Mind Up Time, '. . . although this seems entirely crazy . . . I think I'd prefer it if it were Jack's.'

'But I thought you loathed the man.' Henrietta was stunned but, being Henrietta, not speechless. 'You think he's overbearing and opinionated and selfish . . . not to mention faithless and, what was it, irresponsible. Oh and there was something about being a terrible father . . .'

Fran blushed. 'He is. But I seem to love him anyway. It's the thought of him holding my handbag when I was being sick that did it. I can't seem to get the image out of my mind.'

Henrietta sighed gustily. 'Go on, then. Though I have to say your taste in wooing techniques is somewhat bizarre.' She pushed her friend towards the door. 'Go and tell him, for God's sake. No point wasting everyone's time. Laurence will kill you. Your mother will have a nervous breakdown.

But they'll recover. Here.' She handed Fran the wheel back. 'On yer bike.'

As Fran dashed out of the shop, avoiding the assistant's wrathful expression, she heard Henrietta muttering darkly, 'Just as well we bought something that could be used again afterwards.'

Outside the shop, Fran could breathe freely for what seemed the first time in months. The sky, now that she viewed it from her new position of certainty, had never looked so blue. The stone of the cathedral glowed. Even the pigeons seemed to be hopping about cheerfully. Coo-coooo-coo, they congratulated, milling about her as she fitted Sean's wheel back on his bike. For once technology, usually a sworn enemy, was on her side and the nuts tightened up effortlessly. In ten minutes she would be at Jack's office. What she would do or say when she got there she didn't want to think about.

Recklessly, on pedals of love, Fran fought her way through the afternoon traffic, avoiding tourists, smiling at lorry drivers, stopping for children at a zebra crossing. It was all she could do not to sing. The world could at least be spared her off-key contributions.

By the time she reached the *Express,* Fran was grinning like a mad woman. It was all so easy. She would tell him she loved him and he would sweep her against his tweedy chest and they would bathe together in the light of a truth finally discovered.

When the receptionist told her Jack wasn't in, she thought it had to be a mistake. She already had the script worked out.

The receptionist, keeping a watchful eye on her odd appearance, agreed to call up his office. 'They're sending someone down now,' she soothed.

Fran waited, telling herself this was just a small setback. Jack would be here later.

Hearing a light step on the stairs, she turned and put down the copy of the *Express* she was pretending to read.

'Hello, Francesca, I'm afraid Jack's not coming back today.' To her immense irritation, instead of Jack's assistant the person facing her was Miriam.

Fran took the decision to be generous. After all, Miriam was going to be very annoyed with her. 'Oh. Right. When's he expected in then, do you know?'

'I've no idea.' Miriam paused, a small glint of satisfaction in her eyes. 'You see his wife's just come back to him from Australia. I should think they've got a lot to talk about after seven years, wouldn't you?'

Fran almost laughed out loud. Miriam had to have got it wrong. She had to have. Jack had never mentioned the slightest chance of a reunion with Carrie, in fact he'd barely mentioned his wife at all.

All Fran knew was that Carrie had left him seven years ago, furious at finding he was having an affair, so badly hurt that she'd taken their daughter with her. Her hand slipped unconsciously down to her burgeoning stomach. She couldn't even begin to imagine how terrible it would be to lose a child.

Panic slid a sharp knife between her ribs. If losing a child was so terrible, wouldn't regaining the same child be a powerful incentive for Jack and Carrie to get back together again? Now that she thought about it, Miriam's revelation had an appalling ring of probability.

As she got back onto Sean's bike she told herself that she'd know the truth soon enough.

She pedalled back to the *Citizen*'s offices and handed the bike to a startled Sean before snatching up her car keys and heading for Jack's.

Ben must have seen her coming because he was outside waiting for her, standing in front of the door as if to stop her going in, like a TV policeman protecting the scene of the crime. Who from, she wasn't sure. 'Hello, Francesca. Dad isn't here . . .' He was about to add that Jack had moved into the Cathedral Arms when the door opened behind him.

A slender woman with short dark feathered hair stood in the doorway. Fran had always thought Miriam exception-ally pretty, now she saw the real thing, the imitation dimmed like a candle against the sun. Carrie Allen was ravishing. Poor Miriam, she thought before the full impact of who else she ought to feel sorry for hit her, to be so comprehensively outshone.

'Well, Ben,' Carrie smiled, 'aren't you going to introduce us?'

'Francesca Tyler,' Ben mumbled, 'my mother.'

'What can we do for you?' asked Carrie, her manner so relaxed and at home it was as if she'd never left.

For a fraction of a second Fran was lost for words. *I've come to tell your husband I'm in love with him* might be the truth but lacked something in terms of social graces.

Sensing her distress, Ben came to her rescue. 'She's come to see Ralph. Ralph is Fran's father.'

Carrie studied Fran with sudden interest. So that was why the old man was here, because of the daughter. Of course. That explained – along with the anger and hurt which she'd expected and was sure she could deal with – Jack's curious air of reluctance to get anywhere near her, something she had found far more unsettling. Carrie needed to be up close for her charms to catch fire.

So Jack thought he was in love with Francesca Tyler. She would have to give this little hitch some thought.

Behind them a sudden commotion made them turn to find Ralph, still in his dressing gown, coming towards them with Wild Rover clinging playfully to the cord.

'Franny, darling,' boomed Ralph, 'what a pleasure to see you. What are you doing out here? Come inside, won't you? Can I offer you a cup of tea?'

'Of course,' seconded Carrie. with the faintest of frosts, 'do come in.'

A child, who was sitting on the sofa, jumped up to meet them. Not that introductions were necessary, she was so extraordinarily like her mother. 'This is my daughter Louise. Francesca Tyler.'

'You must be Ralph's daughter.' The child's impish smile was pure Jack. 'He often talks about you.'

'And you must be Louise.'

'Lou actually, I hate Louise.' Meeting her, Fran found it even more shocking that Jack could have ever risked losing this beautiful child and even more so that he had simply let her go without constantly trying to get her back. How must he have humiliated Carrie to make her act in so brutal a manner? A furious, kicking anger at Jack began to well up in her. To be so predictable. To behave in such a hackneyed male way. It was almost inconceivable. But here was the proof.

'Ralph's been teaching me how to play poker,' Lou boasted proudly.

'Hardly needs teaching,' chipped in Ralph. 'She's a natural. Like you were.'

Fran laughed. 'It's still one of the most useful skills I learned.'

'My daughter, Francesca,' Ralph announced with unexpected solemnity into the lull that fell on the conversation, 'is getting married soon and has asked me to give her away.'

'Congratulations.' Carrie's tone implied that madness clearly ran between generations. 'Who's the lucky husband?'

'His name is . . .' and with a look of sudden terror and confusion, Ralph looked to Fran for guidance. 'Franny darling, I'm so sorry. I've forgotten what his name is.'

'It's all right, Dad,' Fran took his arm and led him back to the study.

'As a matter of fact,' Ben announced, making Carrie jump because she'd almost forgotten his presence, 'his name is Dr Laurence Westcott.'

And he waited for the bomb to explode under his mother.

Chapter 20

After she'd tucked her father into bed, Fran drove away miserably. She couldn't face going back to the paper, and all plans to move her father had been scuppered for today at least. After forgetting Laurence's name he had descended into tearful confusion and it was obvious even to Carrie that a move was out of the question.

Strangely, Carrie hadn't seemed to mind the imposition at all. She'd simply stood there looking like an automaton.

Today had made one thing clear. The sensible thing would be to forget Jack. Meeting his child had convinced her of that. Brave little Lou had weathered one storm with surprising strength but two might sink her.

It was one of those early evenings when even the Pope himself would have been hard put to stay at his desk and the whole town had emptied itself out into pubs and cafés and riverside walks. Just beyond the cathedral the sun was beginning to sink in the sky and take on a pinkish glow. Lovers' weather. Fran wondered if Laurence had answered the lure like everyone else or stayed inside to open one more file. Probably the latter. Laurence cared about his patients too much to be distracted by a flibbertigibbet sunset.

Fran got out of the car and sat by the riverbank alone. There was one harsh truth she had to face. She might love Jack, but it was too late. She'd had her chances and thrown them away, sprinkling them like bread to these overfed ducks. Besides, loving Jack meant betraying Laurence, and Laurence was a good man who deserved better. She should settle for what she'd got and be grateful she'd seen the light in time.

A couple in their forties passed holding hands, plain and unremarkable except for the glow they seemed to carry with them, and which had nothing to do with the beauty of the evening. They stopped yards from Fran and watched the river for a moment, then melted into a passionate kiss, oblivious now to the sunset or anything else around them.

Could she ever feel like that about Laurence, now or in ten years' time? Guilt and panic sliced into her, shredding her emotions. Laurence loved her. The wedding was only a week away. He was a man who cared about being humiliated, who found it hard to get close but who had opened his heart up to her. He had already been hurt by another woman who abandoned him: his real mother. Fran had a duty not to do the same thing to him.

And yet could she really marry Laurence when she'd just realized she was in love with Jack?

The clinic was just closing by the time she got there and Moira, Laurence's nurse, was locking the door. 'You've just missed him,' Moira informed Fran in her usual tone of reverence. 'I think he's gone to his mother's.'

'The flowers are going to be glorious,' Camilla enthused. 'I was really lucky to get Prentice and Proud to do them. Philip Prentice is in demand for all the society weddings. He was a bit worried about a late August wedding. The best flowers are finished, he says, but then he came up with this fabulous sunflowers idea.'

Laurence only half listened and the half that did wished Francesca could have bothered to organize the flowers herself. Certainly it was nice for Camilla to be involved, but not if it meant he'd be standing at the altar with sunflowers towering over him like bloody Bill and Ben. 'Are you sure sunflowers are such a good idea?' he asked.

'Of course they are, dear. It's going to be such a stylish wedding people will talk about it for months. I'm sure Francesca will love them.'

Fran herself, meanwhile, was standing in Camilla's hall gazing at the presents piled up on the table there.

One of them, clearly a bottle, stood out from the others in the cheapness of its wrapping. 'To Dr Westcott,' read the label, 'the finest man on God's earth. Without you we would have given up hope. May your own babies be as beautiful as ours. From June, Bill and Tracey (2 yrs) Standish.'

It was too much for Fran.

'Francesca, darling, what on earth's the matter?'

She felt Laurence's arms close round her and she shut her eyes, wishing she need never have to open them again.

'Just pre-wedding nerves,' offered Camilla, arriving in Laurence's wake. 'I almost called the whole thing off the week before mine.' She patted Fran's shoulder with surprising kindness. 'I've been worried you were doing too much, launching your paper so close to the wedding.'

'It's nothing to do with the paper,' insisted Fran and immediately regretted her tone. Camilla was trying to be helpful, and had revealed much more about herself than she usually did. It was horrible of Fran to throw it back in her face.

'I'm sorry. I didn't mean to sound such a bitch. It's just that I need to talk to Laurence alone for a moment.' Camilla would certainly think her a bitch after she'd done so.

Camilla looked as if she'd been stung. 'Fine. Suit yourself,' she bristled. 'If you need me I'll be in the garden.'

'Calm down,' Laurence said gently as if she were a patient who needed to be comforted after great stress. 'It can't be as bad as all that.'

'It is. The thing is, Laurence,' Fran searched desperately for a way of doing this well, but there was none, 'I can't go ahead with the wedding.'

Laurence laughed. 'For once, my mother was right. You have been overdoing things.'

Anger rescued her. 'It's nothing to do with that,' she insisted. 'I *like* overdoing things. I'd be miserable if I weren't overdoing things.' She took a deep breath. 'I can't tell you how sorry I am about this, Laurence, but I'm absolutely serious. You're a marvellous doctor and a wonderful human being – but I don't love you.'

Laurence's face hardened. For a brief moment his tender

concern for mankind looked as if it might disintegrate into something far less humane. Fran took a step backward, and found herself up against the cool stone of the mantelpiece.

'This is something to do with Jack Allen, isn't it?' Laurence demanded furiously. 'What has he told you? The man's a shit. Don't listen to him.'

'I know he's a shit.' Little Louise's face crowded into her mind, reminding her of Jack's faithlessness. Here she lied a little. 'But it's nothing to do with Jack Allen. Anyway his wife has come back to him from Australia and they've decided to get back together.'

She pulled off her engagement ring and put it on top of the most ornate of the presents. It toppled off again and she had to bend down to pick it up. So she missed the expression on Laurence's face when the impact of this news hit him. It had gone as blank as a magic slate.

'I know you won't think so now but I'm sure this is the right thing to do.' She knew it sounded sanctimonious but she couldn't think of any better way of putting it. 'This way I hurt you once but if we married it could go on for years. Not loving someone, even if you desperately want to, is a kind of betrayal too. I know. I watched my parents doing it. I'm so incredibly sorry. And I know all this is my fault, not yours, Laurence. Goodbye.'

She didn't look behind her as she half ran down the front path away from the house piled with wedding presents and plans and flowers. If she had she would have seen her fiancé staring in front of him as if he'd just seen a ghost. Then he turned and walked towards the nearest telephone.

*

'Damn,' Jack swore softly, as he realized yet something else he needed was at home. The pleasure of staying in a hotel, even one as pleasant and unpretentious as the Cathedral Arms, had already worn off after one day. He was missing Ben, and Ralph, who had in some eccentric way established himself as one of the family. He was even missing Wild Rover, for God's sake. Though not the dog's antisocial habit of impaling himself on your shoe at delicate moments or farting disgracefully then leaving the room at a swift and self-satisfied trot, causing the remaining occupants to look at each other suspiciously. And most of all, he longed to see Louise.

He also needed to find out exactly how long Carrie intended to stay. In typical Carrie fashion she had invited him to a family dinner tonight, which was rich considering it was his home and his family. He wasn't sure quite how it had happened but within five minutes of being back she had magically made it seem as if he were the erring husband and she the innocent, long-suffering victim. It was quite a feat.

Even as he packed up his briefcase after work, Jack admitted that tonight filled him with apprehension. Carrie was quite likely to lay on the full Martha Stewart number. Look, aren't we a happy family, the succulent roast would exclaim from its platter. How can you suggest there's anything dysfunctional here? What's seven years of hate and rancour between husband and wife? After all, that's history now, a silly mistake. Why can't you wipe the slate clean?

And he mustn't fall for any of it, Jack told himself sternly as he opened the front door and was hit by the aroma of pork crackling. Even if Francesca Tyler was getting married to someone else next week.

The sight of Louise curled up on the sofa with Wild Rover nuzzled next to her, flanked by Ralph and Ben attempting to play Monopoly, a hazardous choice with Ralph since he always forgot everything he owned, tore at Jack's heart.

'Glass of wine?' offered Carrie, her small neat body encased in Gap black, totally inappropriate to country life, yet somehow she carried it off with such confidence that everyone else looked as if they were the ones wearing the wrong clothes.

The wine was expensive, Australian, and not taken from the eclectic selection of supermarket plonk Jack laughingly thought of as his wine cellar. There was no question of laying wine down in this household. Most bottles only had time for a quick nap.

'Can I sit next to you, Dad?' piped up Louise, catapulting herself into the seat alongside Jack's. Carrie, he noted, had not only seated him at the head of the table but assumed he would do the carving. Even though he felt uncomfortable at such an obvious attempt at playing happy families, Jack had to admit the meal was delicious and the atmosphere seductive. At the beginning of their marriage he had hoped passionately for scenes such as this. But Carrie had had other ideas.

Only Ben seemed uneasy and edgy. Jack wanted to hug him and say, 'It's still you and me, it'll always be you and me,' but Ben refused even to look him in the eye.

After the meal was over and Louise dispatched for

bed, the mood shifted subtly. Carrie edged nearer to Jack and began to fill his glass even though he'd hardly touched it.

At the far end of the table, Ralph leaned over and nudged Ben. 'I get the impression we're not wanted on voyage, old son,' he whispered. 'Time we took the hint.'

Ben stood up awkwardly. Your parents getting back together was supposed to be every divorced child's dream, but he kept wanting to say 'Don't do it, Dad' without knowing what it was he wanted to stop.

'Night, Dad, Night . . . Mum.' His pause said everything, yet Carrie, eyes fixed on Jack and ever so slightly drunk, didn't seem to notice.

'Good night, darling,' she said. 'Isn't it great to all be back together?'

Ben mumbled something incoherent, still avoiding Jack's eyes. and obediently carried his plate to the dishwasher as his father had taught him. He looked up suddenly, fixing his mother with an intent and distrustful stare.

On the pad next to the phone his mother had scribbled a number with someone's initials beside it. And Ben had just worked out whose they were.

Fran ducked her head under the warm, scented bath water and wondered if she'd ever been more miserable. She had done the right thing, but that knowledge didn't bring any comfort. Instead she was conscious only of the hurt she'd caused – that she'd treated Laurence abominably, let down her mother, humiliated Camilla.

And what about herself? Good old Fran, another relationship down the tubes. And this time she had the responsibility of another life to consider.

Don't think like that, she told herself, or you'll fall apart. 'I am going to be strong,' she repeated to herself, tying her hair up in a knot and refusing to look in the mirror in case she hated what she saw. 'And the first strong thing I am going to do is go and tell my mother.'

It was only nine by the time she got there, but Phyllis had already been up since six, a lifetime habit. Fran wondered what on earth she did with all that time. The house was always so immaculate that to find a single mote of dust to vacuum would be an impossible task.

Looking around at the familiar house, Fran saw that without her father it no longer seemed quite like home. Ralph had somehow defied her mother's obsessive attempts at order by his very presence.

As if she sensed this too, Phyllis kissed her daughter briefly and asked how Ralph was.

'He's fine.'

'Is he?' Phyllis turned and straightened the already straight books on the coffee table where no one was allowed to put their coffee in case it spilt on the beige carpet. 'You must think me very unfeeling where your father's concerned,' she said unexpectedly.

Fran listened. Her mother never talked liked this.

'It was the dependency I couldn't take. We stayed together because we had separate lives, really. Him with the paper; me with my bridge. The illness would have changed all that. I'm glad he's giving you away. He'll be

347

proud to do that. I was jealous, you know, of him and you. Pathetic, isn't it, to be jealous of your own husband. But he had a way with you ever since you were a baby. You always went to him, not me.'

For the first time since she was a child, Fran felt able to reach through the years of silence and take her mother's hand. 'I loved you too, Mum. It was just that you seemed so unapproachable, so busy and bustling and sealed into your domestic world. I thought you disapproved of me for wanting to work, to be a journalist like Dad. You thought I was rejecting your values.'

Phyllis squeezed her hand for just a moment. 'Then I was very stupid.' She paused, hesitating. 'I am proud of you, you know.'

The unexpected tenderness in her mother's voice undid her. Fran broke away and tried to hide her tears in the pink damask curtains. 'Don't be. I've done something awful, Mum. I've broken off the wedding.'

But there was none of the furious disapproval she'd anticipated, the accusations of selfishness, the lack of thought for her parents' standing locally, the fear of gossip at bridge. 'I expect you had your reasons.'

'I realized I didn't love him.'

'Then you did the right thing. Perhaps if your father and I had admitted something like that everyone's lives would have been very different.'

The regret in her mother's voice was hard to bear. Her usual brisk efficiency was disintegrating before Fran's eyes, and spurred her on to greater confidences.

'The thing is, Mum. I'm going to have a baby.'

Again her mother's reaction surprised her. A ghost of a smile appeared on Phyllis's face. 'Isn't that usually the reason to go ahead with a wedding rather than to call it off?'

'Not if you aren't sure who the father is.'

'Ah.' There was no hint of shock or condemnation in her tone. 'You'll make a good mother, Francesca. Not like I was. Maybe I'll be a better grandmother. Now, I suppose you want me to try and smooth down Camilla's ruffled feathers?'

'That would be very kind of you.'

'Have you told your father yet?' The sympathy in her voice warmed Fran in its sheer unexpectedness. 'I don't think the news will break his heart. He was thrilled that you wanted him to give you away, but I suspect he was scared he'd do something foolish and embarrass you in public.'

'Thanks, Mum. You're a brick.'

Phyllis smiled creakily. 'Better than being a pain, I suppose.'

Everything at the *Citizen*, when she finally arrived, was mercifully normal. Reporters shouting, Keith Wilson cracking jokes at Mike Wooley, and Sean McGee, ponytailed and intense, pursuing a wicked villain who was dumping illegally or cheating the consumer or generally making the planet a more evil place in Sean's estimation. Stevie pounced on her before she'd even got her coat off.

'Fran! At last! Are you working part time these days? I need an answer. As a matter of fact I've needed it for two days. Do you want to devote more space to the Personal

Ads section, seeing as it's the most popular thing in *Fair Exchange*? Or are you too busy fantasizing about the honeymoon suite to care?'

Fran sat down beside her and lowered her voice.

'It's all off,' she blurted out.

'The Personal Ads section?' Stevie was stunned. Ads had been pouring in ever since the first issue.

'No, the wedding. I've told Laurence I can't marry him.'

Stevie felt like cheering but for once had the sensitivity to refrain. It was always a great mistake to say 'Thank God, I never liked the bastard anyway' in case the engagement was back on by lunchtime.

'Because you love someone else?' enquired Stevie hopefully.

'Don't you start. Because I don't love Laurence.'

'You won't be interested, then, in the fact that a certain London laboratory phoned to say that the result of your test was ready. Now what test would that be? Not a pregnancy test because you already know you're pregnant.'

Fran avoided her hawklike eyes. How did Stevie know everything almost before she knew it herself? She reached for the phone.

'Uh-uh,' Stevie shook her head. 'They won't give the results out over the phone. They were most particular about that. You have to go and pick them up in person. I suggested tomorrow would be a good day after we've got this week's paper to bed and they said that would be fine.'

'Oh God, Stevie,' Fran longed to put her head in her hands or just scream. 'I'm not even sure I want to know any more! As I haven't got either of them, what does it really matter?'

Stevie smiled like a wise and slightly self-satisfied monkey. 'Did you like surprises for your birthday, when you were a child, or did you want to choose what you got?'

'Point taken. I hated surprises. I don't suppose you've consulted the train timetable for me.'

'Eleven-o-two from Woodbury. Arrives Liverpool Street thirteen-o-eight. Return fifteen-o-four. Home by seventeen hundred. It has a buffet. I'll hold the fort.'

'Stevie. What would I do without you?'

'Not get drunk and sleep with men without taking precautions?' enquired Stevie, in her element, as she bustled off to remake the Personal Ads section single-handed.

The train to London was full of tourists who'd ticked Woodbury off their list of English cathedrals, gasped at its medieval closes, ignored its large industrial hinterland and marvelled at how unchanged it was by the centuries. Fran could have disabused them and told them about its homelessness and drug problems but that wasn't what tourists came for. They had that at home.

London was limping towards the end of summer in unexpected heat, looking dirty and up to its knees in rubbish. No wonder Woodbury looked good by comparison. It was a straight run on the Underground with no changes, so Fran made for the tube station, promising herself a cab on the way back. The train was warm and womblike and she almost fell asleep and missed her stop.

When she finally found the lab, which was tucked down

a tiny side-street, a friendly receptionist waved her upstairs to the first floor where she was handed a typed white envelope. Did the technician know what was inside it? she wondered. From the way he discreetly avoided her eye, she guessed he did. She wrote the cheque and tucked the envelope into her bag.

In the cab back to the station she asked herself why she'd collected it at all. How could knowing help her? If it was Laurence then she would feel guilty; if it was Jack she would hate herself for her lost opportunities. Perhaps she should just tear the envelope up? It might be better to simply never know. The baby would be its own person. As if in confirmation she felt a sharp kick, almost making her spill her drink down her front.

The irony was, she reminded herself sternly, this was exactly what she'd wanted in the beginning. A baby without a father.

But that was before she'd gone and fallen in love with Jack.

She still hadn't opened the letter by the time the train stopped at Woodbury. The station forecourt was crowded with wives waiting for husbands returning on the first of the evening commuter trains. Irrationally, Fran longed to see Jack standing there.

Instead it was Stevie.

'Thought you might need a bit of moral support.' Despite the heat, Stevie was wearing an ancient Barbour that looked as if it might have been the prototype for the very first waxed jacket before any whisper of its iconic status among the green-wellied classes. Stevie pulled out an Extra Strong Mint from its capacious pockets. 'Fancy one?'

Fran shook her head.

'So. Who should we call Daddy? Tweedledum or Tweedledee?' Trust Stevie to turn it into a joke.

'I haven't opened the envelope yet.'

'I see.' Stevie negotiated a way through the crowds of tired tourists and wailing children towards her car. 'You went all the way to London to get the results in order not to open them.'

'I didn't know I wasn't going to open them until I got them.' She knew how crazy this must sound. 'I don't suppose Jack has rung, has he? I mean he hasn't got to hear of my no longer impending wedding or anything?'

'If you want Jack Allen to know you've called off your wedding you'd better go and tell him. His wife's already got her feet firmly under the table from what I hear. Fran?'

'Yes?'

'You're a bloody fool to have let that happen.'

Fran's chin shot up. 'She's the one who's the bloody fool. Jack betrayed her and cared so little about his daughter he didn't see her for seven whole years. Who in their right mind would want a man like that?'

'You would. But you might be too late from what I hear.'

'Stevie,' Fran exploded as they parked outside the *Citizen*, 'thinking you know better than anyone else may be a perfect qualification for journalism, but so is occasionally admitting you're wrong. I am not in love with Jack Allen.'

'Right,' agreed Stevie in an infuriating tone, as they

entered the newsroom, 'then it won't bother you that he's sitting over there talking to Keith Wilson about cricket results.'

Fran felt herself flushing like some ridiculous school-girl. Especially when Jack jumped to his feet at their approach.

'I'm sorry, Jack,' Fran cast about frantically for something to say, 'I can't invite you into my office because I no longer have one.'

Jack grinned. 'Just as well it's Stevie I've come to see then. I've got a proposition I want to put to her.'

Fran was left furious and floundering while Stevie led Jack away to the café across the street. God, he was infuriating. Waltzing in here as if he owned the place and carrying Stevie off without a mention of the wedding being off.

Panic winded her suddenly. What if the proposition he was offering Stevie were a job? The *Citizen* without Stevie was unthinkable. She'd accepted the idea of having a baby and going on with the paper, maybe opening new editions of *Fair Exchange*. But only with trusted Stevie there to help out. Surely even Jack Allen wouldn't have the gall to poach her quite so publicly?

It was half an hour before Stevie swanned smugly back into the office announcing that Jack had simply wanted her advice.

'Did you tell him?' Fran demanded, before she could stop herself.

'Tell him what?'

'That I'd called off the wedding.'

Stevie tutted. 'Sorry, Francesca. It must have slipped my mind. But in a small town like this he must have heard by now.'

Fran's spirits drooped. Stevie was right. Gossip in Woodbury travelled faster than the speed of light.

'Of course, there's only one way to be a hundred per cent sure. And that's to tell him yourself.'

Fran turned away. That was the one thing she couldn't bring herself to do.

Chapter 21

'You don't need to pay me rent, Ralph,' Ben explained for the tenth time, tempted to throw the whole Monopoly board to the ground. 'I don't own Park Lane. You do.' They were sitting outside in the big garden, shaded by the ancient apple tree.

'There you are, sixty-six pounds.' Ralph happily ignored him, delighted that he had remembered he was the little silver boot.

Ben gave in and took it. Today was one of Ralph's difficult days when the wires in his brain didn't seem to be making any of the right connections. Ben understood for the first time what being the mother of wily but stubborn small children must be like.

'Ben,' shouted Carrie from the kitchen door, 'I'm going out now. Back at six.'

Ben watched her. As a matter of fact, he knew exactly where she was going. All that he didn't know was what he should be doing about it.

'Ralph,' he asked, knowing it was hopeless but desperately needing to sound out someone. On a good day, there were still shades of the steel trap that had once been Ralph's mind. This was not one of those days. 'I wondered if you could give me some advice.' Ralph looked more alert, as if he could sense the importance of the question to come. 'If you loved your father very much and you found out your mother was deceiving him, would you tell him?'

'Tricky question.' Ralph put down his cards with great deliberation. 'But if you really want my opinion . . .'

Ben leaned forward. This sounded like the Ralph he used to know. 'I think I'd decide it wasn't my place to interfere. Meddling in parents' affairs is a dangerous business.'

Ben's shoulders heaved with disappointment. If this was the old Ralph then all he could offer was conventional wisdom.

'On the other hand,' Ralph added, fixing Ben with a gaze that was now as clear and blue as a winter sky, 'I might make sure he found about it from someone else.'

Ben jumped up and hugged him. He'd just thought of the perfect person to do the telling.

Fran tried to banish all thoughts of Camilla writing little notes of apology to all the present givers and concentrate on putting that week's edition to bed. The flowers would probably have to be paid for anyway, and the catering. She would have to send a cheque. And she still hadn't found the right moment to tell her father he wasn't going to be giving her away after all.

She was in the middle of composing a headline on the subject of kitchen units when Ben burst nervously into the far end of the empty newsroom. By now almost everyone but she and Stevie had gone home and as neither of them had anyone to go home to, they had settled down for a long night's work.

'Ben! How lovely to see you!' Fran beckoned him over to the corner where they were working. He was so tall now it was hard to imagine him as Jack's son at all. As he approached she saw he looked pale and worried. An awful idea occurred to her. 'It isn't about Dad, is it?'

'No, no, he's cool.'

Fran laughed aloud. She'd heard Ralph described as many things but never this. 'And you must be thrilled to have your mother back.' Fran watched him slyly, yearning to find out more.

'I wish she'd stayed in bloody Australia as a matter of fact,' Ben flashed.

'But isn't it a good thing she's forgiven your father after all these years?' Fran realized it was a tactless question the moment she'd asked it. Maybe Ben hadn't even known his parents had split because of his father's infidelity.

'Forgiven *him*?' Ben almost spat out the words. 'You really don't understand anything about it, do you?'

Fran was taken aback. Ben always seemed such a gentle boy. 'No I suppose I don't.'

'It was Dad who had to do the forgiving. She was the one who had the affair, not him. They thought because I was only eight I didn't know what was going on. But I did. I heard all the rows about how she wanted to run off with this man. But Dad said he would expose them and the man's career would be ruined, so Mum ran off to Australia instead and took Lou with her. And to punish Dad she wouldn't let him see Lou for seven years. It nearly broke Dad's heart.'

Fran listened, her pulse racing, her stomach knotting up in panic. This couldn't be true. All these years she'd disapproved of Jack and refused to get involved with him because he'd tossed aside his family when all the time it had been the other way around.

Fran saw the hurt in Ben's own face. His mother had not only abandoned Jack but her own son. How could anyone be that callous?

'Oh, God, Ben,' she jumped up and hugged him. 'I didn't know!'

'And now she's back here and she's going to do it again and I'm so scared for Dad.' He stopped shyly, amazed at his own nerve. 'And you're the only one who can stop it.'

'I am?'

'You must know Dad's in love with you. He has been for months. He plays soppy songs and gets drunk and stares at your paper. If I hadn't walked in that day everything would have been all right between you. But I was embarrassed and tried to be cool.'

'You did very well at it.'

'Yeah. And made you think Dad bonked women right left and centre but the truth was you were the only one he was ever serious about. Please, Francesca. You're the one person who can stop him being hurt again.'

'How?'

'By telling him you love him too and calling off your stupid wedding.'

'As a matter of fact, I've already called off my stupid wedding. Doesn't he know?'

Ben grinned. 'Maybe you should tell him yourself. He left a message on our machine. He's gone to the Cathedral Arms to have a drink with some client. He said he'd be there for half an hour.'

Fran didn't need to think about it. She left all the papers spread across her desk and grabbed her coat. 'I might just do that. And if he turns me down I'll hold you responsible for the public humiliation.'

She skipped down the stairs, too excited to wait even minutes for the lift, and out of the front door of the *Citizen*, to find the streets were drenched with rain. The hot and heavy atmosphere of the last few days had suddenly broken and stair-rods of water were hitting and bouncing up off the pavement. With no raincoat to protect her she'd look like a wrung-out J-cloth by the time she got to the pub. She'd just have to hope love really was blind.

There were some old copies of the *Citizen* in the entrance and she grabbed one to hold over her head. It might at least stop her mascara running. As she did so a woman emerged from the close next door. It took her a moment to recognize the dripping and dishevelled figure.

'Camilla! What on earth are you doing in the pouring rain?' Camilla's normally immaculate hair was sopping and rat-tailed and her beige linen suit stained and shapeless.

'I've been waiting for you out here.'

Fran felt a jolt of apprehension. 'Why didn't you just come up?'

'Because what I want to say needs to be said in private. You selfish bitch!' Without warning she swung her gloved fist at Fran. Fran was so shocked she didn't even move and the glove caught her a glancing blow. 'How could you humiliate my son like that?' Camilla screamed. 'I don't think you ever wanted to get married. You showed not a blind bit of interest in the wedding. All you care about is your stupid paper! What do you think all this has been like for him?'

Fran staggered, shocked by the blow and Camilla's words, and recognizing that there was a painful truth in them. 'I imagine it's been pretty bloody awful and I can't say how sorry I am. You're right. I have been a selfish bitch.'

But Camilla wasn't listening to Fran's apology. 'I thought at least I could get this one thing right for him. I could plan the perfect wedding!' The wild pathos in Camilla's tones was painful to hear. Camilla's usual bone-china manner had slipped away leaving a desperation that made Fran ashamed of herself. She had certainly been anything but the perfect bride to be.

'I thought,' Camilla went on sadly, 'maybe then he might forgive me for my mistake in not telling him about his real mother.'

'I'm sure he's already forgiven you,' Fran held out a hand to the older woman, but she slapped it away. 'I'm sure he understood you were doing it for the best.'

'You don't know him very well, do you? Even if you

were supposed to be marrying him. Do you know, I think he's had a lucky escape.'

'So do I.' Fran's mood of happy confidence had melted away.

Camilla still stood there in the pouring rain, her face glowing with devotion, like an early Christian martyr.

'Let me get you a cab, Camilla.' Even as she said it she knew she couldn't just leave the distraught woman in front of her in a taxi. She would have to take her home; she owed her that at least.

Fran thought of the minutes ticking away. Soon Jack would be leaving the pub and she was stuck here with a hysterical Camilla. The meanness of her thought shamed her. Camilla was right. She was totally selfish.

'Look,' she heard herself offer, 'my car's just round the back. I'll drive you home.'

Camilla, all the fight gone from her, seemed to sag invisibly into the seat as Fran strapped her in and drove her back through the bad-tempered traffic to her pretty cottage on the outskirts of the town. When they got there she even had to look in Camilla's bag for her keys. Once Camilla was installed by the fireside Fran tried to ring Laurence and tell him to come but, unusually early for him, he'd already left.

The clock on the kitchen wall told her that almost an hour had passed since she'd come out of the *Express*. Camilla didn't even seem to notice when she slipped out.

The rush-hour traffic was thinning as she fought her way back to the Cathedral Arms, the after-work drinkers all going home to ready-cooked meals and ready-for-bed children.

Fran tried to put Camilla's desperate face out of her mind as she scanned the pub for Jack.

He wasn't there.

'Left fifteen minutes ago,' offered the barman politely when she enquired. Fran's spirits drooped. Missing the moment was becoming a skill of hers.

Outside the rain was beginning to stop and taxis to empty. One stopped just behind her and a striking young woman in black with short dark hair stepped out, clearly reluctant to let go of the man who was still inside. She leaned back in and kissed him. Fran's heart thumped against her rib-cage when she recognized the gamine features of Carrie Allen.

Fran pulled up the collar of her coat to give her more cover as she craned to see who the other person might be. The taxi window went down and for an instant a face appeared.

The man in the cab was Laurence.

Chapter 22

Now that the evidence was in front of her, it was all so obvious. Why Jack despised Laurence and why Laurence hated Jack. Jack's familiarity with the clinic.

It had been with Laurence that Carrie had had the affair all those years ago. And from what had passed between them it was still continuing now.

How could Laurence have done it? It must have breached every code of ethics doctors were supposed to espouse. Only minutes ago she had driven Camilla home, tortured by guilt at having wronged her good and honourable son for shallow and selfish motives like loving someone else. All Fran could think of was the narrowness of her escape. Had Laurence ever really loved her at all, or did she provide a useful dampener to the threat of buried scandal? Married to the editor of the local paper he would have at least enjoyed a kind of immunity.

And even if his affair with Carrie were simply the result of weakness on his part, he must have known how vulnerable she'd be after years of fertility treatment, how easy it was for a patient to mistake the consultant for God.

Anger scorched through her at Laurence's hypocrisy, posing as the patron saint of fertility, the doctor who cared only for his patients' welfare, while he was actually jumping into bed with one of them.

Fran stepped forward into the light just as the taxi set off. For one split second her gaze locked with Laurence's. It was he who looked away first.

'We were amazed you didn't see it sooner,' Carrie said softly, unlocking her car, parked a few feet away as the taxi containing Laurence sped off. 'Some journalist you are. He wasn't just leading you on, by the way. He actually thought he loved you till I got back. I understand him better, you see.'

'And what about Jack in all this?'

'He doesn't know yet.' Carrie's dark eyes challenged her insolently. 'Are you going to be the bearer of the good news?'

Fran got into her car and waited for Carrie to drive off. Then, feeling more dumb and dismal than she could ever remember, she took herself home.

There was a chill in the air after the rain, the first foretaste of autumn. She shrugged off her work clothes and put on the beloved white silk kimono her father had brought her back from a trip to Hong Kong. It was fraying now but she would wear it until it disintegrated. She snapped on all the lights in her empty flat and ran a bath.

She was standing naked with one toe in the bath when the phone rang. She cursed herself for forgetting to put on the answering machine. With incredible strength of character she ignored it until eventually it stopped. She lowered her whole body into the water just as it started up again, insistent and faintly threatening. This time she couldn't resist it.

'Fran?' The voice was Jack's. Perhaps Carrie had told him what had happened. She dripped hopefully onto the hall carpet.

But the tension in his voice told another story. 'It's your father, I'm afraid. He's disappeared. Ben usually looks after him but he dashed off somewhere this afternoon and forgot all about Ralph. The old scoundrel must have taken the chance to slip off. We've looked everywhere round here. Have you any idea where he might have got to?'

It was getting dark outside and she knew Jack was trying to be calm about her father's disappearance to protect her. But they both knew anything could happen if they didn't find him soon. 'Have you told the police?'

'Yes. They're keeping an eye out.'

Fran reached for her kimono and pulled it on. 'I'll look too. He might have gone to one of his old haunts. The racetrack, perhaps. Or the cricket club. I'll get the car.'

She tried to keep panic at bay as she drove through the darkening streets to all the places Ralph might have gone.

After almost two hours she was too exhausted to go on. She'd forgotten her mobile and decided to stop at the paper to call Jack. Maybe Jack had found him hours ago, playing murder in the dark at the bottom of the garden, and hadn't been able to reach her.

The lights were on throughout the second floor of the *Citizen*. Fran raced up, her heart thumping. But it was only Flo, the cleaner, emptying the waste-paper baskets and tutting about the selfish state the coffee machine had been left in.

'I ask you,' Flo demanded, holding up a furry pork pie she'd just found behind a filing cabinet, 'who works here? Journalists or a pack of wild animals?'

Fran ignored this tricky question. 'Flo, you haven't seen any sign of my father, have you?'

Fran slipped into her old office for a moment of privacy. It was dark in there and Fran slumped for a moment against the door, fighting off despair. What if he'd decided to feed the ducks and fallen in the pond, or was just wandering round somewhere, not recognizing any of the landmarks that had once been so familiar and comforting?

She turned on the lights and gasped. Ralph sat, still wearing his silk dressing gown, on one of the chairs, a telesales headset over his ears.

He smiled benignly as if his presence and his outfit were the most natural in the world. 'Don't worry, Franny darling, I've put the edition to bed. Just tell me one thing. How do you get the cricket score on this damn thing?'

'Oh, Dad!' Fran ran across the room and knelt at his feet. 'We thought we'd really lost you this time.'

'Silly girl. I'd like to get back now.' Ralph smiled indulgently. 'Unless you can make these confounded things work.'

'Sorry, Dad,' the relief she felt made her want to laugh,

'I never was any good at technology. I've got a better idea. Come back to my flat. I've got cable television.'

'No, thanks, Francesca.' Ralph acquired a mulish set to his mouth. 'I prefer it at Jack's. It's like home there,' he twinkled at her wickedly, 'only without your mother.'

'All right. Just for tonight.'

Jack must have heard them coming up the drive and was waiting at the front door, his arm round a red-eyed Ben who had clearly been blaming himself for the whole thing.

'A reception committee,' chortled Ralph, blissfully unaware of all the anxiety he'd caused, 'how thoughtful.'

'You old bugger. Ralph,' Jack greeted him, helping him out of the car. 'Can you just let us know you're off next time?'

For answer Ralph fixed him with a particularly beady gaze. 'I know you from somewhere, don't I?' he enquired. 'I remember,' his voice rang with joyful certainty at retrieving the memory, 'you come every Tuesday and pick the rubbish up.'

Ben sniggered behind them.

'Less of that, thank you very much,' hissed Jack. 'He probably thinks you're from Dyno-Rod.'

'Come on in, wanderer,' Jack invited, 'and I'll find you something tempting on the television.'

Ralph followed him like a lamb.

'Won't Carrie mind?' Fran glanced around her for signs of Jack's wife, trying to forget the image of her reaching down to kiss Laurence earlier this afternoon.

'Not unless she's psychic,' Jack replied, tucking a rug

over Ralph's knees. 'She left for London two hours ago. She couldn't stand the narrowness of Woodbury. And it turns out I wasn't the main attraction here after all.'

'And Laurence was?'

'You worked that one out then.'

'Have they got together again?'

Jack shrugged. 'I gather not. Laurence was too nervous of a scandal. He's going to try and get a job in London where having affairs with your patients is apparently more acceptable.'

Fran tried not to smile. 'I'd better go now. I'll come and get Dad and his things tomorrow. You've been good to him for far too long. If Stevie can hold the fort I'll look after him myself till we find a permanent solution.'

'I think you may find Stevie is contemplating giving in her notice.'

'Jack!' Fran had been so sure he wouldn't steal her. 'You aren't poaching Stevie for the *Express*?'

'No, I took the liberty of seeing if she'd come and look after Ralph. To say she jumped at the chance would be an understatement. Pole-vaulted would be a better term. As long as you agree, that is. I thought you'd quite like the idea of her looking after Ralph when we're married.'

Ben decided this time he might try very hard not to interrupt and crept off towards his bedroom.

Fran sat down, feeling suddenly overcome.

'She can always help out with the baby too,' Jack continued amicably. 'She says she feels like its granny already.'

Fran was speechless. 'How long have you known about the baby?'

'You don't think I swallowed all that crap about Henrietta being pregnant? You told me she met Laurence Westcott when she was having her coil fitted, remember?'

'Coils do fail,' Fran said weakly. 'Babies are sometimes born holding them.'

'Not this one. Besides, there's Lou to think of. Carrie has left her with me, thank God. She needs a bit of stability.'

'But, Jack, we can't let Stevie throw in her job like that. She'll lose so much pension.'

'I think you'll find Murray Nelson is about to try and buy a share of *Fair Exchange*. It's quite taken the gilt off my little launch. So perhaps you could give Stevie a payoff?'

'Jack!' Fran tried to be appalled and failed. 'Who said we were getting married anyway?'

'We don't have to if you'd rather not. You can keep your flat and your life if you need to, but I would love to be involved with my baby.'

Fran bristled. 'How the hell are you so sure it's your baby?' She thought of the unopened envelope containing the incontrovertible proof burning a hole in her bag.

Jack grinned. 'Because I happen to know Laurence Westcott can't have children. He told Carrie that years ago. She didn't mind because she already had two. Didn't he get round to mentioning it to you?'

Fran gasped. Laurence must have known all along and he'd let her believe he wanted to settle down and have a family with her. He'd been deceiving her as much as she had him.

'So,' Jack dipped down so that his eyes were on a level with hers, 'unless there are any other contenders it seems it has to be mine. Look, Fran, I'm not asking to marry you out of duty. You could bring up a baby fine on your own. But having kids is the biggest adventure I can think of, and I want to share it with you. Ben's the best thing that ever happened to me. I lost Lou but I've got her back now, for the moment anyway. I don't want to lose this child too. But it has to be your decision.'

Before she could answer he took her hand.

'There's one tough thing you need to face though: Ralph's going to get a lot worse in the years ahead. He may not even seem like the father you know. But at least we could face it together.'

Fran raised Jack's hand and kissed it. 'I know he'll get worse. But at least he'll be well enough to get to know his first grandchild.'

Ralph, who'd been sitting happily watching the racing Jack had recorded for him, still in his striped dressing gown, perked up. 'You're a very confusing young woman, Francesca.' The old Ralph was clearly back. 'I thought it was Laurence you were marrying.'

Fran laughed. 'So did I.'

'Never mind,' Ralph clucked contentedly. 'I always preferred Jack anyway.'

'That's all right then,' said Fran faintly.

'There's only one thing that worries me about marrying into your family,' Jack announced, perching on the arm of her chair.

'Not everything is hereditary you know.'

Jack ignored her. 'And that's your disconcerting habit of all walking round in your nightwear.'

'Don't worry,' Fran giggled, suddenly aware that she was still in her skimpy silk kimono, 'once we're married I promise you I won't wear anything at all.'

Jack finally pulled her into his arms. 'Why do I not find that reassuring?' he asked. 'And before we go any further, I want one promise: the next time we conceive,' he kissed her so hard it took all her breath away, 'I want witnesses. All right?'